Beautiful Lies

Beautiful Lies

Clare Clark

HOUGHTON MIFFLIN HARCOURT
BOSTON · NEW YORK
2012

First U.S. edition

Copyright © 2012 by Clare Clark

www.hmhbooks.com

First published in Great Britain by Harvill Secker in 2012

Library of Congress Cataloging-in-Publication Data
Clark, Clare.
Beautiful lies / Clare Clark.— 1st U.S. ed.
p. cm.
ISBN 978-0-15-101467-5
1. London (England)—History—19th century—Fiction. I. Title.
PR6103.L3725B43 2012
823'.92—dc23
2012023346

Printed in the United States of America
DOC 10 9 8 7 6 5 4 3 2 1

For my parents, with much love

Truth is beautiful, without doubt; but so are lies.

— RALPH WALDO EMERSON

1

THE ROOM WAS DARK. In the gloom it was possible to make out a three-legged stool leaning drunkenly against a wall and, on an ancient tea chest, an unlit stub of candle jammed in a ginger beer bottle. Otherwise it was bare, save for a heaped-up pile of sacks and dirty straw on which a small child was sleeping. His elbows poked through the holes in his shirt and the soles of his bare feet were black. Above him the ceiling was criss-crossed with sagging lines of laundry.

The silence was thick, constricted, as though the room held its breath. Then, very slowly, a hand insinuated itself between the tatters on the washing line and a dark figure leaked into the room. His face was obscured by a greasy wide-brimmed hat, its shallow crown dented and scuffed. His shoulders were stooped, his whiskers wild and grey. Instead of a coat, he wore a grimy flannel gown that trailed its frayed hem along the floor. He glanced around him, his eyes flickering from side to side, before, silent as syrup, he slunk across the room, his fingers dancing before his face as though he counted coal smuts in the air.

Beside the tea chest he hesitated, fumbling in his pockets. There was the rattle of a matchbox and then the scrape and flare of a match. Shadows leaped from behind the lines of laundry as he lifted the candle to his face. Beneath the snarl of his eyebrows his sharp eyes flickered like a snake's. As for his nose, it swept from his face like the buttress of a great abbey, the hook arching away from between his eyes before curving in a wide arc towards its tip, a point so sharp it might, if dipped in ink, have done duty for a nib. Although the bridge was narrow, the fleshy parts of the nose around the nostrils appeared almost swollen, rising from his cheeks like tumours, the nostrils beneath slicing the polyps in two thick black lines. His skin was a sickening grey.

The old man reached into the straw and pulled out a small brass-cornered chest. Unlocking it with a key on a string around his neck, he raised the lid. For a moment he simply stared. Then, plunging his hands inside, he drew out handfuls of treasure, bringing them up to his titanic nose as though he might inhale them, the glistening chains of gold, the vivid jewels in scarlet and chartreuse and cerulean, the milky ropes of pearls.

Immediately there was a commotion from behind the washing lines. The sleeping child started up in fright. Scrambling to his feet, he ducked beneath the laundry and was gone. Before the old man could scrabble his treasures back into the chest there emerged from behind the curtain of laundry a strange lopsided beast. Its back was humped, its white face crowned with curled horns. Emitting a strangled bleat the beast raised its hoof and jabbed it towards the old man, who cringed, the backs of his hands pressed to his eyes. The creature wheeled around, the sharpness of the manoeuvre almost breaking its back in two, and buried its face in the laundry.

A footman entered the room. Resplendent in scarlet livery and a white wig, he snapped his fingers at the old man, who grudgingly surrendered his treasure. The fanfare of a lone trumpet sounded as a small round lady made her stately entrance. Her hair was pulled back into a tight bun and topped with a large golden crown that threatened to slip over one eye. Pinned to the blue silk sash that she wore over one shoulder was a gold

2

brooch as big as her fist. Though unnaturally small for a lady of her advanced years, her substantial girth coupled with the imperiousness of her expression more than made up for any deficiency of stature and she brandished her sceptre as though it were a bludgeon. The footman bowed. There was no mistaking her. It was without question the Empress of India, Her Majesty Queen Victoria herself.

The old man whispered something to the footman. Hurriedly he stepped forward and presented the treasure chest to the Queen. She received it with stately froideur. Then, unable to contain her glee, she grinned at the villainous old man. He winked at her and blew out the candle.

Abruptly the darkened room was filled with light. The Queen curtsied, her skirts held wide. Then she clapped her hands.

'Well?' she demanded, jumping up and down. 'Can you guess?'

Maribel glanced over at Edward as the Charterhouse children began excitedly to shout suggestions. He stood with one elbow propped on the corner of the mantelpiece and one long leg crossed over the other, a faint smile on his lips. Behind him a housemaid quietly drew back the curtains. The weather had not improved. The wind rattled the window sashes, sweeping the rain across the terrace in veils. Beyond the lawn the sodden trees huddled together like cattle.

'Treasure? Chest? Hide? Steal?'

'Gold!'

'No, look, he's pointing at himself. It's him. The first syllable is him.'

'Old man?'

'Thief?'

'Crook?'

'We're getting warmer. A particular crook, then.'

Charades had been Arthur's idea, of course. Ordinarily,

released from the strictures of their London lives, his children behaved at Oakwood like animals returned to the wild, coming into the house only to eat and to sleep, but it had been a miserable Easter, the wettest anyone could remember. Confined indoors, they had relied heavily upon their father's passion for parlour games. In the afternoons, when in other years there might have been croquet or riding or an outing to the beach at Cooden, Arthur gathered the entire party together in the drawing room for frenzied contests of Hunt the Slipper and Blind Man's Buff.

Several of his games were so outlandish that Maribel could only assume that he invented them on the spot. The previous day, the party swelled by several neighbouring families invited for luncheon, he had insisted upon playing something he called Poor Pussy, in which one of the players was required to crawl on all fours among the assembled company, miaowing piteously. The other participants were then obliged to declare 'Poor Pussy!' with the gravest of expressions. Any player whose mouth so much as twitched was seized upon immediately and set in turn on their hands and knees. The Charterhouse children had demonstrated an alarming aptitude for the sport and had frowned grimly at one grovelling victim after another, until Arthur in a fit of impatience had taken it upon himself to be Pussy and had wound himself around his children's legs, rubbing his head against them and purring with the combustive power of a steam engine until they wept with mirth.

'So like Fagin but not Fagin.'

'He's pointing at his nose.'

'Nose?'

'Hook?'

'Jew?'

'Jew is right!'

'Jew? That's the word?'

'Not the whole word, you silly. The first syllable.'

'How many sybabbles are there?'

'Three, of course. Don't you ever listen?'

'Not to you or I'd die of boredom.'

From across the room Edward caught her eye and smiled. Maribel smiled back and straight away she thought again of the letter hidden in her writing box and the smile tightened over her teeth. To distract herself she fumbled in her bag for her cigarette case. Edward had bought it for her in Mexico City just after they were married. The soft silver was scratched now, the initials on the small raised plaque at its centre almost rubbed away.

She struck a match and inhaled, sucking in the shock of the harsh Egyptian tobacco. Beside her on the chesterfield little Matilda wriggled restlessly, pressing her small fingers into the buttoned cavities of the upholstery. Arthur disapproved of Maribel smoking, of course, but then she disapproved of charades, and Arthur had never paid the slightest heed to that. In Arthur's world only fast women smoked.

'What words begin with Jew?'

'Juice. Juice begins with Jew.'

'Juice is only one syllable, silly.'

'Don't call me silly! Mama, he called me silly.'

'Sneak.'

'Now he called me a sneak!'

'Hush now, both of you,' Charlotte soothed. She held out her hand to Kitty, who glared at her brother before crawling triumphantly into her mother's lap. 'Let's think. What other words begin with Jew?'

'Jupiter?'

'Juvenile delinquent?'

'Judica.'

'Jew-what?'

'Judica,' thirteen-year-old George repeated, rolling his eyes. 'Passion Sunday to you ignorami.'

George had only been at Eton half a year but already he had learned enough disdain for a lifetime. Bertie, who was to join him the following year, stuck out his tongue behind his brother's back.

'It's not that, is it, Papa?' Kitty asked.

The old man shook his head firmly. His nose wobbled.

'Of course not,' he said. 'It's a word you all know.'

'Papa!' Queen Victoria hissed, poking a finger into his ribs. 'You're not supposed to talk.'

The old man gurned guiltily, clamping his lips between thumb and forefinger. The children laughed. Beside Maribel Matilda squirmed. Then she tugged at Maribel's sleeve. There were dimples at the bases of her fingers where the knuckles should have been.

'I'm four,' the little girl whispered confidingly.

'Goodness,' Maribel murmured. Her accent was neither French nor Spanish but a husky tangle of the two that a certain type of Englishman found irresistible. 'Very nearly grown up.'

'How old are you?'

'How old do you think I am?'

Matilda looked thoughtful.

'Are you seven?' she asked.

Maribel smiled distractedly. The letter had come that morning. Alice, their maid, had had the post sent on to Sussex from Cadogan Mansions and, as she had every morning, Maribel had flicked through it idly in the breakfast room, her only thought a faint hope that the milliner had not remembered her bill. The shock of the familiar handwriting on the envelope had caused her to spill her tea on the tablecloth. Arthur had called her a butterfingers and had the maid bring an infant mug with a spout.

'What came after the Nose Man?' Kitty asked her mother.

'That animal, wasn't it?'

'Yes, but what is it?'

'A horse?'

'It has horns!'

'So it does. A cow, then?'

'A sheep?'

'Now we're getting warmer.'

'Like a sheep.'

'A rabbit?'

'A rabbit is nothing like a sheep, you clodpoll.'

'I is not a clodpoll.'

Maribel took a last drag of her cigarette and stubbed it out. Mopping at the spilled tea with her napkin she had apologised to Charlotte for her clumsiness and slipped the letter into her pocket without opening it. Upstairs she had pushed it beneath the envelopes in her writing case and hidden the case at the back of the wardrobe, and still she had not been able to rid herself of the throb of it, the relentless thump of its pulse in the pit of her stomach.

'You've been very quiet, Maribel dearest,' Charlotte said, smiling at her. 'Have you already solved the mystery?'

Maribel blinked.

'The animal,' Charlotte prompted. 'Can you tell what it is meant to be?'

'Goodness. I – is it a llama?'

Matilda giggled.

'Llama,' she said. 'You say it funny.'

'Tilly, hush!'

Matilda frowned.

'Well, she does.'

'That's because Mrs Campbell Lowe is from Chile where llamas really live and therefore, unlike a little English girl, knows exactly how to say it right. Come on, we must put our thinking caps on. An animal with horns.'

Maribel fiddled with the clasp of her cigarette case. She did not know how Charlotte managed always to sit so placidly amid

7

the commotion, a contented smile upon her lips, her arms open to any child who might skid up to her, breathlessly relating their father's latest escapade. Charlotte was always there to laugh at the childish jokes and kiss better the bumps of those who had been knocked down in the rush, rummaging in her sewing box for foil-bright chocolates. Sometimes she read aloud as the children tumbled like puppies around her, her voice sweet and steady amid the hullabaloo. In all the years Maribel had known her she had never once seen Charlotte lose her temper.

Beside her little Matilda swung her legs sulkily, kicking at the wooden trim of the chaise with the heel of her boot. Thump. Thump. Maribel pressed a hand against her forehead. She was suddenly impatient with herself, with her uneasiness. It was just a letter. As soon as this wretched game was over she would go upstairs and open it.

'How about a goat?'

'They're nodding.'

'That was a goat?' George said. 'It looked more like an ass to me.'

'That's quite enough, George.'

'Not goat. Another word for goat.'

'Is there one?'

'How about nanny?'

'Oh my! Boiling hot!'

'Billy?'

'Billy!'

Onstage, the four-legged creature whooped.

'Billy's right!'

'Jew-Billy,' Kitty said, puzzled. 'What's Jew-Billy?'

'Jubilee!' Bertie shouted triumphantly. 'That's what Ursie was with the crown. The Queen's Golden Jubilee!'

'Jubilee, of course, how clever you all are, my darlings. Well done, well done!'

The motley band of performers took a bow before wriggling

through the audience to receive their kisses from their mother. Arthur pinched the lapels of his grimy gown between his thumbs and forefingers and grinned at Edward.

'Any wipers for me, my dear Dodger?' he asked.

Edward raised an eyebrow. 'What a big nose you have, Grandmama.'

'Papier mâché. I fear the entire day nursery is now upholstered with the *Times*.'

'You know, it's a great shame you don't go to more trouble with these things.'

Arthur laughed.

'This was nothing. If Theo had had his way it would have been Buffalo Bill's Wild West. With real horses.'

Impatiently Kitty tugged on her father's sleeve.

'Is it our turn now, Papa?' she demanded.

'Tomorrow, Kittycat,' Arthur said, lifting her into his arms. 'Perhaps we might even persuade Mr Campbell Lowe to take a part.'

Edward shook his head.

'Not this time, I'm afraid. I have to be back in London by noon.'

'Isn't the House in recess?'

'I have meetings.'

'No peace for the wicked, eh?'

'Not if I have anything to do with it.'

Behind them Theo and William had taken two of the sacks and were having a sack race between the piano and the window seat where Beatrice and Ursie quarrelled half-heartedly over a tangle-haired doll. A nursemaid came in and took Clovis for his bath. Charlotte kissed his toes as she handed him over, shaking her head at the black soles of his feet.

'Heavens,' she said. 'Did your father rub you with coal?'

Clovis extended a starfish hand and she blew him a kiss. Then she reached over and touched Maribel's arm.

'Where are you going?'

'To my room. There's something I need to do.'

'It can wait, surely? I've hardly seen you all day.'

Reluctantly Maribel settled back on the sofa.

'Must you go back tomorrow?' Charlotte asked. 'I am not nearly done with you.'

'I must. Edward is to address some Fabian Society dinner tomorrow night and I have promised to go with him. It will be perfectly ghastly, of course.'

'I thought the Fabians were rather a spirited lot.'

'They were once. Before they became Fabians and stopped reading novels and going to the theatre. Now they just wear solemn expressions and argue about strikes and slum clearances.'

'The situation is so awful. I suppose at least they're doing something.'

'But that's just it. They don't do. They talk and talk and talk while trying to exceed one another in glumness and the ugliness of their dresses. Oh, Charlotte, when did everyone get so political?'

'Dearest, your husband is a Member of Parliament. They are supposed to be political.'

'If it were only them I might be able to bear it. But it's all of London.'

'Then thank your lucky stars you are buried in the depths of the country where Socialism is yet to be invented. Forget the Fabians. Stay here and talk to me about poetry.'

It was a tempting offer. Though a great number of their friends were writers and artists and composers, nobody in London seemed to talk about poetry any more or painting or music. Instead promising playwrights and eminent poets exchanged grim stories of the sufferings of the match girls in Hackney and the coal miners in Yorkshire. Conversations, which had once drawn deeply upon intuition and imagination, had become lists of statistics: slum populations, mortality rates, hours of schooling, pence per hour or per gross. The Irish question, universal suffrage, free secular education, trade unions, prison reform, the minimum wage and the eight-hour working day. They lectured, protested, organised meetings, argued for revolution, and bemoaned the exasperating ignorance and passivity of the English working man.

Naturally Maribel did all of these things too. No one knew the arguments better than she did. She lectured and protested and organised and she tried to be glad, because the cause was just and good and it was what all their friends were doing. But for all that she couldn't help resenting it, just a little. There was no beauty in politics. It was all business.

'Stay,' Charlotte coaxed. 'The Fabians will forgive you. One day. Or a week. I don't have to be back in London until next Monday.'

There was a loud shriek from the end of the room. Arthur was chasing the little ones with handfuls of straw that he threatened to stuff down their necks. Ursie, her crown askew, stood on a chair shouting encouragement while, by the fireplace, Edward tossed coins with George and Bertie, who called out their bets as the shillings spun in the air. In the corner behind the piano William and Theo held Matilda by her ankles and swung her backwards and forwards with such vigour that it seemed certain she would fly. The little girl screamed with delight.

Maribel smiled at Charlotte and shook her head.

'If only I could,' she said.

Upstairs before dinner, while Edward played billiards with Arthur, Maribel took her writing case from the wardrobe and unlocked it. The envelope was thick, a rich creamy white, and slightly larger than was strictly conventional. The address was written in dark blue ink and placed, as it always had been, precisely in the centre of the envelope. The handwriting too was just the same, its letters slanted slightly to the right, the loops tucked neatly into themselves like hair ribbons.

She turned the envelope over, running her finger over its sealed edge. *Mrs Edward Campbell Lowe.* The last time they had seen one another, not one of those names had been hers. Very slowly she reached into the writing case, slid the silver letter opener from its leather pocket, and inserted it under the flap of the envelope. The paper sighed as she cut it. Inside was a single sheet of paper. Her fingers trembled as she drew it out.

My dear M,
*   I hope this letter finds you well.*

The letter was very short. Maribel read it through three times, holding the paper with the tips of her fingers as though she meant to tear it in two.

I shall be in London at the end of May and would be most grateful if you would consent to see me. I would not ask if it were not of the greatest importance. Naturally you may be assured of my utmost discretion. I shall write again when I know my arrangements.
*   Your affectionate mother*

Maribel looked at the letter for a long time. Then, returning it to its envelope, she slid it once more beneath the unused envelopes in her writing case. On the mantelpiece the clock struck the hour. She should bathe or she would be late for dinner.

Instead she sat on the window seat, looking out over the garden. The rain had stopped at last and the evening light was as pale and new as the inside of a shell. Somewhere a pigeon cooed. She fumbled her cigarette case from her pocket and snapped it open. The symmetry of the white cylinders, the way in which they fitted precisely into the silver case, was soothing somehow, a refutation of human error. Maribel had her cigarettes rolled for her at Benson & Hedges in Old Bond Street and sent over in packages of one hundred. Mr Hedges boasted to his customers that his rollers were the most dextrous in London, that they could produce forty immaculate cigarettes in a single minute. Maribel had never been able to imagine that. Her fingers shook as she set a cigarette between her lips, struck a match. She smoked fiercely, her shoulders hunched, drawing the smoke into her skull. When the smouldering tobacco threatened her fingers she used the stub to light another.

She would have to tell Edward, of course. She could not meet her mother without telling Edward. And if she refused to meet her? She was not sure that she could make that decision without him either. She had told him a little of her family at the very beginning, of course, recounted foolish stories from her child-hood as everyone did, but they were few and quickly forgotten. By that time the past was ancient history and dull history at that. It had nothing to do with her, with what she had become. She was a different person by then.

When other people enquired about her name or her family or remarked upon her unusual accent, she only shrugged and offered the briefest of explanations. Maria Isabel Constanza de la Flamandière was such a mouthful that she had always been known simply as Maribel. The only child of a French father and a Spanish mother, she had spent her girlhood in Chile where she had spoken both languages, French in conver-sation with her parents, a clumsy local version of her mother's tongue with the servants and shopkeepers. At the age of twelve she had been sent to live with her father's sister in Paris, where she attended a convent school which she disliked. In Paris she had met Edward. That was that, the extent of her history. Even the most persistent of questioners could not draw her further.

The story of her chance encounter with Edward was, by contrast, well known to everyone in their circle. One sunny May afternoon, aged only just eighteen, she had been walking in the Champs-Elysées when she was almost knocked off her feet by an unruly black horse. Its handsome rider had dismounted to beg her forgiveness and, in the sweet breathlessness of those first moments, their lives had been altered for ever. The daze of that Parisian afternoon had intensified into an impassioned courtship, conducted in secret, and then an elopement. Five weeks later in London she and Edward had been married.

They had honeymooned in Texas and in Mexico. Back in London with an eavesdropping servant to consider, they never talked of her family again. She had never confessed to Edward that, on their return from America, she had written a letter to her mother. She could think of no way to tell him, no explanation for her recklessness. At the time she had not concerned herself with reasons. When she had unpacked their boxes and discovered the notices of their wedding, cut from the London newspapers and sent to them by Edward's mother, she had folded them into a single sheet of writing paper on which she had scribbled a short note.

Mother,

Given the circumstances of our parting I thought you would be glad to know that, despite your steadfast belief that I would disgrace you, I am now married. We are currently resident at the above address in London, although we travel tomorrow to the family seat in Scotland. How provoking for you that you will not be able to boast about it. I would ask you not to reply to this letter but I should not wish you to worry unnecessarily.

M

She had posted the letter before she had had time to think better of it. That had been nearly ten years ago. Her mother had respected her wishes. She had not replied. Maribel had known that she would not. No doubt that was why she had risked writing in the first place, because there was no danger of the consequences. Her mother was a woman of irreproachable respectability whose abhorrence of scandal was as vital in her as blood. In ten years she had not written so much as a postcard.

And now, out of the blue, this. Her mother disliked travelling. She would not make the journey to London unless her business was urgent. As for her suggestion that they meet, it was frankly inexplicable. What was so important that it could not be said in a letter?

2

THE HANSOM DREW TO a stop at the south end of Halkin Street. Edward swung open the door and stepped down, holding his arm out for his mother. She took it, smiling at him as he helped her out.

'Goodnight, my dear Teddy.'

'Goodnight, Mother. I am sorry you did not enjoy the play much.'

'Yes, well, I suppose I am glad to have seen it. The newspapers were right in one regard. It was an extremely dramatic production.'

'Wasn't it? There were moments when I was sure we would all go up in smoke.'

'But still lacklustre, for all the modern wizardry. A poor translation, of course. *Faust* is not a pantomime. All those bangs and whizzes might stop the heart but in the end it is Goethe's poetry that chills the soul.'

In the cab Maribel rolled her eyes. She did not disagree with her mother-in-law's analysis. She just wished that for once Vivien would simply say thank you and be done with it.

'I wish we could have given you dinner,' Edward said, pulling the bell. 'Blasted vote.'

'Dearest, at my great age, the digestion is glad of the respite.'

'For an intelligent woman you talk a great deal of nonsense.'

The front door opened, the light spilling over the pavement. As Edward kissed her cheek, Vivien Campbell Lowe pressed his face against hers, her fingers pale against the red-gold blaze of his whiskers.

'You must go,' she said. 'Goodnight, my dear boy. Take care of him, Maribel. Try to keep him out of trouble.'

Maribel shook her head. 'You know as well as I that there is no possibility of that.'

Vivien smiled, a different smile than the one she reserved for her son.

'He looks tired,' she said.

'Doesn't he?'

The two women eyed each other for a moment. Then, touching the tips of her fingers to her lips, Maribel blew her mother-in-law a kiss.

'Goodnight, Vivien.'

'Goodnight. I shall expect you for eight o'clock on Friday.'

'I shall look forward to it.'

The courtesy came easily enough. Vivien Campbell Lowe might be provoking but she was a faultless hostess and dinner at her pretty house was mostly very agreeable. Edward's father had suffered from violent fits and, as his behaviour had grown increasingly erratic, Vivien had abandoned the moors and mountains of Argyllshire for the cosmopolitan society of London. There she had established a salon in the Parisian style to which she invited writers and artists and, as soon as he was old enough, Edward and the more charming of his circle. By the time of her husband's death when Edward was twenty she was well accustomed to the life of the prosperous widow. As she grew older her friends grew younger and, even now, she was often to be found at the parties that Edward and Maribel attended, dressed in the dramatic jewel-coloured velvets that flattered her complexion. She was vain of her dark hair and disdained hats, preferring to adorn her carefully arranged coiffures with feathers or diamond clasps. Sometimes when she conversed with her mother-in-law Maribel found herself peering at her, eyes narrowed a little, in the hope of finding the first traces of grey.

'Go inside,' Edward said gently to his mother. 'You'll make me late.'

Vivien lingered, smoothing the hair from her son's brow. She had never remarried, though Maribel was sure that there must have been offers. Instead Edward paid her a pension he could ill afford and, along with Henry, his bachelor brother, escorted her on those occasions when the absence of a husband might prove awkward. Edward worried about her, living alone with only the servants for company, but it seemed to Maribel that she had everything sewn up very nicely.

'My beautiful boy,' Vivien murmured. Then, patting him like a child, she shooed him out towards the waiting hansom. 'Till Friday.'

'Till Friday.'

As the driver snapped his reins Maribel lit a cigarette. Beside her Edward stretched out his long legs and yawned, sweeping away the smoke with the back of his tapered white fingers. His narrow face was drawn. She frowned at him.

'Must you really go back to the House?' she asked. 'Surely this week they have had their pound of flesh.'

'Please, Bo, not tonight.'

'It is you I am concerned for. Your mother is right. You look exhausted.'

'Not so exhausted I can't put flies in the Home Secretary's ointment. Honestly, Bo, something has to be done. If Matthews has his way it won't be long before twelve people in a dining room constitutes an infringement of the law.'

'Don't exaggerate,' Maribel said. 'Even the Mr Podsnaps want England a free country.'

'Free for a man to starve in – that is a privilege the govern-ment is eager to preserve – but not, apparently, if he would rather hold a public meeting. If he is poor and a Socialist, or worse still Irish, then God help him. For such men Mr Matthews espouses freedom in the Russian style.'

Maribel tipped her head back, releasing a stream of smoke from her mouth. It clung to the darkness like hair.

'You work too hard.'

'And you smoke too much. We must bear our burdens bravely.'

Maribel smiled. She might begrudge the incessant demands of Edward's political life but she was not foolish enough to believe that anything she or anyone else could say would alter him one iota. Edward Campbell Lowe was a radical in his blood and in his bones – his father's father had campaigned with Wilberforce for the freedom of slaves, while his maternal grandfather had famously made a bonfire with a valuable portrait of the Marquess of Bute because, he had declared, it was more than a man could stomach to encounter a Tory every morning before breakfast. Even Edward's own father, whom no one liked to talk about, had espoused tyrannicide and knew the *Corn Law Rhymes* by heart. He had also gone mad. He had died in an asylum, bequeathing to Edward his Scottish titles and estates and debts totalling nearly one hundred thousand pounds.

At Cadogan Gardens Maribel stepped down from the cab. Edward made to accompany her but she shook her head, standing on tiptoes to kiss him tenderly on the cheek. He smiled at her, his hair fiery in the gaslight. He had always been a beautiful man.

'Goodnight, Red,' she said softly.

'Goodnight.'

Edward leaned forward, knocking on the roof of the cab with his cane. The cabman slapped the reins and the horse coughed and moved off, its metalled hooves ringing against the cobbles. Fumbling her keys from her evening bag, Maribel hurried up the shallow stone steps of the mansion block and pushed open the heavy front door.

She wished that Edward did not make it his business to provoke people so. As soon as he had taken possession of his seat he had taken up every unpopular cause he could conceive of, including the wholesale reform of the parliamentary system. In the afternoons he liked to caracole in Rotten Row. As a young man he had spent several years as a gaucho in Argentina and he rode with the gaucho's swagger, his bridle arm held high in the Spanish-Moorish fashion, his horse's harness jingling with silver. Neither his radicalism nor his riding ingratiated him with his fellow Members in the House.

There was a narrow slice of light beneath the door at the foot of the stairs. Maribel closed the front door gently, taking care that it did not slam. Once or twice, when they had first come, Edward had failed in this duty and, like a child's jack-in-the-box, Lady Wingate had leaped out from behind her front door to berate him. Edward found these encounters diverting. He claimed that, by provoking the acceleration of blood through Lady Wingate's coarsening arteries, he was performing a duty of medical care, but Maribel had no appetite for the old lady's implacable irascibility. She hurried on tiptoe across the wide tiled hall.

As she reached the stairs, the door to Lady Wingate's flat banged open.

'Mrs Campbell Lowe.'

Maribel sighed. She stopped, one hand on the banister.

'Good evening, Lady Wingate.'

The old woman glared at her. She was dressed in a dark green velvet evening gown with a huge and rather tarnished diamond pin on the shoulder. The dress was low-cut, revealing a good deal of wrinkled décolletage.

'Must you make such an infernal racket?' she demanded. 'I can barely hear myself think.'

'I'm sorry. I tried to be extra careful with the door this time.'

'Bang, bang, bang, that door, day and night. Anyone would

think it was a pheasant shoot. I don't suppose they have pheasant shoots where you come from, do they?'

'In Chile? No.'

'I told my son a flat was a modern abomination. A house, that's the respectable way to live. Not all piled up one on top of the other like plates. We, thank heavens, are not the French.'

Maribel said nothing. The old lady made a low whistling noise to herself and patted her velvet arms.

'No husband tonight?'

'Not tonight. There is a vote at the House.'

'So I shall have the pleasure of being woken by him later.'

'I am sure he will be very quiet.'

Lady Wingate harrumphed, clicking her false teeth.

'My mother would never have allowed my brother to put her in a flat. Not while she was of sound mind. She was of the opinion that only paupers and prisoners managed without stairs.'

'Well. The world changes.'

'The vote for women, now that would really have her turning in her grave. Silly old bat.'

Maribel smiled. 'I should be getting along. I am sorry I disturbed you. Goodnight, Lady Wingate.'

Lady Wingate harrumphed again and did not reply. She stood in her doorway, seemingly lost in thought, as Maribel climbed the stairs to the first floor. As she crossed the landing Maribel looked down. The old lady's door was still open, her shadow a grey smudge on the black-and-white floor. In all the years of their acquaintance she had never once invited them inside her flat and they had certainly never asked her upstairs to theirs. It was the joy of modern mansion blocks. They came unfettered by the tiresome domestic obligations of ordinary houses. Nobody in a flat considered themselves to have neighbours.

She unlocked the front door and let herself in. Inside the lamps were lit and the grandfather clock ticked comfortably. Maribel paused, inhaling the warm smells of beeswax and applewood smoke. In the drawing room the fire was still burning. As she drew off her gloves and reached up to unpin her hat, Alice appeared in the doorway, a tray of supper in her arms. Maribel smiled at her and set the hat on a side table. It was a particularly pretty hat, purchased on her last visit to Paris, and the sight of it cheered her further.

'Just put the tray here,' she said. 'I shall eat in front of the fire.'

Stretching a little she yawned as Alice set the tray on the fender stool. She knew they had been fortunate. When they had first set up home in London Edward's mother had warned them darkly of the difficulty in securing servants in town, declaring the whole business a sea of troubles, but Alice, though sometimes a little rough around the edges, had proved competent and obliging. She had been with them almost as long as they had been married.

'Will that be all, ma'am?' Alice asked.

Ten years in London had done nothing to soften her West Riding accent. She had come to Maribel through an agency, and when she had first opened her mouth to introduce herself, Maribel had almost sent her away without an interview. It was only desperation that had prevented her, desperation and the recognition that Alice, alone among the trickle of dull-eyed, whey-faced candidates that she had seen that day, was a girl who might be trained. Alice was from Knaresborough. When Maribel had asked her why she had left Yorkshire she had only shrugged and said she never thought to stay.

'The master has a late vote,' Maribel said. 'Again. Heaven knows what time he will be home. Leave something for him in case he is hungry when he gets in, would you? And you had better warm the bed in the dressing room. It gets so cold in there.'

Maribel ate supper curled up on the sofa in front of the fire. They had been back from Sussex a week and she still had not told Edward about the letter. Somehow the time had never been quite right. The Home Secretary's proposals to suppress public meetings had caused a furore among the Radical Liberals in the House and, along with impassioned speeches in the Commons, Edward had attended meetings of the Socialist League and the Socialist Democratic Federation, whose ideological differences Maribel was still unable quite to comprehend. Moreover, the Coal Mines Regulation Bill was at the Committee Stage and Edward was lobbying hard on behalf of the Scottish miners. He was scheduled to travel north to speak at working clubs and town halls across the Scottish mining districts the following week and, on the rare occasion that he had no dinner engagement, he worked late on his speeches, several nights not retiring to bed until two or three in the morning. Most days they had seen one another only briefly at breakfast. Breakfast was no time for awkwardness.

She would tell him when he was back from Scotland. They would dine together alone and she would tell him. Until then the news would keep. It had taken her mother ten years to reply to her letter. Another week or so would hardly signify. And what would her mother do if she never replied at all? Surely she would not dare to send another. The possibility that the matter might simply go away on its own had not occurred to Maribel before and she felt her spirits lift a little. Perhaps Edward need never know at all.

Alice had left the evening newspaper on the side table and she glanced idly at the front page. There were riots again in Ireland, strikes in Manchester. Mr Gladstone and his wife were to pay a visit to Buffalo Bill's 'Yankeeries'. A cartoon at the bottom of the page had the Grand Old Man in a feathered headdress above the caption 'Strong Will, Chief of the Opper Sishun Hinderuns'.

It was extraordinary, Maribel thought, how stirred up London was at the prospect of Buffalo Bill's Wild West. The show had not yet opened and still the newspapers followed every detail of its preparation: the amphitheatre big enough to hold forty thousand people, the twenty thousand carloads of rock and earth required to raise the Rocky Mountains in West Kensington, the electric lights equal to half a million candles. It made *Faust* look like one of Arthur's charades. Everywhere in London huge coloured posters bore portraits of Buffalo Bill Cody mounted upon a rearing white horse, the stars and stripes of the American flag unfurling behind him. The whole city was convulsed with cowboy fever. It was hardly possible to venture out without falling over little boys as they stamped and whooped, cardboard axes held aloft, their mothers' shawls trailing from their shoulders. Charlotte's boys were positively cowboy-mad.

Tonight the evening paper took ghoulish pleasure in informing the London public that the scalp of the Indian who had slain Custer at Little Bighorn would be on display at the Wild West. The thought made Maribel shudder. In Texas, on their honeymoon, she and Edward had been shocked by the malice of the American settlers towards the Indians. In towns like Brownsville and Corpus Christi callowness and casual violence were commonplace, contempt a matter of pride. In Reynosa, on the border with Mexico, they had found a small boy huddled beneath a bush, his arms clasped tight round his rickety legs, his dark eyes round and blank. Every one of his ten brothers and sisters had been rounded up by a party of farmers and shot, one by one, in the head.

Edward had been enraged. Like the Scots at Bannockburn, he saw the Indians as patriots, justified in taking up arms against the trespassers who would subjugate them and steal what was theirs. When he received news that the ranch he had purchased near San Antonio had been burned down by an Indian raiding party and the livestock all driven off, he only shrugged. Morality, he said simply, did not yield to

24

self-interest. It was hard to imagine a man less suited to a life in politics than Edward.

In the hall the grandfather clock struck midnight. Maribel knew that she should go to bed, that Edward would be cross if he found her still up when he got home, but she did not move. She would go to bed when the fire went out, she told herself, and, as she burrowed more deeply into her nest of cushions, a slow tingling moved down her arms and into her fingers. Not memory, precisely, but what the Portuguese called *saudade*, a yearning for something long unseen. There was no word for it in English. Perhaps most English people did not feel it.

She closed her eyes, the smell of sun-baked dust suddenly sharp in her nostrils. A wagon train was not every woman's idea of a honeymoon. In Texas Edward had bought a consignment of cotton which he was sure he could sell in Mexico for a substantial profit. They had been warned that the trek would be long and likely dangerous but the two of them had embarked upon the adventure eagerly, as hungry for movement as for money. They had travelled for nearly sixty days across wild and desolate country and, at night, fearful of Indian attack, they had formed the wagons into a circle and lit a great fire at its centre. Danger had suited her, and discomfort. Though time passed slowly, she had not fretted in its traces. She had eaten simply and slept well, her bed a straw-filled box slung beneath the largest of the wagons. Sometimes, when the night was hot and the scream of the cicadas beyond endurance, she had lain with Edward on his palliasse on the ground, gazing up at the vast sky salted with stars.

'For you,' he had whispered the first time, reaching up to cup the moon between his hands, and she reached up too, fitting the shape of her hands inside his.

'For us both,' she had answered and for the first time in her life she did not want to be anywhere else.

The fire stirred, the apple logs sighing into ash as the *saudade* curled in her like the smoke from an incense burner, solemn and sweet. When it had passed she lit a cigarette, drawing the smoke of the tobacco into the same parts of her. The previous winter she had suffered from an infection on the chest and the doctor had asked that she confine herself to twenty cigarettes a day. Maribel had refused to agree to any such thing. Oscar had once claimed that the joy of cigarettes lay in their being both exquisitely pleasurable and profoundly unsatisfying. Maribel had rolled her eyes and told him to inhale. When she drew the smoke into her lungs, the burning tobacco scattered sparks of light that danced in her blood. It was when she smoked that she knew that she could write.

Edward found her there an hour later, her dark head bent over a notebook, her brow creased, her tongue pressed in concentration between her teeth. The fire was almost out. She held a pencil in one hand and a half-smoked cigarette in the other. Torn-up pages, crumpled and abandoned, littered the carpet around her and, on a tray beside her, a soup bowl and an ashtray brimmed with smouldering cigarette ends. He bent over her, kissing her lightly on the lips.

'Whisky,' she said and she wrinkled her nose.

'All those years in Scotland and still you cannot adopt the ways of my mother country?'

'I have adopted parsimony and there is nothing more Scotch than that. You should be grateful.'

'Parsimony, indeed. You have on a very handsome dress, if I may say so, Mrs Campbell Lowe.'

Maribel made a face, though she could not help herself from stroking the silk of her skirts. Edward was right. It was a particularly handsome dress.

'You know quite well that in Paris everything nice is dear,' she protested. 'There is no purpose in spending almost as much money for things which are worth only the half. This dress shall last me ten times as long as a cheap one and prove the better bargain, you'll see.'

Edward laughed and poured himself a drink.

'Dearest Bo, it would not be half so much fun to tease you if you did not rise so eagerly to my bait. I should have you spend ten times what we do not possess to see you happy.'

'You know quite well that is a shocking lie but it is dear of you to say it all the same.' Maribel yawned. 'The vote went your way, I hope?'

'Not a bit of it. Between them, Matthews and that devil Warren have whipped the Tory bench into a roast-beef-and-port-wine frenzy about decency and the safety of our women and children. Why is it, when it is quite apparent that the vast majority of Conservative members dislike both women and children, that the merest mention of their frailties renders the whole herd red-faced and deaf to reason?'

'So they have banned public meetings?'

'Not yet. But it is only a matter of time. Ever since last February's riots the Home Secretary has done his utmost to stir up a terror of the mob. If one-tenth of his enthusiasm had been directed instead into the relief of the misery of the ordinary man, there would be no need for the demonstrations of which he is so afraid. You should be in bed.'

'I have been writing.'

'Successfully?'

Maribel made a face.

'May I read it?' he asked.

'Not yet.'

Edward drained his whisky and set the glass on Maribel's tray. Then he leaned over his wife, took the cigarette from her hand and stubbed it out.

'Bed.'

Putting out her hands, Maribel let him pull her to her feet. There was a fleck of something on one of his silk lapels. She brushed it away. Without her shoes the top of her head barely reached his shoulder.

'It is not so very late,' she said.

'Bed,' Edward said, and in the grate the dying fire sighed, exhaling soft grey ash.

3

TWO DAYS LATER MARIBEL attended a teatime lecture at the home of Mrs Gallop, Treasurer of the Society for Promoting the Employment of Women. They had been promised Mrs Garrett Fawcett, co-founder of Newnham College, Cambridge, but for some reason she had not been able to come. Her replacement was a heavily built woman with wiry hair who had studied at the Slade School of Art. She wore a dress the colour of stewed tea and, wound several times around her neck, a necklace of lumpy brown pebbles. Somewhere in Hampstead, or perhaps Bloomsbury, Maribel thought, there was a tailor who specialised in Attire for the Clever Spinster, apparel of such wilful ugliness that she could not look upon her clients directly but only in the reflection of a mirror.

'Because of her work with animals, it was not long before Rosa Bonheur found the clothing of her sex to be a tiresome inconvenience. It was to that end, and not for the depraved reasons that some have chosen to attribute to her, that she solicited authorisation from the Prefect of Police to wear men's clothing.'

Beside Maribel, Charlotte leaned forward, her head on one side. Maribel thought of the problems in the second stanza of the poem she had begun two nights earlier. There might be something, she thought, in *the airless parlour of the past, glass-eyed under glass*, but, though she worried at it like a terrier, she could not unearth what came next. Their friend Oscar had recently been appointed editor to a new literary magazine, *Woman's World*, and he had promised to look at anything she wanted to send him with a view to publication. Several times in the past weeks she had begun poems but, though in their first moments they seemed new and fresh, bright with a lustre that might, with work, become brilliance, like children's balloons they had by the next day shrivelled to something disappointing and faintly obscene.

She ached for a cigarette, for the carpeted hush of the flat at Cadogan Mansions. She could not think why she had let Charlotte persuade her to come. It was one of her gravest shortcomings, she thought, the impulse towards company. When the invitations arrived she meant to refuse them but instead she consoled herself with assurances that curiosity was as essential to a writer as paper and ink, that the company of other artists would stimulate both the intellect and the imagination, that to perceive the truths of the world one must live among them and not in the isolation of an ivory tower. It was said to be the opinion of William Morris that a poet should not require paying for his poetry, because he would write better poetry if he had an ordinary occupation to follow. That was all very well for Mr Morris, Maribel thought. His ordinary occupation was to make Art to order and sell it at a profit. So far she had managed only to interest a tiny literary journal in a short poem about Paris. However much she wished to convince herself otherwise, inspiration was not the same thing as distraction. Next year she would be thirty. By thirty Emily Brontë was already dead.

'Our Queen has condemned what she calls the "wicked folly" of Women's Rights,' declared Brown Dress. 'But must Bonheur be condemned for unsexing herself, as Her Majesty would have it? At the Slade, where I myself studied, they have at last permitted male models to pose unclothed for their female students. Surely Mme Bonheur's work attire, be it men's clothes or perhaps even none at all, is nobody's business but her own.

As she herself once so notoriously declared, "The epithets of imbeciles have never bothered me." They should no more trouble us.'

The applause was enthusiastic, mostly, Maribel thought, because they could finally have tea. Brown Dress bowed, her pebble necklace swinging violently about her chin.

'She'll put her teeth out,' she whispered to Charlotte, who pressed her lips together to keep from laughing and clapped more vigorously. When at last the appropriate thanks had been given the audience rose as one and moved quickly over to the platters of sandwiches and scones set out on the sideboard. Unable to wait any longer, Maribel pushed up the window sash and, in the shiver of cool air, smoked two cigarettes very fast.

'Did you discover what became of Mrs Garrett Fawcett?' Maribel said when Charlotte returned with teacups and a plate of cake. 'She had better have an awfully good excuse.'

'Apparently she sprained her ankle. Miss Russell nobly agreed to fill the breach.'

'Well, she is certainly wide enough.'

'Hush. She will hear you.'

'Of course she won't. Women of her kind don't listen. Especially not with all those hideous pebbles clattering around her ears. She seems to have appropriated half of Cooden Beach.'

Charlotte laughed and shook her head. 'Maribel! You are incorrigible.'

'Come on. It must weigh five pounds at least. Is it any wonder the woman's neck is thicker than her head?'

'My Aunt Agatha always said that if a person couldn't say something nice, she was better off saying nothing at all.'

'Then your Aunt Agatha was a fearful prig.'

The boom of their hostess's voice cut across their laughter like a noonday cannon.

'Mrs Charterhouse, Mrs Campbell Lowe. What are you two doing skulking over here in the corner?'

Mrs Gallop bore down upon them, driving before her a diminutive woman with thin hair and a timid expression. Maribel squinted into her tea. Charlotte's amused resistance to her more vinegarish remarks always left her feeling vaguely mean-spirited. Perhaps she had judged Miss Russell too harshly. The woman's appearance was dowdy, certainly, but her opinions were sound. It was enough for women to do battle with the full weight of history without being sabotaged by their own side. And yet the truth was that the Miss Russells of the world had always provoked her. Horrified by frivolity, disdainful of pleasure and pretty dresses, they wore their drabness like a medal, proof of their scholarly superiority.

'Maribel? You remember Miss Woolley, don't you?' Charlotte said as Mrs Gallop steamed away in search of new harbour. Maribel was certain she had never met Miss Woolley before in her life. She took the woman's limp hand, shaking it briskly.

'Of course,' she said. 'How do you do?'

'Very well, thank you,' Miss Woolley said. She sniffed.

'You have a cold,' Charlotte said sternly. 'You should be in bed.'

Miss Woolley shook her head. 'I could not have abandoned Florence on her big night. Not when she was so nervous.'

'Florence?'

'Miss Russell. She is part of my Circle.'

'I would not have thought Miss Russell the nervous type,' Maribel said.

'Appearances can be misleading,' Miss Woolley said gravely, with the authority of one asserting a great Truth. There was a silence. A drip was forming on the end of Miss Woolley's nose. Maribel wondered whether, if she stooped, she might be able to see the whole of Mrs Gallop's drawing room captured in its tiny globe.

'I thought Miss Russell's lecture most interesting,' Charlotte said at last.

'She is too modest, of course,' Miss Woolley sighed. She rummaged in her cuff for a handkerchief and noisily blew her nose. 'I should have liked her to talk more about her own work. It would have inspired us all, I think, to hear about the Muse.'

'The Muse?' Charlotte asked.

'Miss Russell draws from life, of course, but, though those works are of course most accomplished, they are not, in my opinion, her very best pictures. They are too rooted in this world, too – too corporeal.'

'You disapprove of naked bodies, Miss Woolley?' Maribel asked.

Miss Woolley's neck flushed pink.

'That's not at all what I meant. It is only that – well, Florence creates her very finest work, in my opinion, not from observation but from a place beyond our understanding.'

'You mean the imagination?'

'I mean the next world. The realm of the dear departed.'

As Maribel opened her mouth Charlotte shot her a warning look.

'The dear departed,' she echoed politely. 'How fascinating.'

'Have you ever attended a séance, Mrs Charterhouse?' Miss Woolley asked, her pink eyes brightening as she tucked her handkerchief back into her sleeve.

Charlotte shook her head.

'Oh, you should. You really should. It is quite something, you know. Why, only last week, Lady Ashworth conversed with her son, Gerald, the one who died of the measles when he was just a boy. The eagerness of the child, the endearments, it was too tender. "Darling Mama," he said, over and over, "don't cry, darling Mama." We were all quite undone.'

Maribel rolled her eyes incredulously at Charlotte, who ignored her.

'Was it a comfort to her?' Charlotte asked Miss Woolley gently.

'Oh yes, what a comfort! To know that our loved ones are near us, waiting for us, that death takes them not from us but only into another room? I –' She broke off and fumbled once again for her handkerchief.

'Forgive me,' Charlotte said. 'I have upset you.'

'Not at all. It is just that I – I lost both my parents last year. If they could only find a way through to me – to feel their presence near, to hear their voices, it would be such a consolation.'

'Of course it would.'

Miss Woolley put her hand flat upon her breastbone, drawing in a deep breath. Then she smiled bravely.

'You have not suffered as I have, I hope, Mrs Charterhouse?'

'My parents are too busy disparaging Mr Gladstone to allow for infirmity,' Charlotte said. 'Conclusive proof that it is outrage, not Salt Regal, that is the great tonic.'

'And you, Mrs Campbell Lowe? Do you still have your parents?'

'No,' Maribel said sharply. 'Both my parents are dead.'

'You poor dear. Do you miss them awfully?'

'I manage. It was a long time ago.'

Miss Woolley reached out and patted Maribel's hand. 'Tragic circumstances, I suppose?' she asked, her brow furrowed with sympathy.

Maribel crossed her arms. 'A carriage accident.'

'So fearfully common on the Continent, I fear. You are from Spain, are you not?'

'Chile.'

'But your father was Spanish?'

'My mother. My father was French.'

'Goodness. And you have never attempted to summon either of them?'

'Summon them?'

'Through spirit communication.'

'Good God, no. I'd rather put pins in my eyes.'

'Maribel,' Charlotte said reprovingly.

'For heaven's sake, Charlotte, you think just as I do. All that table-tilting and tapped-out messages and lamps switched on and off with strings beneath the cloth. It is the lowest form of charlatanry.'

'I say, now, come on!' squeaked Miss Woolley.

'Miss Woolley, science has yet to reveal many of God's great mysteries. But if the spirits of the dead could truly be summoned to speak with us, souls who have passed through the veil of death into the glorious mystery of the next world, do you not think that they would find something more momentous to relate to the living than "dearest Mama" and "kiss Dolly for me"? There's only one thing more deplorable than the imposture of the swindlers who conduct such gatherings and that's the feather-headed folly of those who attend them.'

Her hands on her hips, Maribel thrust out her chin. Her heart was beating fast and her cheeks were hot. She had not known her feelings on the subject were half so fierce. The result was startling and not a little triumphant.

Miss Woolley drew herself up to her full height.

'You may call it folly, Mrs Campbell Lowe,' she said loftily. 'I call it faith. It is fashionable to deride matters of faith these days, especially in political circles, but when the ignorant and the cynical dismiss new schools of study as no more than cheap subjects for sarcasm, I call it bigotry. It is like the Hindu prince who denied the existence of ice because water, in his experience, never became solid. It is one thing to demand rational proof, quite another to disbelieve everything outside one's own limited realm of experience.' Miss Woolley pressed her handkerchief to her mouth. The tips of her ears were a dark hot pink. 'You believe in bacteria, I suppose, though your eye cannot discern them? What conceit is it then that permits you to deny the existence of the spirits, which is only another form of life you cannot see?'

'The existence of the microscope? The growth of cultures in the laboratory? Controlled experiments? As far as I am aware, the Royal Society continues to favour empirical research and data collection over the science of table-tilting and levitation.'

Mrs Gallop bustled across the room towards them. Charlotte greeted her thankfully, drawing her into their midst.

'How kind you are to have invited us,' she said. 'It has been a most stimulating afternoon.'

Mrs Gallop nodded. 'Miss Woolley, I hate to interrupt so fervent a discussion but Miss Russell says she is ready to leave.'

'Yes. Yes, of course. I shall be there directly.'

'Goodbye, Miss Woolley,' Charlotte said. 'It was a pleasure to see you again.'

Miss Woolley leaned close, turning her shoulders away from Maribel.

'If you were to be interested in joining our Circle?' she murmured. 'I think you would find it most illuminating.'

'How kind,' Charlotte said.

'Then I shall send you an invitation to our next meeting. Miss Russell will be there, of course, and doubtless you will be acquainted with several others in our group. Do you know the Misses Elliott? Such impressive women. I have heard others remark upon the brusqueness of their manner but I find them both perfect sweethearts.'

'Miss Woolley?' Mrs Gallop prompted.

'Goodness, listen to me rattling on. Do forgive me, Mrs Gallop. As my father used to say, "Evaline, when you get on your high horse, you will gallop off – that is, canter off –"'

Charlotte and Maribel watched as Mrs Gallop steered the flustered Miss Woolley away across the drawing room.

'The tigress roused,' Charlotte said, shaking her head.

'I couldn't help it,' Maribel protested. 'She talked such deplorable rot.'

'Not you, dearest. Her.'

'Her?'

'The Miss Woolleys of this world are formidable when provoked.'

'I did not notice.'

'You never do.'

'That isn't true!'

'I wonder if I might go,' Charlotte mused. 'To her Circle.'

'You wouldn't?'

'Why not? If it's good enough for Mr Gladstone it's good enough for me.'

'The Grand Old Man is a member of the Society for Psychical Research, not a practitioner of imbecilic conjuring tricks.'

'It's just a bit of fun. Arthur would adore it, if one could only make him behave. Besides, who knows? There may be more to it than meets the eye. Perhaps Great-Uncle Julius will come back from the other side and finally confess to me where he left the key to the ice house.'

Maribel smiled.

'Don't you find it intriguing?' Charlotte asked. 'Not even a little bit?'

'Not even the slightest littlest bit.'

The tea party was breaking up when the two women took their leave. It was a warm evening, one of the first of the season, and the moon floated like a pale wafer in the darkening sky. Along the river the trees were ghostly with blossom. When the Charterhouses' coachman saw them he jumped down from his box, opening the door of the brougham with a half-bow. Charlotte smiled at him.

'Thank you, John,' she said.

'Is Edward in town tonight?' she asked when they were settled inside.

'Yes, but not at home. He is dining with Buffalo Bill.'

'Really?'

'Apparently Mr Gladstone thought the Wild West quite the thing so he invited Buffalo Bill to the House. Why he accepted I cannot imagine. The debate on the Crimes Bill is hardly likely to be a thrilling display of derring-do, and the dinners are indigestible.'

Charlotte laughed.

'And what will you do while he whoops in his warpaint?'

'I shall have supper on a tray in front of the fire and try to write.'

'That sounds perfectly dismal. Come home with me. We have only Arthur's brother with us tonight and he would love to see you.'

Maribel shook her head. Though she did rather dread the prospect of yet another evening alone she was not equal to the demands of the Charterhouse household. One had to be in particularly vigorous humour to enjoy the clamour at Chester Square, the swarm of children and guests, Arthur's jokes and pranks and insufferable gusto.

'Thank you,' she said. 'But not tonight.'

Charlotte made a face. Maribel squeezed her friend's hand. She knew that Charlotte worried about her, pitied her even. Charlotte could not imagine a life without children.

The sun had set and along the Embankment the strings of electrical lights were slowly coming into bloom. Maribel gazed out of the window, watching the tilt and dip of the brougham's side lantern, idly tracing the shape of the buttoned seat with one gloved finger. She could not help envying Charlotte the carriage. Though even her mother-in-law had to acknowledge the considerable efforts Maribel had made to coax a profit from the estate at Inverallich, there would never be money for a brougham. Edward had no interest in business and not the least aptitude for it either. It took hardly five minutes with the estate accountants to reduce him to peevishness. Arthur Charterhouse, however, who hadn't a cultured bone in his body, seemed to make money simply by looking at it.

'I don't understand it,' she had said to Edward, the very first time they stayed with the Charterhouses at Oakwood. They had been married less than a month. 'The two of you have absolutely nothing in common.'

Edward had simply shrugged. 'We have known each other almost all our lives.'

'He took an egg out of my ear at breakfast this morning.'

'You should be flattered. He doesn't do that to everybody.'

'When Mrs Luckhurst tried to talk to him about *In Memoriam* he claimed that the only form of poetry he has any time for is the limerick. Is it really possible to love a man like that?'

Edward had smiled, then, and kissed her, very tenderly.

'Dearest Bo, when one has known someone all one's life as I have known Arthur, one doesn't choose to love them. It's simply too late to stop.' He tipped her chin up, so that the tips of their noses touched. 'Just wait and see.'

'But he is such a fool!'

'Arthur plays the fool. It doesn't make him one.'

Maribel shook her head. 'It's her I feel for. If you had to be married to him you wouldn't last a day.'

'Charlotte is quite content. As for me, after all these years, I love Arthur quite as much for his faults as his finer qualities. Could you not try to do the same?'

She had thought he asked the impossible. It turned out that she was wrong. She still winced a little when Arthur slid down the banisters, it was true, but she had grown fond of him and not just for Edward's sake. It was because of Arthur that she had Charlotte. For Charlotte she would have forgiven him a good deal more than banisters.

*

They were almost at the park when Charlotte reached out and touched Maribel on the wrist.

'Do you think of them much?' she said softly. 'Your parents.'

'My parents?'

'It's only that you never talk about them,' Charlotte said. 'I wondered if you thought of them, if you even remembered them. You were so young.'

Maribel was silent. She could hear the coachman shifting on the box above them, the jangle of harness, the clatter of the horse's hooves as they passed under Marble Arch.

'I was twelve,' she said at last. 'That is not so young.'

She fumbled for her cigarettes, slid a match from its silver matchbox. The scraped match bloomed orange.

'What do you remember?' Charlotte asked.

Maribel closed her eyes, drawing the smoke inside her. She did not want to lie to Charlotte.

'She always smelled of orange blossom,' she said.

Charlotte smiled. 'What else?'

'She was beautiful,' Maribel said and suddenly she could almost imagine her, seated in the shade of the grape vine at Valquilla, her toes bare, the shadows playing on the pale straw of her wide-brimmed hat. 'She was beautiful and clever and she was always laughing. She hated to wear shoes. She used to sing lullabies to me when I couldn't sleep. *Arroz con leche me quiero casar.*'

'What does it mean?'

'It means *"Rice pudding, I want to get married."*'

'Truly?'

'Truly.'

Charlotte shook her head. 'Your mother had an unfair advantage,' she said. 'Even nursery food sounds charming in Spanish.'

'My mother loved sweet things. *Arroz con leche* and almond cakes and *alfajores*, little tiny pastries filled with caramel. My father used to call her *Jijona. Jijona* was a kind of soft *turròn.* Nougat.'

Maribel took a long drag of her cigarette and dropped the butt to the floor, crushing it out beneath her foot. Charlotte looked at her. Then, leaning over, she took Maribel's hand between hers.

'I wish I had known her,' she said.

Maribel did not reply. The two women sat together in silence, their fingers entwined, swaying a little as the carriage negotiated the uneven flagstones, and in her lap Maribel's other hand made a fist, as though it might squeeze the falsehoods into something true.

4

EDWARD WAS NOT RETURNED from his dinner when Maribel retired to bed at eleven. A little after two in the morning she woke to the soft pad of Edward's shoes on the hall carpet, the click of his dressing-room door. She thought of getting up, of going to him, but the sleep was too strong in her and she only turned over and closed her eyes. She dreamed of her mother, who squatted like a Buddha among Buffalo Bill's warpainted Indians and instructed Edward to shoot glass balls from the sky. In the morning, her head aching, she met Edward coming out of the bathroom and she knew she could not wait until after Scotland. When she kissed him he smelled of tooth powder and soap.

It was their habit to eat breakfast together in companionable silence, Maribel with a book propped up against the toast rack, Edward intent upon the newspaper. Occasionally Edward remarked upon a particularly interesting article but for the most part they communicated only through long-established habits, Maribel pouring tea, Edward buttering toast for them both. When they had finished eating, it was Alice's habit to clear the dirty plates before bringing in a second pot of tea and the first postal delivery of the day, which she placed at Edward's elbow. Edward would grimace at the paper, sigh and set it down. Flipping quickly through the envelopes, he set those addressed to himself to one side and passed the remainder to Maribel, who smoked a cigarette while they opened their letters.

On this particular morning, most of Maribel's were tradesmen's accounts: the greengrocer, the butcher, the laundry. There were several invitations, one of them in the careless scrawl of Edward's brother Henry. Maribel was very fond of Henry, an army officer who shared all of Edward's dash and none of his seriousness. Henry, who had nothing of the bohemian in him and was suspicious of any nation that did not play cricket, had never raised an eyebrow at the unusual circumstances of their marriage. The very first time they had met he had kissed her warmly and told Edward he was one lucky beggar. It had been Henry who had insisted on taking them to the Café Royal and toasting them with champagne, Henry who had decided, on his behalf and his mother's, that Maribel was to be welcomed wholeheartedly into the family. Henry did not believe in complications. As a result he seldom encountered any.

There was a note from Charlotte too, written in haste the previous evening.

> *I wished you had come back with me last night rather than going home to an empty flat. When we parted you seemed so sad and far away. I feared you would spend the evening gazing into the fire and thinking melancholy thoughts and that it would be all my fault. Forgive me, dearest, for pressing you to remember. My affection for you makes me greedy. I need to remind myself that there are certain secrets you are allowed to keep.*

Biting her lip Maribel slid the letter back into its envelope. The generosity of Charlotte's apology made her ashamed. She had grown so accustomed to her own secrets she no longer thought of them as secrets. They were judicious omissions, discreet approximations. They rounded up the numbers. She told herself that she was not so very different from anyone else. It was a truth universally acknowledged, after all, that the details of other people's lives were ineffably tedious, especially when they insisted upon a fastidious regard for the facts. During those long hours spent at the

Charterhouses' dining table as Arthur and his friends reminisced about their schooldays, she had many times been tempted to hurl the nutcracker across the room or stab herself in the back of the hand with the cheese knife, anything to create a diversion.

These days, though, there was seldom any requirement to lie outright. She could not even pretend it was for Charlotte that she lied, that it was a kindness. The truth was that the truth was impossible. Impossible for her and, in particular, impossible for Edward. She was obliged to lie, she knew that, but she could not bear Charlotte to be kind to her for it.

She took up the teapot and poured herself another cup of tea. Edward looked up over his newspaper and held out his cup. Now, she thought, was the time to tell him about her mother.

'So how was the famous Buffalo Bill?' she asked instead.

'Do you know, I was ready to dislike him thoroughly. I had pictured him in cahoots with the despicable Senator Dawes, trailing around Europe like a freak-show proprietor with his stolen Indians in cages while busily selling off the red man's lands to the railroads.'

'And?' Maribel asked.

'It proved quite impossible. The gentleman – and he is a gentleman, for all his American habits – is simply too amusing. His adventures have to be heard to be believed.'

'You were very late.'

Edward laughed. 'There is a rumour that the wives of the Garrick Club have been driven so much to distraction by their husbands staying out all night that they have sent Cody a letter with all their signatures, asking that he forbear from telling any stories after midnight. I am inclined to believe it. The tales of his adventures in the Wild West exceed the imaginings of the wildest Fenimore Cooper.'

'And the stolen Indians?'

'The truth is that Cody is a great champion of the Indians.

The few that survived Custer are a great deal better off with him than they are on the reservations. At least Cody is teaching them a little of the world they are now required to live in. They are fairly paid, well fed, clean. They have proper medical care. If only we could say the same of the miners or the dockers or any other working man in this country for that matter.'

Maribel rolled her eyes. 'You sound as though you have swallowed one of their advertisements.'

'Cody is extremely plausible,' Edward said with a grin. 'Though I am convinced he goes to bed in curl-papers. Nobody has ringlets like that naturally.'

'It is his diamonds I am envious of. I hear they are perfectly enormous.'

'You will have the chance to see them for yourself on Friday. Cody has invited us to the opening performance of the show.'

Maribel looked at him, dismayed.

'Must we go?' she said. 'On Friday you will only just be back from Scotland. I had hoped to have you to myself for once.'

'You have been complaining recently that life has become so dull. I thought you might think it diverting.'

'Me? Watching cowboys galloping about and shooting at one another? No, Red. You should think it diverting. I think I should find it rather tedious.'

Edward hesitated. Then, draining his teacup, he stood.

'I should go,' he said. 'I am due in Committee at ten.'

'When will you be back?'

'I'm not sure. I may have to go to Croydon. A League rally. I promised Hyndman I'd be there if there was no late vote.'

'Croydon? But we are dining with the Pagets.'

'Oh Lord, are we? I'm sorry. You'll have to send my apologies. Better still, apologise for both of us. You always say you find the Pagets tiresome.'

'They are better than no company at all. Red, truly, if I have to spend another evening here alone I shall go stark staring mad.'

45

'I thought you were writing.'

'I am failing to write. It takes up just as much time and is ten times as exhausting.'

'It will come.'

'Will it? I have written nothing for months, or nothing I wasn't ashamed of afterwards. And I am tired of you always, always being out. There are things – I hardly see you.'

'I wouldn't do it if I didn't have to.'

'You find time for the Wild West.'

'To which we are to go together, if you remember.'

'You know as well as I that I shan't see you from one end of the evening to the other. Croydon, for heaven's sake? I shall forget what you look like.'

'Then use the time you have. If you won't write, draw my portrait. Take my photograph. I don't know the last time I saw you with your camera.'

'That's because the camera is broken. It was never much use anyway.'

'And what about you? Are you broken too?' Edward snapped. Then he sighed. 'We make of our lives what we are able, Bo. Don't waste yours being angry with me.'

When Edward had gone Maribel rose and went to her desk, taking from its pigeonhole the book of marbled Venetian paper in which she jotted ideas for poems. She turned the pages. Scribbled sideways across one leaf was a list, written some months before at Inverallich, headed 'Champs-Elysées':

> *flash of silver bit*
> *white scum frothing on arched neck*
> *hooves like arrowheads slicing sky*
> *metaphor for love: coiled sinew, glint of iron*
> <u>*peril bare contained*</u>

Edward was right. One made of one's life what one was able. Taking out a sheet of writing paper she scribbled a note to the Pagets, pleading a head cold. That afternoon, when she was returned from calling on the Wildes, she took her mother's letter from her writing case and propped it against the mirror on her dressing table. There was no purpose in waiting for the right moment. There would be no right moment. The best one could do was to try not to be afraid.

She was sitting at her dressing table when Edward came home that night, brushing her hair in front of the mirror. She heard the click of the front door, the low murmur of voices as Alice took his coat and hat. She reached for her wrap but before she had put her arms into it he knocked at the door.

'Come in.'

She reached out a hand towards him as he opened the door. Under one arm he carried a large package. He set it down on the dressing table beside her and leaned down to kiss her on the top of her head. Glancing at the envelope containing her mother's letter she caught his hand and pressed it against her cheek. He smiled at her in the mirror.

'What a nice surprise,' she said. 'You're early.'

'Early? It's past eleven.'

'That's early for you.' She kissed his fingers. 'I am sorry I was so ill-tempered this morning. You were right. I had no right to be cross with you.'

'I am not so sure. I have neglected you horribly.'

'In the pursuit of a better, juster world. I should stop complaining.'

'Have you been working?'

Maribel shrugged. 'Something like that.'

Putting down her hairbrush she turned to face him.

'Edward, dearest, there is something I have to talk to you about.'

'Is anybody dead?'

'Not as far as I know.'

'Then can it wait till morning? I brought you something.'
Picking up the package he deposited it in her lap.

'For me?' she said.

'For you.'

'What is it?'

'Why don't you open it and see?'

She smiled excitedly as she slid off the string, tearing the paper a little as she unwrapped it. Inside was a wooden box, E. & H.T. Anthony stamped in black letters on the top. She lifted the lid and gasped.

'Edward.'

'It's rather fine, isn't it? It's American. The latest design.'

Very gently she took the camera out of its box. Perhaps ten inches square, a little more in depth, it was made of polished mahogany with exquisitely worked brass fittings and bellows of dark green leather. The lens protruded from its glossy face like the tip of a telescope. She held it in her lap, stroking the smooth wood with her thumb. She knew without asking that they could not afford it.

'It's so small,' she said.

'They call it a field camera. It's designed to be portable.'

'It's beautiful. Almost too beautiful to use.'

'If you say that I shall take it back.'

She smiled. 'I don't deserve it.'

'No. But I thought you would like it.'

'I love it. Thank you.'

She tilted her head up to kiss his cheek. Gently he took the camera from her lap and placed it back on the dressing table. Then, turning her to face him, he kissed her deeply on the mouth, his long fingers loosening the ribbons at her neck, slipping the silk from her shoulders. She sighed as his lips moved down the slope of her neck to her collarbone, finding the dip at the base of her throat, the tilt of her breastbone. She was tired, her body unresponsive, but it was several weeks since he had come to her and she had missed him. She clasped his head, burying her fingers in his red-gold hair, straining to stir in herself the heat of old desire. In the morning she would tell him about the letter. She closed her eyes as his tongue flickered between her breasts and over the cool skin of her belly, his hands tracing the curve of her hips and buttocks, the soft slopes of her thighs, easing her legs apart. She let them fall open. He pressed his forehead against her belly and the push of his tongue was hot and urgent.

Afterwards he fell almost immediately asleep. Maribel slept too, though at about four o'clock she woke and slipped out of bed to smoke a cigarette. On the dark-smudged pillow Edward slept on, his mouth slightly open and his hair tumbled like a child's. Maribel watched him, the jolt of the cigarette bright in her, and the desire that earlier had eluded her flared like a match in her.

In Mexico they had made love almost every night, biting back their cries so as not to waken the dogs. There had been a hunger to her then, a wantonness she had not known she possessed. On the dusty afternoons, as the heavy sun thickened the air and the mules drowsed with their heads low, she imagined him against her and the thought had quickened her breath and set her blood to racing until she burned like the night sky, her skin alive with one hundred thousand white-hot pinpricks of light. She had not known it was possible to feel that way about a man, that a sideways glance might cause her heart to turn over, the taste of his name on her tongue enough to melt her flesh. At the house on the Calle de León, for the sake of discretion, the Señora had assigned the gentlemen names of her own choosing. Edward she had introduced as Santiago.

'Sylvia,' he had said, taking Maribel's hand. 'What a pretty name,' and he had given her a private smile as though he told her a secret. She had not smiled back. Names might mean nothing in a place of that kind but it was discourteous to draw attention to the pretence.

Privately, of course, the girls gave the regular men names of their own. There was Bisabuelo, the ancient lantern-jawed count, and Apestoso, who smelled like an old dog, and Sudoroso, whose perspiration gathered in his eyebrows and scattered like raindrops when he neared the end. Angélique's nicknames were always the unkindest. Her most regular client she called Chinga, or Dog-fuck.

Sometimes, late at night, when the work was over and the lights in the drawing room extinguished, she and Angélique had sat on the balcony, the long windows open behind them, smoking cigarettes to discourage the mosquitoes. Below them, in the courtyard, the fountain sang quietly to itself in the darkness. Angélique was from Marseilles, or so she said. She was saving up her money until she had enough to buy a place of her own. Maribel had not liked Angélique much. She had dark eyes and a full mouth and a body that swelled like ripe fruit inside its skin. Her mother had been a great beauty but her father died and her mother's new husband had difficulty remembering which bedroom was his. Angélique had been obliged to leave. When she talked of men she made scissors with her fingers.

Edward had come to the house every other day for three weeks. Then he went away. Though she did not admit it Maribel missed him, the clean pallor of his skin, the way he talked to her afterwards, as though she were a real person.

A month later he returned and took her away. He had sat beside her as the train bore them towards Paris and, when she let her head rest sleepily upon his shoulder, he had kissed her forehead and told her that no man had ever been happier. In Paris he had invented the story of their accidental meeting, not for him, he was clear about that, but for the rest of them, who were foolish and would never understand. Maribel had thought the tale implausible, had asked how anyone would believe that

50

Edward of all people, who had been riding since before he could walk, had lost control of his horse on a busy thoroughfare, but Edward had told her no one would ever think of such a thing.

He was right, of course. Nobody did. Edward said it was because it was a delightful story and the truth was that most people desired to be delighted. It was the rare cynic who disdained the enchantment of propitious happenstance, where the fate of a beautiful woman might be decided by a chance meeting. Their set was young and gifted and they did not give a spoon for the finer points of Maribel's bloodline. Theirs was a new generation, who spurned the dusty hierarchies of their forefathers and disdained their titles. As for Edward, he was charming and clever and capricious, a gentleman whose pampas swagger was never quite obscured by his elegant tailoring. At Ascot he wore his gaucho knife under his dress suit. Maribel was exactly the variety of exotic bloom with whom a man like he would fall hopelessly in love.

Only Edward's mother had showed little inclination to be charmed by the romance of her son's courtship. Edward had taken Maribel to meet Vivien when they had been married three days. He had sat on the arm of his mother's chair, Vivien's hand on his sleeve, while Maribel stared at the floor and answered her new mother-in-law's questions in monosyllables. In the cab going home the two of them had quarrelled for the first time. Edward had accused Maribel of sullenness, of discourtesy. He demanded to know how his mother was supposed to love her new daughter-in-law if she refused even to look her in the eye. For her part Maribel pronounced Edward cruel and disloyal. She said that it was wicked for a man to care more for his mother than his wife, wicked and unnatural. Both had declared the other impossible. Edward had gone to his club and returned home very late. In the dark refuge of their bed he had held her and her tears had fallen on his face and oiled his dark red whiskers.

Maribel never asked whether Vivien knew the truth. On the whole she thought it unlikely. Even if Edward had tried to tell her, it was not in Vivien Campbell Lowe's nature to hear things that she preferred not to know. Edward knew that better than anyone. Though he had written to Vivien weekly during their time in America he had never once alluded directly to his new wife.

Whatever she knew, the older Mrs Campbell Lowe kept it to herself. She had no desire to attach scandal to the family. Perhaps if Maribel had proved a treasure hunter, she might have sought a way to disgrace her. Along with her unswerving conviction in her own judgement Vivien had friends in Paris. It would have been a matter of little difficulty to establish the non-existence of Maribel's aunt. But there was no treasure to hunt, only debts, and Maribel, unlike Edward, showed some adroitness in the management of money. It was because of Maribel that the estate at Inverallich had at last been persuaded to yield a profit. She could be frugal too, when required, and her frugality never showed. Vivien Campbell Lowe might disapprove of her daughter-in-law, she might even dislike her, but she could not fault her conduct. Besides, she was ambitious for her son. If Maribel was exposed it would mean the end of his parliamentary career.

Maribel's cigarette was burned to a nub. She took a final long inhalation and put it out. In the bed Edward turned over, flinging an arm across her empty pillow. In the Calle de León gentlemen had not been permitted to stay the night. On the train to Paris Maribel had leaned against Edward and it seemed to her a kind of miracle that they had found each other in such a place where the imitation of pleasure was sold by the hour. She wore a new dress she had purchased for herself with the money he had paid her, a pale grey silk that flattered her dark hair and pale skin, and on her finger his grandmother's sapphire ring. When she removed her gloves she set her hand on his, admiring the flash of the stone, hardly daring to believe that, from this day and for the rest of their lives, neither of them would ever again have anything to do with those kind of establishments and, at the same time, unable to shake off the fear that the squalid circumstances of their meeting could not be so easily dismissed, that the disgrace of it would leak like a slow poison into the flesh of their marriage. That he would, in time, find himself ashamed of her.

On both counts, it seemed, she had been mistaken. In all the years of their marriage he had never once alluded to the Señora or to the Calle de León. He had never, in anger or in spite, used the shame of her past against her, never attached any judgement to her situation or to those of other women in similar predicaments. In Parliament, during the debates about the Crimes Bill, he had shown both compassion and practical concern for the safety of girls obliged to work in brothels. Nor was his interest limited to the legislation. She was aware that, since they had been married, he had continued, with more or less regularity, to avail himself of the services such women took it upon themselves to provide.

Edward was discreet but she always knew. The act lifted his mood, much as riding one of his horses did, sharpening his appetite and invigorating his spirits. In the beginning, she had tortured herself with imagining him there, summoning precise pictures in her head of the padded silk headboard, the shaded lamps, the silver-stoppered decanter of whisky on a tray on the dressing table. He would frequent the kind of establishment that prided itself upon its discretion, a place that, insofar as such things were possible, might almost be thought of as respectable.

Edward would be a favoured client, of course, as he had been at the house on the Calle de León, because he was both courteous and appreciative. He would treat the girls as he treated his horses, with consideration and a connoisseur's eye, delighting in the line of a limb, a particular freshness of spirit. Edward might excoriate the failings of his fellow Members in the House but he was not a hypocrite. From boyhood he had determined to make a joyful business of life, to embrace its pleasures as willingly as its responsibilities. He did not censure or condemn the private conduct of others, nor did he speak as other men spoke of the high standard set by his own conscience. He had no wish to play Moses.

Maribel had found that, as long as she was careful not to think about it, it did not matter so very much. Edward was a good husband. She had not had to endure, as William Morris had endured, while his wife conducted an impassioned affair with his dearest friend in the house the Morrises had rented as a summer retreat, or come home, like Jennie Churchill, to find naked girls in her bathtub. She knew she was fortunate. For all their disdain of the ordinary conventions of marriage their friends longed to be happy. They envied Edward and Maribel their ease and affection, the evident pleasure they took in one another's company, the freedom of their lives unencumbered by children. Everyone knew that the Campbell Lowes were devoted to one another. If Maribel had a rival it was only the Houses of Parliament, who proved too frequently a demanding and ill-tempered mistress. As for the other – well, such places were not so very different from the Reform Club or the Athenaeum, private clubs where gentlemen might seek some relief from the heavy responsibilities of work and family. The wife that refused her husband the freedom of such establishments was either a duchess or a damned fool.

5

ON THE DAY THAT they were to attend the Wild West Edward woke in good humour, unable to conceal his enthusiasm. The show had opened its rehearsals to reporters and the newspapers had been full of breathless accounts of its wonders: of trick-riding and sharp-shooting, of buffalo-hunting and steer-roping, of the blood-curdling spectacle of a whooping stampede of war-bonneted Indians as they attacked the Deadwood Stage. They raved about the doll-sized Annie Oakley who could shoot the ash off a cigar while standing on her head and whose *coup de maître* was to stand with her back turned to a man holding up a playing card in his fingers which she then shot, a mirror in one hand and her inverted rifle in the other, straight through the centre of the card. As for the cowboys dared with mounting the wild, unbroken horses in the ring, it was plain that Edward would have given anything to have the chance to do just the same himself.

As usual Alice brought the post and fresh tea. Edward glanced at the envelopes, separating their piles. Maribel emptied her teacup and lifted the lid of the pot. It was not yet strong enough. Opposite her Edward frowned, tapping one of the envelopes against his fingertips. Then he set it on the top of her pile and handed it across the table. It had been addressed to Mrs Edward Campbell Lowe, care of the House of Commons. Someone had forwarded it to Cadogan Mansions. The words

PRIVATE & CONFIDENTIAL were printed across the envelope in capital letters.

'It is one thing to send love letters to a married woman,' he said with a raised eyebrow. 'It is quite another to expect his clerk to act as go-between.'

The letter was written on the same heavy stationery as the first, the familiar handwriting once more positioned precisely in the centre of the envelope. Maribel stared at it, her tea forgotten.

Edward went back to his newspaper. Without raising his eyes, he poured milk into his tea and stirred, setting the spoon back in his saucer. Then he lifted the cup and took a sip. Maribel rested her chin on her cupped hands. The sour smell of the marmalade was making her feel sick.

'How marvellous,' Edward said. 'After the Wild West preview the *Times* reporter asked Chief Red Shirt what he had thought of the British Parliament. The Indian pondered for a while and then answered that he had not thought it very magnificent. "Laws," he said, "could be made much more quickly in my country than in England."'

Maribel tried to smile. Her face felt stiff. Her mother had written to her at the House of Commons. Whatever it was she had to say it was plain that she intended to say it.

Edward put down his newspaper and wiped his fingers on his napkin.

'It is time I was going,' he said, pushing back his chair. 'I shall pick you up at four.'

'Don't go, Red. Not quite yet.'

'Oh?'

'There is something I have to talk to you about.'

'Ah. So it is an admirer.'

'What is?'

'The letter. I notice you haven't opened it yet.'

Maribel clasped her hands together, pressing her knuckles hard against her chin.

'It's not from an admirer. I wish it was.'

'I'm sorry?'

'It's from my mother.'

Edward stared at her.

'Your mother? Are you quite sure?'

'She is coming to London. She wants me to call on her.'

'And you know all this without opening the envelope? I'm impressed.'

'Don't. She wrote before. A week ago, perhaps two. I didn't tell you. I – I didn't know how. She knew about us. I wrote years ago, when we were first married. I should have told you then, I know I should, but I was ashamed. It was such a stupid, reckless thing to do. I thought – it was just that I wanted her to know that I was not dead. Or worse. I never thought she would ever write back. I am sorry.'

'Bo, look at me.'

Maribel sighed. Then slowly she lifted her gaze from the tablecloth.

'I shan't see her,' she said quietly. 'You needn't worry about that.'

'What is it that she wants?'

'She doesn't say. Only that she would not ask if it were not important.'

Edward considered his plate, one finger tapping out a rhythm against its rim. Then he looked up. Reaching across the table, he put his hand on hers.

'Then you should go,' he said.

'I don't know.'

'Bo, your mother was willing to sacrifice her own daughter to avert a scandal. She would not ask if she did not think it essential.'

'To her, perhaps. If the truth were to come out it would finish your career.'

'I seem to be doing a pretty decent job of that without your mother's assistance.'

Maribel smiled faintly.

'There is no reason why anyone should find out,' he said firmly. 'Not if you are both careful. I don't imagine you intend to make a habit of it.'

'No. But why now? And why risk meeting? What is wrong with writing a letter?'

'There are some things that cannot be said in a letter.'

She looked at him, the fear passing over her face like a shadow.

'You don't think – ?'

'There is no purpose in guessing,' he said gently. 'Go and see her. Let her say whatever it is she has to say. It will not be happy news, I fear, but if she has asked to meet you I do not think you can refuse her. How should we live with ourselves if we were to prove ourselves more cowardly than her?'

Major Burke escorted Maribel and Edward to the rear of the tent, where Cody was welcoming his guests. Unlike the inverted cones of the Indian tepees, Buffalo Bill's tent was large and luxuriously appointed, its canvas walls hung with trophies and the floor spread with animal skins upon which were arranged a number of comfortable armchairs fashioned from hide and buffalo horn. Waiters moved among the crowd with trays of drinks, plates of sandwiches and biscuits. The room was already very full.

'I'll leave you here if I may,' Burke said with a bow. A portly man, he wore a wideawake hat tipped to one side, beneath which tightly curled hair spilled in dark profusion over his collar. He had a long scar on one plump cheek and a magnificent stomach which he advertised with a startlingly extravagant waistcoat of gold and purple brocade. His moustaches reached almost to his chin.

'Major Burke is the reason every baronet and beggar in London has heard of Buffalo Bill,' Edward murmured to Maribel as they waited to shake Cody's hand. 'They say that in America he musters more press attention for Cody in a day than President Cleveland's staff can manage in a month.'

The show had been a triumph. From the very first procession, with the full company on horseback galloping around the arena at breakneck speed, yelling and whooping, to the final defeat of the Indians by the newly established pioneers, the audience had sat transfixed. They had marvelled at the skill of the shooters, the pluck of the cowboys as they raced their horses and roped wild steers and held on for their lives as their wild ponies bucked and plunged about the arena. But it was the Indian attacks that kept them on the edge of their seats. As a train of covered wagons was attacked by hostile Indians on horseback in full warpaint, brandishing tomahawks and firing rifles into the air, the round-eyed spectators had gasped as one, and when, in the nick of time, Buffalo Bill on his white stallion dashed to their rescue, his company of scouts behind him, the entire grandstand had erupted in wild applause. Even Maribel had found herself clapping, caught up in the thrill of it. Beside her Edward had cheered like a schoolboy, his hair standing up from his forehead in eager tufts.

Cody greeted Edward like an old friend, grasping his hand and pumping it hard. When Edward was able to extract himself he drew Maribel forward so that he might introduce her. Cody took her hand, bringing her fingers to his lips, and bowed, his eyes sweeping appreciatively across her throat and chest.

'You never told me your wife was so beautiful,' Cody said to Edward, who smiled and gingerly flexed the fingers of his right hand.

'My husband pays me not the least attention at the moment and you are entirely to blame,' Maribel said, laughing. 'He has eyes only for the Wild West.'

'Ma'am, if that is even a little bit true then we are set for success beyond my wildest dreams.'

'Is there any question of that? You are the toast of the town.'

Cody grinned.

'This week maybe. Till the next new excitement comes along.'

'Whoever that is will have their work cut out. Your show is perfectly thrilling.'

'Well, ma'am, it's the truth and that, I think, is the secret to it. No acting or sham, just an exact reproduction of life on the frontier as we have lived it.'

'A romantic version, though, surely?'

'There's fewer chimneys in the West, that's true, and not such a crowd of Englishmen either, but all else wise it's the genuine article.'

Maribel smiled. To her surprise she had enjoyed herself enormously. She had not wanted to come, had complained several times to Edward when he collected her that she had not the faintest interest in cowboys. As they inched their way through the traffic to Earls Court her mood had worsened. From South Kensington railway station the crush of carriages had choked the Old Brompton Road, the press of pedestrians seething among them like boiling porridge. The shouts of drivers and the rattle of conveyances and harnesses and the smell of drains and unwashed bodies had thickened in the unrelenting glare of the afternoon. Never had London been less congenial. And then, as if by magic, the coal smoke and the choke of mean housing had cleared into a wide expanse and the city was gone. Beneath the blue sky the spacious prairie swept upwards in waves of undulating green. At the foot of the hill were pitched clusters of white tents with pathways winding between, and dotted about them, the shrouded figures of Indian braves, their shoulders swathed in blankets of scarlet and blue. Behind them masses of shrub-choked rock rose cliff-steep over thick copses of trees, and further still, in the distance, colossal mountain ranges shimmered purple and gold, like a heat haze. If one disregarded the distant shriek of railway engines and the smoke that rose from one hundred hidden chimneys to smudge the cerulean sky, one might imagine oneself in the New World.

Beside Cody Major Burke gave a discreet cough. He had with him a tall, well-built gentleman with thick dark hair and whiskers, who, despite the hour and the occasion, wore an old-fashioned tweed coat of the kind favoured by prosperous provincials on market day. In demeanour, however, he could not less have resembled a country tradesman. Though he did not speak, there was a vitality to him, a heat that quickened the air about him. Maribel had never seen him before, and yet there was something familiar about his appearance that she could not quite put her finger on. Perhaps he was simply the kind of man who expected to be recognised.

'Colonel, if I may introduce Mr Alfred Webster?' Burke said. 'Mr Webster is the editor of the *City Chronicle*, one of London's most prominent newspapers.'

Maribel blinked. Like everyone else in London she knew of Alfred Webster. She looked around for Edward but he had drifted with the tide of the party and was conversing some distance away with a cowboy of immense height whose ruddy good health made Edward look positively anaemic. Beside him a stand bore a wooden hoop, like an embroidery frame, from which hung a shock of human hair, stuck with feathers. Edward leaned close, examining it, and Maribel shuddered. She wondered what Charlotte's boys would give for the chance to touch such a thing.

'Delighted to meet you, sir,' Cody said, pumping Webster's hand. 'I am so glad you could join us.'

'The privilege is all mine. I thought your show marvellous.'

'Then I shall hope that you make a habit of printing your views in large letters in your newspaper.'

'Oh, I do. It is something of a weakness of mine.'

Cody laughed. His was a face made for laughter, Maribel thought. As soon as he smiled, the planes of it folded neatly into place, like Japanese origami.

'Mr Webster, are you acquainted with Mrs Campbell Lowe?'
Burke asked him.

'Regretfully I have not had that pleasure.'

The newspaper editor turned to Maribel, fixing his gaze upon her as he bowed. While his face was handsome in the ordinary way, his eyes were astonishing, a brilliant blue-white that was both piercing and milkily myopic, like the eyes of an old cat. They gave the unsettling impression of both seeing into the very heart of her and not seeing her at all. She was the first to look away.

'I am, however, acquainted with your husband,' Webster said, like Cody unable to keep his eyes from sweeping the curves of her figure. Unlike Cody's, however, his study was of the utmost seriousness, devoid of the blandness of ordinary propriety. He did not smile. Maribel, who was accustomed to being looked at, was not accustomed to being looked at in that way. Despite herself she flushed.

'Is that right?' she said, pricklingly aware of her hand still clasped in Webster's. Abruptly Webster let her go. He did not take his eyes from her face.

'Did you enjoy the show?' Maribel asked.

'I thought it magnificent. Until two minutes ago, I had imagined it the most remarkable thing I'd see all year.'

From another man such a remark might have been impudent, even improper, but in Webster's face there was no prurience, only wonder. He gazed at her, running his hands through his thick hair. It stood up on end as though electrified.

'You are a flatterer,' she said softly.

'No, I am a newspaper editor. It is my job to tell the truth.'

A waiter brought a tray of champagne. Maribel took a glass. Webster did not. He watched her as she fumbled for her cigarette case, the glass held awkwardly in her fingers, and, though he hardly moved, the energy rose up from him like a race horse, charging the air. Awkwardly she snapped open the case and offered it to Webster. He shook his head.

'Please tell me you are not entirely devoid of vices, Mr Webster?' she asked, attempting gaiety.

'Oh, I have plenty. I am flesh and blood, after all.'

Extracting a cigarette she put it between her lips and hunted for matches. Webster took a box from his own pocket.

'May I?' he said.

Leaning towards her he struck one. The flame was sudden and startling. When she bent down towards it he cupped it with both hands, his fingers brushing hers. The shock of it made her dizzy. She drew deeply on the cigarette, pulling the smoke down into the shiver of her stomach. Webster watched her, turning the spent match over and over in his fingers. His palms were square, his fingers blunt and capable. On the edge of his left cuff there was a smut.

'I hope you do not disapprove of women smoking?' she said.

'Disapprove? No, why should I?'

'Some men do.'

'Some men are idiots.'

Maribel smiled.

'I smoke myself,' he said. 'I can't seem to keep a pipe alight but there is nothing to beat a fine cigar. Useful in interviews, too. A smoking man is more open, I find, he talks a great deal more freely.'

'Oh.'

Webster considered her. She could think of nothing else to say. Then he smiled, the skin crinkling around his eyes.

'Its effect upon the gentler sex, however, requires further study,' he said and he gazed at her, his smile half forgotten, all the vigour in him trained upon her like sunlight through a magnifying glass. She could feel herself burning.

'Why do you smoke?' he asked and she hesitated, considering her answer. It startled her, how much she wanted him to understand.

'It is not about talking,' she said at last. 'I think it is the opposite. When one talks one disperses a little, the words, the breath, it is as though one is making space inside oneself for whatever might be said in return. When I smoke, I become more – myself. The essence of myself. It is as though the smoking concentrates the me-ness, distils whatever I am thinking, whatever I am feeling, to something more powerful, something closer to poetry.'

She faltered, fearful that he might laugh. He did not laugh. He looked at her, his milky eyes bright and curiously still. Above his ears his hair was faintly streaked with grey.

'So you smoke to feel more deeply yourself?' he said.

'Yes, I think I do. Is that strange?'

'No. I think it is – wonderful.'

Behind her a man in an evening cape staggered, knocking her elbow and upsetting her glass of champagne. Maribel gave a little cry of surprise.

'For God's sake, man, what do you think you are doing?' Webster shouted, putting out a protective arm. Beside them several people stopped talking and looked round curiously. A balding man with a sweaty face nudged the gentleman next to him, jerking a thumb towards Webster. The man in the cape doffed his hat and performed a jerking little dance to his companion, who laughed uproariously and dragged him away through the crowd. There was a pause. Then the buzz of conversation resumed.

'Are you hurt?' Webster asked Maribel.

'No, not at all.'

'Shall I fetch you some more champagne?'

'No, thank you. I have had plenty.'

'Not so many vices, then.'

She smiled awkwardly. It had unsettled her to realise how many people there were in the room, how many pairs of eyes. She had barely remembered they were there.

'I am monopolising you,' she said.

'I was hoping you would not notice.'

'I should find my husband.'

There was a pause.

'You know I interviewed him for the *Chronicle*, when he was first elected to Parliament,' Webster said. 'Your husband.'

'I remember.'

She did remember, too. The notion of an interview, a contrivance which Webster had imported from America, was still a new one and Edward had accepted Webster's invitation to converse as much from curiosity as inclination. Webster was then only just out of prison and something of a novelty himself. The two men had eaten a jovial lunch together at Webster's club and afterwards smoked cigars. On perhaps two occasions Webster had jotted a brief note in a leather book. According to Edward he had talked at least as much as he had listened. The article that followed was largely favourable, though in Edward's opinion it bore only a glancing relationship to the conversation that had actually taken place.

'Honest portrait, my eye!' he had declared. 'It is no more than a frame in which to paint the innumerable virtues of Booth and the Salvation Army, an opinion I can hardly object to but on which I do not think I spoke a single sentence during the full length of our lunch. Not to mention the religious feeling with which he credits me. Still, one has to admire the dash of his prose. There is more life to his sketch of me than I could dream of mustering in reality.'

'He impressed me a great deal,' Webster said. 'It is easy to be a radical when you have nothing. Quite aside from the ethics of the thing, it is a matter of simple self-interest. But a gentleman like your husband, with whom God has blessed all he could conceivably want for happiness on this earth, well . . .'

His smile was reluctant, a private smile for one. Maribel felt the prickle of it in the soles of her feet.

'Alfred Webster, as I live and breathe.'

Webster turned. Behind him stood a wizened gentleman with

shrewd eyes and grey hair and whiskers so unruly they might have been scribbled by a child. Webster clapped him on the shoulder. His smile was broad, public, bland with the amiability of the clubbable businessman. Dropping her cigarette Maribel arranged her face into politeness.

'George Fording, what in the name of the Devil are you doing here? I thought you were dead.'

'I knew you would be hiding out here somewhere. Now I know why.'

Fording grinned at Maribel and held out his hand. He had long yellow nails, scaly patches around his knuckles. She shook it reluctantly, leaning back a little so that she might not have to inhale his sour breath.

'I have known Mr Fording since I was a lowly reporter on the *Northern Echo* several centuries ago,' Webster explained.

'Reporter? You were the errand boy!'

'I can't have been a day over fifteen. Fording of course was already ancient, even then. He taught me more in a year than my school had managed in twice the time. Every time I mark up a paper I give thanks to Mr Fording and his rules of thumb.'

'What I remember is how this young man used to catch the office mice and serve them grilled on toast so that we might all understand how it felt to be besieged in Paris!' Fording guffawed. 'So you are not too grand to talk to me these days, now you are a famous editor?'

'Good heavens, if I ever forget where I came from I hope you will restore my memory with a sharp kick to the backside. Pardon the language. The taller the tree, the deeper the roots need to go. There is nothing more intolerable than a man who reaches the top and cannot recall how he got there.'

'So speaks the errand boy. Your father, is he still alive?'

'He passed away eight years ago, God rest his soul, and Joyce has come south to us in Wimbledon. You remember my sister Joyce?'

'Feisty little Joyce with the pigtails?'

'No pigtails these days, though she has lost none of her Yorkshire plainness, I am glad to say. I shall never be permitted to grow grandiose with her about. Do you have sisters, Mrs Campbell Lowe?'

'I'm sorry?'

'I wondered if you had a sister?'

'No. No, I'm afraid I don't.'

'A shame,' Webster said. 'I have found sisters to be like bridge or needlepoint. A pursuit incomprehensible to the young buck but a considerable pleasure in middle age.'

The two men laughed. Maribel did not. She hugged her arms around herself, suddenly desolate. The front of the tent had been raised and clusters of people were wandering outside. The desire to be gone was so strong in her that it was almost a taste in her mouth. To her relief she saw Edward making his way towards her through the crush.

'Might we go?' she whispered. 'I am so tired.'

He nodded, squeezing her arm.

'Mr Campbell Lowe, good evening to you!' Webster said jovially. Maribel held Edward's arm more tightly.

'Edward, dear,' she said. 'You remember Mr Webster. And this gentleman is Mr Fording.'

'Good evening, sirs.' Edward gave Webster's outstretched hand a perfunctory shake. 'And how is the filthy swamp of Fleet Street?'

'The greatest agency for influencing public opinion in the world. And the House?'

'Still the National Gas Works.'

Webster gave an exasperated snort.

'There is nothing done in Parliament because you people are too blasted polite to shake the government into action!'

'Excessive politeness does not appear to be my difficulty,' Edward said.

'It is only with the power of the press behind you that the masses of the people will be raised from their slumbers and true pressure brought to bear!' Webster cried. 'I have spoken to Mr Hyndman about this. His reluctance is madness. I'm telling you, it is public opinion that powers the turbine of democracy, not timid toing and froing in the Chamber!'

'We should talk about this another day, Mr Webster. It is time I took my wife home.'

Webster glanced at Maribel. She dropped her gaze, heat once more suffusing her neck.

'I shall not utter another syllable,' Webster declared, holding up his hands. Then he lowered them. 'But you know I am right. There will be no change to Matthews' position while you have no one behind you but the Socialists and a ragtag of unemployed idlers. Think of Khartoum. Was it politicians who forced Gladstone into sending General Gordon? No, sir. It was the press, the Chamber of the Fourth Estate. Without the public clamour and the outrage and the letters to the newspapers do you think Gladstone would have conceded? Of course he would not. And nor will the Tories now, not with Ireland and half of your lot on their benches. If you are remotely serious about forcing the government to relieve the plight of the working man, you need us. Believe me, sir, you need us.'

'And my wife needs her rest. Goodnight, Mr Webster. Mr Fording.'

Maribel murmured her goodbyes and hastily turned away. She did not look at Webster, nor offer him her hand. She did not look at Edward either. She hurried towards the exit, leaving him to follow in her wake.

Outside the crowds had dispersed and the stallholders were packing up and closing their shutters. The ground was littered with spilled popcorn, torn tickets, a silk flower fallen from a hat. In the light of a gas lamp a man in a corduroy waistcoat stacked piles of volumes into a wooden box, while a boy beside him extracted the pins from a luridly coloured poster. The poster showed Cody on horseback at full gallop, a rifle in his hands. Above his hat in fat scarlet letters was printed BUFFALO BILL NOVELS 164: *BUFFALO BILL'S DEATH-DEAL or THE WANDERING JEW OF THE WEST* 4d. The evening was warm, the air soft. Somewhere a dog howled.

Maribel walked ahead of Edward, inhaling the charcoal-scented air, exhaling Mr Webster. She knew the stories, of course. Mr Webster had taken over the *City Chronicle* from Lord Worsley several years earlier and had proceeded to turn it from one of the glut of stodgy Tory newspapers that filled the racks at gentlemen's clubs into the best-selling newspaper in London. Though his first campaign had been to bring down a Liberal Member of Parliament accused of adultery (which the Liberal Member strenuously denied), it was not until his Sink of Iniquity articles that Webster had truly contrived to convulse the capital. After a frank and widely disseminated warning, in which he alerted his readers to the potentially offensive content that would follow over the next weeks, and suggested to those of a delicate constitution that they might wish to desist in the paper's purchase until such time as the story was exhausted, he launched a month-long series of features committed to the uncensored exposure of the entrapment, abduction and procurement for sale of London's poorest young women and children.

The Sink of Iniquity was not inspired by events, by the reporting of a particularly heinous crime or notorious court case. It was Webster's personal crusade. He vowed to force change, most specifically by compelling Parliament to raise the age of consent for girls from thirteen years of age to sixteen, and in this he proved rapidly successful. Week after week, the paper had revealed to the breakfast tables of respectable London the

69

Gomorrah in its midst, a subterranean world of reeking brothels, monstrous procuresses, forcibly administered drugs and padded chambers where wealthy gentlemen might indulge in private in the pleasures of an unsullied child. No detail was omitted, no outrage left unexamined. One by one the abhorrent proclivities of some of London's richest and most respectable citizens were picked over with disgusted precision. Demand for copies was so urgent that for days at a time the paper could not be found on a news-stand in the capital and frenzied crowds of newspaper vendors laid siege to the *Chronicle*'s offices for reprints. The pressure of public opinion proved irresistible. Weeks later Parliament passed an amendment raising the age of consent. Even those who disdained Webster's methods had to agree that they had been extraordinarily effective.

'Summer is truly come,' Edward said, catching up with her, and he tipped his head back, gazing up at the sky. 'What a beautiful evening.'

Maribel did not reply.

'I am sorry I abandoned you to Mr Webster. Did he try to persuade you to the canonisation of Oliver Cromwell?'

'Astonishingly the subject of Cromwell never arose.'

'Don't tell me you liked him?'

Maribel shrugged, not meeting his eye. 'I thought him perfectly agreeable,' she said.

'You liked him.'

'Yes, I did. I thought he was – vigorous. I could see how he makes things happen.'

'That, dear Bo, is precisely what is wrong with him. It is not the job of a newspaperman to make things happen. I cannot work out whether he is an evangelist, a fraud or a complete maniac.'

'He spoke very favourably of you.'

'Today. But I wouldn't trust him further than I could throw him. He regards it as his mission to raise a prodigious stink about whatever takes his fancy without the faintest concern for the consequences.'

'I had understood that to be the duty of the honourable Member for Argyllshire.'

Edward made a face. 'At least they have not yet thrown me in jail,' he said.

It was the laundrywoman's daughter from Whitechapel who had done for Webster. In order to prove to his readers how simply such a thing might be managed, he had procured a thirteen-year-old girl from her mother for the sum of five pounds. Disguised as a roué, he had witnessed the girl's abduction and consequent drugging with chloroform, before having her bundled off to a Salvation Army hostel in Paris.

Unfortunately for Webster, upon reading of her daughter's fate in the newspaper, the girl's mother had gone to the police. Charges of abduction and indecent assault were duly brought against Webster and his accomplices; Webster had been sentenced to three months in prison. That story had made the front pages on all of London's newspapers.

Maribel tried to imagine Mr Webster confined in a cell ten foot square. She could not do it.

'The man is a charlatan,' Edward said. 'Did you know that he attends séances to assist him in his editorial decisions?'

Something in Maribel shrivelled. She shook her head.

'I don't believe it,' she said.

'He has a medium come weekly to the *Chronicle*'s offices.'

'Surely that can't be true.'

'Burns's friend Jamieson worked for him. Or he did until Webster had him try to procure a copy of de Sade's *Justine* to add a little spice to his Sink of Iniquity stunts.'

'De Sade? Wouldn't that have been illegal?'

'Come on, Bo. Surely legality is but a trifle when one's dead relatives have gone to all the trouble of bringing instructions from the Other Side?'

At the main gate a jostle of cabs waited at the stand, the horses stamping and jingling their harnesses. Edward helped Maribel into the foremost carriage. It smelled stale and she pulled the leather strap to slide down the sash as the cab jolted forwards, breathing in the cool evening air. Beyond the window the sooty houses of West Kensington hunched along the narrow pavements in cramped, provisional rows.

'It's funny,' Edward said. 'I had almost forgotten we were in London.'

When Maribel did not answer he put a hand on her arm.

'I am sorry I abandoned you,' he said. 'I lost my head. Burke introduced me to Chief Red Shirt.'

'Was he all you had hoped?'

'He is wary. I don't know if he has been coached in the subject but he was very careful to give a good account of the American government and their treatment of his people, though I suppose it is conceivable that the interpreter simply excised any seditious remarks from his translation. The ways of the white man have certainly rubbed off on him. He told me that he had visited the Palladium and then he sold me this for a shilling.'

Edward reached into his coat and pulled out a studio portrait of Red Shirt dressed in his feathered war bonnet, a pistol cradled in his hands. The Indian chief did not look directly at the camera but gazed downwards, a slight frown between his eyebrows. A scribble of ink across the bottom corner of the mount passed for an autograph.

'For you,' he said, passing her the photograph. 'A memento. I should have got one of Webster but it seems that signed photographs are the one form of self-promotion in which he does not engage.'

Maribel frowned, coughing a little on the smoke of her cigarette.

'This one will do very well.'

At home she propped the picture of the Indian up against the mirror on her dressing table. It was a poorly composed photograph, she thought as she brushed her hair. The background was ill conceived and badly lit so that it lacked depth and shape. As for Red Shirt himself, with his clasped hands and anxious expression, he resembled nothing more than a harried bank clerk in a silly hat.

'If you cannot convince yourself you are adorable, my dear, what hope do you have of convincing an audience?'

The inflection of Mr Corelli's Italian-London drawl came back to her precisely. Maribel had not thought of the old photographer for years. He had been old even then, unimaginably old to the hopeful girls who trooped up to his third-floor studio in Soho Square to pose against the heavy velvet curtains he had suspended from his ceiling. There were plaster pilasters, a little chipped, that rocked when you touched them and a screen of wrought iron. Mr Corelli's portraits tended towards the classical. The studio was shabby, the floor marked with fraying crosses of tape. The velvet curtains smelled of greasepaint and dust and the dark red fabric was faded into stripes by the sun. Even as she pretended herself Juliet, one hand at her throat and the other set lightly on the unreliable pilaster, Maribel had wondered if Mr Corelli might soon become similarly striped, his back and shoulders a fresh black from being concealed beneath the dark cape of the camera, his trousers bleached to grey. It was said that he had photographed Ruth Herbert at the height of her theatrical career.

In those days, as she imagined Italian sunshine and waited breathlessly for fame to find her, Maribel had looked around his dilapidated studio and she had pitied him. His life was as good as over, hers only just begun. Now, sitting at her dressing table in her high-ceilinged bedroom with its silk-draped bed, she wondered if he might still be found in Soho Square, still taking photographs of young girls who dreamed of Ophelia and Guinevere and audiences at their feet, the tears wet upon their faces.

'One day,' Maribel had said to him then as she counted out his money coin by coin, 'one day perhaps you will tell people that you photographed Sylvia Wylde.'

'Perhaps I will at that, Miss Wylde,' he had answered as he slipped the money into his pocket.

It was the kindest thing that anyone in London had said to her.

6

O N THE DAY SHE was to meet her mother Maribel rose
early. The room was close and her nightgown clung
to her damp skin as she crossed to the window, pulling
back the curtains and raising the sash. It had been sultry for
days and the weather showed no sign of breaking. Though it
was not yet seven o'clock, the sun was already hot in the dazed
sky. In the street below, the milk woman peered through the
railings of the house opposite, calling out to an unseen maid-
servant as she lowered a can of milk into the area. Her handcart
was propped against the lamp post, the churns glazed with
sunlight. The milk would be souring already, knots of white
gathering in the yellowing rim. Maribel watched as the milk
woman pulled up her empty rope and, curling it around her
hand, tramped back to the cart, her hobnails ringing on the
flags. The lettering on the side of the cart declared it the property of *Kemp, 36 Eccleston Street*. Perhaps, Maribel thought, she
would allow herself to be photographed. Milk women were a
dying breed in London, now that the trains brought milk in
from the country. In some parts of the city the dairies delivered
the milk ready measured in glass bottles made especially for
the purpose. A milk woman, however diligent, would not be
able to depend forever on Mr Kemp of Eccleston Street.

Maribel fanned herself with one hand and glanced at the clock
on the mantel. In four hours the hansom would be here. It
seemed an eternity and yet hardly any time at all. The dress

she had decided upon hung sponged and ready in the press but she would need Alice's help with her hair if she was to wear the hat she had purchased for the occasion, a pale straw with a pleated silk band and a wide enough brim to obscure her face. Perhaps she should ask Alice to serve breakfast early. Then again, in this weather she had hardly any appetite. The thought of hot tea was impossible.

Her mother had suggested that they meet at a house on Milton Terrace, a quiet slip of a street hidden among the wide stuccoed villas of Kensington, where she had arranged to stay for the duration of her visit to London.

Maribel could not picture her mother in London. She had talked of cities as others talked of darkest Africa, with bewilderment and a delicate shudder of distaste. When Maribel tried to summon an image of her, she could only think of her in the house by the river, sitting at the walnut desk in the window that looked out over the garden, her head bent over her letters and a dog asleep at her feet. There had always been dogs, brown-and-white King Charles spaniels with chocolatey eyes and foul breath and pink tongues like pansies. Her mother used to clutch them in her lap when her father shouted, her head bowed, her breath and the dog's coming together in shallow snuffles. There was nothing that mortified her mother more than open exhibitions of emotion.

And yet she had travelled a considerable distance to confront face to face the daughter she had not seen for thirteen years. In none of her three letters had she given the slightest intimation of her purpose. It was surely too late for recriminations. Someone was dead, more likely, dead or dying. That was what Edward had meant when he said there were things you could not write in a letter. She thought perhaps that, if it were her father, she might not mind too much, or any of them for that matter, any of them at all just as long as it was not – She shook her head, screwing up her eyes and pressing her fists against her temples. There was no purpose in any of it, the remembering or the wondering what might happen next. She could torment herself with possibilities until she drove herself mad.

Restlessly she padded about the bedroom, picking things up and putting them down. On the floor by the press her evening dress lay abandoned where she had left it, the bodice collapsed into the crust of its skirts like a failed soufflé. The previous night she and Edward had dined with old friends of his mother's in their house at Carlton House Terrace. On their way there, as they neared the Palace, Edward had asked the driver to take them through St James's Park and up to Trafalgar Square.

Despite the lateness of the hour the park was crowded, but in place of parasols and perambulators, the lawns and benches were heaped with bundles and ragged camps had been set up beneath the trees. The heat had brought out the destitute like lice. At the centre of the park, beside the lake, workmen in shirtsleeves busied themselves on the construction of a band-stand in preparation for the Queen's Jubilee celebrations. A smith crouched over a fire, the flames illuminating his face. The heat of the furnace turned the sticky air to water, scarlet sparks darting like fish.

As the driver entered the square, turning the horses towards Pall Mall, Edward called up to him to stop the cab. Families huddled around the fountains, drawn by the promise of refresh-ment and a free wash. A few ragged infants played in shallow puddles on the flagstones, shrieking and slapping the dirty water with their hands, but the prevailing sense was one of dull-eyed enervation. On the south side of the square a pair of constables stood in the shadow of a statue, sweating in their serge uniforms. Maribel watched from the window of the cab as Edward crossed over to speak to them. With his fastidious grace and elegant evening clothes he seemed to Maribel as much unlike the two thickset policemen as the Indian Chief Red Shirt himself.

The anger had stayed fierce in Edward all evening. The

policemen had told him that the number of vagrants sleeping in the square was growing, that everyone knew it was the bread vans that were to blame for they attracted 'loafers' on the make. They said that the Home Secretary himself had said that it was a disgrace to the city. As dinner progressed Edward's wit, always caustic, took on a savage edge. He gave an uncomfortably close impression of Lord Salisbury caressing a capitalist, his hand sliding suggestively between the buttons of his evening shirt. He pretended himself an African savage abandoned in the slums of the East End, tugging on the bone in his nose and enquiring querulously what precisely the English meant to teach him of civilisation. When he proposed a revision to the rules of Glorious Twelfth where, in place of grouse, the guns might be permitted to shoot Tory landowners or even, for a price, the lesser-spotted German princelet, his hostess was provoked enough to speak sharply to him, but neither her disapproval nor the obvious embarrassment of his fellow guests had the least effect upon him. As the women withdrew from the dining room Vivien took Maribel to one side.

'Whatever is the matter with Edward?' she asked. 'He is behaving appallingly.'

Maribel shook her head. 'We came through Trafalgar Square this evening,' she said. 'It shook Edward a good deal. You know as well as I how heavily the injustices of the world weigh upon him.'

'The world's injustices provoke a man to indignation,' the older woman said tartly. 'It is his private dissatisfactions that render him offensive.'

Maribel had been saved from the necessity of a reply by her hostess who, passing through the hall, seized upon them both and bore them into the drawing room. By the time the gentlemen joined them Edward's fury had sunk to an ashen gloom. They left soon afterwards and travelled home in silence, Maribel drawing greedily on the cigarettes that she had refrained from all evening out of affection for her old-fashioned hostess and the reluctant conviction that at least one of them should try to abide by the conventions of good manners. Edward had slept in the dressing room. He had left for Scotland before dawn. Maribel had woken briefly, had heard his low cough as he passed her bedroom, the muffled slam of the front door. He had not come in to say goodbye.

The clock chimed the half-hour. Time would pass, as it always did. In five hours, perhaps less, it would all be over. She sank down on to the bed and tucked her legs up beneath her. In the drawer of the bedside table she kept a leather-bound notebook and several much-chewed stumps of pencil but she did not take them out. It was too hot for words. Instead she reached for her cigarette case and, lighting a cigarette, leaned back her head, rounding her lips to release the exhaled smoke in a series of neat rings. There was consolation in the circles' perfect round-ness, their steady progress towards the ceiling.

Milton Terrace was an unobtrusive row of perhaps twelve white-painted houses set back from the road behind black iron railings. There were no houses on the opposite side of the narrow street. Instead a walled garden exploded from its crumbling brickwork, ivy like unkempt hair, a tangle of rose bushes heavy with browning blooms. The houses of the terrace were austere, narrow and flat-fronted, their windows discreetly pedimented. The only embellishment was a modest stone balustrade that ran the full length of the first floor, divided into twelve by fans of iron in the same plain style as the railings. The front doors were all painted black, their brass numbers polished, their steps scrubbed clean. There was no mistaking the street's respectability. Tucked behind the splendid villas of the adjoining streets with their pillared porticoes and extravagant stucco mouldings, the houses bore themselves with the prim self-effacement of maiden aunts.

Maribel straightened her hat and tugged the creases from her gloves. Then, descending from the cab, she walked slowly up the four shallow steps to the front door of number 8. When she pulled the bell the loudness of it startled her. She touched her tongue to her dry lips. She could hear the sound of footsteps from inside the house. She arranged her features into an expression of polite enquiry.

The young woman who opened the door wore a dress of ice-blue silk, stiffly ruffled and bustled in a style that was no longer quite fashionable. Her hair, swept up in a knot, was mousy brown, with a short fringe frizzled over her shallow forehead. She stared at Maribel, her eyes round and pale as sucked sweets. Maribel frowned.

'Is Mrs Bryant not at home?' she asked stiffly. 'I am expected.'

The woman blinked, her mouth wide open in an O. She bounced a little on the balls of her feet, her hands flapping at her sides. Maribel stared at her.

'Edith?'

'Oh my, oh my, Peggy! It's really you!' Glancing in alarm along the deserted street, she seized Maribel's hand and tugged at her like an impatient child. Her own hand was hot and very damp. 'Oh my goodness, come in, come in! Quickly, before anyone sees you. Oh, Peggy, look at you! I can't believe you are really here.'

Peggy. No one had called her Peggy for thirteen years. She had always hated it. No proper actress could be called Peggy, or Margaret for that matter. They were starchy schoolgirl names, names made of needlepoint and piano lessons and conjugated French verbs. Girls called Peggy were not breathless with passion, magnificent with anger, devastated by grief. They did not raise armies or plot murder or love so entirely that they would swallow poison rather than live without their beloved. They never stood before a rapturous audience, their arms filled with lilies, to receive a tearful standing ovation. Girls called

Peggy mouldered for ever in the provinces, where nothing good ever happened and the only prospect was to become the wife of a red-faced squire.

'I am Maribel now,' she said.

Pulling her sister into the house, Edith closed the door hurriedly behind her.

'Oh, Peggy,' she said. 'I mean, Maribel, oh, I don't know if I can call you that, it's – well, it's so pretty, exotic even, but – I can't believe it. It's really you! Mother, it's her! It's Peggy! Oh, Peggy, you look just as you always did! Mother would have had me at the Ragged School – Tuesday is my day for Good Works – but I simply couldn't. You don't mind, do you? I shan't breathe a word, I promise. Mother has sworn me to secrecy. And the children are gone to the museum and the maid sent out on some fool's errand and Cook won't come upstairs, she never does, so you are quite safe.'

Maribel blinked. 'You are married then?'

'For five years. So I suppose I've changed my name too, how funny. I am Mrs Hubert Birtles now. You look a little pale, Peggy. Can I fetch you some water?'

Maribel shook her head. Perhaps it was the heat that made her so dizzy.

'Mother!' Edith cried. 'Look, it's Peggy. She's come! Except that she is called Maribel now. Isn't that a pretty name, Maribel?'

'Hello, Peggy dear.'

Maribel turned round. Her mother stood in the hall. She wore the three-stranded pearl necklace she had always worn when Maribel was a child and a green dress with a high collar. A green dress. So she was not in mourning. Maribel swallowed, silently thanking God. If it was Ida at least she was not dead.

'Mother.'

For as long as she could remember Maribel had known that her family did not belong to her, that she had somehow accidentally been exchanged at birth. Apart from Ida, her sisters were timorous, biddable, so awash with docility that it made Maribel want to scream, and the boys were just dolts. When she railed against the dreariness of her existence, her mother had made the face she made, when her mouth pinched and the tip of her nose went white, and called her histrionic. Mrs Bryant considered impetuosity in women intolerably vulgar. Maribel had lain in bed at night listening to Lizzie sucking on her tongue as she slept, and imagined herself Lady Jane Grey, imprisoned in the Tower, or better, Joan of Arc at Rouen, for, although Joan of Arc was not so beautiful, she was a soldier and a Catholic which was more dramatic.

Ida had loved Joan of Arc almost more than she had. For years Ida had kept a picture of the saint tucked inside her Bible so that she could look at it during the sermon on Sundays. She said it was so that she would remember that being clever and fighting people was sometimes what God wanted you to do, even if you were a girl. On the days that Ida did not want to be an elephant keeper when she grew up, she wanted to be a soldier-saint like Joan of Arc. Sometimes they slipped out late at night, when the others were all asleep, creeping across the garden and into the woods beyond. The woods were full of strange loud noises, foxes screaming and owls hooting and trees moving restlessly in the earth. Maribel held Ida's hand and told her it was essential for an actress to understand fear, but Ida was not afraid. She turned cartwheels on the lawn, her night-gown a pale ghost in the darkness, and said that in the night the world was more exciting because you could not see where it ended.

Ida had been twelve when Maribel ran away. Maribel had not given a straw for the rest of them, but Ida, brave, dogged Ida, had been her ally, her confidante, the only one who understood her, who loved her for herself and not the insipid dullard they wanted her to be. She had promised to take Ida with her. In the end she had not even left a note.

Her mother stepped forward and kissed her lightly on the cheek. She smelled, as she always had, of face powder and rose water. Maribel's face felt stiff as a doll's. She hardly trusted herself to move. Beside her Edith issued a low moan, pressing her hands against her mouth and hopping from foot to foot.

'It is good of you to come,' Mrs Bryant said. Her mouth twitched a little, as though fingers plucked the nerve strings beneath the skin. 'Did you have a tiresome journey?'

'No, no. The traffic was light. And it is not so long a distance. You never said Edith would be here.'

'Well, it is her house, dear. That is a fetching dress. Unusual.'

'It's from Paris. Nobody in Paris wears the bustle any more.'

'Is that right? We are rather insulated from the fashions, in Yorkshire.'

There was a pause. In the corner a large grandfather clock ticked loudly. Mrs Bryant pursed her lips. Then she smiled, stretching her lips over her teeth.

'Well, you certainly look well. You are hardly changed at all.'

'Nor you.'

It was true. In the thirteen years since she had seen her, her mother had grown perhaps a little looser around the jaw but for the most part she looked exactly as Maribel remembered her, her hair parted in the middle and caught in a low roll at the nape of her neck, her soft pale face barely fretted with wrinkles. On her left hand she wore the pearl and ruby ring that Maribel had liked to play with when she was small. Even the shape of her nails was familiar.

Maribel thought of her beautiful Spanish mother, who had not existed until Maribel and Edward had invented her, and who, as the years passed, Maribel seemed more and more vividly to remember. In Madrid, when Edward took her away from the Calle de León, they had lain in bed in the afternoons in a small hotel near the railway station and imagined a third life for Maribel, not Peggy Bryant or Sylvia Wylde but Maria Isabel

Constancia de la Flamandière. The details of her new childhood were shaped in part by practical considerations – she spoke good French and, because of Victor, tolerable Spanish, and Chile, unlike France or Spain, was conveniently far away – but also by the shape of things as she had always wished them, as they were meant to have been. Maribel's Spanish mother had died tragically young but she had lived as life should be lived, joyfully and without restraint. On sleeply summer afternoons she had held her only daughter in her lap and stroked her hair and told her mischievous stories about the starchy matrons of Buenos Aires, whose priggishness was surpassed only by the English.

'How is Ida?' she blurted out before she could stop herself.

Mrs Bryant's mouth pinched.

'Your brothers and sisters are all quite well, thank you for asking, and your father too, though he suffers these days with his ankles.' She frowned, her head on one side. 'Surely you don't need to keep up that peculiar accent? There is no one here but us.'

'Mother –' Edith giggled.

'Goodness, Edith, I suggest it only for your sister's sake. One would think she'd be glad to have the chance to drop the pretence. Be herself for an hour or two. It's hardly as if you and I don't know who she is.'

Maribel shook her head.

'Actually, you don't have the slightest idea,' she said, her Continental lilt more pronounced than it had been for years. 'You never did.'

There was a silence. Edith shifted from foot to foot. Then Mrs Bryant sighed, fanning herself with one hand.

'It's unspeakably warm, isn't it? I wonder how long it can hold. Edith, won't you invite us to sit down? You can't want us cluttering up your hall all morning.'

'I don't mind,' Edith said and, thrusting out a hand, she clumsily squeezed Maribel's arm. Maribel flinched. With a strangled gasp, Edith pushed past her mother and, shoulders hunched, scurried down the narrow hall towards the parlour.

Despite the brightness of the day the room was dim, the windows obscured by heavy curtains with stiff fringes, and crowded with rugs and sofas and footstools and tables inlaid with mother-of-pearl and papier-mâché screens and spindly-legged chairs upholstered with spaniels in needlepoint. Beside silk-swathed standard lamps and vases bristling with bunches of dried grasses and peacock feathers, claw-footed tables were laden with glass bowls in pastel shades, each filled to the brim with waxen fruit or marble eggs or flowers made from seashells. Between these curiosities prowled a small menagerie of birds and animals in glass cases, while from his place beside the fire-place a large Negro boy stared at Maribel with beady glass eyes, clutching at his arsenic-green draperies. Above him on the mantel a green marble clock of similarly poisonous hue could just be discerned behind a barricade of porcelain figurines, brass candlesticks, ornamental plates and fans decorated with découpage. The coal scuttle bore a picture of Warwick Castle.

'Won't you sit down?' Edith said.

How many times had she said that to Maribel when they were children? As a girl Edith had only ever wanted to play house. Whenever it was her turn to choose the games, she had insisted upon endless wearisome tea parties with dusty water poured from the dollies' teapot and oak leaves for sandwiches. When Maribel had on one occasion attempted to inject a little excitement into the proceedings by staging a fit, Edith, awash with tears, had declared her sister the cruellest creature the world had ever known.

Maribel perched on the edge of an overstuffed sofa and slowly peeled off her gloves. The room was stifling. On the stool before the empty grate a jug sweated, beads of moisture sliding over its belly. They might have been back home in Ellerton. Nothing would have changed there, of course. There would still be the fat dust-pink chesterfields crowded around the fireplace, the pink-trimmed curtains with their pattern of bloated roses, the fender stool embroidered with peacocks, the fringed lamps and the painted miniatures and the china shepherdesses and the poker with the handle shaped like a pine cone. Trapped there on tedious afternoons she and Ida had sometimes used the shepherdesses as puppets, setting them in dramatic tableaux along the mantelpiece, but the housemaid always put things back the way they had been before. Nothing in that house had ever changed. She had thought she would go mad with the overstuffed sameness of it, month after month, year after year, until she could hardly breathe.

'You must be in need of refreshment,' Mrs Bryant said. 'Edith has had Cook make fresh lemonade. I can't stomach tea in this weather, can you?'

'Lemonade would be nice.'

Mrs Bryant poured.

'Laurie writes that in India they drink tea all the time, despite the heat. And all those ghastly curries! I have to keep reminding myself he is a grown man and won't get the stomach ache.'

Maribel took the glass. A grown man. When she had last seen Laurie he had been eleven years old, a thin, shy boy with a mop of unruly hair and a passion for toy soldiers. He had lain for hours in the nursery on his stomach, arranging them in lines. The others had made an eager audience for her performances, settling themselves cross-legged, the little ones in their laps, as, dressed in trailing chiffon, she was Cleopatra or Lady Hamilton or Héloïse whispering the secrets of her heart to Ida's Abelard. Not Laurie. Even as she wept, Mark Antony's dying body cradled in her arms, she could hear the boom from the back of Laurie's throat as his heavy cannon decimated the massed ranks of Napoleon's Imperial Army. Occasionally a small lead figure bounced dully off the wall.

'Still, I suppose one should be grateful, if only for the sake of

Her Majesty's Golden Jubilee. Edith says there are all manner of celebrations planned so one must hope it holds. After such a long hot spell poor weather would be a terrible disappointment.'

Maribel sipped her lemonade. It was weak and over-sugared. She pushed the glass into the jostle of knick-knacks on the side table.

'Mother,' she said.

'I imagine your husband has a good deal to do with the arrangements, being a Member of Parliament?'

Suddenly Maribel could endure it no longer. She flushed furiously, fifteen again.

'Damn the Jubilee,' she said.

'Peggy!'

'I mean it. Damn the Jubilee. Damn the weather. Damn the Queen while we are at it. All these years – you summon me here to talk to you and we waste time on this nonsense. Why can you not just get to the bloody point?'

Mrs Bryant touched her fingers to her brow.

'Really, Peggy,' she said faintly, 'there is no call for such offensive language.'

'Isn't there? I have come here as you asked, as you demanded, at considerable risk to my husband's reputation, not to mention his parliamentary career, and you prattle on about nothing as though we were at tea with the vicar. Well, damn it, Mother, say what you have to say and be done with it. And, by the way, my name is not Peggy. It's Maribel.'

Furiously Maribel tore open her silk bag. Snapping open her cigarette case, she jammed a cigarette between her lips and struck a match. Edith stared at her sister, her pale eyes glazed. Maribel drew the smoke into her lungs and held it there, then tipped back her head, closing her eyes, and blew out a long, deliberate column of smoke. Her head was swimming, the knock of her heart rapid in her chest.

'I cannot believe it,' Mrs Bryant murmured faintly.

'Oh, I am sorry!' Maribel exclaimed. 'Where are my manners? Mother, Edith, would you like a cigarette?'

Edith's eyes grew rounder. She glanced at her mother, who waved a disgusted hand at the smoke, her lips tightening into a thin white line.

'I had thought that marriage might civilise you. I see that I was mistaken. A lady smoking tobacco at all is shocking enough but in your sister's good parlour? Edith will never be rid of the smell. It is just like you to spoil things for everyone else. You always did.'

'Mother,' Edith said in a small voice, 'it doesn't matter.'

'It matters a great deal. It is unspeakably discourteous. I am quite sure Hubert would not tolerate it for a moment.'

Edith hung her head, mottled circles of red flaring in her cheeks. Her neck was blotchy. Maribel stared at her cigarette, watching the red smoulder climb the paper. She took a fierce pull and then another. The scarlet flared. Then, leaning forward, she crushed it against the empty grate and threw it into the fireplace. It winked its red eye dully and exhaled a grey curl of smoke.

There was a silence.

'Forgive me, Edith. I should not wish to cause difficulties with your husband. Now, Mother, perhaps you might tell me why you have asked me here.'

Mrs Bryant bowed her head for a moment, her lips pursed, one finger toying with her pearl and ruby ring. Then, patting her hair, she sat up a little straighter.

'Edith's husband is in insurance,' she said stiffly. 'Coulson Brown, no less. Edith was very fortunate. After what happened – well, it was not easy for any of them. There was no mixing with other young people after that, not for a long while.'

Maribel looked over at the Negro, who fixed her with his glassy gaze. Ida was the only one she had ever considered. If she had thought of the others at all after she left it had been to picture them like horses on a carousel, rising and falling forever in the same stifling circle of trap rides and tea parties and whist evenings. She had disdained their conformity, their stupid contentment, and she had comforted herself always, even on the worst days, that at least she was not them, crushed slowly to death beneath a creeping and relentless onslaught of tedium. She had not once stopped to think what difficulties they might have suffered by her running away.

'Mother was ill for months,' Edith added. 'They said it was the shock.'

There was another silence. From behind its fortifications on the mantel the marble clock clicked and whirred, gathering itself to strike midday.

'Well, heavens,' Mrs Bryant said. 'What gloomy talk and on so fine a morning. Perhaps it will be cool enough to walk out this afternoon, Edith. It would be pleasant to take a little air. More lemonade, Peggy?'

Maribel shook her head. She felt weary all of a sudden, oppressed by the whole wretched rigmarole.

'Mother, if you have something to tell me, I insist that you say it. Otherwise I shall leave and I shall never so much as open a letter from you ever again. You may be sure of it.'

Mrs Bryant bit her lip. Clasping her hands tightly in her lap she glanced at Edith. Edith looked away. 'Very well,' Mrs Bryant said, her back straighter than ever. 'I – well, yes. There was one thing. We thought, I thought – well, it seemed foolish not to ask, really, with everything so long in the past and your husband a Member of Parliament and Scottish too. I mean, it is not such a big place, is it, Scotland, and I am sure they must be acquainted, how could they not be? And family is family, after all, whatever water flows under the bridge.'

'I haven't the faintest idea what you are talking about.'

'Hubert, Edith's Hubert, is an insurance broker. As I think I mentioned. Shipping. Doing well. Very well. In the main.'

Edith tittered. Her mother glared at her.

'Sorry,' Edith said and put a hand over her mouth.

'For many months he has been working to secure the business of the Maddox shipping line on its route to Cape Colony. The company has the mail contract, you see, between London and wherever it is that mail goes to in Africa. It seemed that the arrangements were as good as finalised. Mr Coulson had gone so far as to offer Hubert a partnership on the strength of it. A partnership, can you imagine!

'Only then the manager or director or whatever he was of the Maddox Mail Packet Company passed away quite unexpectedly. Such terrible luck. The new man's a Boer, if you can believe it, and Hubert says there's no talking sense with him. Apparently Boers have no idea at all how things are done here in England. He fears that it must all come to naught, all his months and months of hard work, unless of course he can secure an interview with Sir Douglas Maddox himself. Hubert is certain that it would be a small matter to convince him of the wisdom of it. But Sir Douglas is a very busy man who would not usually concern himself with matters of this kind and Hubert has no letters of introduction. So, you see, he finds himself in an impossible situation.'

Maribel watched a fat drop of lemonade quiver on the lip of the jug and then fall. She thought bleakly of Edward's admonitions of courage.

'That's it?' she said. 'You want my husband to help Edith's husband to get his name on the company stationery?'

'I hardly think that is the way to describe a position on the board of Coulson Brown. But yes, I know Hubert would be very grateful if you were able to – to oil the wheels a little. You must know Sir Douglas, after all? I understand his constituency borders your husband's. One must assume you are acquainted.'

'We are acquainted.'

'You see, I knew it. Just a letter, that's all I ask. Hubert doesn't

90

need to know a thing, just that an acquaintance of mine turned out to be a cousin of yours.'

'On my mother's side, I suppose?'

Mrs Bryant looked flustered. 'If you wish.'

'And that is it? That is the entire reason you asked me here?'

'Well, it is pleasant to see you, naturally, but yes, that is why I took the liberty of insisting. It matters so to Hubert and there are the children to think of. I knew you would want to help your sister if you were able. I have no more appeals up my sleeve, I assure you.'

She laughed, an artificial tinkle. Maribel gaped at her. A letter of introduction for her aspiring son-in-law. It was so preposterous it was almost funny.

'Why on earth could you not have asked me this in a letter?' she demanded.

Mrs Bryant looked aghast. 'A letter, on such a delicate matter? It would have been quite unseemly.'

'More unseemly than risking my husband's career?'

'Come, Peggy, we have been the souls of discretion. Nobody need ever know you were here.'

'But you would gamble with my husband's future, for Edith's husband's sake.'

'Heavens, well, I never meant for – it was simply that –'

'I'm glad she didn't write,' Edith said softly. 'I am glad you came.'

Startled, Maribel turned to look at her sister. Edith's pale eyes were pink, her nose pinker still. Between her fingers she twisted a handkerchief.

'Lizzie always thought you had gone to America to be a famous actress,' Edith said. 'But Laurie – Laurie said he thought you were dead.'

'That will do, Edith,' Mrs Bryant said.

Maribel thought of Laurence's tin soldiers, scattered by the force of his cannon.

'Laurie would have had us all dead every day by teatime,' she said. 'As for Lizzie —'

Edith's face twitched. She bit her lip, twisting her handkerchief into a knot.

'Edith,' Maribel said, 'would you see me out?'

Standing, Maribel touched her cheek briefly to her mother's. The smell of rose water had faded. She noticed the crow's feet at the corners of her mother's eyes, the way the loose skin crinkled around the curve of her ear. Her jawline was downy and dusty with powder.

'Goodbye, Mother,' she said.

'You will ask your husband, won't you? About Sir Douglas?'

'I don't know. Perhaps.'

'We would be so grateful if you would.'

'I said I would think about it. You will have to be content with that.'

Mrs Bryant hesitated. Then she nodded.

'Very well. Thank you, my dear.'

They looked at each other for a moment. Then Maribel picked up her gloves.

'Take care of yourself, Peggy,' her mother said.

'Maribel.'

'Yes, well. We old aren't good at change.'

It was strange, Maribel thought, knowing that you looked at someone for the last time. When she had left Yorkshire she had been too young to think of it.

In the hallway she kissed Edith.

'I will do what I can,' she said.

'I know you will.'

Maribel pulled on her gloves, busying herself with the buttons.

'Tell me about Ida.'

'Ida? She married a doctor, an associate of Father's at the hospital. She is Mrs Maitland Coffin now.'

'Her husband is Dr Coffin?'

'Yes, but you mustn't laugh. She hates it when people laugh.'

Maribel said nothing. The Ida she remembered would have thought Dr Coffin uncommonly funny.

'They live in London too,' Edith said.

'They do?'

It was a shock, though she knew it should not be. It was just that she and Ida had always planned to come to London together. They had thought Regent's Park the most suitable place for a house since it would be convenient both for the theatres and for the Royal Zoological Gardens. Their house was to have electric lighting and modern plumbing and wallpaper and a library full of novels, French as well as English as Jumbo the elephant had been brought up in the Jardin des Plantes in Paris and Ida thought it would be comforting for him to be read to in his childhood language. The windows would look out over the park so that on fine days they could watch boys sailing their boats on the pond and hear the animals talking to each other. There would be two cats, Punch and Judy, both tortoiseshell, who would be encouraged to sleep on the sofas, and a freckled maid called Sally, and crumpets with honey for tea every day. It was important to eat well before a performance.

'Yes,' Edith said. 'Not all that far from here, actually. I see her quite often.'

Ida was in London. Somewhere, quite near here, Ida was speaking, walking, breathing. The thought made her breathless.

Edith hiccupped.

'What is it?' Maribel demanded. 'Why are you crying?'

'I am not crying.'

'Yes you are. What on earth is it? Is it Ida? Is something wrong with Ida?'

Edith shook her head, squeezing her eyes shut.

'For heaven's sake, Edith, spit it out!'

Edith looked up and the tears spilled down her cheeks. 'Oh,

Peggy, I mean Maribel, I can't bear it. I thought you were dead and yet here you are, standing right here in front of me, and then you will leave and I will never see you again.'

Maribel sighed. Then she patted Edith lightly on the arm.

'It is for the best, you know,' she said. 'Think what harm it would do, if there was a scandal. Think of Mother and Father. Think of your husband.'

Edith sniffed. 'But might we not meet again?' she pleaded. 'Here, in secret? I wouldn't tell a soul.'

Maribel looked about her, at the grandfather clock and the paintings of ringlet-headed infants and the Chinese vases that crouched beneath their china hats like fat constables, and she shook her head.

'I don't think so. But I shall think of you, of course.'

She turned away but Edith caught her by the arm, tugging at her sleeve. Her tear-stained face was swollen and shameless, like a child's.

'What happened, Peggy, after you left us? It was Miss Phillips, wasn't it? You went to Miss Phillips.'

'Goodbye, Edith.'

Outside the sun blazed in a bright blue sky and the air was thick as soup. Maribel paused at the bottom of the steps and put up her parasol. At the far end of the terrace a greengrocer wrestled a crate from his cart as his horse waited, its harness loose, its head low beneath its heavy collar. In the garden behind the wall birds sang.

Maribel opened the gate and began to walk in the direction of the High Street. She did not turn, and so she did not see Edith watching her from behind the door nor her mother, half concealed at the parlour window, one hand on the heavy drapes. She thought instead of Ida, who was twenty-five years old, a woman, and neither a saint nor an elephant keeper but only a wife, as Maribel was.

Maribel should never have gone to London without her. She

should have waited. For thirteen years she had carried with her the weight of her betrayal, like rocks in her pockets. Now, at last, Ida had come. The thought quickened Maribel's feet and her heart.

7

EDWARD WAS OUTRAGED, OF course. Maribel could not blame him. She knew the courage it had taken to urge her to go. His intimates would mostly have forgiven him the deception – they were men of the world, after all, and Maribel sufficiently unlike their own wives to allow for latitude – but in the House his provocations were tolerated only because of his standing as a man of the highest integrity in public life. If Maribel were to be exposed as a fraud and a liar the scandal would not only end his political career, it would profoundly threaten the work of the Radicals in Parliament. That he had risked their cause solely that he might promote the career of a man too incompetent to do it for himself made Edward furious.

For all his principles, however, Edward was not entirely devoid of common sense. He understood that the more rapidly he answered to Mrs Bryant's demands the more quickly she would be dispatched. Besides, what she asked for might be granted easily enough. The machinery of the House, like that of his class, was oiled with quiet words and mutual favours, and, though Edward found the back-scratching distasteful, there was nothing unlawful in it. His only condition was that Maribel make it quite clear to her mother that this would be the end of it. There would be no more letters, no more secret rendezvous. Maribel had not the least difficulty conceding to his terms.

The next time he saw Sir Douglas in the House, Edward approached him and offered his somewhat rusty skills as a batsman in the upcoming House of Commons cricket match. When Maddox accepted, Edward admitted that he had a favour to ask in return. An acquaintance of his wife's cousin had some manner of business proposal in which he thought Sir Douglas might be interested and had asked if an introduction might be arranged. Edward confessed that, besides his understanding that the young man in question was considered something of an upstart, he knew next to nothing of the proposal and he understood perfectly if Sir Douglas did not wish to comply. Indeed, he urged him to decline immediately and put an end to the matter there and then. Edward had no doubt that the young man would manage quite well without Sir Douglas's assistance.

It was not much of a gamble. Edward had known Sir Douglas for years. He knew quite well that, even if propriety had not required Maddox to concur, his vagueness as to the nature of the business venture on offer would prove irresistible. The third son of a Greenock barber, Sir Douglas had left school at fourteen to take up his vocation as a capitalist. The flash of profit drew him like a salmon.

'May the dogs please now be put back to sleep?' Edward asked Maribel when it was done. She smiled at him and adjusted his tie.

'Can't you hear the snoring already?'

Edward had a dinner in the City, something to do with the party. When he was gone Maribel sat down at her desk. She had meant to write a note to Charlotte, who, after considerable encouragement, had finally been persuaded to sit for her first photographic portrait, but somehow the words came out differently.

My dearest, dearest Ida,

You are in London. It is so sweet to write those words, to think that we are close again at last. Perhaps you are looking out of your window as I write and watching the swifts I

can see making patterns in the sky. Perhaps you are walk-
ing along streets that I too walk along, looking into win-
dows that I gaze into every day. Not seeing you is so much
harder now that I know you are so close. There is so much I
have to tell you. I never made it as an actress. For a while
I thought – but life does not always come out as you hope. I
don't expect you are an elephant keeper either. Or Joan of
Arc, for that matter. Do you remember you used to ask me
if I'd forget you once I was famous and I promised that I
wouldn't? I never broke my promise, Ida. I forgot all about
Peggy Bryant as soon as I was able and the dreadful Miss
Phillips sooner than that but I never once forgot about you.
My name is Maribel now and I am from Chile. It turned
out that Sylvia was not who I was either. But you – you
were always Ida.

She stopped, unable to continue. Then, very carefully, she
capped her pen and stood, too quickly perhaps, because the light-
headedness caused her to sway and she had to close her eyes to
compose herself. It was the past, the great chasm of it, that did
for her. It was always a mistake to look down.

She hadn't thought of Miss Phillips for years. A temporary
governess, hired hurriedly when Miss Finton's mother was taken
unexpectedly ill, Miss Phillips was a soft-voiced, soft-fingered
sigher, much given to wandering about the house in bare feet,
her mousy hair loose about her shoulders. Devoted to the poetry
of Christina Rossetti, she had the girls study 'Goblin Market'
and rhapsodised with breathy intensity about erotic desire and
moral redemption. When she read *Sonnets from the Portuguese*
aloud she wept. The boys laughed at her which made Maribel
furious, both with them and with Miss Phillips who, for all her
sensitivity, was unable to desist from idiotic pronouncements
on the Beauty of Nature.

Still, Miss Phillips was the first person Maribel had ever

met who shared her passion for the theatre. It was Miss Phillips who insisted upon taking Maribel to the Theatre Royal in York to see Henrietta Hodson as Imogen in *Cymbeline*, Miss Phillips who took her afterwards to the stage door and persuaded the doorman to let them pay their respects to the actress, Miss Phillips who confided to Miss Hodson that 'dear little Peggy' had ambitions to go on the stage. Maribel, struck dumb by the momentousness of the occasion, had hardly spoken. The tiny dressing room with its mirrored wall, the costumes hanging on the door of the press, the proximity of Miss Hodson in her wrapper who had until a few moments before *been* Imogen, the poetry of Shakespeare upon her lips, his breath in her chest – all these wrapped like ribbon around the intense magic of the play, shaping it into something real, something meant for her.

'Are you any good?' Miss Hodson had asked and when Maribel stammered that, yes, she thought she was, the actress had pursed her mouth as though she meant to apply lipstick.

'It is a hard profession. Few enjoy success.'

'I shall,' Maribel said fiercely. 'I must.'

'You sound very sure.'

'It is all I have ever wanted. It is only when I am acting that I feel – real.'

Miss Hodson had given her a hard look, her head on one side.

'Then you must act,' she said. 'You have the looks for it, at any rate.'

'What should I do? How should I start?'

Miss Hodson had shrugged.

'By starting. For God's sake don't rot out here in the provinces. Go to London. Go to the theatres. Persuade them to give you a try. If you really want to be an actress you have to act.'

'Like you.'

'Like me.' Miss Hodson had smiled. Then on impulse, she had taken a card from a silk purse on her dressing table. The card had her name on it and the address of a theatre in London. 'Here. When you make it to London look me up. I know a good many people. I might be able to help you.'

Some weeks later Miss Phillips had been dismissed by Maribel's mother, who declared that she could no longer endure her unpinned hair and extemporaneous outbursts of weeping. Miss Phillips had written to Maribel a few days later, a secretive letter that she begged Maribel not to mention to Mrs Bryant, filled with impassioned quotations and declarations of sisterly love.

> *My own dear girl, hold tightly to your dreams. This world we must live in is a cold place, cruel and careless. Do not let it crush you. Think of me when your spirits fail and let my faith in you be the wings that raise you upward. I believe in you, my sweet fairy, and always shall. I shall not let you fall.*

Maribel had thought she meant it. Three months later she had crept downstairs on a grey pre-dawn morning. When she saw Ida's mud-caked boots on a sheet of newspaper outside the pantry door her nerve had almost failed her. Then she thought of Miss Phillips's letter with the address in Praed Street carefully printed at the top and Miss Hodson's card and her carefully saved money and she turned the key and ran across the lawn to the woods, as she and Ida had done so many times. Two weeks earlier Lizzie had been married. When Lizzie had changed into her honeymoon clothes she had clung to her mother, her face white with apprehension, and her mother had patted her cheek and told her to be brave and obey her husband. Later on the station platform, as the train bearing the newly-weds pulled away, Mrs Bryant had turned to Maribel with a look of brisk self-satisfaction.

'You next,' she had said.

It had rained all the way to London. The droplets raced across the window, cross-hatching Maribel's reflection, her face pale beneath her felt hat. There were smears on the glass. It was very early. All the way to London she had sat there, her shoulders hunched, terrified that someone would recognise her. More than once a train screamed as it passed on the other track, steam streaming behind it like a rain-soaked flag, dashing for home, and she had tried not to think of Ida waking up, finding her gone.

Miss Phillips's house in Praed Street turned out to be an attic room in the decaying home of a decaying old lady with whom Miss Phillips had found a post as companion. Miss Phillips looked smaller in London than she had at Ellerton. Her hair was tangled, her dress not quite clean. When she saw Maribel she had wailed and wrung her hands and threatened to write to her mother, though Maribel was quite sure that she would not. Miss Phillips was a coward. Maribel had walked away without saying goodbye.

Maribel breathed in, inhaling steadiness, the familiar warm smell of the flat. Then, dragging her desk chair to the small rosewood cabinet behind the door, she stood on it, reaching in to slide the wooden cigar box from its place at the back of the highest shelf. The box was battered, unvarnished, clumsily inked on its top in Spanish. As well as a small iron hook it was tightly tied with string.

Unpicking the knots, Maribel opened it. Inside, on top of several faded photographs, was a folded pile of letters perhaps half an inch thick. The letters were in her own hand, its loops and curlicues practised over and over in the ink-scented chill of a Yorkshire schoolroom. Carefully she placed her new letter on top of the pile and closed the box. The string was frayed. It was difficult to make a neat job of retying it.

She knew it was foolish, foolish to write and even more foolish to keep the letters, but she could not help it. She had written her first letter to Ida when she had first come to London and somehow she had never broken the habit of it. For thirteen years she had written to her sister, sometimes at length, sometimes a scribble hardly three lines long. She had never sent any of them, of course – most were not even finished – but somehow, through the writing and the keeping of them, better than no letters at all.

'Remind me why I agreed to this?' Edward said a week later as he sat at breakfast, dressed in a newly acquired set of white flannels.

'Because you are a man of your word,' Maribel replied, pouring tea. 'And because it is entirely your fault I visited Milton Terrace in the first place.'

Edward frowned slightly, jerking his head towards the door. Maribel nodded, conceding the warning. In all the years she had been with them Alice had never shown herself to be anything but trustworthy but she was still a servant. It was important to be careful. Edward tapped his paper.

'This is funny. It says here that the gossip columnist of the *Referee*, who goes by the soubriquet of Dagonet and clearly has a jester's sense of humour, offered a prize of a portrait of the Queen to any British newspaper last week that did not once mention the words "Jubilee" or "Buffalo Bill". Apparently he did not receive a single entry.'

Maribel smiled and held out the toast rack. He took a slice, setting it on his plate, and reached for the butter dish.

'You know, I think I shall encourage you to play cricket more often,' she said, considering him. 'The costume becomes you.'

'Do not push your luck, Mrs L. This is a once-in-a-lifetime favour which I have no intention ever of repeating.'

'You old curmudgeon. I have a sneaking feeling you are rather looking forward to it.'

'Soothe your conscience with as many sweet deceptions as you like. You will suffer a thousand agonies of remorse when I return with a fistful of broken fingers and a black eye.'

'Perhaps you will bowl someone for a century. Or bat a duck or something.'

'Your grasp of the game is impressive but I fear the black eye is infinitely more likely. I suppose I should be grateful that it is June and not the depths of the rugby football season. Six months in plaster of Paris would have been a kindness too far.'

For all his complaining there was no mistaking Edward's cheerfulness as he kissed her goodbye. She watched him stroll up the sunlit street towards the cab rank at Sloane Square, the canvas holdall containing his schoolboy bat and pads slung over one shoulder. It had transpired that his mother had kept them all this time, not in one of the damp attics at Inverallich as Edward had suspected, but at the bottom of a wardrobe in Halkin Street. When Edward had pulled them out the pads had been a little discoloured but the bat was true. He had struck at an imaginary ball and Vivien had laughed, raising an artfully darkened eyebrow.

'Edward has always derided team sports,' she had said to Maribel afterwards, as they drank their soup. 'It did not stop him from being an exceptional cricketer. Considerably better than Henry, though Henry was much the keener. It would seem that if one is blessed with ability enough, one can achieve excellence without enthusiasm. Edward played in the First XI from the age of fourteen, though he was never captain, unlike Henry. They do not allow boys like Edward to be captain.'

Alice put her head round the door.

'Are you done, ma'am?' she asked.

Maribel nodded.

'Thank you, Alice,' she said. 'And Mrs Charterhouse will be calling this morning. We shall need refreshments.'

'Anything in particular, ma'am? We've not much in.'

'Something cold to drink. It is so hot already.'

'I'd do lemonade only there's not enough lemons,' Alice said, stacking the dirty breakfast dishes onto her tray. 'I suppose I could go out.'

'Definitely not lemonade,' Maribel said firmly. 'Ginger beer from the barrow on Elizabeth Street. And some strawberries too, if you can find some. It is just the kind of day for strawberries.'

Strawberries were an extravagance but Charlotte loved them. She loved ginger beer too. It pleased Maribel to picture her friend's pleasure. Besides, the news from Inverallich was good. The apple orchards continued well and, with the improvements finally completed, the farms might at last be coaxed into something resembling a profit. She hummed to herself as she set a chair in the window bay and scrambled onto it, reaching up to drape a length of muslin over the curtain rail so that it strained the morning sunlight into a pale pool on the carpet. Several times she took the chair from the window and put it back again.

'I feel like I am dressed for bed,' Charlotte complained when Alice showed her into the drawing room. She frowned at the unfamiliar bareness of the room, the furniture pushed back against the walls, the half-drawn curtain. 'My goodness, you are in earnest.'

'Did you ever doubt it?' Maribel asked, lighting a cigarette.

'No. But I hoped.'

Maribel smiled, exhaling a long, satisfied stream of smoke.

'Hope is never enough,' she said and she nodded at Alice. 'If anyone calls we are not in. We shall take refreshments at noon. By then Mrs Charterhouse will be in need of distraction.'

'I am in need of it now,' Charlotte said. 'However, I am ready to do my duty. Is Edward at the House?'

'Edward is playing cricket.'

'Cricket? Edward? Are you sure?'

'I am afraid so. Now take off that bonnet. It hides too much of your face.'

'You are fearfully bossy,' Charlotte said, but she reached up obligingly and began to unpin her hat. 'Will you be nicer to me once we begin?'

'I shouldn't think so, should you?'

Charlotte smiled. Maribel took her friend's bonnet and set it on top of a pile of papers on the writing desk. As commanded, Charlotte had worn the embroidered blue dress with the trumpet sleeves and her dark hair hung in a plait down her back. In the heat her pale skin glowed pink. She looked, as Maribel had hoped, like an untroubled Lady Macbeth. On impulse, she kissed her friend on the cheek.

'Thank you for coming,' she said. 'Now come and stand here. In the window.'

'I thought you said I was to sit.'

'You are. But you will stand to do it.'

Charlotte looked about her curiously.

'Is that really the camera? It is so small.'

'Welcome to the future.'

There was a pause while Maribel fiddled with the tripod, adjusting the height. The lit cigarette hung from between her lips and she squinted through the smoke.

'Cricket, though,' Charlotte said. 'I cannot imagine Edward in a team.'

'Vivien says he was rather good.'

'Your mother-in-law, so moderate in her praise? I find that almost harder to imagine than Edward on a cricket pitch.'

Maribel laughed. 'What she really said was that he was the hero of the First XI.'

'Do you think mothers cannot help it? In ten years' time shall I be boasting to my boys' wives about their skill with a hoop or their astonishing aptitude for Musical Statues?'

'With luck they will have acquired some other skills by then.' Charlotte sighed.

'I doubt it. Not one of them seems in the least interested in books or schoolwork or anything at all except balls and cowboys and giving one another bruises. Truly, Maribel, I tear my hair out over them. Why is it that women hanker so after sons? I swear a single day spent at Chester Square would cure them of their delusions.'

Maribel did not answer. She frowned, peering at the tripod.

'Dearest, I am sorry,' Charlotte murmured. 'I didn't mean —'

'Charlotte, do be quiet,' Maribel said briskly, putting out her cigarette in an overflowing ashtray. She bent down, looking at her friend through the viewfinder. 'You know perfectly well that Edward and I are quite happy as we are and a great deal happier than most. Now turn to the left a little. A little more. Yes, like that. And stop talking.'

It was work that steadied her, work that drew a curtain over the flash and glint of memory and softened its sharp edges. For the first time in weeks Maribel was grateful for the unfaltering brilliance of the morning. Other amateur photographers used professional studios where the electrical lights gave a more predictable result, but they were expensive and, besides, Maribel disliked the flattening effect of artificial illumination. She disliked too the sense of occasion imposed by a studio, the atmosphere of anxiety and expectation that stiffened limbs and fixed expressions. Maribel was no more interested in formal composition in photography than she was in poetic tropes. The complexities of construction overworked it, so that the resulting work was dense and heavy. It was Maribel's belief that it was necessary to come at both poetry and photographs obliquely, to make their creation as much of an accident as possible. It was not about pressing images into a preordained shape. It was about capturing a moment of unconsciousness, something fleeting and true. She could quite see why Livingstone's savages

106

considered photography to be stealing. Perhaps poetry was stealing too.

In the drawing room at Cadogan Mansions the light was itself a subject, the buttery weight of it in the drapes of muslin behind Charlotte's head, the filtered column of silver that turned, dust-spangled, in the shadows by her skirts, the splashes of bright white spattered on the ceiling by the diamond solitaire Charlotte wore on her left hand. Maribel knelt at her friend's feet, arranging the spill of her skirts, observing how the silk shimmered with dark lights, and she thought of the loch at Inverallich on a fine day, the breeze puckering its smooth skin. One day there will be photographs in colour, she thought, and the beauty of the world captured so, without our veil of not seeing, will be unbearable.

'Lift the muslin away a little with your right hand,' she told Charlotte. 'As though you were looking out of the window but did not want to be seen.'

'Like this?'

'Just like that.'

The sun had moved a little and no longer shone directly through the window. The gentler light caught in the pearls around Charlotte's neck and in the soft arc of her hair. Maribel gazed at the composition through the viewfinder, at Charlotte pinned beneath the glass like a butterfly. The brightness from the window caused her to squint just a little so that, as she stood there, her features, usually so animated in expression, gave way to the heavy-lidded somnolence of a medieval madonna. The woman in the frame was Charlotte and yet not Charlotte, her eyes and mouth, her chin tilted a little upwards, and yet without the quickening essence of Charlotte that claimed them and made them hers. The observation unnerved Maribel a little. Wasn't that what they said about the bodies of the dead?

She was almost ready. Taking up a collodion plate in its holder she slid it into the camera. She checked to see that the plate was in place, then carefully extracted the cover and set it to one side. In the window Charlotte blinked a little, pressing her lips together to suppress a yawn.

'I know you think you have suffered enough already,' Maribel said. 'But the worst is still to come. I am going to talk now and, however much you desire to contradict me, you are not allowed to answer back. However overwhelming the temptation, you must let me continue in my delusions uncorrected, do you understand?'

Charlotte grinned and immediately she was Charlotte once more.

'It won't be good for you,' she said.

'Perhaps not,' Maribel agreed. 'But it will be very good for you.'

She leaned down, one hand loosening the lens cover. As she talked, rehearsing the old jokes, the well-worn stories, memory moved over Charlotte's face like weather, changing the light and the angles, shifting the shape of her beneath her skin. Maribel watched her friend intently, her fingers alert on the lens cover, readying herself for the shot. The new dry plates required no more than a fraction of a second for exposure, allowing for the capture of the most fleeting of atmospheres. It had been quite different in the old days, with wet plates. Then a model had been required to hold quite still for five or six seconds, a single expression pinned to her face, and the slightest movement could ruin a picture. Mr Corelli had always said that he could tell which of the girls would have a successful career by the discipline that they exhibited when being photographed.

'You cannot hold an expression for the count of five?' he had once declared disdainfully to a girl who complained. 'Then you're no actress.'

The girl in question had gone on to have moderate success in music hall. Afterwards Mr Corelli was heard to mutter that it was fortunate for Hetty Farnshaw that she had the kind of figure that fogged men's brains. Those girls could get away with not being able to count.

Charlotte turned her head imperceptibly, her full lips softening as she raised her chin. Maribel steadied herself and pulled away the lens cover. For perhaps one half of a second, the camera held Charlotte in its unblinking gaze. Then she shuttered it again.

'That's it?' Charlotte asked without altering her position.

'That's the first. You can move a little if you wish. It will take me a moment or two to change the plates.'

Charlotte stretched, turning her head from side to side to loosen her shoulders, as Maribel slid the plate cover back into the camera, obscuring the exposed area of glass. Then, slowly, she extracted it and placed it in the cloth-lined box at her feet. Mr Corelli had been a great talker, hardly drawing breath as he worked. He had always claimed that silences were as bad as the cold for cramping muscles. Victor's photographer had hardly spoken at all, or not to her. He had conferred quietly with Victor behind a screen and, when they were finished, it was Victor who had instructed her as to the requirements of her arrangement. When she asked him who she was supposed to be, Victor had raised an eyebrow.

'The Rokeby Venus,' he had said, and he had laughed and looked at her in the appraising way that he had, with his head on one side. The photographer had spoken only to murmur instructions to the boy who was his assistant. The studio had been stiflingly hot and relentlessly red, with scarlet shot silk on the walls and crimson velvet drapes, like the inside of somebody's mouth. All the glass in the windows had been painted black.

Maribel frowned at the camera, forcing herself to concentrate, but the memories pressed in on her: the ache in her neck from holding the pose, the pins securing the draperies around her hips, the stick of rouge with its dirty paper wrapper. The tightness of her hair in its elaborate twist had given her a headache. Victor had insisted upon the hair, had summoned a woman to the house to assist with its arrangement. The woman had smoothed the hair with wax and spit rubbed into the palms of her hands. It was a matter of tastefulness, Victor said, of refinement. The effect must be of Titian or Giorgione, never Francisco de Goya. Maribel had known hardly anything of paintings then. She had known only that Victor knew people and that he was her best hope. Afterwards she had found twin stains of rouge like spots of blood in her bodice.

The sun was high beyond the window and the parlour uncomfortably warm. Maribel strode over to the window and threw open the sash.

'You are doing wonderfully,' she said to Charlotte. 'Can you endure another?'

Charlotte proved herself a trouper. She managed four more plates, though Maribel did not think any as good as the first. Just as she removed the fifth from the camera, Charlotte closed her eyes and gave a little moan.

'Save me,' she said.

Maribel rang for Alice. The ginger beer and strawberries cheered Charlotte immeasurably.

'A picnic,' she declared happily. 'What heaven.'

'Next time we shall go out to the country, to the river perhaps,' Maribel said. 'And I shall photograph you outside.'

Charlotte shook her head firmly. 'No next time,' she said. 'Once is enough, strawberries or no strawberries.'

'You will change your mind when you see the pictures.'

'I doubt that very much. Isn't the camera obliged to tell the

Truth, however disagreeable? I myself favour the Flattering Deception.'

'That is such hokum,' Maribel said, waving a cigarette in one hand and a strawberry in the other. 'Those photographs that do tell the truth only do so by accident. Most are dishonest as any painting. More so, because they pretend to be real. Talking of which, I have something for your boys.' Setting the cigarette between her lips she rummaged with her free hand in the pile of letters on her writing desk and drew out the photograph of Chief Red Shirt. 'The photographer has rendered him more Stuffed Shirt than Red Shirt but he is still a real live Indian. He has even signed it, after a fashion.'

'Thank you,' Charlotte said. 'The boys will adore it. They are all desperate to go to the show, of course, and complain bitterly that they must be the only children in London not yet to have seen it, but I have promised George faithfully that we shall not go without him so we must wait for the holidays.'

'Have you met him yet, the famous Buffalo Bill?'

'Only briefly at the Mansion House.'

'He came to a party at the Wildes' last Tuesday,' Maribel said. 'The fawning over him put Oscar's nose quite out of joint. He squatted like a toad in the corner of the drawing room and told anyone who would listen that Cody had never been a colonel and that the Honourable came from belonging to an American State Legislature slightly less important than the Essex County Council.'

'Oscar is a brave man. Imagine risking the ire of all the doting peeresses of the realm.'

'Worse still, he accused Cody of eating peas from his knife.'

Charlotte shook her head.

'Dear foolish Oscar. They will flay him alive.'

Maribel laughed. 'He has asked me to write a short piece on the Italian exhibition for *Woman's World*. Will you come? I thought we might go tomorrow if it is not too unbearably hot.'

'I can't tomorrow, I fear. I have an appointment.'

'What appointment?'

'I promised myself I should not tell you. You will only get cross.'

'I shall get much crosser if you don't tell me.'

'How extremely unreasonable you are.'

'How true. So where are you going?'

Charlotte hesitated.

'No. I am not going to tell you.'

'Then you oblige me to draw my own conclusions. You have taken a lover. You have taken a trade. You are become a – a tanner. A crossing-sweeper. A child prostitute. You must dispose of the decomposing body of your murdered love rival. Am I getting warm?'

'Positively scorching, dearest. You see now why I do not have time for the Italian exhibition.'

'Charlotte, Charlotte. You know, don't you, that I shall have to tell Arthur? He is a good man, your husband, in spite of his deplorable fondness for parlour games, and he does not deserve to be so misused. Of course, if you are prepared to buy my silence with a little more information –'

'Will you ever let this go?'

'Probably not this week.'

Charlotte sighed.

'Well?' Maribel demanded.

'I am going to St John's Wood,' Charlotte said at last. 'Lady Rawlinson is giving a tea party for Mme Blavatsky.'

Maribel snorted. Mme Blavatsky was a Russian émigré newly arrived from New York, who had brought with her an exotic wardrobe of scarves and a considerable reputation as a spiritualist and medium. Said to be shamelessly penniless, she had been put up in London by a wealthy American widow who had taken to describing herself as the Russian woman's 'disciple'. There had been much discussion in the drawing rooms of London of Mme Blavatsky.

'You are not?' said Maribel.

'Yes, I am. And Constance Wilde is coming with me. She is as intrigued as I.'

'Charlotte, how could you? Constance, perhaps, but you?'

'Perhaps because, unlike you, I do not believe that we know everything there is to know. And don't frown at me like that. Mme Blavatsky is not a circus act. She does not rig strings under tables or blow lights out. There is no essence of violets wafted about the room. Her investigations have to do with the complexities of human consciousness, the unexplained laws of nature and of matter. Clairvoyance, clairaudience, thought-reading, hypnosis, these phenomena are real, Maribel. They have been proven. Did you know that, even when our brains, the generators of our consciousness, are comatose, deep in sleep, scientists in Europe have found proof of intense and inexplicable mental action? Something must account for that spiritual energy.'

'You disappoint me, Charlotte.'

'Oh, pooh. The fact that all the swans you've ever seen are white doesn't mean that all swans are white.'

'So you truly believe this Blavatsky woman can communicate with the spirit world?'

'I don't know. That is the point, Maribel, I don't know. But at least I am prepared to allow that I don't know and to hold my mind open.'

'You say that as if it is a good thing.'

'Well, of course it is.'

'Why?' said Maribel. 'It is as foolish to hold open your mind as it is your front door. It does nothing but encourage undesirables.'

'Spoken like a true Radical. Your husband would be proud.'

Maribel waved her hand, reaching once again for her cigarettes.

'Do not think you can distract me with politics,' she said. 'Edward has tried it and it does not work.'

'Then let me do it with ginger beer,' Charlotte said.

Sloshing more of the cloudy liquid into their glasses, she handed one to Maribel and held hers aloft.

'To Maribel and the closed mind.'

Maribel grinned.

'To Mme Charterhouse, table rapper extraordinaire,' she countered and she struck her glass firmly against Charlotte's.

When Alice peered into the parlour some minutes later she saw the two ladies seated like children upon the floor, their stockinged feet tucked up beneath them. They were laughing uproariously, their heads thrown back, their hands clutched over their mouths, and their fingers were stained scarlet with strawberry juice.

8

T HE MORNING BEGAN BADLY. It had been another unspeakably hot night and Maribel had slept only fitfully. Edward had come in a little after one and she had lain awake, smoking and listening to the small noises as he readied himself for bed. She did not go out to him. Instead she watched the ghosts that the smoke made in the darkness and thought of Ida. It was hard to imagine her in a house, especially in London. Perhaps it had a garden. Ida had always been happiest out of doors. Perhaps there were children. Maribel tried to imagine Ida with an infant in her arms but all she could think of were her unravelling plaits, her ink-stained fingers, her child's face fierce with concentration. When Ida did sums she twisted her plaits with one finger, the tip of her tongue caught between her teeth. The knots in her hair had driven their mother to distraction.

At breakfast she was raw-eyed, irritable with lack of sleep. When Edward enquired why the marmalade was not the thick-cut kind that he liked she snapped at him. She answered only brusquely when he enquired after her plans for the day. She was tired of his parliamentary commitments and constituency business, and aggrieved by his new infatuation with the Socialist League and the SDF and the myriad subcommittees that such organisations always seemed to spawn. On those few evenings he was at home he stayed up late writing articles for the *Commonweal*. The articles were good and she knew she should be proud of him. She *was* proud of him, but she was also resentful of his neglect and weary of apologising for his absences. She was not supposed to confess it, the New Women would be horrified that she even thought it, but the truth was that without a husband one spent too much time with other women and too many of them were tiresome.

When Edward announced that the second vote in the House might prevent him from accompanying her to dinner with the Wildes that evening, the anger exploded in her without warning. Before he could fold the newspaper she had accused him of negligence, of callousness, of a vaunting political ambition that left everything else in its wake. Perhaps, she said bitterly, if he dug deep into his memory, he might recall that he had a wife. Perhaps he might even consider it prudent to see her from time to time so that he might remake her acquaintance. Or if, as seemed apparent, he meant to take the Liberal Party as a wife, perhaps he might inform his present wife of his decision so that she might release him from the obligations that he plainly found so burdensome.

Edward waited in silence until, like a wind-up toy, she ran herself down. Then, with a perplexed expression, he set his teacup back in its saucer. His apology, though conciliatory, was tinged with a fastidious disdain. He acknowledged that he was busy, promised that he would do what he could to limit the number of dinners and evening votes he was obliged to attend. He wished for easier times ahead. It was plain that he considered her display of temper entirely unreasonable. When he left the flat soon afterwards, he did not kiss her goodbye.

Maribel sat at the table for a long time after he was gone, the shame of her harangue congealing in her cheeks. When Alice came in to clear the table she retired to her bedroom to lie down. She lay there for perhaps half an hour, staring up at the ornate plasterwork that decorated the ceiling. The tears leaked from her eyes and dampened the hair above her ears.

Then, patting her face with a handkerchief, she rose. She put on the old dress she wore to develop her photographs and arranged her hair. When she took her satchel from the hall cupboard she could hear Alice in the parlour, humming tunelessly to herself as she dusted the furniture. She packed the satchel with her plates, her cigarettes and an apple for her luncheon.

Outside the heat was worse than ever. It took only a few minutes to walk down Lower Sloane Street to Mr Pidgeon's Turks Row studio, but by the time she pushed open the heavy green door she had almost regained her composure. It was not in Edward's nature to bear grudges. By the time he got home that night their spat would be quite forgotten.

The green door opened directly into the back stairwell of the large red-brick building that housed Pidgeon's Photography. Mr Pidgeon was a gentleman of dour expression and irreproachable respectability whose business was mostly in the line of captivating family groups, for which the demand appeared inexhaustible. His studio was dominated by a large rocking horse and a plywood doll's house in the Palladian style. There was also an upholstered chaise, large enough to accommodate comfortably a mother and several of her entrancing offspring without irreparably crushing her skirts.

It was plain that the boisterous behaviour of his clientele told upon Mr Pidgeon, for his complexion was yellow and the pouches beneath his eyes slack and bruised, but his attitude of harried resignation did nothing to dampen the appetites of his eager clientele. There seemed always to be at least one child galloping a hobby horse up the stairs or bowling a hoop in the hallway and often, above the shouts and the kicks to the skirting boards, the siren cry of an infant wailing inconsolably. The corridor outside the studio teemed from ceiling to floor with framed photographs of moon-faced moppets in curls and ribboned sailor suits.

When Maribel had first approached Mr Pidgeon about renting his darkroom he had been startled by the suggestion that she attend to her own plates. Mr Pidgeon was of the opinion that the darkroom was an uncongenial and even dangerous place for a lady and had suggested that it might be more appropriate if he were to develop them for her.

'Consider me a trusted midwife,' he had said. 'In my care you may be confident of a safe delivery.'

Maribel had winced a little at the metaphor and firmly declined. Mr Pidgeon had not pressed the matter. With the air of one accustomed to rebuff, and once he had satisfied himself that neither she nor the darkroom would come to any harm, he allowed her to continue in her work unmolested. When they happened to meet in the corridor he nodded politely. He never asked to see her work and she was glad of it, for it saved her the otherwise inescapable courtesy of pretending interest in his.

After the heat of the street, the stone stairwell was cool as a church. Maribel climbed the stairs to the studio on the first floor. The key to the darkroom was kept on a nail inside the studio and it was customary, when Maribel knocked for it, for Thomas, Mr Pidgeon's gap-toothed apprentice, to answer the door. He was a bashful boy with a shock of dark hair, who ducked his head respectfully as he handed her the key but never ventured to speak. Maribel had several times wanted to ask if she might photograph him. Today, however, there was no need to knock. The door to the studio was open. In the corridor a man stood at the window looking out over the street.

Maribel's heart turned over.

'Mrs Campbell Lowe?'

'Mr Webster!'

Flushing a little she extended her hand. He shook it, smiling at her, his brow creased with what seemed to be astonishment. His eyes really were extraordinary. They drew the heat in her out like a poultice.

118

'You are here to be photographed?' Webster asked bemusedly. Self-consciously Maribel put her hand to her hair. She was wearing the bandanna she always wrapped around her forehead when she was working so that her hair would not fall into her eyes. She looked down at her old ticking dress, her battered canvas apron. The front of the apron was badly stained, the strap that fastened it about her neck torn and tied with a knot. *Titian or Giorgione*, she thought, *never Francisco de Goya*. She batted at her skirts with her hands, mortified that he had seen her in so slovenly a costume.

'Heavens, a fine picture that would make!' she said gaily. 'You must excuse my appallingly disreputable appearance. I have come to use Mr Pidgeon's darkroom and the chemicals – well, I'm sure you can imagine.'

'Disreputable? On the contrary, you look perfectly charming. The epitome of artisanship.'

Maribel made a face. 'May God forgive you the excesses of your chivalry.'

'The Lord is merciful,' he said, his mouth twitching.

Maribel looked at the ground. She was sure that those milky eyes of his saw the blush that crept up her chest, the trickle of sweat between her breasts. He was wearing a tweed coat and waistcoat quite unsuitable for the heat and a stiff collar. He did not look hot at all.

'So you are a photographer,' he said. 'How remarkable. I too am an enthusiastic practitioner of the science. A collector too, particularly of portraiture.'

'You collect Mr Pidgeon's work?'

'Goodness me, no. Photographs of plump-cheeked infants do not interest me, however prettily arranged. Mr Pidgeon and I are members of a small society that meets from time to time to discuss the art and science of photography. I am something of an evangelist for the role of photography in Art.'

'How fascinating. Was it an illuminating meeting?'

'Regrettably I am here today with plump-cheeked infants of my own. A family portrait. My wife insisted. You have caught me truanting, I fear. I told Mr Pidgeon that I was in need of some air.'

She smiled. 'I am quite sure you were,' she said.

'I dislike being photographed, don't you? As a newspaperman I am more accustomed to the position of observer. The camera fascinates me. To have the world in which we live presented to us without artifice, not through a glass darkly but face to face, it must alter the way we understand it altogether.'

Before Maribel could answer there was a clamour at the door of the studio.

'Papa, Papa! Arthur has Grace's doll and will not give it back!'

Webster looked round. A small girl in an organdie frock tugged at his coat. He bent down, kissing her upon the nose, and took her in his arms.

'Come now, Patience. Remember your manners and say how do you do.'

The child gazed up at Maribel with round china-blue eyes and said nothing.

'I must be getting on,' Maribel said. 'If I might just collect the darkroom key?'

She gestured towards the studio door. Mr Webster stepped to one side. She felt his eyes on her as she tapped the jamb of the door with her knuckles. Inside, the studio was hot with lights and the hive thrum of children's chatter. Thomas looked up and hurried over, unhooking the key from its nail and handing it to her.

'Thank you,' she said. She weighed the key in her hand as she turned back to Mr Webster. 'Good luck with the portrait.'

He smiled at her.

'Papa!' the child hissed, wriggling to be put down. 'I promised I'd bring you. Grace is crying!'

'I shall be there presently. Good day, Mrs Campbell Lowe.'

'Good day, Mr Webster. Goodbye, Patience.'

As she turned towards the darkroom a faint breeze stirred through the open window, bringing with it the clatter of traffic. Behind her Webster murmured something to the child.

'How do you do, ma'am?' the child chanted in a high sing-song voice, as though reciting times tables. Maribel turned, smiling back over her shoulder.

'Very well, thank you,' she said.

The child twisted her face away, burying it in her father's shoulder. Webster patted her absently. Maribel nodded and walked away, aware as she shifted the satchel on her shoulder, as she slipped the key into the lock, that he watched her, that he knew as she did the quickened beat of her heart, the faint tremble in her fingers as she turned the key in the lock and pushed the door open. The darkroom smelled as it always did of chemicals and used-up air. She inhaled the smell gratefully, leaning against the door. Then, sliding the key back into the lock, she did something she never usually did. She locked herself in. She would not be able to work, she knew, if she did not keep him out.

The darkroom was hardly more than a cupboard lined with shelves, crammed with bottles and boxes and piles of plates awaiting exposure, each marked in white ink with the name of the family group. Maribel took her box of exposed plates from her bag and put them to one side. Then she took down the three developing trays and set them on the lowest shelf, which had been widened so that it might serve as a work table.

When she had filled one basin with clean water she pulled on a pair of leather gloves and, standing on tiptoe, reached down several brown glass bottles from the shelf above her head. Their labels were stained and torn about the edges but it was still possible to make out the names written in faded green ink in

Mr Pidgeon's tiny meticulous script: pyrogallic acid, potassium bromide, ammonium carbonate. She murmured the names to herself as she measured out the compounds and prepared the two plate baths, tasting the poetry in the words, their alchemical promise of transformation. In the small warm room their powerful smells insinuated themselves into her nostrils so that her eyes watered and her head swam a little. She inhaled, the caustic air ravishing her lungs, and the shimmer of anticipation quickened inside her. Where the spirit does not work with the hand there is no art, she thought, and, holding her breath, she took the first plate and slid it from its cover.

She had not expected to be so disheartened. All manner of difficulties could bedevil both the preparation and the development of dry plates and she was inexperienced. She was also clumsy and horribly tired. It was no wonder that she made mistakes. Perhaps she had touched the surface, mixed the chemicals incorrectly, allowed a foreign object into the plate holder of the camera. Perhaps, in her ignorance, she had somehow contrived to expose the plate twice. There were all manner of explanations, each one of them enough to ruin a print, but knowing them did nothing to ease the bitterness of her disappointment. She stared at the spoiled picture disconsolately. In Julia Margaret Cameron's portraits of her daughter, the light fell like a veil over the young girl's face, and her eyes were huge with innocence and fear. It was not as easy as she made it seem.

Her head ached from the fumes of the developing chemicals. Locking the darkroom door behind her, Maribel slung her satchel over her shoulder and hurried along the corridor. The sun was high and she squinted a little, raising one hand to shade her eyes from the brightness of the light. Against the dirt-etched glass of the high window, the sky was a deep Prussian blue.

It was hardly the end of the world, she told herself. Charlotte would sit for her again, and tomorrow she would return to look more calmly at the developed photographs. Proper examination would surely reveal what fault of hers had occasioned such unfortunate results. Mistakes were inevitable, especially among novices. She would improve.

Abruptly a line came back to her from her childhood, a favourite of the Scottish governess, Miss Finton, who had something of a weakness for Samuel Smiles: 'The apprenticeship of difficulty is one which the greatest of men have had to serve.'

'And ladies, mind,' Miss Finton had liked to add, waggling a finger at the girls arrayed before her as she corrected their fractions, and Maribel had rolled her eyes at Ida because she had known what Miss Finton did not, that there were those who had something and those who did not, and no amount of industriousness could change that one jot.

9

THE WEEKS THAT FOLLOWED brought no respite from the oppressive weather. The heat stunned the capital, stifling appetite, curiosity, the process of intelligent thought. Though several times she roused herself to contemplate the work clothes hanging in her press, Maribel did not return to Mr Pidgeon's studios. She felt heavy, too heavy to work and certainly too heavy to chance another encounter with Mr Webster. As for the spoiled photographs, the thought filled her with weariness. It was too hot to write, too hot to walk, to hot even to dress. For the first time in her life she was grateful to Georgie Burne-Jones, who several years ago, in an attempt to recruit Maribel into her Aesthetic movement, had bestowed upon her a flowing dress in the medieval style, slit-necked and wide-sleeved and embellished upon the skirts and around the neck with sunflowers worked in free-form art embroidery. The terracotta fabric had been coloured with a natural vegetable dye which gave the silk its distinctively faded appearance. It might, Georgie had declared proudly, pass for an antique.

Maribel had privately considered the dress an abomination and had refused ever to wear it. It seemed to her a kind of madness that a woman who could dress in ravishing gowns from Paris would choose instead to disport herself in a hideous brown sack. There was nothing liberating about ugliness. Besides, Maribel was neither tall nor willowy. Hers was the kind of hourglass figure shown to its best advantage in stays.

All the same, as the temperature in London continued to rise, it was with some relief that Maribel abandoned the stifling confinement of her undergarments and draped herself in Georgie's loose brown folds. The first time Edward saw her he laughed so much he had to sit down. When he was recovered enough to speak he promised her that as soon as Parliament rose for the recess he would take her to Le Touquet, so that she could parade her exquisite taste before all the aristocracies of Europe.

The days dragged. Invitations were sparse. Those who could left town. Half mad with boredom, Maribel agreed one afternoon to accompany Charlotte to a meeting of the Fabian Society in Fitzroy Square to hear a lecture by Mrs Marx Aveling entitled 'America and the Unconscious Socialist'. Charlotte was to depart for Sussex the next day and Maribel was eager to see her before she left. All the same, the effort of leaving the flat almost defeated her and by the time she arrived in Fitzroy Square, the lecture was starting. Hastening to cross the road, she was surprised to see Edward step down from a cab. She might have called out to him if something in his bearing had not impeded her. His habitually loose-limbed stroll was hunched, furtive as a furled umbrella.

Drawn by the low angle of his hat and a sinking sense of inevitability, she had followed him at a distance to a house in Whitfield Street. The house was pale brick, flat-fronted, its white-painted windows bland with respectability. Beside the black front door there was a neatly clipped box tree in an iron tub. She watched as Edward climbed the three stone steps and pressed the brass doorbell. He did not step back from the door while he waited. Instead he stood very close, as though he might press his lips to its glossy paint. A moment later the door opened and closed swiftly, like a mouth swallowing. Upstairs, on the second floor, the curtains were drawn.

She waited but he did not come out. After perhaps ten minutes another gentleman emerged from the area steps, his hat similarly pulled down low over his face. At the second-floor window a woman's face appeared fleetingly. It was then that Maribel knew for sure. Terrified that Edward would find her there she stumbled along Tottenham Court Road, pushing her way through the early-evening bustle. Even so late in the day it was still unpleasantly close and the perspiration dampened her hands and sent a trickle of moisture between her breasts.

She had thought to take the Metropolitan Railway but the entrance to the station was crowded with clerks and shopgirls in gay bonnets and she did not have the strength for it. Instead she took a cab. As the hansom inched around the traffic-choked snarl of Trafalgar Square she had put her face to the open window, trying to find a breeze, trying not to think of Edward, his elegant fingers, his narrow back, the long white stretch of his limbs. Beside the cab, an old woman shuffled along the pavement, a darned shawl over her head. The back of her skirt was worn, fringed with tattered threads. From somewhere in the melee, a man shouted something. The woman turned, gesturing obscenely and with such vigour that her shawl fell back from her face, and Maribel saw that she was not old at all but hardly more than a girl. Her eyes were yellow as a lion's. Beneath her skirt she wore men's boots without laces.

The box tree outside the house on Whitfield Street had been pruned into a perfect ball, its leaves so uniformly green and pristine that they might have been fashioned from wax. At the Calle de León, in the central courtyard, cascades of purple bougainvillea foamed over the iron balustrades and water danced in a stone fountain. She covered her eyes, her thumb and forefinger clamped against her temples. In the drawing room, the Señora had served pale gold white port in tiny glasses like vials of sunlight.

At the Calle de León they had spoken Spanish, sometimes French. Never English. It would be different in English, she thought. Then she shook her head, impatient with herself. The traffic was finally moving and the cab soon passed the high railings that bordered the private lawns of Belgrave Square. She would be home directly. She was not sure now what had possessed her to follow Edward when he could so easily have turned round and seen her. She imagined his courteous perplexity, his faint embarrassment at her impropriety, and the thought of it made her squirm.

It was on the longest and warmest day of 1887 that Victoria, Queen regnant of the United Kingdom of Great Britain and Ireland and first Empress of India, celebrated her Golden Jubilee. Along the length of the processional route the streets were wreathed and swagged, every house arrayed with velvets and tapestries and hanging baskets filled with roses and flags of every imaginable nation. Embroidered banners bore loyal mottos and greetings to Her Majesty in tall gold letters, triumphal arches of extravagant design spanned the thoroughfares, festoons of brightly coloured silk hung from windows and from roofs. Between them profusions of flaunting flags and bunting and clusters of Union Jacks criss-crossed the air so that, as the Queen drove from Constitution Hill to Westminster, flanked by her mounted princes, it was as though she traversed a single great avenue of brilliant colour.

Immense crowds thronged the streets, the swell of their cheers like the roaring of an ocean. From their place on a sweltering balcony in a window at the foot of the Haymarket, Edward and Maribel observed the crush of Her Majesty's subjects stretch as far as the eye could see in both directions. Despite the sweltering temperatures, the people greeted every part of the parade with unwearying enthusiasm, whooping in loud approval for the handsome German Crown Prince, a chivalrous apparition clothed all in white, and louder still for the Prince of Wales and his brothers who followed, mounted on three fine bay horses. Sunlight flashed on helmets and epaulettes, on scintillating cuirasses and buttons. When at last their Queen passed in her golden carriage, her eight cream-coloured horses bedecked in golden harness hung with crimson tassels, her footmen gleaming in their livery of gold lace, the bellows grew deafening. All along the street men doffed their hats. Many threw them in the air. Among all the dazzle of the procession, the gold and the blazonry, only the Queen was plainly dressed in a gown of sombre black-and-grey stripes, its sole embellishment the broad blue ribbon of the Garter across her shoulder. In place of a crown, she wore a simple grey bonnet.

'Why, she wore that very same bonnet to the opening of the People's Palace,' remarked the wife of the Member for Croydon as the Queen raised her hand to the crowds arrayed in windows and on roofs, delight lighting her plain pale face.

'Such thrift,' Edward said.

When darkness fell there were fireworks in the park. The streets were thronged with people until late into the night, their drunkenness exceeded only by their good humour. The next day, despite the heat, Maribel took her camera and walked the route taken by the Queen's procession. She photographed the sagging swathes of bunting, the wilted flowers, the heavy-eyed huddles of weary merrymakers, the flotsam of the great wave of celebration that had surged so triumphantly through the capital. At the gates of Hyde Park a cordon of policemen blocked the roads in every direction. The park itself was closed. Thirty thousand of London's children had been invited to a fete presided over by the Queen herself, a constable told Maribel. As well as magicians and tumblers, the children had been promised tea, with sandwiches and three kinds of cake.

That night, as the Campbell Lowes attended a dinner given by Frederic Leighton in the Arab Hall of his house in Holland Park, a mob broke into the enclosure where the children's party had taken place and set fire to the marquees. In the days that followed, fearful of a repeat of the riots of the previous winter, newspaper editorials called for a clearing of Trafalgar Square, where the number of men and women sleeping rough had swollen to several hundred. They thundered warnings of respectable citizens once again attacked, carriages overturned, shops smashed and looted, property stolen. Unless repressive action were taken immediately, they roared, law-abiding London would once more fall victim to the savageries of the mob.

Only the *Chronicle* took the side of the poor. Throughout July the newspaper ran a series of fervent articles about the men Webster dubbed the 'unemployed', who, he argued, lived barely quarter lives; stunted physically and morally, deprived of any kind of education, they could not live as God had meant them to live but were instead reverting to a race of brutes, a miscegenation of debased humanity capable of every kind of evil. He wrote of godlessness, of foul language and fouler lodgings, of the lack of thrift that forced wives to seek work outside the home, of the cursed affliction of promiscuity and casual marital relations, and laid the blame for all squarely at the doors of an inhumane and profit-hungry society. In particular he condemned the landlords of pestilential dwelling houses as no better than brothel keepers, for both profited from the moral and physical ruin of the weak and the destitute. For several consecutive days he published the names and addresses of landlords in the East End whom he deemed particular offenders. When the *Chronicle* received a letter from a prominent firm of lawyers threatening a libel action, Webster published that too.

'He speaks his mind,' Maribel observed as she glanced through the paper one evening. 'There is no doubting his courage.'

Edward turned from the window. The weather was finally breaking. Beyond the roofs purple clouds massed, hastening the evening towards darkness.

'A facility for making enemies is not the same thing as courage.'

'But his writing is vigorous,' Maribel said. 'He will not be ignored.'

'He enjoys whipping himself into a frenzy of righteous fury.'

'But if he can whip up his readers too, surely it will help you?'

Edward shrugged.

'I defy him to whip up Parliament,' he said. 'He could plug the entire House into Deptford Power Station and provoke not so much as a twitch.'

Maribel did not answer. She thought of the heat in her skin when he looked at her, the quickening of her pulse, and it occurred to her that for once Edward might be mistaken.

A week after the Jubilee celebrations, Maribel and Edward dined at Chester Square. Edward's brother Henry was there, and several other of Arthur's friends who had known one another at school and shared Arthur's uproarious sense of humour. The conversation during dinner was dominated by an enthusiastic reminiscence of the practical jokes that these men had played upon one another, both as boys and in later life. Maribel listened in silence to tales of tapioca spiked with frogspawn, shoes filled with ink, boys tied to their bedsteads or held out of windows by their ankles, and thought of the stories Edward had told her of the *payadors* of Argentina, gaucho troubadours who vied to out-verse one another in contests of song that could go on for hours. It was the custom among the gauchos, whenever they were paid in silver, to fix the coins to their belts or to their horses' bridles. In Chester Square the silver was displayed on the dining-room table, shaped into gleaming forks and candlesticks and coasters and artfully feathered game birds with open beaks.

It was not until the ladies retired to the drawing room that Maribel had the chance to talk to Charlotte. When the coffee had been served, and the other wives settled on the sofa, they stood together before the empty fireplace. Maribel licked the crystals of coffee sugar from her spoon and lit a cigarette. Beyond the thick curtains rain spattered lightly against the windows.

'London has been very dull without you,' she said to Charlotte.

'And Sussex just as dull with me,' Charlotte replied. 'Even the children were insensible with the heat. I had forgotten what silence sounded like.'

'Was it heavenly?'

'It should have been but after one day of it I longed for riots. I seem to have become accustomed to them.'

'We must adapt to survive. That Mr Darwin was no fool.'

Charlotte smiled, her attention distracted by one of the other women. Maribel talked desultorily to someone's wife about the servant problem. When at last the gentlemen joined them from the dining room, bringing with them loud laughter and the smell of cigars, Edward pleaded fatigue and an early train the next morning. A cab was summoned. In the hall Charlotte kissed them goodnight and pressed upon them an umbrella. The rain was falling hard, the sultry night restive with thunder.

'I've hardly spoken to you.'

'I know. Come to tea tomorrow, won't you? I want to hear about the photographs. Were they good?'

Maribel wrinkled her nose. 'They should have been, or three of them anyway. The light was perfect, absolutely perfect, and you too of course, but somehow I managed to spoil the plates. I don't even know what I did wrong, some kind of double exposure, maybe, or dirt on the glass. Whatever it was I botched them. I am sorry.'

'Don't be a silly,' Charlotte said. 'We will just have to try again.'

'Seriously? You could bear it?'

'Of course I could. We must adapt to survive.'

Reaching out, Maribel squeezed her friend's hand.

'Thank you.'

'Thank Mr Darwin.'

'I mean to develop my Jubilee photographs tomorrow morning. Fingers crossed I do better with them.'

'Maribel,' Edward said wearily from the doorway, gesturing towards the cab. His wife's inability to leave a party promptly was one aspect of her nature to which he refused to become accustomed.

'Tomorrow, four o'clock,' Charlotte said and pushed her towards the door. 'Take her home, dear Edward, I beseech you. We have had quite enough of her.'

The rain drummed on the roof of the cab, piercing the light from the street lamps like a cascade of silver needles. The heaviness of the downpour required them to keep the windows up, and the cab smelled strongly of stale sweat. Maribel lit a cigarette.

'How were the gentlemen? Awash with blue jokes and tales of schoolboy high jinks?'

'Gossip, mostly. They are as bad as a bunch of wives when they get together. They were full of salacious stories about your Mr Webster.'

'He is not my Mr Webster.'

'Dearest Bo, you rise like a salmon.'

'Then don't be a fly.'

Edward smiled.

'Do you remember when you saw him at Turks Row that he told you he collected photographs? Well, it turns out that his is rather more private a collection than he might have intimated. Arthur's friend Woodhouse went to dinner at Wimbledon the other night, strictly gentlemen only, and they all had a good deal too much to drink. The collection was brought out with the cigars. Woodhouse, who had been dreading a pious lecture in aesthetics, was perfectly delighted. It was basically naked ladies. Webster of course calls it Art.'

Maribel was glad then that they sat side by side and that in the darkness he could not see her face.

'One might have guessed, of course,' Edward added. 'It is always the Congregationalists.'

'I thought it was the Scots.'

Edward laughed. 'The Scots too. What we bury under our tartan blankets would make a sailor blush. By the way, I have suggested to Henry he come up to Inverallich this summer. It would be nice for Mother.'

'Did he say he would?' Maribel asked, glad of the change of subject, and she leaned forward, pressing her crossed arms hard against her stomach. The thought of Mr Webster looking at photographs of naked ladies with those milky eyes of his was peculiarly unsettling.

'He said he would think about it. He is preoccupied with the Prince of Wales, with whom he has taken to playing poker. To my lasting credit I refrained from vulgar jokes about knaves.'

'Your self-restraint is commendable. Will he be bankrupted?'

'Henry? On the contrary, he is confident of riches. Apparently he and Prince Edward have been receiving instruction in the game from Buffalo Bill and they are become quite expert. It may of course be that they will soon become expert in losing money to Buffalo Bill. We shall have to hope for the best.'

At Cadogan Gardens Edward descended first so that he might open the umbrella. Maribel took his arm as they crossed the street.

'Henry told me that the Prince has had Cody arrange a shooting match between his little sharp-shooter Annie Oakley and the Grand Duke Mikhail of Russia,' Edward said, pushing open the front door. 'Apparently the Queen hopes that a humiliating defeat by a girl half his height will be enough to send the Russian home and put an end to his unsuitable interest in the young Princess Victoria.'

Maribel laughed, then put her finger to her lips, gesturing towards the door of Lady Wingate's flat. Edward nodded, his face stern. Folding the umbrella he twirled it like a walking stick and, his knees raised high and his feet pointed, he tiptoed stagily across the hall. Maribel giggled. She closed the front door as quietly as she could manage but, as Edward set his foot on the first step, it emitted a loud creak. Lady Wingate's door flung open.

'Madam,' Edward said with a bow. 'Good evening.'

Lady Wingate glared at him. She wore a loose gown of a vaguely oriental design, her long grey hair in a plait over one shoulder. Her eyes were bright as a bird's.

'Good evening?' she scolded. 'It is the middle of the night! And yet in you slam, rousing the whole lot of us with your racket. It will not do!'

'I'm sorry,' Maribel said.

The old lady ignored her.

'You are in all sorts of trouble with the papers again, you know,' she said, gesticulating at Edward. 'More Irish than the Irish, they call you. Will you bomb us? Or do you mean simply to smash things up?'

Edward grinned.

'Dear Lady Wingate, if I bomb or smash anything you'll be the first to know.'

'I don't know how you can live with yourself, consorting with common criminals. You should watch your step.'

'I shall do my best. This one in particular,' he said, pointing to the one beneath his foot. 'We shall have someone come and look at it tomorrow. There must be something we can do about the creak.'

'In Burma it was the frogs that kept one awake,' Lady Wingate said. 'That and the cicadas screaming their heads off. One was required to sleep under a net, of course, because of the mosquitoes. My mother hated it, she said she could not breathe, but I always found it rather romantic. Like sleeping in a cloud.'

'Goodnight, Lady Wingate,' Edward said.

The old lady hesitated, then waggled a reproving finger. Her knotted hand was bunioned with rings.

'It won't do, you know,' she said. 'That child this afternoon and now all this rumpus in the dead of night. It won't do at all.'

Halfway up the stairs Edward stopped. Lady Wingate waited in her open doorway, her shadow staining the tiled floor.

'Goodnight, Lady Wingate,' he called down. 'Tomorrow I shall buy you a mosquito net. One should always sleep in a cloud.'

It was Alice's night off. Inside the flat Maribel turned on the lamp by the coat stand and removed her hat. The window at the far end of the corridor had been left open and the undrawn curtains stirred, rain glinting in a puddle on the sill.

'That woman gets dottier by the day,' Maribel said, loosening her hair. 'The door's one thing but disturbed by a child? She knows quite well that there are no children here.'

'That woman has the hearing of a bat,' Edward replied. 'She could hear a child sneeze six streets away.'

'She's lonely,' Maribel said.

'She never leaves her flat.'

'She's old.'

'She's the same age as my mother.'

At the bedroom door Maribel turned her back to her husband.

'Would you?' she said, bending forward a little.

Edward unhooked her dress. Halfway down he paused, sliding his hands inside the bodice to cup her breasts, kissing her softly on the back of her neck.

Maribel thought of Whitfield Street and the house with the box tree.

'I thought you had an early train,' she said.

'Not so very early.'

She turned towards him, stroking his tired face. There were lavender shadows under his eyes.

'And what about Lady Wingate and her bat hearing?' she murmured.

'I promised I should watch my step.'

With his hand still inside her dress he guided her into the bedroom. When he kissed her she closed her eyes, suffused not only by the first stirrings of desire but also by the reassuring familiarity of his mouth against her mouth, his hands on her skin. Beyond the uncurtained window the rain was still falling. Taking Edward's hand she pulled him over to the window, pushing the sash up as far as it would go. A light breeze was blowing and, when she slipped free of her sleeves, flecks of rain gleamed on her bare arms. The coolness of the air was exquisite. Thunder rumbled, a deep belly growl, and fell silent. There was a moment of stillness and then a crack of lightning that broke the night in two. In the knife-white light Edward's hair was black.

Afterwards, when he had returned to his dressing room, Maribel rose to smoke a cigarette. Dragging a chair to the window she threw open the curtains. The storm was dying. The rain had stopped and the sticky night air clung about her like a sigh. She smoked slowly, holding the smoke in her chest, lighting a second from the stub of the first. On a night like this one, in a narrow alley behind the Criterion Theatre, Victor had taken her into his arms and promised to make her a star.

'You know why the sun sets in the evening, Sylvia?' he had asked her in his soft Spanish drawl, standing on tiptoes slightly so that he might kiss her. 'Because that is your moment. Even the sun knows when it is beaten.'

She had held him in her arms and known he was a gift from God. She had begun to despair. Victor might be small and rotund, and a great deal older than he chose to admit, but he had money. He knew people. He had invested in a play that had toured in Europe. He could do for her what Mr Corelli's photographs had not – put an end to the ceaseless rounds of auditions, the dusty couches and the snatched bit-parts. Victor's next project was a charming piece about a beautiful ingénue. The West End, Broadway, even Paris and Vienna, they would take them all by storm. Sylvia Wylde would be bigger than Sarah Bernhardt, bigger even than Charlotte Cushman in her heyday. The washed-up Miss Hodson would read of her triumphs in the newspapers and weep.

Three days later she had moved out of her cramped room in Rupert Street and into a small and comfortable cottage he had rented for her close to the canal in Maida Vale. It had a little wrought-iron balcony and a large porch over the front door, creamy with clematis. In the mornings she sat on the balcony, watching the sun on the water and the ducks as they squabbled in the reeds, and her bright future was so close she could feel the warmth of it like breath on her face.

The photographer in the crimson studio had made only two hundred prints. Victor had had them expensively mounted. He said that it was all about exclusivity, that he did not mean to have her picture fingered by grimy-fisted working men. She was not a music-hall chanteuse, a sly-winking wanton. She was a leading lady and a leading lady was not handed around in the public house, hidden under the mattresses of miners. Twelve years ago he had looked at the portrait of her, her hand set coyly between her thighs, and declared it a Work of Art. Were those the kind of pictures Mr Webster collected and showed to men after dinner when they were red-faced with port? Was that why he looked at her like that, because he had seen her before? The fear rose in her sharply, a spike in her throat like vomit. She inhaled deeply, swallowing it down. It could not be. The chance of such a coincidence – surely it was less than infinitesimal. Twelve years was a very long time. A photographic print was not made to last twelve years.

All the same she stood, shaking her head as though she could shake her thoughts loose. Pushing the sash of the window as high as it would go she leaned out. Above the roofs the moon slid clear of a silver-trimmed tatter of cloud and drifted slowly across the night. The London moon was so small, she thought, a moon not so much to be cupped in the hands as pinched sharply between finger and thumb. She was not in the least bit sleepy. She thought of her notebook, the unfinished poem, but it was words from the schoolroom that stirred in her, verses recited long ago at Ellerton, her hand pressed to her chest, her childish voice straining for pathos.

> *And like a dying lady, lean and pale,*
> *Who totters forth, wrapp'd in a gauzy veil,*
> *Out of her chamber, led by the insane*
> *And feeble wanderings of her fading brain,*
> *The moon arose up in the murky east*
> *A white and shapeless mass.*
>
> *Art thou pale for weariness*
> *Of climbing heaven and gazing on the earth,*
> *Wandering companionless*
> *Among the stars that have a different birth,*
> *And ever changing, like a joyless eye*
> *That finds no object worth its constancy?*

10

THE NEXT DAY, AS promised, Maribel went to tea at Chester Square. She was late. As she was shown in, a posse of boys mounted on wooden hobby horses descended the wide staircase in a stampede of boots and whooping, the smallest one whirling a loop of rope around his head. Ducking their heads to avoid the ordinary courtesies, they careered across the hall and thundered, with a slam of doors, towards the garden. The maid sucked in her cheeks as she took Maribel's parasol.

Charlotte was in her sunny sitting room on the first floor. She smiled as the door opened.

'Dearest, you are come after all,' she said. 'I'm so glad. I thought you might have forgotten.' Kissing the tousle-haired child on her lap, she set it onto its feet beside her chair so that she might stand up. Toys lay scattered across the Aubusson rug and, on the footstool, a mass of picture books, some open, was piled in a precarious heap. 'Beatrice, say good afternoon to Mrs Campbell Lowe.'

'Good afternoon, Mrs Campbell Lowe,' Beatrice parroted and, sidling up to the tea tray, she snatched a bun, took a big bite from it, and slipped the rest into the pocket of her pinafore. Charlotte shook her head.

'That will do, Bea dearest. Now go and find Ellen and the others in the nursery. There will be tea there too, you know.'

The child darted out of the room. Charlotte smiled.

'How other mothers manage to bring up their children to be civilised human beings is beyond me. My lot remain resolutely feral.'

Maribel managed a smile. She felt giddy, thick-headed, as if she might be coming down with something.

'You must be longing for tea.' Charlotte peered into the pot. 'Oh dear, I shall have to ring for more. This pot is quite stewed.'

'I like my tea strong.'

'Not as strong as this, surely?'

'Possibly stronger.'

Charlotte shook her head and poured, adding milk and offering Maribel the sugar. Maribel took two teaspoonfuls and stirred, gazing into the rich brown swirl of her cup.

'So you brought the Jubilee photographs, I hope?' Charlotte said, gesturing at Maribel's battered satchel. 'Are they good?'

Maribel shrugged.

'I don't know. I have yet to develop them.'

'I thought you were going to do them this morning? If I remember rightly it was the reason you were obliged to refuse my kind invitation to the Foundling Hospital recital.'

'Ah.'

'Quite right "ah". Anyone would think you didn't care for my children's wilful destruction of the works of Schubert.'

Maribel smiled faintly. She removed the spoon from her tea and set it in the saucer. A cluster of tiny bubbles circled slowly around the edge of the cup. Charlotte looked at her.

'I was only teasing.'

'I know.'

'Is something the matter?'

'No, of course not.' Maribel fumbled for her cigarettes. 'It's been a busy day, that's all. If I can only sit here peacefully drinking my nasty stewed tea and smoking my nasty Egyptian cigarettes I shall be quite restored. Tell me about the recital.'

'Must I? I shall bore us both half to death. Besides, we have much more important matters to discuss. Did I tell you that we dined the day before yesterday with the Rawlinsons?'

Sir Gerald Rawlinson was an illustrious physicist and member of the Royal Society whose most recent preoccupation was the proof, through scientific means, of the existence of God. As Charlotte described his latest experiments, Maribel sat quietly in a pose of attentiveness, sipping at her soupy tea, but she hardly heard a word. She kept losing the thread of what Charlotte was saying.

She had not lied to Charlotte when she had told her that it was her intention that morning to develop her Jubilee photographs. That morning she had indeed gone to Mr Pidgeon's studio. As usual Thomas answered her knock but, to her surprise, instead of handing her the key, he blinked at her and asked if she might wait where she was. A moment or two later Mr Pidgeon himself appeared at the door.

'Mrs Campbell Lowe,' he said. 'You are come at last.'

Maribel frowned. 'Is there something wrong?'

Mr Pidgeon glanced behind him into the studio. Then he stepped into the corridor, closing the door behind him.

'Excuse me,' he said. 'I wonder if I might talk with you for a moment?'

The gravity of his expression was discomfiting.

'Why?' she said uneasily. 'What on earth is the matter?'

'Dear me, I have alarmed you. Forgive me. That was not my intention, I assure you. It is just the photographs, the ones you left in the darkroom to dry. It is not my business, I know, but in the circumstances it was not possible to avoid seeing them. Suffice to say, I have secured them in my private office under lock and key. I hope you forgive my presumption. I knew you would not wish them left in the darkroom.'

'Oh, those,' Maribel said. 'You are kind but you need not have gone to any trouble, I know they are spoiled. The fault was plain as soon as I developed them, though I cannot think what it was I did wrong. Was it the bath, do you think, or something to do with the plates? I wouldn't want to make the same mistake with these ones.'

Mr Pidgeon peered at her.

'Mrs Campbell Lowe, am I right in believing that you have no children of your own?'

Maribel frowned. Mr Pidgeon had never before presumed to make enquiries that were clearly none of his business.

'I'm afraid I do not see what –'

'Forgive me but there were no children present when you took the photographs in question? Or at any time while the plates were in your possession?'

'Not at any time. Mr Pidgeon, are you quite well?'

'Indeed I am, madam. Indeed I am.'

'Then perhaps you might explain to me what this is all about.'

'Can it be that you do not yet know what you have?' Mr Pidgeon was so enlivened that he bounced a little on the balls of his feet. 'I had not imagined – why, how extraordinary. The image is quite clear, there can be no mistaking it.'

'Mr Pidgeon, you are alarming me.'

'Forgive me, I beseech you. It is only that, as a photographer by profession myself, I have naturally taken an active interest in spirit photography. I myself have on occasion experienced phenomena, interference if you like, in my work that cannot easily be explained away, but yours? It is unambiguous. Unmistakable.'

'I am sure I don't know what you mean,' Maribel said firmly.

'Then come in, come in. Come and see for yourself.'

Mr Pidgeon held open the door to the studio. Maribel hesitated. Then she stepped inside. On the far side of the room Thomas was sweeping the floor.

'Thomas, Mrs Baxter and her family will be here presently,'

Mr Pidgeon said. 'Please ask her to wait. Mrs Campbell Lowe, if you would come this way.'

The office was a small, cluttered slice of a room cut from one corner of the studio. Mr Pidgeon removed a pile of papers from an upright chair and, depositing them among many others on the large wooden desk, invited Maribel to sit. From high in the long, thin strip of window came the persistent whine and thump of a bluebottle banging against the glass. Taking a key from his pocket, Mr Pidgeon unlocked the narrow top drawer of the desk, and drawing out a manila envelope, handed it wordlessly to Maribel. She fingered the flap. Mr Pidgeon smiled at her encouragingly, showing his yellow teeth. Slowly she drew out the pictures.

'Might I?' Mr Pidgeon said excitedly.

Taking the photographs from her, he spread them out across the desk. Maribel leaned forward. There, five times over, was Charlotte, her hand raised and her face tilted away from the camera, a pose that, as Maribel had hoped, succeeded in capturing something of both her gentleness and her intelligence. Two of the photographs were overexposed. In two more Charlotte had moved so that the lines of her face were blurred. Mr Pidgeon picked up the last one. Maribel sighed. There, like a veil of smoke thrown over Charlotte's skirts, was the greyish smudge that spoiled the work.

'Look here,' Mr Pidgeon said, tapping the photograph with his index finger. 'A child, quite plainly. May I ask you where you took these?'

Maribel gazed at the photographs. She felt a little dizzy.

'I do not see a child.'

'But you must,' Mr Pidgeon insisted. 'See the hand here, against the woman's skirt, and here the face, half turned away. It is faint, of course, and indistinct in places as one would expect, but there is no mistaking it. It is most definitely a child, a boy I would hazard, perhaps eight or nine years old.'

Maribel pressed her nails into the palms of her hand. There was a pressure like a knuckle in her throat.

'The blotch you call a face I call a thumbprint,' she said.

'It is a child. A spirit child.'

She shook her head dumbly. 'No,' she whispered. 'I do not believe in ghosts.'

'What about the resurrection of the body and the life ever-lasting? Do you believe in the Apostles' Creed, Mrs Campbell Lowe?'

Maribel did not answer.

'Are we not told that God works in mysterious ways? It is He, after all, who has blessed us with the scientific abilities necessary to invent and produce the camera so that we might better understand the miracles of His creation. This is possibly an unhappy question and most certainly an impudent one but forgive me for I must ask it – is it possible that you might by any chance recognise the child in this picture?'

It was like fainting. For a moment everything stopped. The drift of dust in the sunlight, the murmur of voices in the studio next door, even the rumble of traffic from the street outside ceased. The restless bluebottle fell silent. Maribel touched her dry lips with the tip of her tongue. Then, carefully gathering up the photographs, she stood. She could hear the sing of blood in her ears.

'That is quite enough,' she said. 'You forget yourself, Mr Pidgeon. I shall see myself out.'

'Mrs Campbell Lowe –'

'Enough, do you hear me?'

Dashing away the tears with the heel of one hand, she flung open the door of the office and fled across the studio. From their perch on the chaise a mother and her clutch of plump-cheeked children regarded her open-mouthed, their picture book abandoned in mid-sentence.

'What is wrong with that lady, Mama?' a piping voice

enquired as she banged open the studio door and clattered down the stairs towards the street. She did not slow her pace until she reached the iron railings of the Ranelagh Gardens. The horse chestnuts were in full leaf and the shaded paths were busy with children and starched nursemaids pushing perambulators. Maribel hesitated, drawing a handkerchief from her pocket to blow her nose. Her eyes were sore, her throat swollen. A boy in an oxford jacket eyed her suspiciously as he rattled a stick between the palings. Then he stuck out his tongue. Maribel stared at him. He stared back. Then she went in.

For a while she walked, watching the children as they threw their balls and bowled their hoops and made elaborate shapes in the air with their skipping ropes. On the brittle dun lawn two little girls fussed over a chocolate-coloured spaniel with a ribbon around its neck while, beside them, an infant in a white knitted bonnet and white wool leggings stumped stiff-legged like a diminutive Egyptian mummy.

At the Embankment end of the gardens Maribel found a vacant bench in the shade of a high hedge and sat down. The pile of photographs lay face down in her lap, their edges curled by the damp warmth of her hands. She did not turn them over. Instead she leaned forwards, her elbows on her knees, her forehead resting on her fingertips, and in the darkness of her hands closed her eyes.

'He's a peculiar fish, though, isn't he?' Charlotte was saying.

Maribel blinked at her. She had the lurching sense of waking without ever having quite known that she was asleep.

'Those disconcerting eyes. Cataracts, I suppose, though he appears to see perfectly well.' Charlotte frowned. 'Dearest, are you quite all right? You haven't touched your filthy tea.'

'I'm sorry.' Maribel gave herself a little shake and reached once more for her cigarettes. 'I am just a little tired, that's all.'

'You do look pale. Must you smoke so very much?'

'You know I must.'

'You know, Mr Webster was fearfully interested in your work. He kept asking me what you were working on.'

'Mr Webster?'

'Have you not been listening to a word I say?'

'Of course I have. It is just that I cannot understand why everyone is so interested in Mr Webster all of a sudden.'

'Because he is so excessively interested in you, that is why. The man is positively smitten.'

'Charlotte, really.'

'It's perfectly true. I tried several times to change the subject but he would have none of it. He wanted to talk only of his beloved.'

'Well, I can't imagine why,' Maribel snapped. 'I have done absolutely nothing to encourage his interest.'

'Oh, I don't think Mr Webster needs encouraging. According to Arthur, he is mad on everything to do with sex and turns the air blue the moment the ladies are out of the room.'

'Stop it.'

'Arthur is convinced it is only his unrelentingly Nonconformist self-discipline that prevents him from becoming quite the debaucher. Apparently his father was a Congregational minister somewhere ferociously ascetic like York where they think novels the prayer books of the Devil.'

Maribel shook her head unhappily.

'He referred to God as the Senior Partner,' Charlotte added.

'No.'

'I'm afraid so.'

Maribel tried to smile. She took a sip of her tea. Everything about Charlotte's sitting room was familiar, from the pattern of roses and forget-me-nots on the teacups to the yellow silk sofas and the Dresden clock on the mantelpiece. Even the jumble

146

of wooden bricks on the floor at her feet seemed always to have been there in that precise arrangement, blue on yellow, the letter T facing upwards. She set her cup and saucer down on the table beside her.

'Charlotte, I – there's something I have to show you.'

Reaching into the bag at her feet Maribel drew out the photographs. Taking the top three she set them in a row on the fender stool. The lump in her throat made her cough.

'Please,' she said. 'Tell me what you think.'

Charlotte leaned forward. 'Are these the ones of me?'

Maribel nodded. Charlotte picked one up and then another, her brows drawn together in concentration. The point of her tongue showed pink between her teeth.

'Well?' Maribel prompted.

Charlotte looked up and smiled. 'Maribel, these are really good. The way you catch the light in this one – it's just beautiful.'

'I – this part here –'

'That's a shame, yes, but it hardly ruins the picture.'

'You don't think – you don't think it could possibly be a spirit?'

'Very funny.'

'I'm serious.'

Charlotte rolled her eyes. 'You, the arch sceptic? Don't be a tease.'

'So you think it is ridiculous too? I – it is only that the photographer whose darkroom I use tried to convince me that it was the ghost of a child. A ghost! I mean, really.'

'Except that it has happened, hasn't it?' Charlotte said, and she peered again at the photograph. 'There was that man in America, what was his name, the one who made those portraits of Abraham Lincoln's widow –'

'And who was prosecuted for fraud.'

'He was acquitted. They were never able to prove anything.' She stared at the photograph in her lap, her head on one side. 'I suppose it *could* be a ghost. It is just not a very good one.'

She looked up at Maribel, her eyes wide. Maribel's face twisted a little and then she started to laugh. When Charlotte laughed too she laughed harder, the tears spilling over and running down her cheeks. She laughed until her cheeks ached, her arms wrapped round her stomach. When at last she stopped laughing her tea had gone cold.

'Poor Mr Pidgeon,' she said at last, wiping her eyes. 'He will be so disappointed.'

'I doubt it. His kind make do with a great deal less than this.'

'Mr Pidgeon will have to make do with nothing at all. These photographs are going on the fire and that is that.'

'How very selfish you are, dearest.'

'I know, denying the Spiritualist crackpots their fun. Not to mention the penny press. I can see the headlines in *Tit-Bits* now: MEMBER FOR ARGYLL IN SÉANCE SCANDAL. FOREIGN WIFE SEES DEAD CHILDREN.'

'No one expects anything else of foreigners. And Edward is never happier than when people are complaining about him.'

'Then how about THE HONOURABLE MRS ARTHUR CHARTERHOUSE IS THE GHOST LADY!'

'Arthur might object,' Charlotte conceded. 'But it would be rather thrilling for the children.'

Maribel smiled.

'Fortunately for you, we have thrills aplenty already,' Charlotte said, leaning back in her chair as Maribel picked up the photographs and slid them into their brown envelope. 'We go next week to the Wild West – at long last. The boys are quite beside themselves. What they know about Buffalo Bill and his cowboys would fill an encyclopaedia. You aren't leaving, are you? You only just arrived.'

'I can't stay much longer. Edward is only just back from Scotland and we are dining with the Webbs.'

'The Webbs? And you refuse cake? Have you taken leave of your senses?'

'I told you, Charlotte, I am not hungry.'

'What has hungry got to do with it? See how thin you are. Are you sickening for something, do you think? If only you ate more and smoked a little less –'

'Hush your fussing. I am quite well.'

'Perhaps you should see a doctor, just to be sure.'

'I don't need to see a doctor.'

Charlotte shook her head. Then she grinned. 'Did I tell you that the medical officer assigned to Buffalo Billeries is a Dr Coffin? The boys think it killing.'

Maribel stared at her. 'Dr Coffin? Are you sure?'

Charlotte giggled. 'Isn't it marvellous? A Yorkshireman, apparently. I know Northerners have a reputation for bluntness but one might have hoped someone would have had a quiet word in the man's ear. I mean, it hardly inspires confidence, does it?'

That night Maribel pleaded a headache. When Edward had gone she sat at her desk for a long time, a sliced apple on a plate beside her. It was Alice's night off and in the dining room tomorrow's breakfast table was already laid. When the slices of apple were parchment brown she took out a sheet of writing paper from one of the desk's many compartments and set it on the blotter in front of her.

My dearest sister, she wrote. *I wish –*

She stopped, the pen nib resting on the page, her gaze fixed somewhere above the paper, and the past moved in her like blood. She had never told Edward about the child. She had told him most of what had happened and no doubt a good deal more than she should have, but she had known better than to talk of the child. What would there have been to say? A whitewashed room with an iron bedstead and a wooden crucifix on one wall and orange trees beyond the window. Around the perimeter of the walled garden a circle worn by her feet in the dusty earth, round and round. The days measured out by bells. The old woman who brought her her food and waited while she ate. The silence. When at last it came it took a very long time. They had to use forceps and she thought she would die. Afterwards she expected they would take it away. She did not want to see it. All that mattered was that it was over. She had to get back to Victor, to London. She had already lost so much time.

Instead they brought it to her to nurse. She had refused, pulling the sheet over herself, turning her face away. The old woman had waited until she was quiet and then put the infant on her breast. It was a boy. His skin was olive-toned like his father's, his head covered in downy black hair. His fingers clenched into tiny fists. When she held him his skull fitted perfectly into the cup of her hand.

She nursed him for nearly three months. There was a sickness in the village and no wet nurse could be found. He was a strong child, always hungry. Sometimes when he sucked she could feel the pull of him in the curve of her spine. She did not name him, or not out loud, but she grew accustomed to the weight, the warmth of him, the way he opened one sleepy eye to watch her as he fed. Once he pulled away from her breast, the milk gleaming on his chin, and he smiled at her. A few days later the old woman took him away. She did not know what was to become of him. Perhaps the old woman would have told her, she was not unkind, but she did not ask. She could not. She asked only how soon she could leave. When her breasts filled with unwanted milk the ache in her spine was unendurable.

They took her to Victor's remote country estate in Galicia. She was ill for a long time. Victor was in America with *Iolanthe* and nobody at Valquilla mentioned the baby. The house was crumbling, the ochre plaster peeling from the walls, but the furniture was dark and smooth and heavy. The walls were covered with paintings of Victor's frowning ancestors. The days were warm and slow, the nights endless. The cook, who was from Chile, baked *alfajores* and *arroz con leche*, soft, sweet foods to tempt her appetite. She sat on the wide *terraza* beneath the grape vines, her toes bare, the shadows playing on the pale straw of her wide-brimmed hat, and waited for the pain to go away. There was a mark on the underside of her finger where the gold ring had pressed.

Victor's *Iolanthe* was a smash. He married his Phyllis in New York City. The actress, an American, had blonde curls and a heart-shaped face and sufficient celebrity for Maribel to have seen her picture once in a periodical. The newly-weds planned to honeymoon in Europe: France, Italy, the lakes of Switzerland. Apparently the actress did not care for Spain. The house in Galicia was to be packed up, its staff dispersed. It was understood that by the time the happy couple sailed for America in the autumn Maribel would be gone.

She had remained at Valquilla as long as she was able. It was a particularly hot summer, the sunlight thick as treacle on the stone steps to the *terraza*. She no longer liked to sit beneath the grape vines but there was nowhere else for her to go. Inside the high-ceilinged rooms the furniture that could not be moved was covered with dust sheets. There were marks on the walls where the pictures had hung. At night the darkness pressed into the hole inside her, muscular as a snake. She suffered from paralysing stomach cramps. When autumn came and the house was finally closed up she travelled to Madrid, where Victor had arranged for a sum of money to be made over to her. The heat made her stupid. She wondered afterwards if the lawyer had cheated her. The money did not last long.

She had managed. She was resourceful and it no longer seemed to matter much what happened to her. A year later, she met Edward and returned with him to England. It was almost a happy story, in the end. In London a doctor told her she would not have more children. She had known he was right. That part of her was shrivelled, desiccated, the soft pink flesh shrunken yellow-tight. When she bled, which was not often, the flow was sparse and brown. The fierce spark of life was not in her. But the child? The thought that he might be dead was unendurable.

Maribel gazed down at the paper, the pen in her hand. Then with elaborate care, she wrote his name. Then she wrote it again, more urgently this time, and again and again, scrawling it in great loops across the page until the paper was almost entirely black, and as she wrote Ida leaned close, her arms caught around her bony knees and her frown fierce with concentration.

When there was no more room on the page she stopped. She felt spent, bereft. Her hand was shaking. She closed her eyes. When she opened them again she knew what she had to do. She set the letter to Ida aside. Then she took a fresh sheet of paper and, inscribing the date at the top of the page, began, very quickly, to write.

11

EDWARD PEERED AT THE post, squinting at the envelopes
as he sorted them. In recent months he had grown
long-sighted, holding the *Times* at arm's length to read
it as Maribel's father once had. The oculist had prescribed
spectacles but Edward refused to wear them. This small vanity
touched Maribel. She had not thought a man of his intellect
would object to growing old.

When she had refilled his teacup she took her letters and
flicked through them. Edward had already provided her with
the address of Colonel Cody's lodgings on Regent Street, and
the letter, duly stamped, waited on the hall table for Alice to
take to the post. If she was lucky, Maribel thought, she might
have an answer by the end of the week. During his time in
London Buffalo Bill had acquired something of a reputation for
punctiliousness. Besides, she hoped that her proposition might
intrigue him. In her letter she had taken care to assure him that
she would be delighted to grant him permission to use any of
the photographs he wished without charge for publicity purposes
and if one thing was certain it was Cody's enthusiasm for
publicity. She had pointed out that, while Major Burke was eager
to describe the Wild West not as a show but as living history,
its scenes scrupulously recreated from real-life events, the only
photographs she had seen of the braves were posed, stilted
things, rigid with artifice. With their careful props and painted
backdrops they resembled theatre bills or cigarette cards. It

would be quite another thing to capture the Indians in their camps and tepees, going about the everyday business of tending their horses and their weapons, of smoking their pipes and applying their warpaint, while their squaws cooked or cradled their papooses. Such an undertaking might be managed in a matter of days and with a minimum of disruption or inconvenience.

Maribel had slept fitfully. A little after dawn she had risen and, in her nightgown, had written another brief note, this time to Henry, beseeching him to be a dear and do what he could to persuade his new American friend to indulge her. *Tell him I am a precociously talented amateur,* she coaxed, *and that, as the wife of a Member of Parliament, I have tremendous influence with the newspapers. Please feel no obligation to cleave too closely to the facts. As Buffalo Bill knows all too well, the truth is often improved by some judicious embellishment.*

As she sealed the letter she had wondered, as she had several times during the night, whether it might not be a much simpler matter to write to Edith and ask her for Ida's address. Except that it was impossible to imagine that it would end there. Edith, ever alert to opportunity, would surely insist upon a part in whatever followed. She would squeeze herself into the space between them, as she had squeezed herself into the gap beneath the rhododendron bush at the bottom of the garden, noisily clamouring for attention, and everything would be spoiled.

'Must we go up to Scotland as soon as the House goes into recess?' she said, fiddling with her unopened envelopes. Edward did not look up.

'Why?' he asked. 'Do you have reason to stay?'

'It is only that, if Colonel Cody does grant me permission to photograph the Indians, there will not be a great deal of time.'

'But, Bo, the arrangements are all made. Can the Indians not wait until we are back?'

'Perhaps. But then there's Paris for dress fittings, and the likelihood of poorer weather. And they are not here much longer. They go to Europe, I think. Charlotte said something about a show in the Coliseum.'

Edward raised an eyebrow.

'That glorious monument to imperial power and cruelty? Isn't that a little too ironic for comfort?'

'Fortunately the Americans haven't the faintest grasp of Old World history.' She did not pursue the matter of delaying their departure. Edward did not appreciate being pestered. 'Have you time for another cup?'

'No, I should be going,' Edward said, folding his napkin and setting it on the table. 'I am due to meet Hyndman in less than an hour.'

'Again?' When Edward did not answer she frowned. 'You won't be late tonight, will you? I promised your mother we should call for her on our way to the Burfords'.'

'I shall have to meet you there. I have appointments this afternoon.'

'At the House?'

Edward pushed back his chair.

'I am lunching with Alfred Webster, did I tell you?'

Maribel hesitated. It disconcerted her, the frequency with which Mr Webster seemed into insinuate himself into ordinary conversations. It was almost as if he pursued her. Impatiently she shook her head.

'No. No, you didn't.'

'He claims to support our position on paid work for those seeking poor relief, says his paper has influence with the vestries. With luck he might be persuaded to side with us on the Eight Hour Bill.'

'I thought you disliked him.'

'I do, but, since he will write on the subject whatever my opinion of him, I may as well endeavour to persuade him to our point of view. Things are bad, Bo. Wages are falling so fast that the numbers of the unemployed increase literally week by week. It seems to astonish the government that men cannot be induced to starve working when they have the liberty to starve idle. When winter comes, it will be worse than last year. Perhaps Webster can do what we cannot and force the Tories to open their eyes before the storms break.' Edward dropped a kiss on the top of her head. 'Don't worry about Mother. I shall not be late, I promise.'

Maribel nodded but did not get up. She stayed at the table, cradling her teacup, as Edward moved about in the hallway, gathering his things. She heard him say something to Alice, then the click of the flat door as it closed behind him.

When her tea was finished she set down the cup and began to open the post. Among the bills there was a letter from Mr Pidgeon, written in tiny and precise copperplate, begging her pardon for offending her and beseeching her to return to the studio. When Alice came in to clear the breakfast table Maribel took her letters to her desk to answer them. She sat there for some minutes, her pen uncapped, the fingers of her left hand tapping out a pattern on the paper. Then she set down her pen.

'Alice,' she called, putting on her hat, 'I am going out for some air. I shall take the letters with me.'

She meant to walk to the park. The sun was shining but, though the sky was cloudless, there was a pleasant breeze and it was not oppressively warm. She would take a turn around the bandstand, she decided, and perhaps a cup of tea at the tea rooms by the Serpentine. It would be soothing to watch the brightly coloured boats on the water, to listen to the distant laughter and the plash of oars. In her bag, along with her cigarettes, she carried a book of poetry and a notebook and pencil. Perhaps she might write a little.

At the corner of Sloane Square she hesitated. Then she crossed to the centre of the square to the cab stand and hired a hansom. It was not yet ten o'clock when she reached Earls Court. The cab set Maribel down at the entrance to the American Exhibition, where a clutch of slack-faced tourists milled irresolutely at the turnstiles. A large sign above the ticket kiosks declared the exhibition's opening hours to be '10.30 A.M. TO 10.30 P.M. DAILY, 1s ADMISSION'. Behind the sign the track of the switchback railway, the exhibition's main attraction, stretched vertiginously into the sky, while, beside the kiosks, a woman in a white apron sold refreshments from a wooden barrow bearing the legend 'AMERICAN SODA POP' in scarlet letters. There was a flurry as the wooden blinds of the kiosk windows lifted like eyes opening, and the tourists, also appearing to rouse themselves from sleep, arranged themselves into an orderly queue.

Maribel did not join them. Instead she followed the boundaries of the exhibition site until she reached the entrance to the Wild West showground. The tall iron gates were locked, several chains slung about the palings, and beyond them the broad boulevard that led to the arena was deserted, the grass trampled to brown dust. There was a sudden noisy wheeze and then the rattle and shriek of a railway engine, unnervingly close. Maribel grasped the handles of her bag more tightly and straightened her spine. Inside the gates, on either side of the entrance way, were small wooden huts, each with a split door like a stable. In one, visible through the open upper door, sat a uniformed guard, his chair tipped up on its back legs. He pursed his lips, whistling softly under his breath. Maribel gestured through the bars, brandishing her letter.

'Excuse me,' she said. 'I have a letter here for Colonel Cody. I should like to deliver it to him personally.'

The guard blinked, jerking forward as he rocked his chair back onto four legs. Opening the lower door of the hut he walked over to the gate.

'Do you have an appointment, ma'am?'

'Not exactly. But perhaps you might tell him that Mrs Campbell Lowe is here to see him. I am happy to wait.'

The guard grinned. 'Then I hope you brought sandwiches, ma'am. First show's not till three and Mr Bill ain't never here till lunchtime.'

She hesitated, one hand on the iron gate. For the first time she wondered exactly what it was she was doing here.

'If it's a letter you can leave it with me,' the guard offered. 'I'll make sure he gets it soon as he gets in.'

Maribel fingered the envelope, then shook her head.

'No. Thank you.'

Slowly she turned away from the gate. By the deserted cab stand there was a pillar box. Pushing the letter through the slot she followed the painted finger that pointed towards the Underground Railway. The broad path skirted the Wild West camp and, beyond the high fences, the sky was criss-crossed with the clustered poles of tepees. At a distrustful distance, and half hidden by a newly planted coppice of trees, a terrace of yellow houses huddled in the dust, their small windows and low roofs lending them a sullen air.

Somewhere, in a house in a street not far from this one, Ida sat, stood, slept, ate. Charlotte had told Maribel that Dr Coffin was not in fact an angel of death but so fierce a proponent of hygiene that he inspected every tent in the camp daily and had the Indians turn out their beds for ventilation at half past seven sharp every morning. Such a regime surely demanded that he be lodged close by. Maribel felt the skin on her arms tighten. She walked faster.

The railings became a whitewashed wall of planks. People had carved their initials into the wood, hearts pierced with arrows. The name FANNY was gouged in uneven capitals. She could hear voices, the stamps and whinnies of horses. Beyond the wall the railings began again. She was almost at the station when she saw two patched-up boys squeeze themselves through a gap in the palings. They dragged behind them a small dog on a piece of string.

The taller one eyed her as she passed, his face sharp with calculation. There was no one else about.

'Penny to spare, miss?' he called out.

She hesitated, slowing her pace. The boys glanced at one another.

'Tuppence if you got it,' added the other hastily.

Maribel stopped, turning to face them. The boys' eyes travelled over her, taking in the silk dress, the garnet brooch on her collar.

'Have you boys proper business with the Wild West?' she asked. 'Or were you trespassing?'

'Trespassing, miss?' the taller boy said with great affront. 'Course we wasn't trespassing. Me mum works at one of the stalls inside, don't she? Selling programmes and that. We was bringing her her dinner.'

'Do you do that often?'

'Most every day. Me or me brother.'

'So you know the doctor then? The one who takes care of the Indians?'

'S'pose.'

'Well, do you or don't you?'

'What's it to you?'

'I'll give you a shilling if you can tell me where he lives,' Maribel said.

The boys exchanged another look.

'Awright,' the taller boy said and he jerked his head left, tugging at the dog, whose nose was buried in a patch of groundsel. ''S up there. Ward Street, number 16. Third street on the right.'

'You are quite sure? Dr Maitland Coffin?'

The boy grimaced, holding up a grimy palm.

'Course I'm sure. Everyone round here knows old Coffin.'

'Very well then,' Maribel said, fumbling in her purse for a shilling. 'Thank you.'

Ward Street was no less spiritless than the terrace she had observed opposite the showground, and hardly more respectable. In Ward Street at least the houses did not open directly onto the pavement but had narrow front gardens, boxed with low wooden fences, and some of the window frames looked freshly painted, but like the other it had a mean and temporary air. The yellow bricks were sandy-looking, as if they might crumble when you touched them, and, beneath the low roofs, the yellow was streaked brown with damp. Maribel had not thought of Ida in a place like this.

Number 16 was neither the best nor the worst house in the terrace. Its front garden was neat, with paving laid to the front door, and the brass door knocker was only slightly tarnished. There was a dried-out attempt at a border, edged with pebbles. Maribel exhaled, convulsed by the sudden urge to smoke a cigarette. Then she marched up to the door and knocked.

There was the sound of voices from inside, the thump of feet descending the stairs. Maribel smoothed her hair, her lips moving uncertainly as they searched for a suitable expression. There was a pause. Then the door opened. A red-faced woman in a faded dress eyed Maribel suspiciously. She held a swaddled infant in her arms, while, from among her skirts, another child, a girl, peered out with bright bird eyes. Yellow stains crusted the infant's blanket.

'Yes?'

Maribel stared at her and the anticipation ran out of her like sand.

'This is not the home of Dr Maitland Coffin, is it?' she said.

'Coffin?' The woman's face twisted with disgust. 'What is this, some kind of joke?'

'No,' Maribel said. 'I have made a mistake. I am sorry to have disturbed you.'

The red-faced woman frowned.

160

'Are you all right, miss?' she said less brusquely. 'You need a drink of water?'

Maribel shook her head. 'I am quite well, thank you,' she said.

As she turned away, the infant began to wail, a sharp high scream like the shriek of a dog fox. Maribel kept walking. There had been foxes in the woods behind their house in Ellerton. Once a vixen had made its earth near the woodshed and there had been cubs, four of them, that tumbled over one another for the sop of bread and milk that the children set out for them. Ida had named them all, though no one believed she could tell them apart. She had begged their mother to let her keep one as a pet.

Ida would never have allowed her child to be taken away.

Maribel walked for a long time. The featureless streets sprawled for what seemed like miles, a profuse and desolate undergrowth of brick that snaked greedily over the sour earth. The few trees were scrawny things, hardly more than branches jammed in the ground. It was neither prudent nor quite respectable to walk alone in such a place but Maribel walked all the same and it was not the wilderness of the voracious city that she saw but the moors of her childhood, the green hills scabbed with rock, the spring of the heather as she lay on her back watching the larks rising in the empty sky, silvering the air with their song.

The reply from Colonel Cody was both as punctilious and as favourable as Maribel could have hoped. He wrote that he remembered her well, and that he would be delighted to permit her to photograph his Indians at any time convenient to herself, though the twice-daily shows did mean that she might be better to attend the camp in the mornings if she wished to see the Indians at their ordinary business. He asked that, once she had decided upon a suitable date, she write to Major Burke at the

Wild West office so that he might meet her upon arrival and act as escort during her visit. An interpreter would also be provided for her convenience.

Maribel set the letter to one side. She was glad of it, of course, but the fierce urgency that had possessed her had quite gone. The thought of seeing Ida no longer thrilled her. She told herself it was Edward she thought of, that she acted from conscience, from scruple, but she knew she deceived herself. It was not all about Edward. He was not even the biggest part of it.

She had returned from her exertions in Earls Court exhausted, her feet aching, and taken to her bed. An hour later she had roused herself and, asking Alice for tea and paper, had sat up, an ashtray balanced on her chest, and tried to write. It was not the poverty of the streets she had walked that she strove to capture. It was the emptiness. Maribel had visited with other members of the Socialist League the slums of the East End, had borne witness to the rags and the tallow lamps, the rotting beams and stinking basements, the wretchedness of the squalid lanes. Ward Street and its ilk were nothing like these. They were respectable neighbourhoods, moderate and mostly law-abiding. In Ward Street ragged children did not cluster in doorways. The women were not poisoned in lead-works, exhausted in nailworks, worn haggard and ancient by ceaseless toil. They did not squat dead-faced in the mud and dust, their hands extended in grim appeal. Ward Street was quiet, the lives of its occupants hidden from view. These were the homes of ordinary working men, thrown up so quickly the builders had not troubled with foundations. They would fall. Till then the walls were shored up with fear and fatigue and the frantic struggle for propriety. It was a blank brick waste-land of cheeseparing and quiet desperation.

All afternoon Maribel had smoked and scratched out lines in her notebook. By evening the bed was littered all about with torn-up paper, scraps of words that drifted across the coverlets like snow, but the stone still lodged in her chest and the enchantment never came. She thought of her beloved Ida, the elephant tamer, boxed into one of those cramped little houses with an infant that cried like a dog fox, and she thought of Sylvia Wylde, the actress in the whitewashed room whose soaring ambitions had been nothing but the vain fantasies of a child, and she knew she could not write it because to write it was to admit that it was so.

When Edward consulted her about the final arrangements for their journey to Inverallich, she did not attempt to persuade him to delay their departure. The knowledge that Ida was nearby had settled in her. The violent jolt of it, electrical in its force and urgency, had waned to a bruise that, as long as it were not touched, might be forgotten. In place of the urgent need to see her sister was a kind of grief, the anguished assurance that there would be no purpose in it. There could be no repairing a bond of sisterhood long severed, no blessing in reminding them of what they had lost. Ida was her memory, her truth. The truth now was that she did not want Ida to remember. With Ida she would see the distance she had travelled, the void between what she had wished for and what she had become.

Maribel had made another self since then. The Edward Campbell Lowes had a wide circle of illustrious and influential friends. Among their acquaintance they numbered many whose names were familiar across the country: artists, politicians, writers, the more bohemian of the aristocracy. Edward was Laird of Inverallich, even if he did not care to use the title, and distinguished enough to be lampooned in *Vanity Fair*. Maribel had had a poem accepted for publication. She had presented a well-received lecture to members of the Socialist League on 'Socialism and the Modern Woman'. But she was not yet ready. One day, when she was established as a poet or perhaps as a photographer, she might be able to present herself to Ida and see, reflected in her sister's eyes, the version of herself that she had left home for, the version of herself for which she had risked everything. Then it would be time.

She packed for Scotland briskly, impatient to be off.

12

B Y THE TIME THEY reached Inverallich the heatwave of London felt as distant as a dream. High summer in Argyllshire that year was cold and wet, the wind-lashed rain like hurled pins against their cheeks. Even on dry days clouds muffled the mountains, burying the peaks in their rolls of grey flesh. Maribel shivered in her shawls and knitted gloves. The house, situated at the northernmost tip of a peat-stained loch, seemed to drink in the damp and chill from the black earth. The sheets mildewed and, in the grates, the sodden firewood hissed and smoked. It was the kind of place, she wrote to Charlotte, where it was possible to recall Miss Woolley and her Circle with nostalgia.

She was seldom alone, though she saw Edward hardly more than she had in London. Five hundred miles from the wretched encampments of Trafalgar Square, the raised fists and placards of the Socialist demonstrators protesting angrily outside the Whitehall offices responsible for the Poor Law, there was no reprieve for the poor of rural Scotland and, despite the powers of the new Crofters' Commission, unrest prevailed. Impatient with their plight, Salisbury's government showed no qualms in using troops to quell their protests. Edward's days were taken up with appointments, rallies, visits to local smallholdings and crofting townships, speeches at public meetings. Maribel attended those at which she was required, making polite conversation with slab-faced ladies whom she knew would afterwards declare her accent unfathomable. Edward was always at the other end of the room.

It was not just constituency business either. The Coal Mines Regulation Bill was in the Committee Stage and in the course of two gruelling weeks in August Edward addressed more than fifty meetings across the Scottish mining districts, mustering grass-root support for the wider publication of safety reports, an unqualified ban of child labour in the mines, and a compulsory eight-hour day. In the last few months the gap between his politics and those of his party had widened sharply and the satirical cartoons in *Punch* and the *Daily News* made much of the correlation between the colour of his hair and that of his opinions. As Trafalgar Square swelled with the homeless, with agitators and demonstrators and sightseers eager to enjoy the circus, Edward and his kind were denounced by the city's newspapers as provocateurs, reckless rabble-rousers intent upon violent confrontation. Only Webster at the *Chronicle* held steady, his support of the Socialists unwavering, his impassioned editorials in defence of the poor a persistent thorn in the government's side. Edward had the newspapers sent up from London and, though Webster's muscular Christianity raised his hackles, he was grateful. They were in no position to be choosy.

Maribel was left often to her own devices. She had much to occupy her. She managed the estate accounts. She organised the cook and the two raw-faced maids. She counted the silver. She wrote one or two indifferent poems, took some indifferent photographs which, lacking a darkroom, she parcelled up with the still undeveloped plates from the Jubilee and sent to be printed at Oban. She visited the Inverallich cottages, taking baskets of freshly baked bread and cakes, and admired children and sheep. The tenants asked after Mr Edward and the affection in their voices was unfeigned. Mr Edward was much loved at Inverallich. After the election, when he had won his seat for the Liberals, two hundred tenants and feuars had gathered to greet them at the railway station. There had been cheers, speeches, boys whistling on blades of grass set between their thumbs. Then, instead of horses, fifty men with ropes had pulled their carriage to the house just as the Skye crofters had pulled the carriage of Henry George, the radical social reformer, two years before. They had travelled the short distance in silence, Edward's hands clasped on his lap. It was the first time since Maribel had known him that he had had nothing to say.

Maribel occupied herself as much as she was able but still darkness came late and the days were long. Vehemently opposed to the annexation of the great Scottish estates as playgrounds for the wealthy, Edward did not shoot or stalk but, on those few days that he was home, he walked or rode out into the hills. For all the urbanity of his manner the bleak landscape of Inverallich was his *querencia*, the Spanish word for the home territory of an animal, the mists and mountains as much in his blood as the pampas of Argentina. Sometimes Maribel went with him on these expeditions. More often he went alone. On horseback he covered great distances and returned exhausted and content, his breeches crusted with spatters of peat.

This summer, and despite his punishing schedule, he rode more than ever. In Glasgow, where they had stopped for a few days with friends on their journey north, Edward had, to his astonishment, encountered a spirited Argentine mustang in the traces of a tram-car and had, after some negotiation, persuaded the owner to sell the horse to him for fifty pounds. It was only once the animal was settled in the stables at Inverallich that he had discovered that she bore the brand of Javier Casey, an old friend of Edward's from his gaucho days. Delighted as much by the caprices of Fate as by the mare herself, he named her Pampa.

Maribel had never before seen him so charmed. He smiled whenever he talked of Pampa, which he did often, declaring her the finest and most mettlesome horse he had ever known. He had Maribel take her photograph and pressed unwary guests into inspecting her. Several times Maribel came down for dinner to find the drawing room empty and the men in their evening suits in the stable courtyard, treading cautiously over the cobbles in their thin-soled slippers. Edward had determined to bring the creature to London, though the livery costs were exorbitant, so that he might ride her through the winter. A great deal of time was taken up by the complicated plans for her conveyance.

Letters came regularly from Charlotte in Sussex, from Oscar and Constance and Edward's brother Henry in London. Edward's mother visited. There were games and parties and balls in other people's draughty houses, with much bellowing and dancing of Scottish reels. It was too much and, at the same time, not enough. The society at Inverallich was narrow, the demands of the estate wearisome. Both were relentless.

In Scotland it was not as easy as it was in London for Maribel to close her eyes to their financial difficulties. With agricultural prices continuing to fall they had had no choice but to increase the allowances to their beleaguered tenant farmers. Rents were down. The interest on their mortgages swallowed any profit raised on the estate, leaving them only a few hundred pounds on which to live. Such an amount did not come close to meeting their day-to-day expenses, let alone provide funds for additional repairs and improvements. She had managed, after much difficulty, to persuade Edward to sell a small section of the estate closest to the town to raise capital, but prices were depressed and the money was quickly swallowed. With the expenditure required to support his political career and the necessity of supporting even a frugal household in London, they had not only failed to reducing their borrowings, they had been obliged to add to them. When Henry arrived, lured north by the promise of the Glorious Twelfth, she confessed to him that, if things did not improve, she feared that, sooner or later, they would have no alternative but to sell up altogether.

'Poor Mar, how dreadfully you would mind that,' Henry said with a grin and Maribel laughed and swatted at him with her book.

'Edward would mind horribly. I can't imagine how he would manage without it.'

'It is our father's fault, not yours. Teddy knows that. You have done wonders.'

'Not wonders enough.'

'Wonders,' Henry said firmly. 'But you should tread carefully. I'm afraid Mother will blame you.'

'For debts accumulated by her own husband?'

'For obliging her to remember their existence. My father was packed off to the madhouse when I was, what, nine? Mother has had more than twenty years to revise her recollections of marriage.'

It was a great comfort to Maribel to have Henry at Inverallich. Henry loved shooting game almost as much as his brother abhorred it but, unlike Edward, he was discouraged by poor weather and, when it rained, he preferred the fireside to the moors. Maribel was only too happy to abandon her duties in order to keep him company. The two of them sat together companionably, reading and writing and smoking and drinking tea, every so often exchanging stories from the newspaper or titbits of information from their letters.

As witty as he was worldly, Henry was a wonderful gossip. He related in glorious detail the latest spat between Oscar Wilde and his old friend James Whistler, and his descriptions of the waspish American painter hissing like a djinn in his monocle and pointed slippers made Maribel laugh out loud. He told her of the son of a well-known peer discovered at the Café Royal with a stolen lobster in the leg of his trousers when it became apparent that the creature was not half as dead as the young man had presumed it to be. He told her about the party thrown by Lillie Langtry to celebrate the the divorce from her long-suffering husband, which the Prince of Wales had had to be forcefully dissuaded from attending, and about the letter that had arrived at the Wild West from his wife, Princess Alexandra, informing Buffalo Bill that she wished to attend the show incognito. Given that the Princess's face was about as well known in London as the face of Big Ben, this had presented Cody with something of a difficulty.

Even Henry could not keep himself from laughing as he related what had happened next. The Princess had arrived in an ordinary carriage and had refused Major Burke's invitation to sit in the royal box, insisting instead on being seated among the people. When Burke had asked why, she had simply replied, 'I like the people.' Burke had duly taken her to the press box which was, to his great relief, unoccupied. Minutes into the performance, however, the door to the box had opened and several journalists and their lady friends had noisily taken their seats alongside the Princess. During a break in the show, one of the journalists had turned to Burke and asked who the other guests were.

'Excuse my inquisitiveness,' the journalist had said. 'It's only that I never saw such a likeness in my life to –'

Burke had cut him short.

'I know what you are going to say. The resemblance is quite striking, though I would ask you to refrain from remarking upon it. Since arriving in London Mrs Jones has heard nothing else. I fear she grows weary of the comparison.'

An introduction was inescapable. Burke, in a cold perspiration, had proceeded to present the Princess and her companion as Colonel and Mrs Jones, friends of his from Texas. He had not breathed easily again until his troublesome charge was once more safely seated in her carriage, at which point she had laughed uproariously and thanked Burke for a grand adventure.

'And Cody?' Maribel asked, amused. 'Where was he in all this?'

'As far away as he could manage. Bill has woman trouble aplenty without the Princess.'

'Oh?'

'He is hopelessly smitten with a young American actress.'

Maribel made a face.

'Pretty as a picture, of course, and like all Americans quite without conscience,' Henry said. 'And don't give me that look. South America is quite a different matter.'

'Go on.'

'The charming Miss Clemmons met Bill at a supper party a few weeks ago. She has travelled all the way from California for acting lessons with Emile Banker, no less, but as far as I can see she has no need of them. Already she has quite persuaded Bill that she has eyes only for him.'

'Perhaps she has,' Maribel said, lighting another cigarette.

'She is an actress, for heaven's sake, with a nose for a wealthy patron. She makes no secret of her desire to be famous.'

'And in exchange Colonel Cody gets a beautiful young girl on his arm. Who is to say he does not get the better end of the arrangement?'

Henry shook his head. 'She is making a fool of him, Mar. You should see him, trailing after her all over the Wild West and out to dinners and plays, introducing her to everyone as his "niece", while his tongue lolls from his mouth like a Labrador's. Behind all that easy pioneer charm Bill is an innocent where women are concerned. The voracious Miss Clemmons will eat him for breakfast.'

Then more fool him, Maribel thought.

'I thought Cody's daughter was with him,' she said instead. 'Surely she knows a fake niece when she sees one?'

'He has packed Arta off with his nephew on a six-week tour of Europe. Still, I suppose when they get back he will have to put a stop to his nonsense.'

'And you men can get back to your poker.'

171

'This is not about the poker.'

'Isn't it?'

'You, Mrs Edward Campbell Lowe, are a fearful cynic.'

'And you, Mr Henry Campbell Lowe, are fearfully fond of cards.'

Henry laughed. 'Shall we play?'

'Why not?'

Stubbing out her cigarette, she took down the large atlas that always served as a tabletop and set it in the centre of the sofa as Henry rummaged for cards among the clutter of dice and coloured counters in the top drawer of the tallboy.

'Poor Mrs Cody,' she said quietly.

'*Au contraire*, disgustingly wealthy Mrs Cody. There are rumours that Bill has been offered a million dollars for the Wild West providing he stays with the show for three years. Even Miss Clemmons would leave plenty of change from a sum like that.'

Taking a pack of cards from the drawer, he slid them from their box and shuffled them. They were a pack Edward had been given by a friend upon winning his seat in Parliament, the cards all pen-and-ink caricatures of well-known politicians. Joe Chamberlain's card was entitled The Rt Hon. Orchid Chain-Em-In, the Baron de Worms's the Baron de Caterpillar. Edward had studied the cards and declared himself duly warned. Campbell Lowe was a name that offered itself all too willingly to parody.

'Will he sell?' Maribel asked Henry as he dealt.

'If the offer is genuine he would be mad not to. The Wild West cannot remain a sensation for ever. There are only so many times an Indian can be slaughtered before it gets tedious.'

'Tell that to the American government.'

Henry won the first round easily, laughing with mock triumph as he swept the cards into a pile. He shuffled again, his fingers dextrous as a conjuror's.

'Did you ever take your photographs of the Indians?' he asked, as they studied their cards.

Maribel shook her head. 'There was not time before we left London,' she said. 'Perhaps when we are back. Colonel Cody has been very kind.'

'Don't leave it too long. The show goes on tour at the end of October.'

'That soon?'

'Your turn to start.'

Maribel was distracted and played poorly. When Henry beat her for the third time she shook her head. She pushed the atlas away. Several Members of Parliament slid to the floor.

'I need some air,' she said. 'Will you walk with me?'

Outside the rain had stopped. The pale grey sky had a white trim and, beyond the dull grey slate of the loch, the heather hazed the moor with purple. They walked through the gardens and took the path down to the pebbled beach. The brambles had flowered and the yellow-spattered gorse filled the damp air with the smell of coconut. Maribel looked out towards the tiny island at the loch's centre, its trees stunted and gnarled as Japanese bonsai. As boys, Edward had told her, Henry and he used to spend whole days on the island. They would take sandwiches and fishing rods and not come back till it was nearly dark. They liked to pretend that they were the only two boys left in the whole world.

'It's a pity you could not be there when Bill took forty of his Indians to the Congregational Chapel at West Kensington,' Henry said. 'That would have made a splendid photograph. Apparently they sang "Nearer My God to Thee" in Lakota.'

'I am not interested in the Indians as curiosities. If I am to photograph them it should be as they really are. The truth, not the myth-making.'

'But the Wild West is all about myth. Bill is the first to admit that no tribe could have afforded to be so gloriously feathered as his troupe, even before Custer. As for all that whooping, no real Indian has whooped in all his life. Cody invented it, to give the Indians a better entrance.'

'That's just the show. My photographs would show them behind the scenes, going about their ordinary lives.'

'What lives? They have no lives in London. When they are not being paraded in full warpaint as a mobile advertisement, they sit in their tepees and wait to be summoned for luncheon.'

Maribel was silent. They walked along the beach, Henry occasionally stopping to pick up a stone which he turned several times in his fingers before sending it skimming across the loch. The stones skipped and spun, drawing six or seven silvered arcs before finally sinking into the water. There was no purpose in arguing with Henry. He spoke as she would have spoken had their positions been reversed, and what he said was true. There could be no photographing the Indians as they had been. Those Indians were gone, wiped out as the herds of buffalo had been wiped out, by the inexorable advance of the white man's civilisation. The few that remained were kept, like the buffalo, in captivity, a souvenir from a past redesigned by those who were not there. The Indians of the Wild West were actors. Worse, they were ghosts.

'Perhaps if I do this that is what I should try and capture,' she said at last. 'The miserable emptiness of it.'

'Oh, they aren't miserable,' Henry said airily, launching another stone across the water. 'Just idle. And a good deal less savage than Buffalo Bill's Wild West would have us believe.'

When Henry suggested walking on to the boathouse Maribel declined. She watched as he strode off before she turned and made her way back up towards the terrace. It was four o'clock and nearly teatime. By now the Indians would be in the middle of a show. For the sixth time that week they would attack the stagecoaches and cabins of the white men only to be summarily dispatched by Buffalo Bill and his band of cowboys. *The only good Indian is a dead Indian* – wasn't that what one of the American generals had said? She could not remember which, though she supposed it was Custer. Custer had not been fond of Indians.

There was no shame in dying, of course. It was the measure of a great actress, she had always told Ida, to die well. In the school-room in Ellerton, trembling and resolute, she had died again and again. Juliet, Antigone, Lady Jane Grey, Joan of Arc, she had whispered her final words like a prayer before, with a poignant grace, she finally succumbed. One had to learn to fall beautifully, she informed Ida, because it was much too late to rearrange your-self once you were down. To fall beautifully and not to breathe. The effects were ruined if the audience could see you breathe.

She missed the theatre. She had never before permitted herself to admit it. She missed it. Not the realities of her brief career, the awful rooms and the worse auditions in the seedier theatres the wrong side of Leicester Square, the producers with their shiny coats and their squint-eyed hangers-on, the sighing and the sucking of teeth, the if-onlys and the not-this-times. What she missed was the promise of a magnificent future, the intoxicating certainty that if she could only escape the barred cage of her childhood she would fly.

At night, in her bed in Ellerton, she had closed her eyes and listened to the roar of the audience like the roar of a great sea and she had curtsied and smiled and kissed the tips of her fingers and pressed the flowers in their swathes of ribbon and crinkly tissue paper against her chest and she had thought she would burst with the need of it. When she was thirteen a girl she knew vaguely had died from a swollen heart. For weeks after-wards Maribel had lain in her bed, her own heart bloated with longing in her chest, certain that hers would kill her too.

She had slipped the door of the cage but she had not flown. She had fallen, like a fledgling pushed too soon from its nest, and thought it flying, till the ground came up to meet her. Now she watched from the ground as others made patterns in the sky for posterity, and her heart was small and hard, like a walnut.

The little notebook she carried with her was in her pocket, a stub of a pencil attached to it by a ribbon threaded through the spine. On impulse she pulled it out, leafing through it for an empty page. The wrought-iron bench that encircled the largest of the beeches was wet. She sat all the same. Poems had to be written quickly, before the act of thinking corrupted their simplicity.

> *The clear white page on which I set to write*
> *In sky-high letters, curlicued, sun-bright,*
> *Is grey with jottings, doodles, words rubbed out,*
> *Thoughts half strangled, half forgotten,*
> *Mangled verses misbegotten,*
> *Discarded truths I never thought to doubt.*
> *Fierce June of hope now chill November:*
> *What did I dream? I daren't remember.*

She let her hand drop, staring down at the poem in her lap. A friend of Edward's, impressed by his political articles for the *Commonweal*, had recently asked him if he might be interested in writing a series of pieces on his travels as a young man in South America. There was a possibility of a book. Edward had said he would think about it but he had already begun to write. Several days ago he had shown her a short piece that he had written about two gaucho brothers from the pampas on the River Plate. Though he had dashed it off in hardly more than an hour it was a polished piece, witty and wise. When Maribel asked him how much of the story was taken from his own experience, and how much made up, Edward had only laughed.

Write what is in your heart, that was the advice someone had once given her, and she had tried to. Perhaps, she thought, her poetry revealed what she had so far managed to conceal even from herself, that her heart was full of platitudes, platitudes served up in a gravy of doggerel. She could not even bring herself to cross the poem out. The hammy symbolism of such a gesture was worse even than the lines themselves.

Summer was coming to an end. In the newly planted orchards the apples had begun to ripen. Henry and Edward played Wild West with them, throwing the little green windfalls into the air for the other to shoot. When they came in for tea they had little bits of apple in their hair.

When Henry departed to stay with friends in possession of a proper grouse moor Maribel did not return with quite the same staunchness to her neglected duties. Though she continued to conduct estate business in the mornings, in the afternoons she found herself often taking refuge in the library. It was not a room that she and Edward were accustomed to using. Edward's father had contrived to lose a fortune during his lifetime and the library at Inverallich was his greatest legacy, proof of his ability to part with money without the slightest thought or purpose. He had favoured the purchase of books by the boxload, weight being, in his opinion, the best estimate of a book's value, and the resulting collection, for the most part, stood as a testament to the ability of man, by way of Mr Caxton, to set down on paper more words than most speak in a lifetime and still say almost nothing at all.

Maribel had half intended to begin some kind of clearing out of the collection and several tea chests, half filled, stood in the corner of the library. During her excavations, however, she had discovered that, among the stolid discourses on heraldry, the outdated travelogues and the collections of poor sermons and poorer poetry, there was to be found the occasional jewel: some essays of Montaigne, Cervantes' *Don Quixote* translated into Scotch, a hand-inked volume, bound in sheepskin, containing a monk's sworn account of his conversations about God with a mule. There was an entire shelf of books of natural history, translated long ago from Latin or Greek, and another dedicated to the obscurer sciences. Several had elaborate illustrations. Maribel, filled to the brim with the poetry of her contemporaries, found herself entranced by these volumes, by their blend of the prophetic and the preposterous, the peculiar beauty of their language. As she immersed herself in the arcana of alchemy or astral magnetism, the words, so long dormant, began to move in her.

Most days, when Edward came in from the stables, he found Maribel curled up on the old chesterfield in front of the fire, a book open in her lap, a notebook and pencil on the seat beside her. He would sprawl next to her then, his stockinged feet propped on the fender, and drink what was left of the tea from her cup while she read out to him passages that had caught her eye and breathed in his smell of rain and horses. Sometimes she would have found a book he had mentioned, or one that she thought would amuse him, and they would read together, their shoulders touching, the warmth of the fire pink in their cheeks, until it was time to bathe and change for dinner. Occasionally Maribel would reach for her notebook, her head bent as she scribbled. The bathwater grew cool and, in the kitchen, the cook tapped her spoon restlessly against the iron pots.

It was some nights before their own departure for London that Edward arrived back at the house to find Maribel waiting for him in the stone-flagged hall.

'You're cold,' he said to her, kissing her on the nose. 'Where is your shawl?'

'I am warm,' Maribel said. 'And I have something I want to show you.'

Taking him by the hand she dragged him into the library. Two large books bound in battered brown leather lay open on the table in the centre of the room. Maribel picked up the first, turning it over so that Edward could see the spine. The book was the second of two heavy volumes of Pliny's *Natural History*, translated into French. She turned the pages, searching for something. Many passages were underlined or marked with exclamation marks, and the margins were crammed with pencilled comments, also in French, declaiming Pliny's inaccuracies with Gallic disgust.

'What on earth is that?' Edward asked.

'Pliny. I was reading it this afternoon.'

'Good God. Has it really come to that?'

'I was browsing in the first book through the parts about Lusitania. A lot of it was about the geography, the flora and fauna of the region, but Pliny also writes a lot about gold mines. Apparently the Romans obtained a great deal of their gold from Lusitania, which of course is part of modern-day Galicia. And it occurred to me that even when I was there the country people used to go to the River Sil and wash for gold. There were endless folk stories about the treasure people had found and about a mine in the Vierzo where, long ago, before anyone could remember, gold had been brought from the ground in blocks so heavy it took three men to lift them.'

'That sounds like a typical Galician story.'

'Well, yes, but then I read Pliny's chapter about minerals in Book II and I found this: "In all gold there is some silver, in varying proportions; a tenth part in some instances, an eighth in others. In one mine, and that only, the one known as the mine of Albucrara, in Lusitania, the proportion of silver is but one thirty-sixth; hence it is that the ore of this mine is so much more valuable than that of others.'''

'I am not sure I understand your point.'

'My point is that I know where Albucrara is. Not the mine but the valley. I've been there. Pliny describes it exactly, the oxbow lake, the S-shaped twist in the river, the mountains to the south. He's describing the Val de Verriz. I know he is.'

'Bo, Galicia is a big place. It is filled with lakes and rivers.'

'Not exactly like this one.'

Edward kissed her and pushed her lightly away.

'Your nose is icy,' he said. 'Bath time.'

Maribel allowed herself to be led upstairs. It was not until later, when dinner was over and Edward was helping himself to cheese, that she returned to the subject of Pliny. This time she did not allow Edward to discourage her.

'Very well,' Edward conceded at last. He held his glass of port up to the candle in front of him, contemplating its garnet gleam. 'Let us say you are right and Pliny's Albucrara is indeed in your Val de Verriz. You are not the first person to have discovered Pliny, even in French. If there was a gold mine to be found there, someone would have stumbled on it by now.'

'But why? The Val de Verriz is in the middle of nowhere. It's a part of Spain most Spaniards don't even know. No one there would have ever heard of Pliny, let alone read him. I'll wager the area has never even been surveyed.'

Edward made a face. 'Do I deduce anxiety at the parlous state of our finances?'

'What harm would it do to make some enquiries? You have friends still in Madrid. We could write to them, see if they knew someone who might help.'

A knock on the door interrupted them.

'Will you take your coffee in the drawing room, ma'am?' Cora, the maid, asked, nudging the door open with her knee. She had the tray in her hands, its side wedged against her belly to keep it steady. Maribel nodded. By the time the tray had been set down, the coffee poured, and they were settled in front of the fire the conversation had moved to practical matters. Maribel was content to leave it so. As one of his Socialist associates had once observed, one was obliged occasionally to plant an idea with Edward Campbell Lowe but one should never make the mistake of trying to water it.

When they had drunk their coffee they rose. It was still light. Beyond the window the sky had lifted its padded grey skirts, revealing petticoats of startling pinkish blue, and the late roses tapped their white faces against the glass.

'Perhaps tomorrow will be fine,' she said. 'Wonders will never cease.'

Edward came to stand beside her. She could feel the warmth of him, the quiver of energy in his long lean limbs.

'Do you think about it?' he asked softly. 'About Spain? About Madrid?'

Maribel hesitated.

'It was a long time ago,' she said.

'There is a picture I carry in my head from that house on the Calle de León. You are sitting up, your knees pulled up to your chin, and your hair is tumbled about your shoulders and you are looking at me in that way you have, so intense it is almost angry, and you are so beautiful, so – absolute, that I know without doubt that this is why I have come. This is why Madrid is here.'

Maribel looked up at her husband, an ache rising in her throat as she touched him very gently on the cheek. He smiled. She longed for something to offer in return but, to her bafflement, she found that she could summon almost nothing of those dusty months in Madrid and, as for Edward, no trace at all. Absently she found herself recalling how the shadowy parlour of the house on Calle de León had always smelled of almonds. It had been the Señora's strongly held belief that men who liked women also liked cake.

In the convent on the edge of the oxbow lake the old woman had baked her a cake of almonds on Kings' Day, when the people of her village celebrated the visit of the three wise men to the baby that lay in the manger in Bethlehem.

'Come,' she said softly. 'It is time for bed.'

13

THE LOW AFTERNOON SUN spilled into Charlotte's drawing room. The horse-chestnut trees were turning, their leaves yellowed and spotted with age. It was the end of September. Soon the leaves would be gone.

'We have some news,' Charlotte said.

Maribel smiled. 'Do you?' she said.

'I – you already know, don't you?'

'Perhaps. A little.'

'Am I so very fat already?'

'You look radiant. How do you feel?'

'Fat.'

'And happy?'

'Very happy. I thought when Clovis came I – but . . .'

She smiled, the sedated smile of a Lippi saint. Maribel smiled back. Charlotte had borne a child regularly every eighteen months for the length of their friendship and Maribel had known as soon as she saw her that she was pregnant again. It was the same every time: Charlotte's lassitude, the fullness of her face, the abstracted vagueness with which she trailed off in the middle of a sentence, a slight frown of bemusement denting the pale flesh between her eyebrows. Just a few minutes earlier she had hunted across the tea tray and even on the floor for her teaspoon before Maribel had realised what it was she was looking for and gently pointed out that she was holding it in her left hand. Charlotte had shaken her head then, and smiled.

'I'm sorry,' she had said. 'You must think me quite dotty.'

Maribel had laughed but she had not denied it. The conversation had progressed in fits and starts, Charlotte frequently lapsing into a soft-faced reverie.

As a girl Maribel had been repelled by pregnant women, by the misshapen bulk of them. They reminded her of the picture in her encyclopaedia of the great African snake which dislocated its jaw so that it could swallow an antelope without having to chew. It was a surprise then to observe Charlotte, who did not carry her children so much as merge into them. With each of Charlotte's pregnancies Maribel had been struck most not by her friend's size but by her softness, the blurriness of her edges. It reminded her of baking as a little girl when, on rainy afternoons, she was sometimes allowed to take the cut-off parts of the pie crust and roll them together to make something new.

'I almost forgot,' Charlotte said, rousing herself. 'I have a present for you.'

'For me? Surely I should be the one giving presents.'

Fumbling in the workbox beside her chair Charlotte drew out a small package wrapped in tissue paper.

'What is it?'

'Open it and you'll see.'

Maribel unwrapped the parcel to reveal a small box. She lifted the lid. Inside was a curved wooden block. She glanced at Charlotte, who grinned.

'It's a studio stamp. Look.'

Taking it out of the box she showed Maribel the rubber plate on the underside. In reverse, in neat capitals, the rubber letters spelled out

'My own stamp,' Maribel said, gazing at it.

'All the professional photographers have them. Promise you will use it.'

'I promise.' Maribel ran her thumb over the raised letters. 'Thank you.'

After tea the younger Charterhouse children were permitted a few minutes with their mother. When they came in like a whirlwind, jumping on the sofa and upsetting the milk jug, Charlotte did not remonstrate with them as she usually did. She only smiled and closed her eyes, inhaling their child smell of soap and starch. Pregnancy was Charlotte's laudanum. Maribel saw how it enfolded her in its soothing embrace, drawing her down into a pure and private place where there was no world and no pain and only the light at the heart of her, behind the shutters of her closed eyes. Like laudanum she seemed unable to break the habit of it.

'Read it!'

Two of the younger children thrust a book beneath Maribel's nose, flapping it up and down.

'Say please, Tilly,' Charlotte said mildly.

'Please read it!'

Reluctantly Maribel took the book. The story was a slight tale about a girl who dressed her kitten in a lace cap and took it for rides in a perambulator. Maribel thought it perfectly dreary, but the children leaned up against her, their thumbs jammed in their mouths, and gazed with big slow-blinking eyes at the pallid pictures as if they were windows they could see right through. She turned the last page. Opposite her Charlotte opened her

185

eyes, watching sleepily as the other two children stacked wooden bricks one on top of another.

'"Tomorrow, said Emily, we shall go to the zoo",' Maribel read and, with a flourish, she snapped the book shut.

'Again,' commanded Matilda.

'Clovis pulled the thumb from his mouth with a pop.

"Gain,' he said.

'Please,' reminded Charlotte dreamily.

'Pease,' he echoed.

'Not today, dear,' Maribel said. 'I have to go home.'

Extricating herself from the warm weight of the children she stood. Charlotte did not seem to notice. She sprawled in her chair, her head back and her mouth slightly open, gazing at the tower of bricks as though entranced.

'Charlotte, dearest, I am leaving.'

Charlotte blinked, rousing herself. Behind her there was a clatter of bricks, a high wail.

'You clumsy! You ruined it!'

'Did not!'

'Did so, you — you ninny! You knocked it!'

'Ow! Get off me!'

'Children, please,' Charlotte murmured. 'Dearest, must you go?'

'I am afraid I must.'

Behind the arm of Charlotte's chair the children jabbed and kicked at one another surreptitiously, their faces pinched with fury. A thrown brick struck the table leg.

'I've bored you,' Charlotte said. 'Don't bother to deny it, I know I have. I've bored myself.'

She made a face, turning down the corners of her mouth. It still looked like she was smiling. Maribel smiled back.

'Don't be silly,' Maribel said, kissing her, but she was glad when the front door closed behind her and she stood alone on the wide pavement, breathing in the smoke-scented air. The sun was sliding like a gold coin behind the houses, washing the porcelain sky with streaks of pink and gold. Across the street, behind the high iron railings, the smooth-lawned gardens were empty, the nursemaids all gone home. In early summer the branches of the horse chestnut blazed with blossom like Christmas candles and beneath the avenue of limes the raked gravel paths grew sticky with sap. Now the horse chestnut drooped wearily, its withering leaves extended like hands, palm upwards.

Maribel picked up a fallen conker shell and ran her thumb over its green flesh, pimpled with spiky nubs. It was too early for conkers. The shell opened reluctantly, displaying a small sleek nut nestled in its centre. Its skin was a rich, marbled brown, the scar at its base chalk-white. Charlotte's children were ferocious conker players, always quarrelling over the finest specimens, and in the autumn it was customary to find Charlotte with a bottle of witch hazel in one hand and a wad of cotton in the other, tending to the casualties of battle. The children were full of theories about the best way to harden conkers and tried each year to persuade the cook to bake them in the range. Charlotte had grown used to finding them forgotten in the airing cupboard or tucked into crevices behind a fireplace.

They had collected conkers when Maribel was young too. There had been a horse-chestnut tree at the bottom of the lawn of the house at Ellerton and, every autumn, Maribel and her sisters had gathered them, piling them up in glossy heaps in their pinafores. Lizzie and Edith had not cared about shape or size but Maribel had discarded the misshapen and the flawed, the ones with the yellowed scars or the flat corners. She had kept only the perfect ones, their rich brown lustre cool and silky against her cheek. Lizzie and Edith had kept theirs in a box for months, taking them out from time to time to make patterns with them on the schoolroom floor, but Maribel had refused to join in. She forgot every year how quickly conkers shrivelled and lost their shine. Every year the disappointment was fresh in her.

'Why, Maribel!'

Maribel turned. Charlotte's husband Arthur stood beside his carriage. He raised his hat.

'Would it be impolite to ask whether you are coming or going?' he asked.

Maribel smiled. 'Going, I am sorry to say.'

'Then let John run you home.'

'Thank you, Arthur, but it is such a pretty evening. I would enjoy the walk.'

'Nonsense, I won't hear of it.'

He held open the door of the brougham with a theatrical bow and Maribel allowed herself to be helped inside. When Arthur Charterhouse was set upon benevolence there was no resisting him. He waved a hand as the carriage drew away, then turned towards his front door. She knew what came next. After all the years she had known Arthur his habits were almost as familiar to her as Edward's. He would stand in the doorway, legs astride, and bellow his return, skimming his hat like a plate towards the hatstand. Even as it missed its hook, the boys would thunder down the stairs, tomahawks brandished, and he would whoop and roar as he chased them, wrestling them to the floor and tickling them until they wept for mercy. As the carriage turned out of the square, the low sun buttering the white stucco, she fancied that she saw the windows of the house shake in their sashes.

It was only a matter of minutes before the brougham pulled up outside Cadogan Mansions. Clicking reassuringly to the horses, the coachman jumped down from the box and opened the door.

'Thank you, John,' Maribel said as he unfolded the step.

'Madam,' he said in his Irish brogue, smiling as he touched his hat with his whip. John had been with the Charterhouses since before their children were born and was adored by all the family for the placidity of his temperament. Charlotte liked to claim that in fifteen years she had never once seen him frown but Maribel refused to believe it. She did not see how it was possible these days to be Irish and never angry. The outrages piled one upon the other, each more monstrous than the last. Only a few days before, in County Cork, thousands had gathered outside the Mitchelstown courthouse to protest the prosecution of Edward's friend William O'Brien, the Irish MP, under the new Coercion Act, for his part in inciting yet another rent strike on one of Cork's largest estates. Though the protest had been peaceful, the police had opened fire on the crowd, killing three estate tenants and wounding many more. Edward, without so much of a drop of Irish blood in his veins, had been unable to contain his fury at the violence of it.

'Are they not content with evicting these men, with starving them and forcing them to live in hedgerows and heaps of stinking rubbish? What have they to add, that they must then slaughter them in cold blood?'

Even Charlotte, whose brain had softened to cheese, had been roused enough at tea to deplore for almost a full minute the plight of the Irish before her attention had been diverted. But John only nodded and smiled and touched his hat, his broad face placid as a cow's. Perhaps it was best, Maribel thought, if you were Irish, to be incapable of anger. Otherwise, once you had started, how on earth would you stop?

14

EDWARD HAD SENT WORD from the House, telling her not to wait up. She ate supper from a tray and went to bed early. She dreamed of crowds, and when the blast of a gun startled her into waking, she lay for a moment in the darkness, her pulse fast, before she quite understood that she was awake. Somewhere in the flat Edward was banging about. Maribel peered at the clock. It was just after two thirty in the morning. Frowning, she rose, slipping her wrap around her shoulders.

Edward was in the drawing room, a glass in one hand and the whisky decanter in the other. Maribel squinted at him in the brightness of the electric light.

'Red, what is it? What's wrong?'

Edward drained his whisky. Then he poured himself another.

'What's wrong? I'll tell you what's bloody wrong. What's bloody unspeakably immeasurably bloody wrong is that an assembly of dyed-in-the-wool dunderheads, not one of whom occupies his seat for any other reason than a blind accident of birth, a bunch of petrified anachronisms who sleep through most of the proceedings and talk through the remainder, not only dare to dictate to us, who have been elected by the people, but have the legal right to do so, while we who are the people's spokesmen are forbidden to speak in their defence. What is the point of it, Bo? What is the damned point of any of it when we can say nothing, do nothing?'

Maribel's heart sank. She put her arm around him, steering him towards the sofa.

'Sit,' she said. 'Tell me what happened.'

Edward sat, Maribel cross-legged at his feet. It was the Coal Mines Regulation Bill, he told her. He had been working on the bill for months, arguing in the House, lobbying in the tea room, returning again and again to the coal-grimed men's clubs and the church halls not only of his own constituency but of Yorkshire and the Black Country. A workable bill had finally been jostled and wheedled through the Commons, only to be subjected by the Lords to a series of amendments, amendments that, in Edward's opinion, not only cut the heart from the bill but extracted its teeth, one by one. The final provocation came with an amendment from Lord Cross which would prevent the appointment of checkweighmen, the trusted agents of the miners themselves, as safety inspectors. Incandescent with rage, Edward had risen to his feet to condemn the indefensible powers of the Upper House and the fundamentally undemocratic nature of the English Parliament. The House had erupted. Calling for order, the Speaker had demanded that the honourable member withdraw his remarks. Edward refused. In the vote that followed the motion was passed by a heavy majority. The Member for Argyllshire was to be suspended from the House.

'For how long?' Maribel asked, lighting two cigarettes and passing one to Edward.

'Seven days.'

Maribel thought of Mr Engels, who had patted her arm at one of his famous Sunday parties and told her that her husband was a fine man in sore need of a manager, of pale po-faced Miss Potter, who hankered moonily after the revolting Mr Chamberlain and who had once declared in Maribel's hearing that Edward Campbell Lowe was generally agreed to be a *poseur* and a fool. She wished she did not feel ashamed.

'Seven days is not long,' she said. 'Will you keep your seat?'

'It hardly matters. If I can't say what must be said openly to defend the interests of my constituents, if I am to be gagged for speaking out in the service of democracy and of reason, then that seat is worth nothing.'

'Will you resign? Is that what the party will expect?'

Edward shrugged.

'The party expects me to disappoint them. They take comfort in my predictability. As for me, how can I leave when there is so much left to do?'

He leaned forward, his glass cradled in his hands. Maribel put her hand on his shoulder and they both watched as the whisky turned in slow honeyed circles around the crystal. Then Edward raised the glass to his lips, tossing it back in a single swift swallow.

'Those damned Tory bastards,' he said. 'What hope do the coal miners have now?'

Edward was summoned by Earl Spencer. The meeting was civil, the rebuke discreet and emphatic. It was made quite clear that it served no one's purpose, least of all that of the Liberal Party, to defy the rules of the House, and that it would be best for both Edward and the party if he were to apologise. When Edward declined, confessing himself unable to apologise for something he did not regret and for which, furthermore, he had already been publicly chastised, Spencer did not press him. He did, however, make it quite clear that no further improprieties would be tolerated. The party, catastrophically split by the Irish question, was already dangerously weakened. Though Trevelyan had been persuaded back into the Liberal fold, Goschen continued to strengthen his position in the Conservative government in the post of Chancellor of the Exchequer, and recent talks with Chamberlain and Hartington about the reintegration of the

Liberal Unionists had collapsed. While the Grand Old Man might share many of Edward's political convictions he had precious little patience for agitators.

Spencer instructed Edward to keep his head down. He urged him to spend the seven days of his exile from the House in his Scottish constituency, addressing matters of local concern. Edward nodded, shook the peer's hand, and spent the next seven days in a frantic whirl of activity, addressing clubs and societies across London on the promotion and protection of the political interests of the working class. Government figures had shown that the previous winter, more than two thirds of dock labourers, building craftsmen, tailors and bootmakers had been out of work for at least a part of that time. Many had not worked at all. The approaching winter looked set to be just as bad. With a third of the country's population living in chronic poverty, and the working classes forming a majority in perhaps two-thirds of London's constituencies, Edward had hoped for an eager response to his petitions. He was enraged by the apathetic response that greeted him.

'It is like crying into the wilderness,' he fumed to Maribel after one meeting in Clerkenwell. 'These men may be desperate but they haven't a radical bone in their bodies. The entire meeting added up to nothing more than a knitting circle of down-and-outs grumbling about the rheumatism.'

'They cannot all be like that.'

'Can't they? They seemed to me more insular, more backward-looking, more in love with the old order than a gaggle of tweed-clad Tories. It is them I strive for, always them, and yet not one in five believes a word I say or even understands it.'

'You have John Burns and that other one you introduced me to the other day, what's-his-name, Harry Quelch,' Maribel said, thinking of Quelch's bright bird eyes, the sharp creases etched between his eyebrows. Afterwards Edward had told her that, because there was no English translation of *Kapital,* Quelch, one-time tanner and packer in a paper factory, had taught himself French from a dictionary so that he might read Marx's words for himself.

'Yes,' Edward agreed. 'We have them. And there it stops. The rest of the sorry lot squirm and cringe their way off the bottom rung of the ladder until their feet are clear of the muck and there they remain, clutching at the straws of their respectability and wiping their shoes on the heads of those who would follow them. Believe me, no one is quicker than the English working man to drop Socialism at the first whiff of social advancement.'

Maribel sympathised with her husband but she could not help wishing that he had taken Spencer's advice and travelled north. Ejection from the House had brought out in him all the contrariness in his nature and extra measures of pig-headedness to boot. He was wild with energy. As the days went on his attire grew more flamboyant, his gaucho swagger more pronounced. He wore bandannas knotted about his neck and, when he rode Pampa about London, he had her wear the bridle he had brought home from Argentina which was made of elaborately tooled leather with heavy silver badges on the reins and browband.

Often he went out without explanation. The flat was empty without him, his absence like a bruise in her chest, but when he was at home she wished he might find somewhere else to go. Whatever his adventures they did not calm him. He paced the flat, circling the sitting room until she thought they would both go mad with the monotony of it. She did not think he intended to provoke her but he could not help himself. He ground his anger against her like a flint.

She could muster little heat in return. A low dreariness had settled upon her which she could not shake. She did not write. Months before she had agreed with Mr Morris that she would lecture for him at Kelmscott House on her childhood in

Chile. The date drew closer but she did nothing to prepare her talk. The thought of it filled her with a light-headed kind of contempt. Instead she sat with a novel open on her lap on the sofa at Cadogan Mansions and, while her eyes moved across the lines of words, her head returned again and again to a whitewashed room with a crucifix on the wall. Mostly it was empty. Sometimes Ida was there, eight years old in rag curlers and a grass-scuffed pinafore, her legs stuck out in front of her, and, on her lap, a baby in knitted garters, its eyes glassy with astonishment. Beyond the tiny window the orange trees were covered in dust.

'When are you going to photograph those Indians?' Edward demanded of her one morning as he passed his teacup for her to fill. 'It says here in the paper that the show leaves for Birmingham at the end of October. You are running out of time.'

Maribel shrugged.

'It can't be helped,' she said.

'Of course it can be helped. You are not to let that expensive camera rot. Or your mind, for that matter. You are bored, Bo. There is nothing that becomes you less than boredom.' Edward gulped his tea, then pushed back his chair. 'I have to go.'

'I am not bored.'

'Then I don't know why not. You've done nothing but moon about for days. Take some photographs. Write. Investigate your gold mine, for heaven's sake. Only do something. Inertia might kill slowly but it kills all the same.'

Soon afterwards he left, banging the door behind him. Maribel sat for a long time at the table, her teacup cradled in her cupped hands, as the silence crept back into the room. When Alice came in to clear the breakfast dishes she pleaded a headache and went back to bed.

15

MARIBEL LEANED TOWARDS THE mirror to fasten the clasp on her necklace. It was a becoming piece, the dark red stones glistening against her pale skin setting off the darkness of her hair, and the sight of it lifted her spirits a little. That morning, his seven days' suspension complete, Edward had returned to the Commons. He had been too long in the House to hope to be garlanded for his outburst but he had not anticipated the chilliness of his reception. There had been, he told Maribel, a palpable silence as he entered the Chamber, a thickening of the air into which the ordinary shuffles and creaks and clearings of throats dropped like stones. When he took his seat on the Opposition benches several of his fellows had glanced away, turning to their neighbour or rummaging with papers on their laps.

'As though they might catch something by looking,' he said.

Maribel said nothing. She had kissed Edward goodbye that morning, had observed as he fastened about his shoulders a black cape edged in silver braid and set on his head his broad-brimmed Spanish hat, and she had known that trying to keep Edward in check was like trying to tame the weather.

'You should dress,' she said, glancing over her shoulder. Edward stood in his shirtsleeves in front of the fire, staring into the flames. 'We are expected at eight.'

Autumn, so slow in coming, had blown in on a sudden flurry of leaves. The wind rattled the windows in their sashes and whistled in the chimney, so that the fire writhed in the grate. At night there was a chill to the air and the fog snagged in the gaslights like twists of sheep's wool. Alice had brought the velvet cushions and the heavy silk counterpane out of storage, and the bed and the chaise were plump with them, as though readied for hibernation. It was snug with the curtains drawn, the lamps and the bright fire spilling their pools of warm light on the thick carpet, and for a moment Maribel wished that they did not have to go out.

Edward turned, running a hand through his hair so that it rose from his brow like a coxcomb.

'Remind me again why we agreed to this?'

'We?'

'It is always "we" when I regret a decision, you know that. If I meant not to go I should have said "you".'

It was his first attempt at a joke in many days. Maribel smiled at him in the mirror, adjusting the diamond clasp in her hair. The clasp had been Alice's idea. It was encouraging to see how clever with hair the Yorkshire girl had become. The dress was becoming too, though not quite as modish as she would have wished. The gowns in the fashion plates in the French magazines were wider in the shoulders this season, exposing the full length of the collarbone, and the skirts were narrower over the hips. She would go to Paris in three weeks. The thought cheered her further.

'Get dressed,' she said.

They were dining with the Worsleys. John Worsley, properly Viscount Worsley of Stoke, was a senior Liberal who had been Chief Secretary for Ireland until the Gladstone government had fallen. He had also, until he retired and ceded the position to Mr Webster, been for many years the editor of the *Chronicle*. He and Edward were colleagues, not friends, and the Worsleys had never before asked the Campbell Lowes to dine with them at home. It was evident that the timing of the invitation, to

197

coincide with Edward's first day back in the Commons, was no accident of fate. The dinner, while an entirely private affair, constituted a public gesture that would not be misunderstood by those in the Liberal Party who wished Edward's exile to continue beyond the term of his suspension. Edward Campbell Lowe was to be forgiven.

The conspicuous generosity of the act infuriated Edward and his instinct was immediately to refuse it. It was Maribel who had, in the end, persuaded him that they must accept, if not for John then for Rose, his wife, who had always been kind to Maribel. The Worsleys had met years ago, while Rose was married to a Mr Atwood, and they had been obliged to wait for him to die before they were able to marry themselves some years later. It was generally agreed among his friends in the Liberal Party that, were it not for Rose Atwood and her unpardonable circumstances, John Worsley might one day have become Prime Minister.

She had known that he might be there. Though Mr Webster's *Chronicle* was a good deal changed from its days under Lord Worsley, Worsley remained chairman of the newspaper's board and was known to admire, if not always appreciate, the journalistic dash of his successor. Besides, Mr Webster remained a staunch supporter of the Member for Argyllshire. While he acknowledged that the Speaker had had no option but to suspend Mr Campbell Lowe he had nonetheless published an editorial echoing Edward's frustration with the filibustering intransigence of an unelected Upper House. Most of the other newspapers had called for Edward to resign.

After the raw swirl of the street the Worsleys' high-ceilinged drawing room was imposingly patrician, the air vibrating like a struck glass with the refined hum and clink of cultivated society. They were late. Several people turned as they entered. Beside her she felt Edward stiffen a little, and she realised for the first time that perhaps this was difficult for him. It was not something that occurred to her often, that there were things he might find difficult. She gave his elbow a tiny squeeze.

Rose Worsley greeted them warmly, gesturing at a waiter who offered a tray of champagne. Maribel took a glass and sipped. When she looked up she saw him and, despite everything, the shock of it was electric, shrivelling the soles of her feet.

He stood by the fireplace in a posture of exaggerated ease, one elbow on the back of a leather wing chair, one foot on the brass guard that ran around the grate. His other arm was crooked outwards, the tips of his fingers dipped into his coat pocket. He was looking directly at her. Immediately she turned away, swallowing champagne and the rush of her pulse. He looked like a bad actor, she thought. Even his dinner suit, with its faint sheen, had a whiff of repertory wardrobe about it. She looked up at Edward, elegant and sardonic in his perfectly cut coat, and the warmth in her face shamed her. She leaned towards Rose, laughing at something the older woman said. And still her heart raced. She pressed a hand to her breastbone, feeling the shape of the garnet necklace beneath her fingers, and she knew, though she did not look in his direction, that he watched her. She could feel the heat of his eyes on the back of her neck. Despite herself, she wanted it to be so.

With an effort Maribel forced herself to join her husband's conversation with their hostess. Soft-faced and plump-wristed, it was widely acknowledged that Rose Worsley's pink-and-white complexion belied a piercing intelligence. Though John Worsley was agreed to be a clever and cultured man, it was whispered that the best parts of his monographs were all written by his wife. Certainly she was crisply intolerant of any kind of intellectual sloppiness. Maribel knew her only a little but she had liked her immediately. She seemed to Maribel the kind of woman who might rescue an injured hedgehog, feeding it warm milk with a dropper while recalling amusing observations on the spiny creature from Pliny and St Antony of Padua. She had no children. Once, at a tea party, when she and Maribel had found themselves stuck with a group of parliamentary wives who could talk of nothing but their offspring, Lady Worsley had reached into Maribel's lap and squeezed her hand. Then she had taken her hand away. Maribel had been startled by the gesture but afterwards curiously touched. They had never spoken of it again.

It was a few moments before Lord Worsley detached himself from a group on the other side of the room and crossed to greet them. He shook Edward's hand.

'Remember Candide,' he said. *"In England it is thought well to kill an admiral from time to time to encourage the others."*

'Then it is fortunate I have no sea legs to speak of,' Edward said.

Worsley chuckled. Then, begging the ladies' pardon, he asked if he might borrow Edward for a moment before dinner.

'Fifteen minutes,' Lady Worsley said. 'No longer. Coddled eggs don't wait.'

Her husband tugged his forelock.

'Aye aye, sir.'

Lady Worsley smiled as he escorted Edward away.

'I suppose I should be glad of the naval allusions. It has been nothing but Robert Walpole here for months. Now who here do you know? Mr Webster, who succeeded John as editor of the *Chronicle*? Everyone in London seems to be acquainted with Alfred Webster. He is the Buffalo Bill of pressmen.' She made a funny little shape with her lips. 'But I shall not permit you to talk to him now. You are seated beside him at dinner.'

*

Maribel was escorted to her place in the dining room by Sir John Billington, a gentleman of florid complexion and military moustaches. Mr Webster was waiting for her, his hands on the back of his chair. Against the snow-white napery and gleaming silver his ill-fitting suit looked clumsier than ever. He made little pretence of listening as on his other side Mrs Van den Bergh, the wife of a visiting American writer, endeavoured to distract him with admiring comments on the flowers. Instead he watched as Maribel made her way around the table towards him, one finger tugging at his collar as though it choked him. When at last she reached him Maribel extended her hand. He seized it with a jumpy eagerness that caused her to flinch, her alarm shot through with a bright thread of excitement.

She glanced at Edward, who had taken his place on the other side of the table beside Lady Worsley. He glanced back, the faintest of smiles tugging at the corners of his mouth. Composing herself, Maribel turned her shoulders firmly away from Mr Webster, nodding with a tremendous show of interest as Sir John described for her in exhaustive detail the improvements he was making to the country estate he had recently inherited from his father. It was only when Sir John's neighbour on his other side embarked upon a long anecdote about a family she was sure must be Sir John's nearest neighbours that she reluctantly allowed her attention to return to Mr Webster.

His milky eyes were fierce as he contemplated her.

'Mrs Campbell Lowe, there is something I must talk to you about,' he murmured. 'It cannot wait.'

Maribel hesitated. Then she unfolded her napkin, smoothing it over her lap.

'Goodness,' she said lightly, swallowing the squirm in her stomach. 'How fearfully cloak and dagger you sound, Mr Webster. I thought we were in Mayfair, not a French novel.'

Mr Webster stared at her. Again she felt the heat spread in

her skin like blotting paper. Frowning, she glanced uneasily across the table towards Edward. Deep in conversation with Lady Worsley he did not look up. Mr Webster followed the direction of her gaze. Then, lowering his head, he stared at the tablecloth.

'Mrs Webster,' Maribel said. 'Is she here tonight?'

Mr Webster shook his head. Maribel watched as with his thumbnail he pressed a long gouge into the tablecloth beside his side plate. Now that he did not look at her she wished that he did.

'Regrettably my wife is not blessed with good health.'

'I am sorry to hear that.'

'Yes, well. You are fortunate not to suffer as she does. You look radiant.'

How can you know, she wanted to say, when you will not look at me? Instead she inclined her head.

'Thank you.'

There was a silence. Footmen moved around the table, pouring wine, setting cocottes on little gilt-edged saucers in front of each guest. A mass of candles burned in branched silver candelabra and drops of molten light caught in polished silver and cut glass and silky white porcelain. On the other side of the table Edward's hair glinted red-gold. He murmured something to Rose Worsley, who laughed. Beside her Mr Webster fiddled with his cutlery.

When the decanter reached them Webster put his hand over his glass and asked for barley water. Maribel took a sip of sherry, inhaling the sun-toasted smell of Valquilla, and contemplated her cocotte. She wondered what it was that Mr Webster so urgently desired to tell her. He was hot-headed, that much was plain, but he was a man of business, surrounded at the table by his fellow pressmen, a married man with, it seemed, strong Christian principles. What on earth could it be that he wished to say?

'I wanted to thank you,' she said for something to say. 'For supporting Edward as you have. It has been a great comfort to him to know that there are people on his side.'

Mr Webster shook his head impatiently. He took up his spoon, plunging it into the cocotte. In France, Maribel thought, the word *cocotte* was slang for prostitute. She wondered what Webster would say if she told him.

'That there can be another side is the great outrage of our times,' Webster said. 'I don't know how the Home Secretary sleeps at night.'

'Perhaps he shan't, if you and Edward have anything to do with it.'

'Then we will have done our job. At least your husband appears to have suffered no ill effects from his banishment.'

'Banishment? You make the House of Commons sound like a fairy kingdom.'

'Now there's a thought,' Sir John interrupted cheerfully. 'The question is whether one considers Matthews Prince Charming or the wicked stepmother.'

'Or Sleeping Beauty,' said the woman on his left archly. Maribel did not know her. She had a heart-shaped face and a mouth like a buttonhole. 'One must only hope someone kisses him awake before those vagrants in Trafalgar Square start smashing up Pall Mall all over again.'

Sir John laughed.

'Be careful what you say about vagrants to Mr Webster,' he said. 'I gather he bites.'

Mr Webster smiled blandly.

'Not at all,' he said. 'It surprises me only when decent-thinking men – and ladies, come to that – place a higher value on the windows of a gentleman's club than on the lives of hundreds of starving poor.'

'Come now,' Sir John said, discomfited. 'I hardly think this is the time.'

'Then when is? When the wretched men and women and children in Trafalgar Square have conveniently expired?'

'Mr Webster, no doubt you think me an old fuddy-duddy but I am old-fashioned enough to believe that political discussion is best kept for when the ladies have withdrawn. Perhaps we might talk of something more congenial?'

Shrugging his shoulders Webster worked his spoon into the corners of his dish. A fleck of cream gleamed white on his chin and under the table his leg jiggled restlessly up and down, as though the agitation in him could not be contained. Maribel could feel the prickle of it in the air between them, in the tiny hairs on her arms.

Picking up her spoon she dipped it into her egg, pressing the bowl of the spoon against the round yolk. It stared up at her balefully. She pressed harder. The yolk resisted and then burst, bleeding yellow into the cream. As she stirred the mixture a muscular swirl of raw white clung to the spoon. She pushed the dish away.

Sir John hesitated. Then he began once more to converse with the lady on his left side. On Webster's other side Mrs Van den Bergh was engaged in a discussion about Atlantic steam-ships. Mr Webster finished his egg and set down his spoon. The conversation of the other guests rumbled around them as the cocottes were taken away and soup was brought, a thick soup of grass green flecked with herbs, a spiral of cream curled at its centre. Webster picked up his spoon and took a mouthful of soup. He swallowed. Then, shaking his head, he set it back down.

'Mrs Campbell Lowe,' he murmured.

Maribel's stomach lurched.

'I meant to ask,' she said hurriedly. 'How were the portraits from your sitting with Mr Pidgeon? Were you pleased with the results?'

'I would rather talk about your work –'

'I am ashamed to say that I have taken pitifully few photographs of late. Having said that, Major Burke at the Wild West has just recently agreed that I might photograph Buffalo Bill's Indians. Not all dressed up like actors for the shows but behind the scenes as it were, the real men without all the whoops and the warpaint. It had occurred to me that perhaps your newspaper might be interested in publishing them.'

She tailed off, discomfited by the intensity of Mr Webster's stare, the coquettish smile stranded on her lips. As she put down her soup spoon and patted at her mouth with her napkin he leaned towards her, once again tugging at his stiff collar with one finger. Instinctively she leaned back.

'We are more than just acquaintances, are we not?' he murmured. 'We understand one another?'

Maribel's stomach lurched.

'I – I am not sure I follow you, Mr Webster.'

Webster leaned closer. Maribel stared at her lap, her napkin twisted in her hands.

'Horace Pidgeon spoke to me about your photograph,' he murmured. 'The one of the woman.'

Maribel's head jerked up.

'I beg your pardon?' she said.

'It was wrong of him, of course, but do not judge him harshly. Mr Pidgeon knows of our acquaintance. He implored me to speak with you, to persuade you to reconsider. Please, Mrs Campbell Lowe, hear me out. This has nothing whatsoever to do with my work at the *Chronicle*. I speak to you not as a newspaperman but as a Spiritualist.'

'And I am supposed to find that reassuring?'

He smiled as though she had made a joke.

'I told Mr Pidgeon you would understand,' he said. 'I thought perhaps I might come to Turks Row tomorrow. So that I might see it.'

Maribel shook her head.

'There is nothing to see,' she said. 'Mr Pidgeon had no right to speak to you, no right at all. The photograph he saw was the result of a spoiled plate.'

'With all due respect, madam, Mr Pidgeon has a great deal of experience in such matters and he assures me that your photograph is genuine. Do you know what that means?'

'I know exactly what that means,' she said angrily. 'It means that Mr Pidgeon is mistaken. The plate was spoiled. It caused a smear on the photograph. That is the end of the matter.'

'Mrs Campbell Lowe, have you ever seen a spirit photograph yourself?'

'Whether I have seen —'

'I take it that you have not?'

Maribel stared at him. 'I do not care for swindles, Mr Webster,' she said.

'As I thought. So it is fair to assume, madam, that you would not consider yourself an expert in these matters?'

'I really don't see —'

'Would you be willing to concede then that you are not the best person to ascertain whether the photograph in question was or was not genuine?'

'On the contrary, I have all the experience I require. I have seen the photograph. You, sir, have not.'

'But Horace Pidgeon has. And Pidgeon knows what he saw.'

Maribel crossed her arms.

'Mr Pidgeon may see fairies at the bottom of his garden for all I care. The photograph no longer exists. Which means that the point is moot, wouldn't you agree?'

'I don't understand.'

'I destroyed the plate,' she said smoothly. 'As for the prints, I burned them. There is no longer any photograph.'

'I don't believe you.'

'Are you calling me a liar, Mr Webster?'

'You wouldn't have done such a thing. You couldn't possibly —'

'Why on earth not? What use did I have for it?'

'And its value to others, to – to the world? You never thought of that?'

'My photograph was a disaster, a failed attempt at portraiture by an incompetent amateur. Forgive my candour, Mr Webster, but spirit photography is no more than a giant fraud practised upon the credulous. The picture was spoiled. It had no value of any kind.'

Webster's fists clenched on the table, his knuckles white. He leaned forward, so close she could smell the soup on his breath. The conversations around the table had grown louder and when he spoke his voice was hardly audible.

'Am I to understand that you wilfully destroyed the work of God?' he hissed, his milky eyes rolling in their sockets. 'What kind of an agent of Satan are you?'

Maribel leaned away from him, disgusted. When she thought of the squirm of excitement she had allowed him to rouse in her it caused her stomach to turn over.

'I beg your pardon?' she asked coldly.

'I should have known it. I should have known it from the start, with your sighs and your sheep's eyes and your oh-so-charming little blushes. I am married, Mrs Campbell Lowe, and a faithful husband, but what does a woman like you care for the sanctity of the marriage vow, for righteousness and ordinary English decency? What does a woman like you care for Truth?'

Maribel clenched her hands in her lap to keep them from shaking.

'Are you quite finished?'

Webster did not answer. He was breathing hard, the stiff front of his shirt heaving queasily, and there was perspiration on his forehead. Maribel took a sip of sherry. Then, setting down her glass, she turned her back on Mr Webster and began to converse with Sir John.

*

The cab rattled briskly through the dark streets. Maribel leaned her head against the cracked leather upholstery and stared out of the window. In Grosvenor Square a gaggle of carriages loitered outside a grand house, the coachmen sprawled on their boxes, knots of liveried footmen trading insults. Lamps burned brightly in the pillared porch, and snatches of music and laughter drifted from the open windows. The windows were vast, like great aquaria. Behind the glass, gleams of bright silk flashed and dipped. The cab skirted the carriages to cross the square, passing into the shadowed gloom of the beech trees that fringed the gardens. Maribel watched her hands grow white and then a greenish yellow as the cab emerged once more into the gaslit dazzle of South Audley Street.

A cab clattered past them, heading north. Otherwise the streets were empty of traffic. At the corner of Curzon Street a girl in a black shawl lingered, one hand at her throat, drawing circles on the pavement with a slippered foot. In the gaslight her scarlet dress had a brown tint, like dried blood. She looked up as the cab slowed at the junction, her eyes like dark holes in her pale face, and for a moment she gazed at Maribel and Maribel gazed back. Then the cabman hissed, the cab jerked forward and she was gone.

Maribel shifted a little on the leather bench, drawing her fur cape more closely about her shoulders. Near the park two policemen leaned against high iron railings, pale brows above the blackout of whiskers and thick serge. A girl hurried past them, a servant of some kind perhaps, her bonnet low and her cloak drawn up around her chin, and one of the policemen called out to her and the other one laughed. The cab turned then to take the park road and, as the clouds parted to reveal a sliver of moon, it was possible to make out inky bundles huddled beneath the trees.

Somewhere a dog barked. Maribel lit a cigarette. Roused by the flare of the match Edward yawned and pressed his hand to the back of his neck.

'Poor Bo, what bad luck to get Webster,' he said. 'The man is quite intolerable.'

'No. He's worse.'

'He gave Worsley the most fearsome lecture after dinner. I can't imagine what possessed him. His position at the *Chronicle* has been precarious ever since the abduction case. Without Worsley's support on the board Webster doesn't stand a chance.'

'That man is a – he's insufferable. What was our poor host's offence?'

'Defending the right of scientists to research without censorship.'

'How can anyone object to that?'

'With the utmost moral outrage, when the study is of human sexual behaviour. Do you remember that doctor, Ellis he was called, whom we met once at dinner with Edward Carpenter? Fellowship of the New Life and all that "peace and vegetables" tripe?'

'"*The cultivation of a perfect character in each and all.*"'

'Exactly. It would appear that Mr Ellis has rather lost interest in the perfectibility of mankind and has embarked instead upon a scientific investigation of sexology in general and sexual inversion in particular.'

Maribel thought of Oscar and of his famished helplessness in the presence of the beautiful and indifferent boy who lodged with them at Tite Street. Then she thought of Mr Webster's milky stare and her insides clenched.

'He hopes to publish an academic analysis along the lines of Krafft-Ebing's *Psychopathia Sexualis*,' Edward said. 'Well, naturally Webster denounced Ellis as Satan's pornographer, and when Worsley objected, Webster saw red. He even had the gall to demand of Worsley how he could look his wife in the eye.'

'Webster's father was a minister,' Maribel said, remembering Charlotte.

'I should have known it. The man is a bigot and a damned

hypocrite, Bunyan on the library shelves and dirty pictures under the bed. The disgust he parades is nothing but blind terror at the voracity of his own appetites. Don't be deceived by the reverential references to the invalid wife. There is no man in the world more infatuated with sex than Alfred Webster.'

Maribel squirmed.

'That is just what Charlotte said.'

'I won't ask how she knows.'

At Cadogan Square Edward paid the cab and helped Maribel out. They were in the hallway when he began to laugh. Maribel put a hand over his mouth.

'Quiet,' she hissed. 'You'll wake Her Ladyship.'

Edward kissed her fingertips as together they tiptoed up the stairs. He was laughing again by the time they let themselves into their flat.

'What?' asked Maribel. It had been days since she had seen him laugh. 'What is it?'

'I just remembered,' he said. 'Lady Worsley told me the most marvellous story about Webster. After all that Sink of Iniquity business, Worsley went to visit Webster in Holloway gaol. He had thought to cheer his spirits, but when he was shown to Webster's cell, he found the man positively elated. When Worsley rather nervously enquired what it was that had made him so cheerful, Webster told him that, while exercising in the prison yard that morning, it had occurred to him that if anyone at that moment had asked who was the most important man alive, the answer would have to be – Webster himself. *The prisoner in this cell*, I believe, were his exact words.'

'No. Really?'

'Apparently. Isn't it wonderful? She also told me that every year, on the anniversary of his imprisonment, Webster insists upon parading about London in his prisoner's uniform for the entire day, cap and all. An act of remembrance, apparently. The irony is that, as a first-class misdemeanant, after the first day he wore his own suit of clothes.'

Maribel thought of Webster's clenched fists, the hatred in his milky eyes.

'I think perhaps he is quite mad,' she said slowly.

'Of course he is. Only the insane believe themselves always to be right.'

Much later, she rose and went into the drawing room. It was cold. She shivered, huddling into her nightgown as she unlocked the drawer at the back of her desk and drew out the photograph of Charlotte. The edges of the photograph curled a little. They had grown velvety with handling. She should mount it, she thought, but she knew that she would not. She ran her thumb very gently over the blur that smeared Charlotte's skirts, touching the place where an overheated imagination might see a face. It was possible to see anything, she thought, if one wanted to enough. For a moment she pressed the photograph against her chest with the flats of her hands. Then, impatiently, she pushed the picture back into the drawer and, locking it, went back to bed.

16

H ER EQUIPMENT WAS HEAVY and she travelled to the
Wild West by hansom, her boxes tucked around her
feet. Raw gusts of wind rattled the windows and
tugged at the hats of pedestrians as they hustled, heads bent,
along the busy pavements. Maribel pulled her cloak more tightly
about her, glad of the fox-fur tippet around her neck. She rested
the side of her face against it, rubbing her cheek against the
shivery softness of its underbelly, and hoped it was not going
to rain. She had almost not come. At breakfast she had told
Edward she was not feeling well and thought it might be
prudent to cancel the Wild West and spend the day in bed. He
had considered her over the top of his spectacles. Then he had
lowered the newspaper.

'My father once told me that one only regrets the things one
does not do,' he said. 'Aside from the inescapable fact that it
would have behoved my father to regret a good deal more of
the things he did do, it is one of the few wise things he ever
said.'

'I don't mean not to go. Just not today. If I am coming down
with something –'

'Why are you so nervous?'

'I'm not nervous.'

'Good. Because you have no need to be. You will be wonderful.
And you will go if I have to drag you there myself.'

If the Speaker of the Commons had hoped that the

mortification of exile would put an end to the excesses of the Member for Argyllshire he was to be considerably disappointed. In the days after the Worsleys' dinner Edward returned to Parliament with a new and bitter determination, his old irony ground by the seven-day absence into something sharper and more vicious. When he left Cadogan Mansions in the mornings he slammed the front door. Maribel had taken to holding her breath as she tiptoed across the hall. She had no desire to face the wrath of Lady Wingate.

At Drayton Gardens an overturned dray blocked the road. Maribel stared out of the window at the scrofulous bark of the plane trees that lined the pavement. When Edward had asked if she meant to write a plan for her day at the Wild West she had been emphatic. A plan constrained possibility, she said, and precluded the taking of risk. The preconceived shape of it limited what the eye could see, the heart feel. It was only in those spaces in oneself that opened when one was afraid that inspiration could truly take hold.

She had been right, she thought as the cab driver touched his whip to the horse's rump and the hansom began very slowly to edge forward. All the same she wished she had a plan. She had told too many people about her expedition to return with nothing. She thought again of the coquettish way in which she had suggested to Mr Webster that he might want to publish the photographs in his newspaper. Though almost a week had passed she still felt a sour squirm of nausea whenever she thought back to that night. She had not made a fool of herself, not quite, but she had come very close. When she had turned away from Webster to talk to Sir John he had made a sideways remark about political passions running high and the lady on his other side had pressed her buttonhole mouth tight shut and blinked her eyes in a way that had made Maribel want to pour soup over her head. Again and again she reassured herself that she had not really thought Mr Webster so very interesting, that, until he had revealed himself to be a madman, he had given a reasonably effective impression of an intelligent and entertaining companion whom any woman might have found congenial. Then she thought of the jolt in her stomach, the heat that had suffused her when he looked at her, and she was flooded yet again with shame at her foolishness and her mendacity.

Major Burke met Maribel at the small side gate to the Wild West through which he had once smuggled the Princess of Wales. When the cab pulled up, he stepped forward to open the door for her. He wore his usual wideawake hat and, beneath his coat, a waistcoat of scarlet silk decorated in appliqué with a lurid pattern of orange and purple. Maribel gazed at it in astonishment. A hat could not help being wideawake in the company of a waistcoat like that.

'I am delighted to see you, ma'am,' Burke said, lifting his hat. 'We feared that perhaps you had forgotten us.'

'Of course not. Thank you for accommodating me.'

'Please, it is our privilege to have you here.' He bowed. 'It is not every day we play host to glamorous lady photographers.'

Maribel smiled. His courtesies were almost as shameless as his waistcoats.

'Then let us both make of the most of it,' she said.

'Amen to that. Now where do you wish to start?'

The translator's name was Molloy, an American originally of Irish extraction who, according to Burke, spoke more than ten different Indian dialects. Molloy was a lean, sharp-faced man with a gold watch chain and a derby hat. His eyes were set slightly too close together. When Burke introduced him to Maribel he bowed, doffing his hat, and kissed her hand. The wet press of his lips put Maribel in mind of egg white, which in turn made her think of Mr Webster. The association did not favour Mr Molloy.

Molloy, Burke and Maribel walked together slowly around the Indian camp. The wind had dropped and a thin sunlight strained through a muslin of cloud. From behind the rock-strewn embankments came the submerged rattle and whistle of trains entering the Earls Court cutting. The camp was much smaller than Maribel remembered, no more than fifteen tepees for the approximately one hundred Indian performers and their handful of children. Only those squaws with a role in the show had been permitted to travel with the company.

The Indians were drawn from a number of tribes, not only Sioux but Cheyenne, Pawnee, Kiowa and Arapaho. In the past these tribes had sustained their own enmities. Now they squatted together outside their tepees or sprawled on benches hewn from split trees. The men's black hair fell in hanks over their shoulders and their naturally harsh features were further brutalised by slashes of vivid paint in every shade and hue. One face was bright yellow, the eyes outlined in blue and the nose adorned with a brilliant red streak. Another was blue, yet another green with yellow stripes across the cheeks. Beside the men, two tangle-haired infants scratched in the dust with a stick. A few of the women sewed, garments of fabric or leather piled in their laps, their beads bright drops of colour in the flat white light. The rest stared ahead of them or down at the ground, their hands slack between their knees.

'They are grown rather accustomed to visitors,' said Burke.

The tepees were arranged in a circle, their sides elaborately decorated with patterns and pictures of buffalo and birds. The ground about them was hard and dusty, the grass worn away, and the canvas was stained with soot. And yet there was none of the usual detritus of camp life that she had seen with Edward in Mexico, no smoke-blackened pots and pans, no stone circles or raked-over fires.

'They eat in the dining tent,' Burke explained. 'We get through six hundred pounds of fresh meat a day.'

'It is as though they are waiting for a train that will never run,' Maribel said.

'That is the life of the travelling show,' he agreed cheerfully.

'What exactly is it you are looking for?' Molloy asked her. It was the first time he had spoken. His voice was high-pitched, slightly nasal, and he drew out his words like elastic, stretching the vowels and pressing down into the inflections. Like a whining child, thought Maribel, or a woman wheedling a favour.

'For what's there,' she answered.

The men took her to the stables, where several Indians and many more white-skinned men busied themselves with horses, and to the blacksmith's forge. The blacksmith too was a white man, his eyes blue in his dirty face, but several Indians squatted there, watching him as he went about his work. Another held the head of a wild-eyed bay, murmuring something unintelligible under his breath as the blacksmith nailed a new shoe to the horse's nearside back hoof. Behind the forge men unloaded wagons full of straw and animal feed. Not one of them was a redskin.

'The Indians do not do work of this sort?' Maribel asked Burke.

'Our Indians are performers, not labourers. We hire navvies for the heavy work.'

They circled the warehouses, following the path to the Medicine Tent, a kind of sweat house filled with steam made by pouring water over heated stones. When she asked if she might go inside, Burke shook his head. The Medicine Tent, he said, was for the use of men only.

'In the old days the Indians would take a sweat as a ritual purification before battle,' Molloy explained. 'Here it is a place for them to relax and unwind. The Sioux call it *inikagapi*.'

They walked around the dining hall. The sides of the hall were rolled up. On the beaten earth floor battered trestle tables were set out in rows, like a school.

'The tent behind the mess tent there is the sanatorium,' Burke said. 'Mercifully we have had little cause to use it.'

Maribel looked at the tent. She could feel her pulse in the roots of her teeth.

'Your doctors,' she said. 'They work there?'

Burke raised an eyebrow.

'That is the idea.'

She hesitated.

'If I wished, needed – for my work – to meet your doctors, might that be arranged?'

'You'll be disappointed, I'm afraid. We feared a red-skinned medicine man might cause more trouble than he cured so we hired them here. Both our men are English.'

'You can say that again,' Molloy said.

Burke grinned.

'Nothing wrong with pride in your homeland,' he said. 'If it weren't for that we'd not have made a dime.'

A little later Burke excused himself. It was Molloy, the translator, who remained with Maribel as she set up her equipment in the corner of a small tent provided for her use. He leaned against the table and watched her as she worked, his arms crossed over his chest, his foot swinging backwards and forwards.

'Do the children go to school?' she asked him as she polished the plate cover.

Molloy shrugged.

'The kids are in the show, them that are old enough. It don't leave much time for schooling.'

'And how old is old enough?'

'The youngest'd be Master Bennie, I guess. He's coming up five and plenty grave enough for adulthood. It's one of them peculiar things with Indians. Born ancient, the lot of 'em, yet even the wizened-up ones stay kids their whole lives.'

'Why is that?'

'Damned if I know,' Molloy said.

Maribel looked up, startled by the coarseness of his language. He saw her looking but he did not apologise. He hummed under his breath and his leg swung like a pendulum. Maribel busied herself with her plates, stacking them in their cases in her battered satchel.

'You ready?' he asked her.

'Not quite.'

Molloy drummed his fingers on the table.

'Major Burke tells me you speak a dozen Indian languages,' Maribel said to distract him.

'Something like that, I guess.'

'Where did you learn so many?'

'It's a long story.'

'The best ones always are.'

Molloy fished his watch from his pocket, studied it, shook it. He held it to his ear and, frowning, wound it, rubbing its face on his waistcoat before setting it back in his pocket again.

'I ran away from home,' he said at last. 'When I was a kid. A Lakota chieftain accepted me into his tribe.'

'You ran away to live with the Indians?'

'I ran away because I couldn't stay where I was. Unless that's happened to a body he ain't never going to understand it but it's what happened to me. I was thirteen years old and a runt too. Not so much as a hair on my chin. The Indians took me in, taught me to fend for myself.'

Despite the chief's kindness Molloy had not stayed long with that first tribe. He had drifted from place to place, and from tribe to tribe, learning their customs and their languages. The Indians he met taught him to ride and to hunt. He grew skilful with a bow and arrow. When he was old enough he joined the US Army as a courier. They gave him a gun, for protection. It was not long before his language skills were noticed by senior officers and he was promoted. He acted as guide to the soldiers and as an interpreter. It was a better job with better pay.

'So you went over to the other side.'

'A man's gotta make a living.'

'But you turned informer. You betrayed the very people who had taken you in.'

'It wasn't that way. The old life was over by then. The West was as good as won. The Indians were promised that if they ceded their tribal territories they'd be given land, rations, schools. A future. The way I saw it, it was the best chance they had. I didn't know the government'd end up treating 'em like dogs and half of them starving to death for lack of food. How was I to know that? If they'd ended up with one quarter of what they'd been promised they'd have been just fine.'

Maribel was silent. She slipped the leather strap of her camera around her neck, feeling the weight of the camera against her belly.

'I didn't know,' she said.

Molloy shrugged, brushing dust from his lapels. Then he jammed his derby hat a little lower on his head and stood up.

'You ready now?' he asked. 'Then let's get this show on the road.'

17

I N THE DARKROOM SHE watched as the first of her photographs bloomed in its bath of developer. When the exposure was complete she extracted it, the tips of her gloved fingers touching only the very edges of the glass, and set it in the stop bath for a moment before sliding it cautiously into the tray of hardening fixer. She leaned forward, peering in the low light at the submerged plate. Her breath stirred the fixer, causing the dark shadows of the picture to shimmer and separate on its surface like droplets of oil.

She moved a little, shifting the gloom of her own faint shadow, and tried not to breathe. The surface of the bath steadied. Beneath it, as though through cheap glass, two men squatted in front of a tepee. Their faces were unpainted, their hair loose. One wore a striped blanket around his shoulders, the other a woollen overcoat, its arms empty flaps at his sides. Both men looked directly at the camera. Their dark faces were grave, almost stern. Their mouths turned down and there were deep shadows beneath their cheekbones. They might have been carved from wood. The tepee behind them was decorated with pictures of buffalo. Behind the tepee the rocky embankment rose steeply, and behind the embankment, crenellated against the white sky, stretched a row of chimney pots, one tipped with a twist of dark smoke. In the corner of the photograph, just visible, was a railway signal, its striped arm raised in salute.

It would not make a beautiful photograph. The day had been overcast, the light flat and insipid. There was no mystery in the picture, no grace, nothing to lift the image from ordinary representation into the realm of art. There was no connection between subject and observer as there was always in the photographs of Julia Margaret Cameron, no tension, no intimacy. The scene was not even picturesque. On the ground beside the Indians was an abandoned Wild West programme, its cover tattered with use. But it was a good photograph. She had managed somehow to capture in it something she had not previously understood. A people on the brink of extinction did not look different because there was anything different about them. They were as they had always been, their grief and their gravity and their primitive instincts as old as the earth. They looked different because the world for which they had been made no longer existed. They were bewigged judges evicted from their courtroom, sleepwalkers who had woken to find themselves on a busy street in nothing but their nightgowns. They were actors in their costumes and their greasepaint, riding home on the Clapham Omnibus.

It had taken some persuading to convince Mr Molloy to lend the taller of the Indians his coat. It was clear that the brave shared Molloy's reluctance. Flatly refusing to put his arms in the sleeves, he slung the coat around his shoulders and muttered something Mr Molloy omitted to translate. It was Maribel who had found the Wild West programme and put it in the foreground of the shot, Maribel who had calculated that, if she stood upon a trestle, the chimneys would be visible above the embankment. The result was an image that, if not strictly true, had the weight of truth about it.

Beauty is truth, truth beauty – that is all
Ye know on earth, and all ye need to know.

It was nonsense of course, a great deal of Keats was nonsense and never more so than when he attempted aphorism, but all the same Maribel felt a prickle of anticipation as she slid the plate into the wash tray. Photography might not be among the higher arts, might not, to some, be an art at all but only a chemical reaction, a scientific tool whose place was in the laboratory. Still, it would be something, she thought, to open people's eyes, to make them see, so that, like a theatre-goer in one of the boxes too close to the stage, they found themselves looking not only at the stage but into the half-light of the wings.

Hurriedly she set about the next plate. Even if she worked quickly the process of development would take her several hours. Major Burke had warned her that time was limited, that the first of the day's two performances began at three o'clock and the Indians would be required to get ready, so, with Mr Molloy's assistance and a boy from a refreshment stall pressed into help with the props, Maribel had worked like a demon, contriving to pack the work of several days into as many hours: a brave in front of the bookstall, surrounded by brightly covered cowboy adventures; a herd of buffalo with pelts like mothy carpets grazing in their enclosure over which towered an almost-finished mansion block, its roof cross-hatched with scaffold; a squaw gingerly holding a borrowed safety bicycle. She had had Molloy ask the squaw to straighten her arms, to frown at the newfangled contraption.

'So that the bicycle almost falls over, yes, just like that. The more uncomfortable she looks, the better.'

Now, in Mr Pidgeon's darkroom, she thought of the advertisement she had seen recently on the end of a terrace of houses, 'PEARS SOAP' painted in curling letters several feet tall, and underneath, more soberly, 'MATCHLESS FOR THE COMPLEXION'. She imagined two dark-faced squaws standing beneath it, their faces sexless and unsmiling, dark-faced papooses in their arms, and wondered if Burke might permit her to take the squaws to Hammersmith.

They had been packing up when Molloy accosted a slight gentleman in a dark suit. His narrow face was trimmed with dark side whiskers that curved towards the corners of his mouth and on his nose he wore a pair of steel-rimmed spectacles.

'Hey, Doc,' Molloy called out to him. 'There's someone here wants to meet you.'

The gentleman cast a glance in Maribel's direction and his face twitched, an almost imperceptible frown. He walked towards them slowly. He wore a sombre suit of black cloth and around his hat a band of black silk.

'Mrs Campbell Lowe, this is Dr Coffin, medical director here at the Wild West. Didn't you want to ask him something?'

'Dr Coffin,' Maribel said faintly.

The doctor gave a peremptory bow. He was hardly taller than she was. On the chain of his fob watch he wore a grosgrain mourning ribbon.

'Madam.' His voice was startling, a rich baritone much too large for his body. 'What is it you wish to know?'

Maribel moved her lips but her voice did not come. The doctor frowned at Molloy, not troubling to conceal his impatience.

'Are you unwell, madam?' Molloy asked.

Maribel shook her head, moistening her lips with the tip of her tongue. Her head swam.

'No, thank you. I just – I suppose – I wondered – do the Indians suffer from distempers unknown to white men?'

He answered carefully, the words rumbling in his chest, but Maribel hardly listened. She held tightly to the handle of her satchel, battling to maintain an expression of polite curiosity.

'I hope that answers your question?'

'Why, yes, yes, thank you.'

'Then good day, madam.' Once again he lifted his hat. 'It was a pleasure to meet you.'

Maribel nodded. The doctor turned away.

'My sympathies,' she blurted. 'For your loss.'

'Thank you.'

'Was it – I don't mean to – it was not a close relative, I hope?'
A shadow passed over Dr Coffin's face.

'My daughter,' he said 'She lived only a few days.'

'Oh God.' Covering her mouth with her hands Maribel stared
at the doctor and the tears in her eyes spilled over and fell down
her cheeks. Reaching out, she touched the doctor very lightly
on the sleeve. He flinched and turned away, nodding at Molloy.

'If that is all, perhaps you would excuse me –'

Maribel thought of the tiny white coffin, of Ida, her fierce
little face shrunken with grief, and her heart twisted.

'I lost a son,' she said. 'He was six weeks old.'

'Then you know our grief,' the doctor said stiffly.

Maribel shook her head, wiping her eyes with the back of
her hand.

'No,' she said. 'No one could know that.'

There was a silence. Beside Maribel Mr Molloy sucked his
teeth.

'Well,' the doctor said. 'Good day, madam.'

'Good day, Doctor. May God grant you peace. You and your wife.'

In the gloom of the darkroom Maribel fumbled one of the
plates, her fingers clumsy in their canvas gloves, and again
tears pricked behind her eyes. At breakfast Edward had asked
her if she might be coming down with something. She had
told him only that she was tired, which was true. Whenever
she closed her eyes she saw Ida. When they were children
Ida had made coffins for dead birds and mice and rabbits that
she found in the fields and woods. Edith had wanted to conduct
burial services with prayers and hymns and solemn readings
from the Bible but Ida had refused. She buried them with

handfuls of stones and wild flowers and lit fires on the turned earth.

Maribel did not know what had possessed her to tell the doctor about the baby. It was as though some kind of madness had come down on her, obscuring everything but him, her sister's husband. She had wanted to take him in her arms. Instead she had told him the truth. He had stood before her, a stranger in a mourning ribbon, the loss of his child like a hole cut out of the middle of him, and she had opened herself up and shown him the hole in herself.

The chemical stink of the bath seared her nostrils and made her dizzy. It was only in the darkness that she began to comprehend the enormity of what she had done. The words she had spoken could never be unsaid. Now Dr Coffin carried them with him, inside him, like a seed. Perhaps it would wither and die, untended and forgotten. Or it might take root, pushing up towards the light. It was not difficult to imagine.

'Dashed troublemaker, that Campbell Lowe,' someone would say, because that was what they always said, and the doctor would look up from his newspaper and nod and remark that only the other day he had met Campbell Lowe's wife at the Wild West and did they know that the Campbell Lowes too had had a child who died?

There was nothing she could do to stop it. The thought was awful and magnificent.

'Mrs Campbell Lowe?' She heard the scrape of the handle of the darkroom door as it turned, the rattle of the door in its frame. 'Mrs Campbell Lowe, are you in there?'

Maribel blinked. Then very carefully she took the last of the plates from the development tray and slid it into the stop bath.

'I am not yet finished,' she said. 'I shall give Thomas the key when I am done.'

There was a silence. Maribel cleaned the excess emulsion carefully from the final plate and set it in the fixative to harden. She took another from the wash tray. She inhaled the caustic stink of the chemicals, feeling the scour of them in her nostrils, their taste in the back of her throat. Mr Pidgeon did not go. His feet made dark shadows in the strip of white light beneath the door.

He knocked again.

'If I might persuade you to spare the time,' he said through the door. 'I have something I should like you to see.'

'I am working, Mr Pidgeon. I do not wish to be disturbed.'

'Of course. I understand. I beg your pardon.'

There was another silence, then the click of footsteps along the corridor. The line of light beneath the door settled and set. She emptied the development tray into the sink and wiped it clean with a handful of rags. She clattered bottles into their places on the shelf.

With Mr Pidgeon gone, the air was clearer, less close. It was strange, she thought, how the presence of another human being shifted something in the atmosphere, how the energy of them or the warmth or the sucking into their lungs of oxygen alerted one to their presence, even if they were quite silent. Edward liked to walk about the flat in bare feet but, though he made no noise on the soft carpets, she knew always when he was near. The flat was different when he was in it. It was not a matter of any of the five senses but of something separate, some kind of unconscious divining of the air that sensed a changing of shape, a shifting of energy.

Often, when she was reading or writing, so absorbed that the ordinary sounds of the room had stilled to silence, something in her would prickle and she would look up to see him observing her from over the cover of his book. The weight of his gaze, wasn't that the phrase so beloved of lady novelists? And yet, in the exasperating way of cliché, there was something of the truth in it. He looked at her and his gaze was like a touch, the heat of it stirring something deep and inexplicable in her so that whatever it was that occupied her was, for a moment, forgotten. There was probably a scientific explanation for it, an ether that propagated human warmth just as the luminiferous ether propagated light or something as simple as magnetism or electricity that set a charge between living things.

A gentleman from the Royal Society had once tried to explain to her at a dinner party the principles of electromagnetism. The air pulsed with hidden patterns, he said, waves of electrical activity that might be discerned by the right apparatus. He had talked earnestly of oscillation and quaternions and she had nodded attentively and, for the most part, let the words wash over her. One particular, however, had aroused her curiosity. For hundreds of years, he had said, mariners had observed that lightning strikes would agitate a compass needle. Nothing holds perfectly steady, she had thought then, not even True North.

When it was time for the final plate to be removed from the wash bath she stacked the boxes containing the plates and pushed them into a corner of the workbench. Then she removed her gloves and apron, balling them up and stowing them in their cubbyhole at her feet. Fatigue pulled at her neck and pinched the space between her eyebrows. She took an apple from her bag and ate it, contemplating between bites the gleam of the white flesh in the gloom. Edward was out and she had given Alice the night off. Supper would be something cold on a tray. There was no reason for her to hurry.

She yawned, throwing the apple core into the old paint tin under the workbench. There was nowhere to sit in the darkroom, no room for a chair. Instead she sat on the workbench, swinging her legs, and lit a cigarette which she smoked very slowly, watching the dull red gleam of the lit tobacco flare vivid scarlet as she inhaled. The paper burned faster on one side than the other, leaving a dark point like the tip of a pencil. She picked at it, scorching her fingers. When it was finished she lit a second cigarette from the stub of the first and smoked that too. Then she let herself out, locking the door of the darkroom behind her. The light in the corridor was grey, grainy. Soon it would be winter.

The sudden appearance of Mr Pidgeon in the corridor made her jump.

'Ah,' she said, thrusting the key at him. 'You'll excuse me, I hope. I am horribly late.'

'I thought you might be interested in this.'

'Mr Pidgeon, as I said, I –'

'Please.'

Maribel looked at the photograph in her hand. An old woman in widow's weeds gazed at the camera. Her hair was parted in the middle and drawn tightly back from her face, stretching the skin across her prominent cheekbones. Her eyes were dark beneath heavy brows, her mouth severe, and in her lap she held a Bible. Her hands were large with prominent knuckles, a man's hands. Behind her to her left stood a tall Chinese vase of ornamental grasses and, half hidden amongst them, stood the shadowy figure of a young man in a stiff collar. Apart from the collar and a halo of pale hair like dandelion fluff it was hard to make him out.

'Frankly, Mr Pidgeon, I –'

'The widow is a Mrs Burwood. I am informed by the family member who graciously entrusted me with this print that the man behind her is quite recognisably her husband. When the picture was taken he had been dead a full year.'

Maribel sighed.

'What nonsense,' she said. 'That "man" is hardly more than a boy.'

'The dead disdain the ordinary conventions of time. He appears to her as his wife first knew him, as a young man.'

'Mr Pidgeon, these photographs are tricks. Hoaxes. Like the bones of the saints the tinkers sell on the Camino de Santiago.'

'Not everything in this world is for sale, Mrs Campbell Lowe. The solace that Mrs Burwood derives from knowing her husband is close by is surely without price.'

'That does not make it true.'

'You are right that there is some fraudulent manufacture of such photographs, but this one is quite genuine. As is yours. I am prepared to make you a handsome offer for it.'

Maribel thought of the narrow streets around the Faubourg Saint-Honoré, the jewel-box shops with their silk stockings and fur stoles and heavenly heady perfumes. She thought of Charlotte and of the child, whose flesh was her flesh, and whose name she had whispered to herself in the darkness.

'It is bad enough, Mr Pidgeon,' she said, 'that you consider yourself entitled to share my private property with Mr Webster, a man with whom my husband is required, as a Member of Parliament, to maintain a professional association. It is quite unacceptable that you continue to harangue me in this insistent and offensive manner.'

'Madam, please. I know I should not have shown your photograph to Mr Webster without your permission. It was only that Mr Webster showed such great interest in you and in your work and it was plain that he held you in such high regard –'

'I am not remotely interested in your excuses, Mr Pidgeon. Your conduct was indefensible. Now if you would step aside –'

Mr Pidgeon regarded her with his bloodhound's eyes. Then he held up his hands in surrender.

'You are quite right. What I did was wrong. I apologise unreservedly.'

'Very well, then.'

'As for the photograph in question, I shall not mention it again. If, however, you should ever change your mind –'

'I shall not.'

'I don't suppose you might permit me to see it just one last time?'

'No.'

'No. Of course not.'

'Good evening, Mr Pidgeon.'

'Good evening, madam.'

Mr Pidgeon did not go back into his studio. As Maribel hurried down towards the street he stood watching her, one hand on the banister, his shadow staining the stairs like spilled tea.

18

A T THE END OF October the west of Scotland was hit by a hurricane. It came at night and quite without warning. The winds were so violent that they uprooted trees and stripped the slates from roofs. In the crofting townships that had sprung up on the fringes of the great hunting estates hundreds of the huts were destroyed, while flash flooding forced many more to be abandoned. At sea the waves were thirty feet high. Scores of fishermen were reported missing.

The next day a cable came from Inverallich. The ancient oak at the back of the house had fallen heavily across the enclosed courtyard, bringing down a part of the stables and damaging the old kennel house. The new glasshouse, only recently completed, had been shattered, the orchards badly hit. A large section of the roof at the northern end of the house had also sustained considerable damage.

It was quite impossible for Edward to leave London. It was left to Maribel to travel north to appraise the extent of their misfortune. She went resentfully, for the change in plans obliged her to delay her usual autumn visit to Paris and she knew there was little chance of her favourite dressmaker being able to reschedule her appointment in time for the winter season. As for the cost of all the damage, she could hardly bring herself to think about it. It was three weeks since the *Illustrated London News* had agreed to take one of Maribel's photographs of the Wild West Indians for a modest fee. The journal had only recently begun to publish photographs at all and already Maribel had permitted herself to anticipate the pleasures of a regular income, a small fund of her own sufficient at least for the small luxuries that might fortify one against the larger privations of indebtedness. It was so much easier to be frugal in a brand-new pair of stockings.

The overnight sleeper was due to arrive at Inverallich station at a little before seven in the morning. Maribel refused the steward's offer of an early breakfast and asked only that she be wakened in time to ready herself for disembarkation. It was still dark when she drew back the curtains of her small cabin. She dressed and washed her face. The edging on one of her gloves was starting to fray. She tucked the loose threads into her wrist as the train slowed, and peered out of the window. Grey light leaked into the black sky and the moon was wan. Even in the stuffy carriage, its air warm with the must of slept-in bedlinen, she could feel the misted chill of the Highlands insinuating itself into her bones.

A grim-faced McDougall met her on the platform. It had not been possible to bring the gig to meet her, he explained. The storm damage had left the roads to the house impassable. He would have a boy come down with a barrow for the luggage but he was afraid that they would be obliged to walk, if Her Ladyship could manage it.

They picked their way in silence along the storm-ravaged lane. The morning was grey but there was no rain. The road was littered with the twisted corpses of trees and branches, their ripped flesh fresh white against the dark banks of mud and rotting leaves. Those that had not fallen stood mutely along the length of the lane in silent vigil, their limbs shattered and amputated, the breaks in their ranks unclosed. The wind moved in sharp eddies through the hedges, setting what leaves remained to fluttering. Somewhere a blackbird sang.

When they reached the stone pillars that marked the entrance to Inverallich, McDougall hesitated, a frown pinched between his brows.

'It's bad, ma'am,' he said.

She nodded, but as they rounded the bend in the drive and the lawn spilled away from her up to the house, she let out a sharp cry, her hands flying up to cover her mouth. Across the lawn the cluster of beeches that had stood there for more than two centuries had been ripped from the ground. Two lay on their sides, their branches reaching almost to the terrace in front of the house, their great pale roots clawing at the air. The iron bench that had encircled the larger one clung to its trunk, its feet pulled from the ground, its delicate filigree buckled and broken. On a mild day it had been Maribel's favourite place to read.

The trees that remained upright huddled together, propped at drunken angles. The lawn was strewn with shattered branches, the terrace with broken pots and slates. Several of the substantial rhododendron bushes that framed the house had been uprooted. All were crushed. Above them, the house, which had always compensated for its lack of beauty with an imposing froideur, had shrunk into itself. The hole in the roof was like a mouth, edged about with broken teeth.

'We were lucky the damage was not greater,' McDougall said. 'If a tree had fallen on the house . . .'

They walked together slowly up the drive. In the sunken Dutch garden to the south of the house the stone sundial lay toppled on its side like a skittle. Maribel thought of Edward at the last meeting of the Highland Land League, his fist in the air as he led the assembled crowd in their rallying cry: *Is treasa tuath na tighearna!* The people are mightier than a lord. The storm, it seemed, was mightier than any of them.

'We'll have a tarpaulin on the roof by evening,' McDougall said. 'The winds were too high yesterday. We couldna keep it down.'

'And the tenants?'

'Praise God no one was hurt. There's some damage to the cottages, some slates off and the like, fences blown down. Most of the sheep found shelter. It's the orchards've come off worst, ma'am. More than half the new trees down.'

Maribel spent the day with McDougall, assessing the extent of the damage. As she had feared, the cost of repair would run to hundreds of pounds, perhaps more. There was no money to pay for it. Late that night, when McDougall was gone, she sat down in the library with the estate accounts. There was no denying the numbers. Once the interest on their mortgages had been met, their free income for the previous year had amounted to a grand total of £298 6s 5d, more than £400 less than the year before. Such a sum barely began to cover their everyday expenses.

The fire was bright in the library, the light from the gas lamps soft and warm. Maribel lit a cigarette and then another, reluctant to abandon her cosy nest on the sofa. Though she had had Cora light a fire in her bedroom grate, she knew from long experience that it would be days before the breath and bustle of ordinary life banished the damp chill from the upper floors of the house. The prospect of the gelid bathroom was dismal.

Maribel turned the pages of the accounts. Business was bad but, with the way things were at present, she doubted if there was a farm in the country, large or small, that was not struggling. It was their interest payments that crippled them. At their last meeting in August Edward's financial advisers had recommended to him that he sell a second parcel of land to the south of the estate in order to disburse a part of the mortgage. Edward had refused. He had argued that current prices were too low, that the sale would make only a small dent in the great mountain of their mortgages, that the income from that land, if properly managed, would be worth more to the estate than the capital sum raised by selling. His advisers had attempted, without success, to change his mind and had left unhappily, their handshakes curt. Edward had declined to offer them even the small consolation of promising to think about it.

It was, he told her later, a matter of principle. There were tenants on that piece of land and he would not betray the trust of his tenants. Maribel, who had a much better grasp than her husband of the principles of bookkeeping, had bitten her tongue. The truth was he could not bring himself to face it. It was not only his mother who could not forgive him the sale of the land to the west. He could not forgive himself. He might baulk at tradition and revile the unthinking attachment of the land-owning classes to the conventions of their forebears, their worship of property and propriety, he might despise the earldoms over which his ancestors had squabbled and mock the hereditists who claimed for him, as descendant of Robert II, the rightful crown of Scotland, but he drew his strength from the black earth and peaty waters of the Scotch land to which he had been born. The peaks and the bogs and the boulders, the curving lochs and hidden springs, these, unchanged and unchanging, were his topography, his dominion, to have and to hold. Centuries of Lowes lay in the little private cemetery near the house, their bones criss-crossing beneath the tussocked ground. One day Edward would be buried with them. Perhaps then he would be at peace.

Maribel leaned forward, throwing the stub of her cigarette into the fire. She watched as it burned, curling her toes beneath her. It was late. She stretched, her fingers intertwined behind her head. The knot of her hair was thick and warm in the palms of her hands. She turned her head idly, releasing the stiffness in her neck, her eyes half closed. Then, brushing the ash from her skirt, she stood. The Pliny was in its usual place on the bookshelf. She put her hand on the spine, tracing the gilded letters of the title with the tip of her index finger. The leather was rough, bubbled where damp had lifted the skin from its binding. Gently she drew the book out, weighing the volume in her hands. It was still there, the frayed silk ribbon she had put in the book to mark the place. She opened it. The words *gold mine of Albucrara* were underlined in pencil and marked with an asterisk in the margin. The asterisk was dark and emphatic, its shape pressed into the pages that followed. Maribel could no longer summon the conviction that had added spike after emphatic spike to that asterisk but before she went to bed she set the book on her desk, its pages open at the correct place, her fountain pen in the dint along its spine. Tomorrow she would write to Edward's friend in Madrid. It was always better to do something.

Edward took the Friday sleeper, arriving in time to meet with the estate accountants at Inverallich after breakfast on Saturday. McDougall's men had worked hard. By then the lawn and the terrace had been cleared of debris, the fallen trees cut up and dragged away. Ladders snaked up the front of the house and work had already begun to repair the roof. Maribel was glad Edward had been spared the worst of it. His face was ashen when he stepped out of the gig, the skin beneath his eyes smudged purple with fatigue. He leaned against one of the gig's wheels, his hat clutched to his chest, one hand buried in his hair.

'Oh my sweet God,' he murmured.

Maribel took his arm, pressing her cheek against his shoulder. They stood together in silence as Edward gazed about him.

'Jesus Christ,' he said at last.

'Come inside,' Maribel said gently. 'Cora is making a fresh pot of coffee. Did you have breakfast on the train?'

Edward shook his head.

'How about some kedgeree? Some eggs? There are plenty of eggs.'

'I don't want eggs. Good God, Bo, why didn't you tell me?'

'You knew.'

'Yes, I knew. But this?' He gestured helplessly.

'It is not as bad as it looks.'

'Isn't it?'

The meeting with the accountants did nothing to raise Edward's spirits. A number of the tenants had suffered damage to their properties and would need assistance in their repair. Several had asked for extended time in which to pay their rents. The orchards, which had been predicted to generate significantly increased profits in the forthcoming year, had been decimated. Again it was proposed that Edward consider the sale of a part of the estate. Again Edward refused, but Maribel noticed the weariness in his voice, the way he rested his forehead in the palm of his hand as he contemplated the figures on the paper they set before him. Even Edward, she thought, could not hold out for ever.

Afterwards the two of them walked down to the loch. Neither of them remarked upon the devastated remains of the beech trees, the drifts of sawdust in the gouged lawn. On the pebbled beach Edward bent down and picked up several flat round stones. Neither he nor Henry could be near the loch without throwing stones at it. The wind was brisk, whipping the brown water into little peaks. The trees on the island huddled low against the chill.

'How was London?' Maribel asked, rummaging in her pocket for her cigarettes.

'Like St Petersburg. It seems ever more likely that Warren will prevail, that Matthews will grant him his ban.'

Sir Charles Warren was a former colonial governor and the new Commissioner of the Metropolitan Police, a hardliner determined to crush the increasing militancy of a city driven to the brink by rampant unemployment. The bitter October weather had not prevented the swelling numbers of destitute men and women sleeping rough in Trafalgar Square, and, under pressure from the Tory newspapers who condemned the situation as a disgrace to the capital, Warren had drastically stepped up police efforts to keep them out. For weeks his officers had been carrying out a campaign of harassment and summary arrest. As the weather worsened, the skirmishes in the square had grown more belligerent and the number of arrests had spiralled. Meanwhile Warren, fearful of a repeat of the riots that had convulsed London eighteen months before, was exerting increasing pressure upon an uneasy Tory government to outlaw all public demonstrations in Trafalgar Square.

Maribel inhaled. Cold air gave a particular pungency to a cigarette, intensifying its flavour and sending sparks of sensation skittering into her limbs. She coughed a little and inhaled again.

'And Matthews has the power to do that, constitutionally?' she asked.

'The Home Secretary can do as he pleases, if he deems it in the interest of national security.'

'But that's outrageous.'

'It is worse than that. It is a declaration by the government of this country that they seek not to fill the mouths of the starving but to gag them. They mean to let them die.'

'Can nothing be done?'

Edward shrugged and sent a stone skimming across the corrugated water. It jumped once, a startled leap that sent it somersaulting upwards, and disappeared with a splash.

'In Parliament? Not a thing. On the street? Perhaps, if we can manage to agree on anything and stop tearing ourselves to shreds.'

'But won't that only mean riots all over again?'

'By God I hope so.'

*

After lunch Edward disappeared to the library to do some work. He had a speech to write, correspondence that required an urgent response. Into his briefcase he had crammed the previous day's newspapers to read on the train and these he deposited in Maribel's lap, along with the post from Cadogan Mansions. Maribel set the letters to one side, flicking through the crumpled stack of newspapers: the *Times*, the stalwartly Tory *Herald*, the almost as steadfastly Whig *Post*, the *Illustrated London News* which had no need of politics because it had pictures, the two popular evening papers, the *Globe* and the *Sun*, and, tucked between them, Webster's *City Chronicle*.

Maribel drew the *Chronicle* out of the pile, opening it at random. It was not a newspaper she saw very often and it occurred to her to wonder as she glanced over its neatly stacked columns of words whether it would be possible to tell from the pages of a newspaper if its proprietor was losing his mind. On the opinion pages there was a strongly worded commentary on the diplomatic mission to divide Africa among her European masters; it pressed the Prime Minister not only to push for Britain's rightful share of Africa's riches but to remember her duty to civilise its savage peoples. It was a well-written piece, coherent and convincingly argued, its economic imperatives finely balanced with a Christian compassion. If Mr Webster had garnered his opinions from a séance, Maribel thought, the realm of the Other Side must be a strange blend of Hampstead and a parlour in Cheltenham Spa.

Yawning, she flipped the pages, working her way backwards towards the front. She was almost at the cover when she saw the photograph. It was grainy, imperfectly reproduced. Above the picture, a title in bold type saluted A HUSBAND'S DEVOTION.

She stared, blinking stupidly. A photograph printed in the pages of a daily newspaper was oddity enough, though not unheard of. One or two of the bigger newspapers had carried photographs of the Queen in her carriage on the occasion of her Golden Jubilee. But this photograph? There was no mistaking it. It was quite recognisably the photograph that Mr Pidgeon had shown her outside his studio, the portrait of the widow, Mrs Burwood, the face of a young man half visible amid a sheaf of grasses in a large Chinese vase.

The article that accompanied the photograph described the photographer, a Mr Frederick A. Hudson, as 'perhaps the most renowned spirit photographer in England'. In despair over the frauds perpetrated by unscrupulous tricksters in the name of Spiritualism, Mr Hudson had submitted to an investigation into his methods by the eminent Society for Psychical Research, whose members included not only Mr Gladstone and Lord Tennyson but a Dublin professor of physics and a Cambridge philosopher. After meticulous inspection of the man and his methods, the Society had conceded that, in their opinion, Mr Hudson's work did indeed offer a scientific proof of the objective reality of spiritual forms.

It was in acknowledgement of the Society's pioneering research that the *Chronicle* had decided to publish the extraordinary portrait of a British widow whose departed husband had appeared to her during a sitting at Mr Hudson's studio. The photograph, never previously published, was the tribute of one newspaperman to the thousands of Christians across the country who had themselves experienced the physical manifestation of their loved ones, believers to whom the Lord in His mercy had permitted a glimpse of the life everlasting, and who might today hold their dear departed a little closer, safe in the certainty that, where faith had taken them, the sceptics of science had duly followed. Rigorous scientific investigation had not undermined the foundations of the Christian faith but fortified them and in so doing they had fortified the purpose of science too, for what greater pinnacle of knowledge was there than proof of the soul's immortality, promised to mankind by God?

The piece, Maribel thought, was a masterpiece of manipulation; the pseudo-science, the shameless bias, the sentimental moral climax. All the same, it was interesting how much more convincing the photograph was when printed on the flimsy paper of a journal. The blurriness of the spirit image hardly mattered when the quality of the print was so poor.

She wondered what had possessed Mrs Burwood to authorise its sale, what Webster had paid for it. She hoped it was a great deal. She thought of the photograph of Charlotte locked in the drawer at the back of her desk. Webster's article did not identify Mrs Burwood by name but the photograph showed her face quite clearly. Perhaps a widow in straitened circumstances was obliged to do what was necessary to support herself and her family. All the same, it was hard to imagine any situation in which money would be adequate compensation for the insufferable intrusion into matters of private concern. Things at Inverallich might be bad but they would have to be a great deal worse before one could be persuaded to sell anything to a man like Webster.

Abandoning the paper on the floor she rose to pour herself another cup of coffee. As she sipped at it she gazed out over the garden towards the pewter gleam of the loch. In the driveway McDougall was supervising the unloading of a cart and several men worked among the broken rhododendrons. The sound of the saws carried mournfully on the wind. Around the window the roses were battered but apparently undamaged. She should prune them while she was here, she thought, or they would grow leggy. Roses could take a terrifying amount of pruning, Vivien had shown her that. The more one savaged them the better they seemed to like it.

Sighing, Maribel put down her cup and picked up the pile of letters. One, in a pale blue envelope, was written in an unfamiliar hand. She turned it over, slitting it open. Her mother had always said that coloured writing paper was for governesses and little girls.

Parkside, Wimbledon

Dear Mrs Campbell Lowe,

I fear that, on the occasion of our last meeting, we parted on less than warm terms. I write neither to apologise nor to seek an apology – I presume to imagine that you, like myself, are of too indomitable a constitution to be distressed by a little plain speaking – but rather to thank you. Only days after our contretemps, I was fortunate enough to have offered to me an extraordinary photograph taken by the great Spiritualist, Mr Frederick Hudson. Had you proved less intractable, I might never have had the privilege of publishing perhaps the most important proof to date of the material existence of the spirit. You described your own photograph with devastating candour as, and I recall your words exactly, a 'failed attempt at portraiture by an incompetent amateur' and, though I flinch at so cruel a verdict, I must confess that, when considered alongside the genius of the peerless Mr Hudson, even the most strenuous of imitations must surely be found wanting.

This letter comes therefore with my grateful appreciation. As editor of perhaps the most widely read newspaper in London I have a duty not only to my loyal readers but to the Truth and to the guidance of those who trust in God. You may wish to purchase tomorrow's Chronicle to see the results for yourself.

Your obedient servant &c
Alfred Webster

Maribel stared at the letter. Then, with a furious shake of her head, she crumpled it up and threw it into the grate. The fire licked inquisitively at the ball of blue paper, scorching its edges before it caught in a sudden burst of green flame. She jabbed at it with the poker, stirring it into a shower of black fragments. She had never told Edward about the photograph. Why would she have? Edward was not interested in a spoiled plate. Like Webster's letter it was not worthy of the paper it was printed on. The *Chronicle* lay where she had left it, carelessly folded on the button-backed sofa. Snatching it up she thrust it too into the fire. It caught immediately, bursting with a sudden and violent heat that sent flames roaring up the chimney.

19

THE LAST DAY OF October fell on a Monday. At the showground in Earls Court, the Wild West played the last of its three hundred London performances. Colonel Cody himself had not missed a single one, though Henry told Maribel privately that on more than one occasion he had needed a little help in mounting his horse. The newspapers, whose gloom at the end of the cowboy bonanza was palpable, estimated that, during its five-month run, two and a half million Londoners had paid to see the show, turning the likes of Buffalo Bill, Annie Oakley and Buck Taylor into household names. As the American Exhibition prepared to close its doors, several of Edward's parliamentary colleagues, under the presidency of Lord Lorne, met with their American counterparts to discuss the establishment of a Court of Arbitration for the settlement of disputes between Britain and the United States.

'It is the opinion of the *Times* that "civilisation itself consents to march on in the train of Buffalo Bill",' Edward announced as Maribel poured his tea. '"It is no paradox to say that Colonel Cody has done his part in bringing America and England nearer together."'

'I thought Miss Clemmons was American too.'

'You, Bo, are a shameless tattletale.'

'Blame your brother. I simply repeat what he tells me for the purpose of your education.'

'How commendably diligent you are. I must go.'

'Already?'

'I have a meeting with Burns. What time does Cody expect you?'

'About half past ten, I believe.'

'Take him this.' He handed her his copy of the *Times*. 'It is not every day a cowboy changes the world.'

Its London season over, the Wild West was to travel to Birmingham and from there to Manchester where it would spend the winter. The packing-up of the showground would take some days and Maribel had been granted permission to photograph the Indians as they prepared to leave their temporary home in west London. She was hopeful that the *Illustrated London News*, disconsolate at the prospect of losing so photogenic a subject as the red man to the provinces, might once again be prevailed upon to publish one of the pictures.

When Edward was gone Alice brought in the letters. Maribel contemplated the pile without enthusiasm. Every post seemed to bring bills, or news of bills. The repairs to the roof at Inverallich had hardly been completed when it was discovered that the storm had somehow damaged the drainage system beneath the house, flooding the cellars. Since McDougall's cable gloomily outlining the painstaking work required for its repair, she had half wanted to poke her letters with a stick before touching them, for fear of what other creepy-crawlies might lurk there. The pigeonhole in which she filed outstanding bills was bursting at the seams.

It was near the bottom of the pile that she saw the letter with the Spanish stamps. The address was written in a bold hand, the words looped with flourishes that tangled them in knots, and the stamps were purple and orange. She would keep the envelope for one of Charlotte's boys, she thought as she turned it over, sliding her letter knife under the flap.

Her Spanish was rustier than she had thought it, the handwriting not always easy to decipher, and she was obliged to read the letter slowly. Sr Rivera regretted that he would be unable to be of help to Edward since he was soon to leave Madrid for Buenos Aires but he had contrived, amid the preparations for his departure, to consult with one Tomas Muñoz, a mining engineer until recently settled in Lima. It was the opinion of Sr Muñoz that it was quite possible that there were indeed mines in the Vierzo region but that no further progress could be made without an inspection of the particular location of the mine, which their letter had omitted to specify. He therefore suggested that Edward and Maribel travel to Madrid to meet with Sr Muñoz and, if an agreement might be found to suit both parties, to continue on to the purported location of the mine, so that a thorough assessment might be undertaken of its potential. To that end he enclosed Sr Muñoz's address. He wished them every success with their endeavour.

Maribel hoped it was her awkward translation that lent the letter its air of faint disdain or, better still, affront on the Spaniard's part that she had not trusted him sufficiently to confide in him the precise vicinity of the mine. She had the uncomfortable sense that Sr Rivera had little time for quixotic fools.

Still, it would do no harm to meet Sr Muñoz. Edward needed a holiday and Madrid was lovely in the spring. They could walk in the Parque del Retiro, take a rowing boat on the Estanque. She had never done that. There was no point in talking to Edward about going away at the moment – with the situation in Trafalgar Square worsening daily she almost had to put on false whiskers and pretend to be John Burns to get his attention – but when things were calmer she would take him away. In spring musicians performed concerts in the bandstand on Sunday afternoons and the flowers would be in bloom. At Valquilla the bougainvillea had spilled over the terrace. In the evenings, when the sun slanted low, its flowers had lit up like hundreds of tiny Chinese lanterns, staining the air pink. She had sat there for hours, the drowsing bundle in her arms, memorising with one finger the crocheted pattern of his blanket.

At Earls Court the sky threatened rain. Work on dismantling the Wild West showground had already begun. The air was coarse with the scream of saws, the whack of mallets against wood. The great backdrop to the main arena with its rolling prairie and distant mountain ranges had been taken down, and from beyond the piled-up foothills of rock and trees that embanked the performance area, the terraces of Earls Court huddled uneasily, their roofs tugged low over their small windows. In the camp the tepees too had been dismantled and were being scrubbed clean. Where the tents had been pitched there were circles of soot-blackened stones.

The tent provided for Maribel on her previous visit was no longer in evidence. Instead she was accommodated in a room in the box tent that housed the Wild West offices. The chairs were made of buffalo hide and on the wall hung a feathered war-bonnet and several newspaper articles, framed in gilt. One was a poem in the style of Longfellow 'from the mouth of Punchiwatha'. She glanced idly at the final verse as she prepared her camera.

To the Queen too the papooses,
Dusky little Indian babies,
Were presented, and she touched them
Gently with a royal finger
That the squaws, the happy mothers,
Might go back upon Kee-way-din,
On the Home wind o'er the water,
To the land of the Ojibways,
To the land of the Dacotahs,
To the Mountains of the Prairie,
Singing gaily all the praises
Of the Gentile Queen and Empress,
And the wonders of the North Land.

Once again Mr Molloy, the translator, had been assigned to her as guide. Several times, as they walked around the showground, she thought she glimpsed ahead of her the diminutive figure of Dr Coffin and each time her heart jumped into her mouth. It was never him. Once it was a boy carrying planks of wood, once a woman, an Indian squaw, squarely built and wrapped in a blue blanket. Neither resembled him in the least. And yet, though she dreaded seeing him, she hoped for it too, even willed it. It required a concerted effort not to ask Mr Molloy about him. When they passed close to the sanatorium her heart beat so rapidly she could hardly catch her breath.

She forced herself to concentrate on her work. She took several photographs of the Indian squaws on their hands and knees scouring their tents, the chimneys of Earls Court belching behind them, and several more of the fierce-faced men who squatted on their haunches, watching as their women worked. She photographed four braves playing poker amid the ruins of the encampment, and three Englishwomen with brooms and dusters, their hair tied up in handkerchiefs, cleaning out the Deadwood stagecoach. Several of the more elaborate tableaux, such as an Indian brave tearing down a large Wild West poster, she had planned in advance. Extracting a copy of one of the thousands of penny dreadfuls relating the exploits of Buffalo Bill from her bag, she had Molloy instruct one of the smaller Indian children to hold it up in front of his face as though he meant to read it, its lurid cover upside down. Another of the children posed in Mr Molloy's derby hat.

She worked methodically and with care but there was a flatness to the photographs, or to herself, that she could not lift. It was not just that she was distracted, nor that the day was overcast. With its great sets dismantled, its camps struck, the Wild West and its occupants had a sad provisional atmosphere. The undulating prairies with their pioneering spirit and their herds of wild buffalo had shrunk to heaps of London rubble, the mighty Indian warriors to a ragtag of refugees.

'That's it?' Molloy asked when she began to pack up her equipment.

'That's it.'

Molloy shrugged. 'OK.'

They walked back towards the tent. Outside an Indian waited. He was very tall and broad-shouldered, with waist-length black hair parted in the middle and tied back in a ponytail. His face, bare of warpaint, might have been carved from mahogany. Most striking of all, he wore, in place of the habitual Indian costume, a dark tweed suit and a shirt with a stiff collar. The knot of his tie was askew and loose as a schoolboy's. She could see his collar stud.

'Who is that?' Maribel murmured, reaching for her camera.

'That's Black Elk. His father's cousin was Crazy Horse, the Lakota chief who led the Indians against Custer at Little Bighorn.'

'Crazy Horse was murdered by the army, wasn't he?'

Molloy twisted his mouth.

'Opinion differs about that but, yes, he died in custody.'

'And Black Elk is compelled to capitulate to his murderers fourteen times a week? How can he endure it?'

Molloy shrugged again. 'He insisted upon it. He told Cody that he had had a dream in which his tribe were allowed to return to their lands. He said that if he could only travel to the world of the Wasichu, the white man, he might discover the secret that would help them.'

'And has he?'

'Somehow I doubt it, don't you?'

Maribel was silent.

'Do you want to take his picture?' Molloy asked.

She weighed her camera in her hands for a moment, imagining the shot. There was something about the Indian in his English clothes that was both outlandish and immensely dignified. One of the newspapers had recently reported the story of a band of Umatilla Indians who had set upon a photographer at their reservation and broken his camera because they feared that, if he took their portraits, their souls would be trapped in the photographs for ever.

'No,' she said.

As she entered the tent she turned. The Indian was looking at her, or beyond her, his dark eyes grave in his mahogany face. It was impossible to guess what he was thinking.

Burke came to bid her goodbye.

'I have asked Mr Molloy to accompany you to the train station,' he said. 'Unless you wish him to find you a cab?'

'The train will be fine.'

Burke reached out and shook her warmly by the hand.

'Goodbye, ma'am. It has been a pleasure.'

'Goodbye, Major Burke, and thank you. Oh, I almost forgot.' She pulled out an envelope of photographs. 'I brought some of my pictures. I thought they might make a souvenir for the Indians.'

'What a kind thought. I shall make sure they get them.'

'And my husband sent this for Colonel Cody.'

Burke smiled as she handed him Edward's copy of the *Times*.

'It's a fine piece, isn't it?' he said.

'You have already seen it?'

'I've seen all of today's newspapers, ma'am. That's my job. Thirty-odd morning editions in the city and we're in twenty-nine. Still, the London *Times* is something special. Bill will get a kick out of that.'

'London will be lost without you. What will the newspapers write about once you are gone?'

Major Burke grinned.

'I'm sure they'll think of something.'

Outside Mr Molloy was waiting for her, his hat tipped over his eyes. He straightened up as he saw her, relieving her of the heavier of her two bags.

'Will the doctors travel with you to Birmingham?' Maribel asked as they passed through the iron gates of the Wild West for the last time. Outside the ticket office was boarded up. The popcorn stalls were gone.

'I don't know,' Molloy said. 'Why?'

'I just wondered.'

There was a silence.

'I keep thinking of Black Elk,' she said. 'About the dream that told him he had to come here.'

'It was a vision.'

'Is that different?'

'Black Elk would say so.'

'What would he say?'

'The Lakota think that, when a man has a vision, he enters the world behind this one where the spirits of all things live. Black Elk would say that world is the real one, and everything in this world is only a shadow.'

'That's not really so different from what Christians believe.'

'I wouldn't know about that.'

'Are you not a Christian, Mr Molloy?'

'Me? I'm not really one for religion. I believe what I know, what I see with my own eyes.'

'And what is that, if I may ask?'

'That Black Elk's people are starving in the reservations. That the less real this world is for them the better.'

20

'EDWARD, DEAR, AT LAST!'

Vivien's delight was plain, as was her irritation. It was past nine o'clock and they had been obliged to begin dinner without him. Maribel smiled up at him and, as he passed her chair, he gently brushed her shoulder with the back of his hand. He smelled of cold fog.

'Apologies, Mother, everyone,' Edward said, taking the proffered seat beside her and accepting a plate of soup. The other guests were already eating poached pheasant with celery. 'Thank you. It has been something of a week.'

'Already? But it is only Tuesday.'

'Don't say that or I shall never make it to Saturday.'

'Oh, Mr Lowe, but you must,' said the American dowager on his other side. 'It is you we are all coming to see.'

'Mrs Rasmussen is throwing a party on Saturday afternoon at Green's hotel,' Vivien explained. 'Apparently the main dining room has several French windows that look out directly over the square.'

'Well, I am not in London long,' Mrs Rasmussen said. 'I wouldn't want to miss all the action.'

'Then march with us, Mrs Rasmussen,' Edward teased. 'We should be glad to furnish you with a flag.'

The old lady laughed girlishly, shaking her jowls.

'It's a tempting offer. I've always rather hankered after a flag.'

'Consider it yours.'

It had finally happened. After months of concerted pressure on the Home Secretary, Warren had finally got his way. The previous Friday, the Commissioner of Police had issued a proclamation summarily announcing that from henceforth it was unlawful to hold public meetings in Trafalgar Square. The ban was in response to a meeting called in the square by the Metropolitan Radical Federation to demand the release of William O'Brien, the Irish MP imprisoned for his part in inciting a rent strike in Cork, a peaceful rally at which the police had opened fire, killing three people. A coroner's jury in Dublin had found the police responsible for all three deaths but the men were never prosecuted. Instead it was O'Brien who had been tried and found guilty. His continued incarceration was for many a sharp reminder of the capacity of a despotic state to exceed its powers.

The protest might ordinarily have been expected to bring out only the usual band of hardliners and troublemakers. Warren's ban, however, carried forward on a building tide of public anxiety about law and order, had done for the Socialists what months of half-hearted compromises had failed to do. It unified them. The great wave of outrage that bore down on them drowned out the bitterest of quarrels. Differences in politics, in principle, in temperament, the faults and failings and festering splits which had been picked over with such obsessive meticulousness, all these were abandoned. For the first time in almost a decade the radicals of London, and a fair number of Liberals too, found themselves bound in common cause. Edward was euphoric.

Henry's old friend Charles de Vere leaned across the table.

'Surely you are not serious, Teddy, old chap,' he said. 'A Member of Parliament attending an illegal demonstration? Won't you be in the most fearful hot water?'

'For what? It is the Commissioner of Police who defies the law, not to mention morality, decency and the fundamental rights of a civilised society. When a British government attempts to outlaw its people's right to peaceful protest what else is a man to do but peacefully protest?'

'Do you honestly believe that the lowest elements of London will be content with that? Last year's protests were intended to be peaceful, remember? Those ruffians broke every window in my club.'

'I would break a few windows myself to protect the fundamental right of the people to freedom of speech,' Edward said. 'We cannot allow Warren's cavalier disregard of English constitutional law to go unchallenged.'

'You cannot challenge it in Parliament, through the proper channels?'

'When the Home Secretary himself shows not the faintest regard for the proper channels, as you call them, one must assume that they have ceased to serve any functional purpose.'

'The Home Secretary does have the small advantage of several thousand police,' Vivien pointed out.

'And the Household Guard, if the *Telegraph* is to be believed,' Charles added.

'But we have the Fourth Estate,' Edward countered. 'Gascoigne at the *Post* and Webster at the *Chronicle* have both come out in favour. The Easter Sunday rally in Hyde Park drew nearly one hundred and fifty thousand people. With the newspapers behind us Hyndman reckons we should get double that. They will not disperse us so easily.'

'Three hundred thousand people,' Maribel said faintly. She had never imagined it would be so many.

'It will be a most extraordinary spectacle,' Mrs Rasmussen said. 'You are quite right to march, Mr Lowe. A man's right to free speech should be inalienable.'

'I hope you mean to ride in on Pampa,' Charles said. 'I can see you now, gaucho cloak tossed over one shoulder, bridle jangling like a Christmas tree.'

'I imagine I shall walk,' Edward said, smiling, but Maribel winced. Even on foot, she knew that his participation would provoke the House. There were already too many Members, even among his own party, who considered him an agitator and an egotist. His participation in the march would, for many, be another proof of his incorrigible exhibitionism.

'You will join my little party, I hope,' Mrs Rasmussen said to Maribel. 'We will provide you with sandwiches and a first-class view of the proceedings.'

'That's most kind, but I am not sure –'

'But of course she will come,' Edward said. 'Mrs Rasmussen and I shall wave at you with our flags.'

Mrs Rasmussen laughed giddily.

'Mr Lowe, truly, you are too much.'

Edward smiled at her. Then he leaned across the table towards Maribel.

'Please, Bo. This is our moment, the one we have been waiting for. They shan't stop us, you know. We shall reclaim Trafalgar Square for the people.'

Edward's face was lit like a boy's. It filled her with tenderness and a sinking sense of foreboding.

'Yes,' she said. 'I know you shall.'

Even Edward knew well enough to keep a low profile during the preparations for the march. The following morning he travelled north to Carlisle. From there he would go to Newcastle and then to Stoke-on-Trent before returning to London early on Sunday morning. It had been recommended that Maribel accompany him. The provincial party faithful liked wives.

Instead, after Edward had left for the station, Maribel went to Turks Row. Though several days had passed since her visit to the Wild West she had not yet had the opportunity to develop the plates and she was curious to see how they had turned out.

To her surprise it was Mr Pidgeon who answered the door when she knocked for the key. It was the first time Maribel had seen him since their contretemps about the photograph. He looked old and tired, his mouth bracketed with deep parentheses. Unhooking the key from its nail, he passed it to her through the gap. The silence was awkward.

'No Thomas here today?' Maribel asked, for something to say.

'He's busy,' he said. 'We have a family due shortly. Eleven children.'

'Heavens. That poor mother.'

The photographer did not answer.

'Well then, I shan't keep you.' She lingered, weighing the key in her hand. 'You know, I saw that photograph you showed me in the *Chronicle*. The widow. I was surprised. I thought you told me not everything in life was for sale.'

Mr Pidgeon frowned but still he said nothing. He turned away.

'Is that what would have happened to my photograph, if you and Mr Webster had persuaded me to sell?' Maribel demanded. 'Would it have been published in his newspaper?'

'Now hold on —'

'You attempted to deceive me, Mr Pidgeon. To take advantage of me.'

'Madam —'

Maribel shook her head.

'I think perhaps it would be best if I found another darkroom. Wouldn't you agree?'

Pidgeon closed his eyes, massaging the arch of his nose with his thumb and forefinger.

'If that is what you wish,' he said.

'You have not left me much choice in the matter.'

'And today?'

'I am here now. I haven't time to take the plates elsewhere.'

'Very well.'

'Send me the account of whatever expenses are outstanding. I shall put the key back through the door when I am finished.'

He watched as she turned and walked away down the corridor towards the darkroom.

'What Webster did was unpardonable,' he said quietly. 'It was beyond the pale.'

Maribel hesitated. She did not turn round.

'He told us that his wife had lost her mother. That the photograph would be a comfort. Afterwards he claimed that he had acted "in the public interest". He said that Mrs Burwood had an obligation to share her experiences with the nation, that glimpses into the next world were a gift to us all. Doubtless he was also aware that impoverished widows are not in a position to sue.'

'Are you saying that the photograph was printed without her permission?'

'Mrs Burwood's sister-in-law shared the photograph with our group in confidence. It was not easy for her. The spirit was her dead brother, to whom she had been greatly attached. She wept when – It was a family matter, a private family matter.'

'And the widow?'

'She knew nothing of Mr Webster's intentions until after the photograph had been published. He has since furnished her with a small cheque by way of reparation.'

'But that's unconscionable.'

'Mrs Burwood is no longer on speaking terms with her sister-in-law. Miss Burwood for her part refuses to see me. The damage is irreparable.'

They were both silent. Mr Pidgeon exhaled heavily, smoothing the lapels of his coat with the palms of his hands. Then he extended his right hand.

'Goodbye then, madam. It has been a pleasure to make your acquaintance and I wish you every success with your photographic endeavours.'

For a moment Maribel hesitated. Then she took his hand and shook it. It was regrettable, but his admissions, as they both knew, made the necessity of finding another darkroom even more pressing. There would be no escaping the awkwardness between them now.

'Goodbye, Mr Pidgeon. I shall return the key when I am finished.'

From the bottom of the stairs came the slam of a door. A cacophony of children's chatter filled the stairwell.

'Children,' an exhausted voice protested. 'Children, please.'

Maribel gave Mr Pidgeon a small smile.

'*Bonne chance*,' she murmured.

He shook his head, raising his eyes to heaven, and hurried to the head of the stairs to greet them.

21

THE FOLLOWING DAY SHE lunched with Charlotte in Piccadilly. An exhibition of Old Masters, several of which had never before been shown in England, had recently opened at the Royal Academy and Maribel, eager for distraction in Edward's absence, had persuaded Charlotte to go with her. They met at Vaizey's, a tea shop in the Oriental style in a narrow street off St James's Square. Convenient not only for the Academy but for the shopping emporia of Regent Street, it was one of a handful in the vicinity considered respectable for ladies lunching without a gentleman escort. The room was attractive, arranged into alcoves colonnaded with narrow pillars, while, in its centre, above an extravagant arrangement of ferns, an octagonal glass cupola trimmed with filigreed brass sifted onto the polished floor the pale grey light of the autumn afternoon. The coffered ceiling was gilded and painted with stars. As befitted its clientele, the restaurant was staffed entirely by women.

Charlotte and Maribel followed their waitress to a table in the far corner of the room. Around them feathered and beribboned bonnets ducked and swayed like a meadow of exotic flowers. Although the baby was not due for another three months Charlotte had already grown fat and she sighed with pleasure as she sat down, smoothing her starched napkin over the jut of her stomach.

'That's better,' she said. 'My feet are so swollen I can barely get my boots on.' Taking the menu from the waitress she opened it, running her finger down the page.

'Shall we have roast chicken?' she asked Maribel. 'I have the most atrocious craving for roast chicken. Heaven knows what that signifies about the baby.'

'That it is unlikely that it is a chicken?'

'One can but hope. Although a chicken might stand a better chance of mastering Latin than Georgie.'

'Talking of Georgie, I brought this.' From her bag Maribel extracted a copy of her photograph of the Indian child reading his upside-down adventure story. 'I thought he might think it amusing.'

The waitress cleared her throat. Charlotte smiled at her.

'Oysters, I think,' she said. 'And then most assuredly roast chicken. Oh, and ginger beer.' She eyed Maribel across the table. 'You agree, don't you, dearest? If we don't decide now we never shall.'

'That sounds perfect.'

Charlotte handed the menu back to the waitress and held out her hand for the photograph.

'But that's wonderful! And fearfully funny with him clutching his penny dreadful. Georgie will be tickled pink.' She turned the photograph over. 'The photographer's stamp. You used it.'

'Of course I used it. I use it all the time.'

Charlotte smiled, her gaze moving idly over the room. Suddenly she ducked, raising the photograph between them like a fan.

'Don't look now but there is Esther Allbright lunching with Lady Coningham. Let's pray they don't see us. Americans are so extraordinary about pregnancy. The agonies they suffer trying not to notice, you would think it was syphilis.'

Maribel glanced over.

'I think you are safe there. From what I hear Esther Allbright is so nearsighted she only recognises her own husband at two paces.'

She nodded towards a wan-faced lady seated alone at a small table near the entrance to the kitchen. As she studied the menu, the lady frowned, jotting with a pencil in a small notebook by her knife. Her hands were small and pink as a mouse's paws.

'What about that one, though?' she said. 'What can she be writing so furiously? Do you think she is working out what she can afford to eat?'

Charlotte considered the woman for a moment.

'Her hat is new. And look at that pearl brooch. No, she means to set up a rival restaurant. She is taking notes on the menu so that she can steal the best dishes.'

'Either that or she is setting it to music. Something jovially Continental, with a part for a squeezebox.'

'Now that is just silly. Her hair is much too neatly pinned for a composer and look at how cross she is. I have it. She is writing the definitive New Woman novel. *A Table for One*. It will be a devastating critique of female education, marriage, the shackles of motherhood and the emancipation of fish with parsley sauce.'

It was a thoroughly cheerful lunch. Afterwards the two women made their way arm in arm along Duke Street towards the Academy under the canopy of Charlotte's umbrella. The afternoon was still and the fine rain hung in the air in veils. At Piccadilly the traffic was at a standstill. They picked their way cautiously between the carriages.

'You know, we could skip the exhibition and go to Burlington Arcade,' Charlotte suggested as they reached the other side. 'I've had over three hundred years to see Titian's *Charles V*. Another week or so won't hurt.'

Maribel shook her head.

'You will not corrupt me,' she said. 'I promised Edward faithfully I would not go shopping.'

'You had no business making promises like that without consulting me first.'

'It is for your own good. If you so much as glimpsed the

horrors of our estate accounts you would go into labour on the spot.'

'That bad?'

'Worse.'

Charlotte clicked her tongue, squeezing Maribel's arm.

'For heaven's sake don't say anything to Arthur,' Maribel said. 'Edward would never forgive me.'

'Not a word, I promise.'

At the junction with Bond Street they stopped as a dray inveigled itself into a gap large enough for a two-wheeled trap. An omnibus driver shouted angrily, brandishing his whip.

'You wouldn't have to shop,' Charlotte said. 'You could carry my packages.'

'That's quite enough from you, young lady. We are going to see these paintings if I have to carry you in myself.'

Despite the respectful notices the exhibition had received in the newspapers the gallery was almost empty. Charlotte had gone on ahead and, apart from an elderly man in a homburg hat and spectacles, Maribel was quite alone. She stood in front of Rubens's *Fall of Man*, her head on one side as she considered the painting. She remembered Oscar's friend Rex Whistler telling her that, as an old man in his fifties, the widowed Rubens had married a girl of just sixteen years old and it was her voluptuous figure that had served as the model for the most famous works of his career. She wondered if this picture was one of those. There was something in the way that Adam reached for Eve, his hand at her breast, his thumb brushing her nipple as she stretched up to pluck the apple, that spoke not just of warning but of unashamed desire.

A woman came to stand beside her. Maribel moved a little to her right, not taking her eyes from the painting. A tousle-headed Cupid leaned down from the branches of the tree, holding out the apple to Eve in a plump fist. Magnificent in her naked-ness, Eve gazed back at the infant, her hand extended, her expression dazed with love, oblivious to Adam and his admonitions. Around the apple their fingers touched. In this way, Rubens seemed to be saying, Adam is expelled from Paradise and every man after him, shut out by the impregnable intimacy of mother and child.

The woman beside her was standing very close, her breathing shallow as a spaniel's. Maribel felt a shimmer of irritation.

'Peg – I mean, Maribel?'

Maribel turned. The woman was Edith, one hand over her mouth. Her eyes were very round. She bounced a little on the balls of her feet.

'I can't believe it!' she hissed in a stage whisper. 'I saw you in the other room but I thought my eyes were playing tricks on me. What are you doing here?'

'Edith.' Furtively Maribel glanced about. The man in the homburg was gone. In the frame of an open doorway she could see an elderly couple conversing in the adjacent room, a guard in uniform staring slack-jawed at the floor.

'Are you here alone?' Edith asked.

'With a friend. I should go.'

'Must you really?'

'She might come back at any moment. It would not do to have to explain.'

'No. No, of course not. I can't believe you're here. Who would have imagined?'

'Goodbye, Edith.'

Edith's mouth snapped shut and her shoulders sagged.

'You're right, of course. Goodbye, Peggy. I mean, Maribel. Sorry. It is only that I . . .'

Maribel hesitated. Then she leaned forward and gave her sister a fleeting kiss on the cheek.

'It was nice to see you, Edith,' she said.

'I am here with Ida.'

Maribel froze.

'I thought she needed cheering up, getting out, you know, well, she's been so gloomy lately, one can't seem to snap her out of it, but the silly thing only went and dropped her gloves. A brand-new pair apparently. Well, of course when I saw how upset she was I said I would buy her another pair, Horace wouldn't mind, he wouldn't ever have to know, but she got quite angry with me about it, I can't think why, and she stormed off. I imagine she went back to the entrance hall to see if anyone has handed them in. Perhaps this is her now.'

Flustered, she glanced over Maribel's shoulder. Maribel pressed her hands together, her eyes on the parquet floor. Her heart was tight as a fist. A double-chinned matron bustled past, a pale young girl trailing three paces behind her.

'Eyes ahead, Eugenia,' the matron commanded. 'There is nothing for us in here.'

The parquet was in need of a polish. Abruptly the thought of seeing Ida filled Maribel with panic. It was too sudden, too soon. She was not ready.

'I have to go,' she said.

'May I tell her I saw you? I mean, I know it is supposed to be a secret but —'

'Goodbye, Edith.'

She fled. She found Charlotte seated on an upright chair in the atrium, her hands crossed demurely over her swollen stomach and her eyes half closed. She blinked sleepily at Maribel.

'Dearest, whatever is the matter?'

'We have to go.'

Charlotte frowned, hauling herself awkwardly out of her chair.

'Are you all right?' she asked.

'Of course. I need some air, that's all. Come on.'

'I'm coming, I'm coming. Hang on a moment. I have to fetch my umbrella.'

The cloakroom attendant was an elderly man with a luxurious white moustache. Maribel shifted from foot to foot as he took

Charlotte's ticket, enquiring after the exhibition and lamenting the inclemency of the weather. When at last he brought the umbrella she had to stop herself from snatching it out of his hands.

Outside the rain had grown heavy. Beneath the arches of the Academy Charlotte paused to raise her umbrella.

'Wait,' she called to Maribel. 'You will get soaked.'

Maribel turned impatiently.

'Then hurry up.'

The shallow stone steps were greasy with rain. In her haste Charlotte lost her footing and fell heavily. She cried out, a sharp yelp of shock and pain, her bag and umbrella tumbling from her grasp.

'Charlotte!' Maribel exclaimed, stricken. Snatching up her skirts she flew to where Charlotte lay sprawled across the steps, her right arm bent awkwardly to one side. Her face was very white. She tried to raise her head.

'My arm,' she whimpered.

Maribel nodded, kneeling beside her.

'I know,' she said, stroking her hair. 'Just don't move, darling. You mustn't move.'

'The baby —'

'Oh God, Charlotte. It's not coming, is it?'

Charlotte shook her head and gasped, her face tightening with pain. Rain spangled her hair, her skirts, her pinched face. Maribel cast frantically about her. The courtyard was deserted, the rain falling in broad sweeps. Beside her Charlotte whimpered and closed her eyes. Maribel felt the panic clotting her chest.

'Help!' she cried. 'Somebody, please help!'

The rain sighed and thickened. It was growing dark.

'Don't move,' she whispered to Charlotte. 'I'm going for help.'

Charlotte whimpered again. The angle of her arm was sickening. Maribel stroked her forehead, her hand trembling, and scrambled to her feet. Stumbling a little she ran to the door of the Academy, flinging it open. It was bright in the lobby, the gas lamps lit. The old man in the cloakroom looked up.

'Fetch a doctor,' she cried. 'There's been an accident.'

'An accident? What kind of accident?'

Maribel turned. In the lobby two ladies stood close together, their faces shadowy beneath the raised hoods of their cloaks. The one who had spoken held a furled umbrella. Her hands were bare. The other was Edith.

'She needs a doctor,' Maribel said faintly. 'She fell. On the steps. She's pregnant. I think she may have broken her arm.'

'Is someone with her?'

It was Ida. She looked no different than she had at ten years old. Perhaps there were lines about the mouth, a faint dustiness to her skin, but it was her, her heart-shaped face, her freckled nose, her bright brown eyes with the flecks like pollen around the pupils. There was no mark upon her to show that she had borne a child, that she had lost a child. She was barely more than a child herself. Maribel stared at her sister and she wanted only to fall into her arms, to weep, to kiss her precious face and stroke her hair and breathe in her Ida smell until her lungs burst. She had never held Ida, except during a performance. In those days they had neither of them had much time for caresses.

Maribel shook her head.

'There's nobody,' she whispered. 'Please come.'

Ida nodded, raising her umbrella to the cloakroom attendant.

'A doctor at the double, if you please. You have brandy? Then once the doctor is summoned, please fetch it and bring it out. Edith, come with me.'

Edith nodded, her mouth open, as Ida followed Maribel out into the rain.

'You have not tried to move her, I hope?'

266

'No.'

On the stone steps Charlotte had closed her eyes. Her lips were white, her breathing shallow. Bundling up her skirts Maribel sat beside her, taking her good hand in hers. It was damp and very cold. She set it against her cheek and tried not to pretend that it was Ida's.

'Hold on, darling,' she said, the tears spiking in her throat. 'Just hold on. The doctor will be here any moment, I promise you.'

'Is she all right?' Edith asked in a loud whisper. 'Is it a concussion?'

'She has fainted,' Ida said briskly. 'And she is extremely wet.'

'I have salts,' Edith offered and she slipped her hands inside her cloak, fumbling with the clasp of her bag. Ida shook her head.

'It is the pain. She is better off as she is. Are those hers?' She pointed to the bag and the umbrella at the bottom of the steps. 'Bring them here. And Edith? Open this.'

She had always been practical, Maribel thought, even as a child. She watched as Ida handed Edith her own umbrella and unfastened her cloak, laying it over Charlotte like a blanket. Underneath the cloak Ida wore a paisley shawl, pinned with a brooch. She undid the brooch, carefully sheathing the pin before slipping it into her pocket, and rolled the shawl into a pillow which she slid beneath Charlotte's head. Charlotte stirred, whimpering quietly. Ida murmured reassurances as she took the two umbrellas from Maribel and Edith, propping them against the steps to create a canopy. 'You'll get wet,' Edith said.

Ida shrugged and handed Maribel Charlotte's bag. She did not look at her.

'My arm is not broken,' she said.

Maribel hugged the bag on her lap and gazed down at her friend's damp, white face, the tails of hair plastered on her forehead. Her breathing was shallow and capillaries sketched faint purple lines in the translucent skin of her eyelids.

'She will be all right, won't she?' she asked pleadingly.

'The doctor will be here soon.'

'And the baby?'

Ida crossed her arms across her chest, rubbing briskly at her upper arms with the palms of her hands.

'That is a matter for the doctor.'

Maribel looked up at her sister. Drops of rainwater clung like lace to the brim of her ugly brown hat.

'I'm so sorry, Ida. About what happened.'

Ida did not answer. They waited in silence. After a time Charlotte's eyelids fluttered and she moaned softly to herself. Very gently Maribel stroked her face, her hair, and still the doctor did not come.

'Where is that fool with the brandy?' Edith said after a while. 'I can't imagine why it's taking so long.'

No one answered. Edith pleated the edge of her cloak between her fingers.

'Immediately, that was the instruction,' she went on. 'An ignoramus could not have failed to grasp the urgency of the situation. A doctor, then brandy.'

It was quite dark now. The gaslights in the courtyard fringed the rain with gold.

'Perhaps I should . . .' Edith said, gesturing towards the lobby.

'Yes,' Ida said. 'Why don't you?'

'I think I should.'

Nodding firmly, she bustled up the steps. Across the courtyard a figure in a dark slick coat hurried, an umbrella held aloft. Then he vanished. Maribel smoothed Charlotte's hair from her forehead.

'It won't be long now, dearest,' she murmured. 'The doctor is on his way.'

She stroked Charlotte's damp cheek with a curled finger. Charlotte closed her eyes.

'I think she's fainted again,' she said.

'Bloody doctor,' Ida said, scowling into the darkness. 'Where the devil is he?'

Immediately Maribel was in the orchard at Ellerton, Ida beside her crossly rattling the bucket of pony nuts for the fat little Shetland that hid when you called it.

'Oh, Ida,' she whispered, swallowing the lump in her throat. 'You have no idea how much I've missed you.'

'I told that idiot doorman that we needed someone straight away. I couldn't have made it plainer.'

'When Edith told me you were in London – forgive me.' With the back of one hand Maribel brushed away the tears that spilled from her eyes. 'It's just – Oh, Ida, your baby. I'm so very sorry. I wish I'd had the chance to meet her.'

Ida made a strangled noise. She bent down, busying herself with the umbrellas.

'Ida, look at me, please. If you knew how many times I wished I had taken you with me . . .'

For a moment there was silence. Maribel held tight to Charlotte's hand. Then Ida exhaled sharply.

'Peggy, please –'

'We were going to have a house in Regent's Park, do you remember?'

'Were we? Mother always did say we children talked a lot of nonsense.'

'I didn't think it was nonsense.'

'No. Well.'

Abruptly there came the sound of voices. The door opened, spilling light into the darkening night.

'I have him,' called Edith triumphantly. 'I have the doctor.'

Ida raised her hand.

'Over here,' she called. Then she knelt down next to Charlotte, two fingers feeling for the pulse in her wrist. 'The doctor's here now. Everything's going to be all right.'

'Write to me,' Maribel whispered and she folded her card into Ida's free hand. 'Promise you'll write to me.'

Ida did not reply Gently she adjusted the shawl beneath Charlotte's head. Then, smoothing her skirts, she stood.

'Goodness me, Doctor,' she said. 'I thought you'd never come.'

22

CHARLOTTE LAY IN BED, propped up with pillows, her arm in its casing of plaster of Paris set on a velvet cushion by her side. She was pale with a bruised look about the eyes, but the doctor had assured Arthur that she was as comfortable as could be expected. She had broken the radius, he explained, one of the two bones which ran from elbow to wrist, and the break would take some weeks to heal. Morphine pills would ease the pain. As for the baby, it was quite unharmed.

'She is to rest,' Arthur said, wagging a finger at his wife. 'Do not let her tell you otherwise. There will be no sledding down the staircase for a month or two.'

Charlotte held out her good hand to Maribel.

'Dearest,' she said.

'Look at you.'

'I know. The children call me the Egyptian mummy.'

'Perhaps if you were to paint the cast it would look more cheerful?' Arthur suggested. 'Something uplifting. Florence Nightingale with her lamp, perhaps, or the dying moments of Admiral Nelson. Ursie is longing to try out her new watercolours.'

'Please make my husband go to his office,' Charlotte said, pressing Maribel's hand.

'Do you hear her, Maribel? She would have me thrown out of my own home!'

'You know quite well you want nothing more,' Charlotte

protested. 'You maraud around a sickroom like a tiger in a zoo.'

Arthur smiled.

'Very well,' he said. 'But I shall be home in time for tea.'

'You are the dearest man in the world but you shall do no such thing. I know how busy you are at present. We shall manage very well without you.'

'In that, Mrs Arthur Charterhouse, you are sorely mistaken. We have great plans for your entertainment, the children and I. If you cannot come downstairs then it is our considered opinion that downstairs will have to come to you.' He kissed her tenderly on the cheek. 'Take care of my wife, Maribel.'

'I shall do my best.'

'And no smoking in the sickroom, do you hear me?' he added, raising a warning finger. 'You shall not poison Charlotte in her own bed.'

'Goodbye, dearest.'

The door clicked shut behind him. Charlotte sighed, closing her eyes.

'Are you in pain?' Maribel asked.

'Just a little tired.'

'Shall I leave you?'

'No. I am just resting for a moment. Then we shall have Hannah bring tea.'

Maribel watched as Charlotte's face slackened and her breathing grew deeper. On the counterpane her good hand turned slowly outwards, the fingers uncurling like a flower. Then, setting the package of books she had brought for Charlotte on the bedside table, she tiptoed over to the wing-backed chair. She was in no hurry. In her pocket she had *She*, the new novel by H. Rider Haggard, which she had purchased with not a little shame and the certain knowledge that many of their circle dismissed it as drivel. She settled herself, opening the book with a sigh of pleasure.

'Did she tell you who she was?' Charlotte murmured some time later.

Maribel dragged herself away from the lost kingdom of Kôr. 'What is that, dearest?'

'The lady at the Academy. The one who helped me. Did she tell you her name?'

Maribel folded her hands, running the tips of her thumbs over her lips. The sudden urge for a cigarette made her cough. She pressed a palm to her chest.

'Her name? Let me think. No, I don't believe she did. Does it matter?'

Charlotte blinked and tried to sit up, sending a spasm of pain skittering across her face.

'Do you need something?' Maribel asked anxiously. 'A pill? Something to drink? Shall I call for Hannah?'

'Stop fussing. You are as bad as Arthur.'

'Perhaps I could dance for you. Pull an egg out of your ear. Recite a poem.' She struck a pose. '*Into the valley of Death rode the six hundred.*'

'Stop it.'

'Some water then?'

'Very well. But only if you promise it will shut you up.'

Maribel held out the glass and Charlotte drank. Then she leaned back against the pillows. The effort had clearly tired her.

'I just wish I had the lady's name,' she said. 'I still have her shawl.'

'What, here?'

'Not in this room, obviously. I think Hannah took it for laundering.'

It was a strange feeling, knowing that something of Ida's was here, in the house.

'Do you think perhaps if I enquired at the Academy?' Charlotte said. 'She might have left an address. It was not a good shawl. Still, one ought to return it. I understand she was very kind.'

'Yes. She was.'

Charlotte sighed, smiling wearily at Maribel.

'Dearest Maribel. What a clumsy muff I am. What in heaven would I have done if you had not been there to rescue me?'

'If I had not been in so much of a hurry you would not have fallen in the first place.'

'Of course I would. Look at me. I don't need your help to trip over my own feet.'

'I am sorry, all the same.'

There was a knock on the door.

'Yes?'

Hannah put her head into the room.

'The doctor's here to see you, ma'am.'

'Very well. Show him up.'

'I should go,' Maribel said. 'I shall come again tomorrow.'

'Thank you for the books. When I asked Arthur for something he brought *Beowulf.*'

Maribel grinned.

'You can have *She* as soon as I am done with it.' She hesitated, her wrap bundled in her arms. 'I shall be in Piccadilly later. Shall I enquire for you, about the shawl lady?'

'Wouldn't it be a bother?'

'No bother at all.'

'Well, then, yes, thank you.'

When Maribel bent to kiss her, Charlotte caught her hand, her pale face tender.

'Yesterday at the exhibition,' she said. 'Something frightened you. What was it?'

'Frightened me?' Maribel shrugged. 'I remember thinking that very bloody St Sebastian by what's-his-name rather gruesome.'

When Charlotte did not smile Maribel made a face.

'Oh, Charlotte!' she remonstrated. 'With all that's happened, yesterday feels two lifetimes ago. How on earth can you expect me to remember?'

*

The attendant at the Royal Academy was apologetic. No one had notified them about a lost shawl. Maribel left Charlotte's address in case the lady should ask for it and went home. Later that afternoon she wrote to Edith. She thanked her for her kindnesses and assured her that the patient and her unborn child were recovering well. She wrote of Charlotte's wish to thank her Good Samaritans and to return Ida's shawl and suggested that, to be quite certain to avoid any difficulties, both Edith and Ida write directly to the Academy on headed writing paper, enquiring after the injured woman. In this way the addresses might be secured without any connection being made between themselves and Maribel.

Mother has been through enough, she wrote. *We must think of Mother.*

She paused, her pen hovering above the paper. Then, in a rapid scrawl, she drew the letter to a close.

> *I shall not write again. Should we ever cross paths again I*
> *think it best we do not speak. If you would be kind enough to*
> *send Ida's address by return I will write the same to her.*
> *M*

23

THE SUNDAY OF THE protest was a bleak day even for November, with a hard ground frost and a raw north-easterly wind. By midday the low sky threatened rain. In St James's Park the trees were bare, the lawns clotted with mud, and the few ducks on the pond huddled together as the icy breeze whipped the water into peaks. As Maribel's hansom edged around the perimeter wall of Buckingham Palace towards the Mall, the crush of traffic slowed and then stopped altogether. Maribel was required to make the last part of her journey by foot.

Four days had passed and she had heard nothing from Ida. Each morning, as Alice brought the post to the breakfast table, she had allowed her hopes to rise but to no avail. Ida was grieving, of course. She mourned her lost child. Maribel knew how grief unhooked one's will, made the smallest action unimaginable. She tried not to think of Ida's brisk efficiency at the Academy. Ida would write when she was ready, when the pain had cleared enough to permit her to imagine a future. Maribel could wait, at least until she received Ida's address from Edith. It exasperated her that Edith did not write. It was her own fault, Maribel thought bitterly as she forced her way through the crush towards the elaborate facade of Green's hotel. Her letter had both requested an answer and forbidden it. She could almost picture the confusion tugging at Edith's foolish mouth as she tried to decipher what was required of her. Maribel did not dare write again. Meanwhile she closed her eyes, summoning again the memory of Ida's hand closing around her card on the steps of the Academy, and wished with all the clench-faced determination of a child for Ida to uncurl her fingers and relent.

The crowds on the pavements, though thick, were orderly, but at Green's security was tight. A barrier had been erected in front of the revolving glass doors of the hotel and Maribel was required to show her invitation to the policeman there and again to a uniformed doorman in the lobby before she was permitted to enter the lift which would take her to the first floor. The rooms that Mrs Rasmussen had taken for her party were elegant and spacious with high ceilings and three pairs of French windows, through which it was possible to see Nelson's Column and the slate-grey dome of the National Gallery. Half-circles of upright gilt chairs had been arranged in front of the windows for spectators but as yet they were mostly unoccupied. It was still early. The Socialist marchers, whose intention was to converge upon the square from all directions simultaneously, were not expected for another half-hour at least.

Mrs Rasmussen greeted Maribel warmly, a snuffle-nosed dog clamped beneath one arm. She attempted to steer her towards a group of people gathered around the fireplace but instead Maribel took a champagne saucer from a waiter in white gloves and crossed the room to the windows. They opened onto a dropping-flecked stone balcony but, when she tried the handle of one, she found it locked. It hardly mattered. Even through the glass the window afforded an almost uninterrupted view of Trafalgar Square. Like most Americans Mrs Rasmussen understood the value of spectacle.

The prospect that greeted her did nothing to ease Maribel's anxiety. The sunken area at the centre of the square had been closed and ranks of mounted police in heavy cloaks scored strict black lines over the mouths of all the streets that emptied into it. Along its southern side, below the window in which Maribel stood, a line of grim-faced policemen stood four deep, their elbows touching. On the other three sides she could make out two ranks of helmets, tightly massed, while to the north, beneath the impervious facade of the National Gallery, further masses of policemen stopped up the steps that led from the street to the fountains. It was impossible to imagine how the marchers might breach such stalwart defences.

She took a sip of her champagne, feeling the fizz of it on her tongue. The party was filling up and the room was stuffy and uncomfortably warm. Behind her she could hear Mrs Rasmussen's tinkling laugh as she greeted her guests, the muffled yaps of her adenoidal dog. Waiters moved around the room, filling glasses, offering sandwiches and savouries. The time was drawing nearer. Below the hotel balcony a substantial crowd was gathered about the police perimeter, among them a considerable number of women and children. Many were ragged but a great many more were not. Groups of gentlemen in whiskers and good coats clustered on steps and in porches, gazing about them with the detached curiosity of tourists. Several carried pairs of binoculars on leather straps around their necks. The noise of the crowd seeped through the gaps in the window frames like the sound of the sea.

She craned her neck, combing the crowd for his hat, but she could not make out Edward among the swarms of men. Perhaps he meant to lead one of the groups of marchers with their banners and their drums. She did not know. He had left Cadogan Mansions several hours earlier, telling her only as he snatched up his hat that he was to meet John Burns and that they would march on the square together.

The electricity in him had frightened Maribel. It was Burns who had spoken with great violence at the demonstration in the square nearly two years before, Burns who had notoriously unfurled a red flag and waved it above his head, shouting that 'unless we get bread they must get lead'. It was Burns who had declared hanging too good for landlords and capitalists and had incited the mob to smash windows and plunder shops. If Edward had chosen Burns as his companion, it was blood that he wanted. In the centre of the square, circled like wagons, were three windowless Black Marias.

'Mr Webster,' Mrs Rasmussen trilled behind her. 'How good of you to come.'

Maribel turned too abruptly, spilling her champagne. She brushed ineffectually at her skirts as the dark stain feathered and spread. Immediately a waiter materialised at her elbow, brandishing a linen napkin and a bottle with which to refill her glass. She waved him away impatiently, glancing over her shoulder. Mr Webster was watching her. He smiled at her over Mrs Rasmussen's head, touching the tips of his fingers to his forehead in a kind of salute. Frowning, she looked quickly away, fumbling for her cigarettes. If Edward had known Mr Webster was invited he would not have let her come. That morning, when he had left the flat, jabbing his fingers into his gloves, Edward had seen the copy of the *City Chronicle* on the hall table. Snatching up his hat he had swept it to the floor.

'That stupid sensationalist bastard,' he had said bitterly. 'He will have blood on his hands tonight.'

He had slammed the door behind him as he left, the force of it fluttering the scattered pages of the newspaper. Maribel had not picked it up. She could not bring herself to touch it.

'Mrs Campbell Lowe, how nice to see you. Is it begun?'

Maribel turned to see Lady Worsley standing behind her, a cup of tea in one gloved hand. The two women greeted one another affectionately, gazing side by side down into the square. The crowd was growing restless. Men jostled and shouted. A small boy wormed his way through the crush and threw a stone at a policeman.

'Are you quite well?' Lady Worsley asked. 'You look as though you've seen a ghost.'

'No ghost. Just Mr Webster.'

'Ah. That would do it.'

'I don't know how he has the nerve to show his face. I am only glad Edward is not here. I don't think I have ever seen him so angry.'

Lady Worsley shook her head.

'He brought the page with him, did you see? In case any of us should have missed it.'

She nodded towards the fireplace. Propped on the mantel in a large gilt frame was the front page of the previous day's *Chronicle*. Its headline trumpeted in large bold capitals quite legible even from the distance of the window: ONWARD, CHRISTIAN SOLDIERS.

Maribel's jaw clenched and the squirm in her stomach hardened into a knot. For days the Socialists had worked tirelessly, rallying working men and women from across the metropolis. This would be, they proclaimed, the largest demonstration of its kind ever seen in London. From suburbs around the capital, from Peckham and Bermondsey, from Battersea and Deptford and Clerkenwell, tens of thousands of men and women and children would march unarmed to defy the Commissioner's arbitrary decree and defend their constitutional right to public protest. The tide of opinion was so strong that the Home Secretary himself had been forced formally to address the House on the matter, offering an assurance that bona fide meetings would not be interfered with.

It was only on Thursday evening, when all the arrangements had been completed, that the Home Secretary had issued an order forbidding processions within the central part of the square. Shaken, the Socialists called an emergency meeting. They would go to the square as arranged, they decided. They would conduct their peaceful demonstration. If challenged by the police, they would protest formally against the illegal prohibition.

The *City Chronicle* had no such scruples. For weeks Webster's newspaper had steadfastly supported the Socialists' endeavour, publishing a series of articles and printing letters from influential radicals, Edward and William Morris among them. The Home Secretary's order, however, provoked a quite unprecedented response. Dismissing peaceful protest as no more than a fly-swat in the face of a bloodthirsty lion, Webster had called upon the people of London to converge upon Trafalgar Square with all the arms they could muster. Peaceful protest was impossible. It was time for a mighty and violent crusade against repression and injustice.

Appalled, the Socialists could only watch as immediately, and in a fever of furious horror, London's conservative newspapers seized upon the story. Front pages across the capital declared Webster's diatribe criminally irresponsible, an incitement to riot. They claimed, of course, that this was what the Socialists had wanted all along, that Webster was the puppet of the SDF and the Socialist League, that, far from the peaceful demonstration that they claimed to want, the Socialists longed for a bloodbath. Calls were made for a doubling, a tripling of the police presence in Trafalgar Square. Londoners were warned to barricade themselves in. Not since the Sink of Iniquity had the *City Chronicle* been so much on everyone's lips.

'It seems he will have publicity whatever the cost,' Lady Worsley said quietly. 'Poor John. That his newspaper, his chosen successor – it is very difficult for him.'

'Lord Worsley is here?'

'No. He is – indisposed. My nephew accompanied me.'

'Ah.'

'And Mr Campbell Lowe?'

'He is down there,' she said. 'Somewhere.'

Edward had thought Webster on their side. Ragingly egocentric, certainly, sensationalist too, perhaps even a little mad, but ideologically a radical. One of them. It had never occurred to

Edward that Webster would requisition the forces of Socialism for the greater glory of himself and his newspaper.

The party was drifting over to the windows. Out of the corner of her eye Maribel saw Mrs Rasmussen chivvying her guests towards the circles of chairs. On the other side of the room Mr Webster said something to a group of gentlemen, who laughed and settled themselves in the window furthest from her. If she was lucky, she thought with a flicker of relief, they might contrive to avoid speaking to one another altogether. She glanced at the mantelpiece but the framed copy of the *Chronicle* was no longer there. No doubt, like everyone else, Mrs Rasmussen had considered the gesture in execrable taste. The seats around her were filling up. She nodded at those with whom she was acquainted but she did not sit down. She remained at the window, one hand against the glass, all of her attention once more upon the square. Thousands of people now choked the perimeter, pressing in on the wall of policemen that defended its interior. The mood, it seemed, was souring. In several places the black line broke and re-formed as skirmishes broke out. Bricks were thrown and punches, batons raised. Mounted policemen urged their horses through the crowd, churning the dense mass, their truncheons thrust like bayonets. Men raised their arms, holding their elbows over their heads. Maribel scoured the crowd anxiously for Edward.

'Where are the marchers?' she said. 'Should they not be here by now?'

A small and dapper gentleman in an impeccable tweed suit leaned forward, one elbow upon his knee.

'I fear there is not the slightest chance of the marchers making it this far,' he said. His accent was American.

Maribel frowned.

'Why on earth not?'

The American smiled and introduced himself as Mr Ackermann. A newspaperman from Boston, he had been in London three months.

'Warren learned his warcraft in darkest Africa,' Mr Ackermann explained. 'He will have no intention of allowing tribes of savages to fight together and on their chosen turf. Don't you agree, Bellingfield?'

Bellingfield, a long, thin man with a face like an emaciated racehorse, nodded.

'Quite right,' he agreed.

'But there are to be three hundred thousand of them,' Maribel said. 'How can he hope to stop them?'

'The Commissioner has twenty thousand constables and the Home Secretary breathing down his neck. After last year do you think he wishes to fight another pitched battle here in the square? Of course not. He will have mobilised his forces to intercept the protesters on their way. Tactically he has the advantage. Confront the marchers by blocking their route, then use the side streets to allow an attack on the flanks as well as to the front. Despite Mr Webster's war whoops in the *Chronicle* most will not be armed. Act decisively and you disarm the columns before they come together, thus preventing a combined show of force.'

'Only the most determined and well-organised militia would have a chance of breaching those defences,' the horse-faced man said.

'Does that sound like the Socialists to you?' Mr Ackermann asked, and they both laughed. Maribel did not laugh.

'Surely it cannot be necessary to have quite so many policemen?' she said quietly to Lady Worsley.

'They seem to have taken no chances,' Lady Worsley admitted.

Mr Ackermann shrugged.

'After last February's debacle what choice do they have?' he said. 'London requires them to keep order and keep order they will. They know that for every man intent upon peaceful protest there are ten roughs who wish for nothing more than broken windows and stolen property. The unemployed may insist upon their right to gather, to demonstrate, but it is rascaldom that has made this square its headquarters these past weeks and it is the honest working man who pays the price.'

'The unemployed in London have rightful grievances,' Maribel said stiffly.

'That is true but it is not they who gather today. The men down there are unemployed only in the sense that they would refuse every honest employment that might be offered them.'

Maribel's mouth tightened.

'If there are ruffians among the crowd Mr Webster is entirely to blame for it,' she said. 'The Socialists want only to defend their right to peaceful protest.'

Mr Ackermann raised an eyebrow, glancing over his shoulder at Mr Webster, who stood at the other end of the room, looking out of the window with his hands in his pockets.

'Mr Webster has added his five cents, of that there is no doubt. But the Socialists are disingenuous. Your English working class has a profound regard for law and order. Were it not for the lumpen seeking the immediate redistribution of wealth from the shops of the West End, the crowd down there would number no more than a few hundred.'

The fact that she knew the American to be right did not endear him to Maribel. She took a cigarette from her case and set it between her lips. She did not offer him one.

'You do not share this gentleman's cynicism, do you, Lady Worsley?' she asked, striking a match, but Rose Worsley only sighed and shook her head.

'I do not hold out much hope for the protesters,' she said. 'Ruffian or Socialist, it hardly matters, does it? This government thinks one as criminal as the other and deals with them accordingly. Marches such as this one simply harden their resolve.'

'The poor are starving in the streets and the Home Secretary would seal their mouths shut,' Maribel protested, Edward's words rising easily to her lips. 'What can we do but march?

How else can we force the Tories to attend to the miseries of the poor?'

The roar rose up from the square so suddenly it seemed that it might knock the glass from the windows. In the parlour of Green's hotel the guests gasped. Mr Ackermann rose to his feet. Across the square, coming from the direction of the Strand, a mass of protesters, banners aloft, stormed the lines of the police. In an answering surge the crowd below the balcony pressed forward. There were women among the crowd, and children too, their heads half submerged as the rushing flood carried them on. Immediately, with the oiled authority of a machine, the first rank of mounted police moved forward, the horses driving into the crowd, while from all sides policemen on foot armed with truncheons and batons weighed into the fray. Men lashed out with fists, hurled stones. They brandished sticks and cudgels, striking wildly above their heads. Arms linked, they charged the unyielding ranks of the foot policemen, throwing themselves bodily against the wall of serge. The air was thick with shouting, the sickening sounds of blows.

Maribel saw two men seize the bridle of a police horse, dragging the creature's head down so that the animal stumbled. The policeman on its back raised his arm, his mouth a black hole in his face, and struck one of the men across the head with his stick, over and over, the blows like the striking of a clock, until the blood ran down the protester's face and he fell, disappearing from view. Beside him a policeman's face contorted as he kicked out with his heavy boots. Maribel pressed so close to the window that her breath clouded the glass, but he did not get up. If the policeman did not kill him, she thought with a sick lurch of her stomach, his fellows would trample him to death.

Somewhere in the madness was Edward. The crowd twisted and writhed as the first rank of mounted police, the solidity of their line unbroken, moved forward with the oiled authority of a great black machine. The protesters fought, fists and sticks flailing frenziedly, but they could not breach the line. A scarlet banner declaring 'THE SOLIDARITY OF LABOUR' in large black capitals sailed forward, hoisted on twin masts, only to slump, its bearers felled by a hail of blows. The words crumpled into a pool of scarlet and were gone.

The people outnumbered the police perhaps fifty to one and yet there seemed all of a sudden to have sprung up a new multitude of black uniforms, policemen proliferating like ants pouring from the ground. Batons carved arcs in the air. Boots stamped. Horses swerved and reared, their hooves slicing through the press of bodies. Faces ran with blood. The crowd eddied frantically, the force of those who shoved forward resisted by those who, in terror, tried to push their way back towards safety. Someone wielded a post, a rag of torn scarlet streaming like a pennant from its top. Already the dazed and bloodied bodies of protesters were being dragged by police through the crowds to the waiting Black Marias, their arms lashed behind their backs. The chaos was unimaginable.

'Lady Worsley, Mrs Campbell Lowe, well, isn't this something to behold?'

There was no avoiding him. He stood so close she could smell the oil in his hair, the faint reek of onions on his breath. As Rose Worsley turned to greet him Maribel forced herself to nod. She could not bring herself to look at his face. He wore a scarlet silk neckerchief and an ill-cut suit of hairy tweed and, against his thighs, his fingers tapped out a restless rhythm. Beside him stood a thickset man with mutton-chop whiskers and a dark coat.

'Ladies, you know Sir Douglas Maddox, of course?' Webster said.

'Yes indeed,' Lady Worsley said. 'How do you do?'

'Sir Douglas,' Maribel said.

'Your reprobate of a husband not here?' Sir Douglas asked,

shaking Maribel's hand. 'I haven't seen the old troublemaker in weeks.'

Maribel attempted a smile.

'I know just how you feel.'

'Making a bloody nuisance of himself in the House, I hear. Offending everyone left, right and centre.'

'Just because he's one of the few Members with principles,' Webster said.

'Thank you, Webster. I shall endeavour to take that the right way. I just hope it doesn't interfere with his cricket career.' Maddox smiled at Maribel. 'Thirty-something runs he scored for us at the Commons match last summer. Highest score of the afternoon. I'm counting on him to do it all again next year.'

'I'm sure he'd be delighted.'

'Just goes to show it's worth doing a friend a favour from time to time. It was your cousin, wasn't it, the Yorkshireman from Coulson Brown he sent me?'

Webster looked at her curiously. 'You have family in Yorkshire, Mrs Campbell Lowe?'

Maribel felt her colour rising. 'No, of course not. How could I?' she said with a Gallic shrug. Over the years the Spanish-French inflections in her voice had mellowed but now the 'h's fell away and the 'th's hardened into 'z's. 'The man was a cousin of Edward's, I think. Or a cousin of a cousin. I hardly recall. I certainly never met him.'

'The boy was a decent sort, as I remember,' Maddox said. 'A sound head on his shoulders.'

'That's the way of the Yorkshireman,' Webster said. 'Says what he means and means what he says. No time for fine words and flimflammery. I hail from that part of the world myself, of course.'

Beyond the window a shout went up. Maribel turned and looked out, glad of the distraction. Her cheeks were hot.

'A proud, proud day,' Webster said with satisfaction.

'It doesn't look as though the protesters are making much headway,' said Maddox.

Webster shrugged. 'They will be defeated, of course. Warren will take care of that. But that is not the point. Win or lose, the oppressed will prove that they cannot be disregarded.'

It had begun to rain. Flecks of water spattered the window-panes. Around the police cordon, which had yet to be breached, the skirmishes had grown more ferocious. On the steps of a building close by the window a man in a torn coat slumped bareheaded. Blood clotted in his hair and ran in dark streaks down his white face. Somewhere in the melee someone screamed, a long agonised cry like an animal caught in a trap. Webster contemplated the confusion, patting his chest. Maribel thought of Edward, down there somewhere, and the fury rose in her like bile.

'Why are you not down there with them?' she said, snapping open her cigarette case. 'I thought it customary for a general to lead his troops into battle.'

'I am a newspaperman, madam, not a soldier,' Webster said. 'I do what I can. The refusal of this government to assuage or even acknowledge the wretchedness of the poor is unconscionable. The cry of starving children, the filth of the slums, the despair of those worn down by miserable labour, these are stains upon us all and an affront to God. If I were a politician like your husband I would argue in the House as he does. If I were a soldier, yes, perhaps I would fight. As a newspaper editor, what I can do is rally God's people, to urge those who seek a better world to rise up and let their voices sing out until the glass shakes in the windows of the great halls of Westminster. Because of the *Chronicle*, the poor of London will finally be heard.'

'The Socialists believe you have done great harm to their cause.'

'All of them? Then I have done the impossible. They have never before managed to agree on anything.'

Maribel did not smile.

'Madam, I cannot say I am sorry. I do not answer to the Socialists. I answer to my conscience and to God, and I am accustomed to making enemies. I regret nothing. There is not a man in all of London who can doubt the fire in my belly.'

'No indeed. You have promoted yourself indefatigably.'

'I have promoted the truth, madam. And I shall continue to do so, for as long as I have breath in my body. I do not care for the admiration of others, only for the courage to do what is right.'

'Courage? It takes such courage to stand up here drinking champagne while others are beaten and imprisoned for the cause you claim as your own?'

Webster's milky eyes were cold.

'You must be very sure of your own virtue, madam, to cast aspersions upon mine.'

Maribel did not answer. In the square more men were being hauled to the Black Marias. Where was Edward?

A girl in a starched cap brought cups of tea on a tray. Maribel took one, though the thought of drinking it made her queasy. Setting it on the windowsill she crushed the remains of her cigarette in the saucer.

'Sweet heaven!' Mr Ackermann cried.

He pointed to the north side of the square. Beneath the lofty pediment of the National Gallery, some fifteen feet above the whirling maelstrom of the mob, a troop of perhaps three hundred Grenadier guardsmen marched in slow formation. They stood, resplendent in their scarlet coats and bearskins, between the great white columns of the gallery, as though making their entrance upon a Greek stage, their chins raised, impervious to the tumult of the fighting beneath them. Then, in a single movement, they took up their rifles and fixed bayonets.

The room drew in its breath.

'They would have the fountains play blood,' someone said quietly.

Maribel clasped her hands, pressing them to her mouth. Almost directly below the window several men were attempting to edge their way behind a column of mounted police. They wore scarves wrapped over their mouths and, though the brims of their hats obscured their faces, it was plain from the respectability of their coats that they were gentlemen. One man's hat was broad-brimmed, low-crowned in the style of the Argentinian gaucho. A police horse tossed its head frettishly, its eyes rolling, and, ducking his head, the man in the broad-brimmed hat ran a hand over its dark flank. The hand was white and narrow, with long elegant fingers. Edward's fingers. Maribel gasped, pressing her forehead against the glass.

'I cannot imagine it is much of a comfort to your husband,' Webster said conversationally, 'that, while he faces the police batons, you are making it your business to estrange what little press patronage he still has left.'

Maribel hardly heard him. Instead she watched in horror as a shout went up. Immediately several of the mounted policemen closest to Edward turned, wheeling their mounts about so that the horses' heads jerked up, spittle flying from their mouths. Standing up in their stirrups, the policemen set upon his band of protesters with their truncheons. The men were trapped, surrounded on all sides by the press of horses. They were not armed. They raised their arms to protect themselves, twisting away as the blows rained down on their heads and shoulders. Clamping their batons in both fists, the policemen smashed them into the men's faces, their skulls, their chests. One horseman kicked his feet from his stirrups, driving his metal-capped boots again and again into the men's ribs and abdomens.

The broad-brimmed hat was knocked aside. Maribel saw the

red-gold gleam of Edward's hair, the curve of his cheek, as he glanced upwards to see a policeman raising his truncheon in both hands. There was nothing Edward could do, nowhere he could go. With all his strength the policeman brought it down on Edward's forehead. There was a hesitation, like a stoppage in time. Then blood burst from the wound, coursing down Edward's face. He raised his hands, his mouth open, his eyes rolling back in his head. The policeman struck again and he crumpled, slack as a doll, and was gone.

She had known immediately that he was dead. It was not possible that a man might sustain a blow like that and live. Edward was dead. They told her afterwards that she cried out, beating the windows with her fists until the glass rattled in the frame. She did not remember.

They took her away to a place where she might lie down. The room was small and hot with buttoned leather chairs and a walnut table, padded on all four walls with gilt-tooled books in cages of gold mesh. Lady Worsley patted her arm. Someone else brought brandy and put the glass to her lips. She swallowed without looking up. The brandy burned her throat.

Some time later a man in scuffed brown boots came to tell her that Edward had been arrested and taken with Mr Burns to Bow Street Police Station. Maribel had not understood. The man, whom Maribel did not think she knew, twisted his hat between his fingers and told her that, though Edward's head wound was severe and he had sustained a number of other contusions, his injuries were not sufficiently acute to require him to be taken to hospital. It was Mr Burns, he told her, who had helped him to safety, albeit with several policemen as an escort, Mr Burns who, using his hat as a makeshift bowl, had brought water from the fountain so that Edward might wash the blood from his face. There were them who did not like Mr Burns, he said solemnly, but Mr Burns was a good man.

Maribel thought of Edward using a hat as a bowl, Edward with his arms behind his back in a Black Maria, Edward walking and breathing with bloodstains on his shirt front, and she wept and gasped to herself, rocking in her chair with her face pressed against her knees. When at last the spasms ceased, and the heaving in her chest was quietened, the man she did not know had gone. She sat up and wiped her face and drank a little of the water offered to her by Lady Worsley.

'You have been very kind,' she said several times. 'Please do not let me detain you.'

Still Lady Worsley looked at her with her head on one side and stroked her wrist and would not go.

'Let me take you home,' Lady Worsley said. 'You have had a terrible shock.'

Maribel shook her head.

'I must go to my husband,' she said.

'My dear, you are in no state –'

'I must go to my husband.'

'Let me at least call you a cab. And have a supper packed for your husband. He will need something to eat.'

Maribel felt the lump rising again in her throat, the threat of tears. She swallowed hard, nodding.

'Thank you. Truly.'

'I am glad to help.'

While Lady Worsley made the necessary arrangements, Maribel asked for pen and paper. At the walnut table she wrote to Edward's mother, and to Henry, informing them of Edward's situation. They would need bail, if they were to get Edward out tonight, and she asked if either might be able to help in raising the necessary sum. When she had signed the letters she sealed the envelopes and took them to the front desk herself, asking that a boy might be found to take them directly.

A doorman escorted her to the hansom under the cover of an umbrella. Trafalgar Square was deserted. The rain fell heavily, pocking the pools of the fountains and scattering the gaslight into tiny fragments of gold. By morning the blood would be washed away. Maribel gathered her cloak about her and, clutching the warm package of Edward's supper like a child in her lap, ordered the driver to take her to Bow Street.

24

ESPITE THE SEVERITY OF Edward's injuries he was not permitted to return home that night. He was charged with assault and unlawful assembly and passed the night with Mr Burns in an unheated police cell. He was not given a blanket. The next morning he was at last released, his bail stood for him by his uncle, Colonel George Wilcox. Wilcox, who was not a blood relative but married to Edward's father's sister, was at pains to stress to his nephew that he acted out of loyalty to Edward's mother and not because he approved in any way of Edward's actions which he considered not only unlawful but contemptible. In the lecture that followed, in which much was made of Queen and country, several allusions were made to Wilcox's Victoria Cross, awarded to him at the Crimea.

Kept awake all night by the pain in his head and the racket of the other inmates, Edward endured his uncle's blandishments without protest. He looked ill and dishevelled, his wound a dark gash in his battered face. His shirt front was splattered with dried blood. In the cab on the way home he closed his eyes, murmuring only that he supposed the old man should not be begrudged his money's worth.

At Cadogan Mansions Maribel drew her husband a hot bath and summoned the doctor who inspected Edward's head and closed the wound with several workmanlike stitches. Edward's shoulders and chest were dark with bruises, his cheek grazed from his fall. His lip was split, his eye bruised. When the doctor pressed his stomach he gasped with pain. The doctor diagnosed a broken rib and likely inflammation of the inner organs resulting from kicks to the abdomen. He was also running a fever.

'Nothing that time will not heal,' the doctor told Edward, shining a light into his blackened eye.

'Oh, I shall get time,' Edward said. 'I am under no illusions about that.'

The trial was scheduled for seventeen days hence to allow sufficient time for preparation of the men's defence, but neither Edward nor his counsel held out much hope for clemency. The mood in the country did not favour them. Bloody Sunday had been condemned by Fleet Street almost without exception. There was little sympathy for the hundreds of ordinary men and women who had suffered injury, many of them critically.

The protesters, the newspapermen asserted, had received their just deserts. The riots had been motivated neither by an enthusiasm for free speech nor a reasoned belief in the innocence of Mr O'Brien but by a sordid zeal for unrest and by greed for the spoils of plunder. Though Edward insisted that the police had attacked protesters without provocation, that they had, under express orders from their superiors, hit out at unarmed women and children, concentrating their assault on those least able to retaliate, the newspapers were, for the most part, unstinting in their praise for Warren and his men. The *Daily News* and a handful of other minor Liberal journals murmured uneasily about coercion and the whiff of martial law, but their protestations were drowned out by jeers and the clamour of exultant Tory indignation. Righteousness had triumphed. The people of London had been protected and defended against ruffians and criminals. If a few of these felons ended up dying in the process, most editors agreed, then they could blame no one but themselves.

Only the *Chronicle* continued openly to back the cause of the protesters. If anything, Webster's leading articles grew more forceful. The newspaper opened a Defence Fund to secure bail and pay fines, the details of which were published daily. It was said that the board of the *Chronicle* were very unhappy, that words had been spoken. The Sink of Iniquity scandal had served, in the opinion of many of its members, to degrade the solid reputation of their newspaper but there could be no doubting its effect on their profits. Webster's obdurate support of the rioters, by contrast, had little commercial advantage. The starving poor were not in the habit of buying newspapers.

The fever, and the blow to the head, left Edward weak and dizzy. For several days he was obliged to remain in bed, his head wrapped about with bandages. The bruise around his eye leaked blue and purple stains into the pale skin of his temple. Visitors were forbidden, except for his mother, who came every morning, insistent that she should take her turn with the nursing. Maribel could hear the murmur of their voices from her desk in the drawing room, as she smoked and pretended to answer letters. In the afternoons Edward occupied himself with writing and with reading the newspapers, which he left strewn in angry despair about the counterpane. His bedclothes exhaled the scent of his mother's expensive perfume.

'Don't read them,' Maribel said. 'They will only make you ill.'

Edward ignored her.

'Listen to this one,' he said, holding up the *Times*. 'Apparently Mr Burns and I led an "insane rush" on the police line before we were captured. Captured? They make us sound like street thieves – or Indians. I should have worn a war bonnet.'

'Red, dearest –'

'"The mob was kept moving by the police." "Kept moving" being the accepted legal jargon for trampling the crowd with horses and beating them indiscriminately.'

Maribel tried to take the newspaper from her husband but he

twisted his body away from her, holding the pages out of her reach.

"'It may be hoped that the magistrates will not fail to pass exemplary sentences upon those now in custody who have laboured to the best of their ability to convert an English Sunday into a carnival of blood." So it has come. Russia is arrived. The victors write the history and it shall be so. No more humbug of "the protection afforded by law to the humblest citizen". The honest man is to be blamed for the unprovoked and brutal assault upon his person and there shall be laurels for the Police Commissioner who incited his uniformed brigands to riot and murder.'

He cast aside the newspaper and picked up another. Maribel sighed and lit a cigarette.

'As for Mr Harrison at the *Morning Herald*, it is his considered opinion that my attitude to law and order is incongruent with the magistracy that I hold in three counties of Scotland and that my criminal behaviour renders me unfit for the offices of both Member of Parliament and Deputy Lieutenant. Of course there is no suggestion of the criminal behaviour of the police. I saw one poor woman in distress begging a police inspector if he had seen a child she had lost. His answer? He called her a damned whore and knocked her down. Do you think that the *Morning Herald* consider that "congruent" with his position?'

'Forget the *Morning Herald*,' said Maribel. 'Look at the letters that have come this morning. See how many champions you have.'

'Among the Socialists perhaps. It is a commonplace for Socialists to be united in defeat. How many letters from my fellows in the House?'

Holding her cigarette between her lips, Maribel leafed through the letters, her eyes narrowed against the smoke. There was one from Charlotte, another from Henry, and a good number scrawled on paper that was not quite clean. She could see no sheets of writing paper stamped with the portcullis of the House of Commons.

'I'm not sure. If they have written personally –'

'They will not write,' Edward said. 'My honourable colleagues share the opinion of the Fourth Estate. I am a revolutionary, a seditionary and an enemy of law and order. Not to mention a disgrace to the Commons.'

'Isn't that what you have always wanted?'

Edward put the newspaper down. His smile was weary.

'It is a dream come true,' he said.

'Red, you fight for the causes dearest to your heart. You provoke people and they do not like it. It has always been so.'

'And the working man is no better off.'

'You know that is not true.'

'I shall go to jail as proof that the capitalist masters of London can treat their slaves in whatever way they choose. It is hardly a worthy cause.'

'You will not go to jail,' Maribel said without conviction, brushing ash from the counterpane.

'There are Irish members imprisoned for simply speaking their minds.'

'They cannot do that here. The Crimes Act only applies in Ireland.'

'Legally perhaps. But do you think our government is troubled by a little nicety like that?'

'They might ban public meetings but they cannot fix your trial. This is England.'

'No. We are Russia now. Whatever my fate, it has already been decided.'

Edward's counsel was Mr Asquith, a skilled advocate and Liberal Member for Fife. The party, it seemed, was not yet quite ready to abandon him.

Mr Asquith, while hardly more optimistic than Edward about his chances of avoiding imprisonment, was of the view that, given the testimony of a number of witnesses, Edward might be acquitted of the more serious charge of assault. He did, however, stress the importance of discretion in the weeks before the trial. Edward was to write nothing, to say nothing. The newspapers had made much of Edward's reputation as an agitator, his contempt for the law. Any further suggestion of impenitence would gravely disfavour his cause. Edward chafed against such restrictions but he was obliged to acknowledge the prudence of Mr Asquith's position. Instead, as soon as he was well enough, he occupied himself with close involvement in the preparation of his defence. The work engaged him and improved his spirits.

Still the days passed slowly. Maribel smoked too much. At night she could not sleep. After the riots of the previous year she had gone with Mr Morris's wife Jane and Mrs Besant to visit several prisoners in Millbank and the miserable gloom of the place had clung to her for days afterwards. The men had been held in narrow cells furnished only with a table, a hammock, a slop tub with a lid and a stick painted red at one end and black at the other. The stick was the only form of communication the prisoner had with his fellow man. If he wanted work he put his stick through a narrow slit in the wall of his cell with the black end out. If his needs were of a personal nature he showed the red end. It had been a mild day and yet the damp and the chill of the place had entered her bones, as though all the weed-clad, mud-scabbed ghosts of the river, the dregs of the desperate and the damned, had risen from the marsh to stake their claim there.

When she thought of Edward in such a place, wordless, wretched, half starved, his long, elegant fingers bleeding from picking oakum, it was with agitation and, increasingly, with anger. In the newspapers' leading articles and on their letters pages, Edward was not only damned as a revolutionary but disdained as a reckless exhibitionist, determined upon exploiting every moment to its dramatic full. Several cartoons lampooned his gaucho style, his broad-brimmed hats, his bandannas, the ornaments of Argentine silver on Pampa's Spanish saddle.

Maribel had never doubted her husband's commitment, the sincerity of his opinions, but she wondered now whether it had been necessary for Edward to storm the police lines, to provoke so direct an assault. Others had not. George Bernard Shaw had decided to abandon the march when the police attacked, Mr Hyndman of the SDF too. Edward had declared them cowards, accusing Shaw of running away, but what was it that he had achieved that they had not, apart from arrest and a severe head wound? Edward was not a trades unionist or a self-taught labourer, after all. These were not his battles. He was a Member of Parliament whose power lay not in his fists but in his ability to press for constitutional reform. He knew as well as anyone that the debacle in Trafalgar Square would only serve to diminish what little authority he still wielded in the House. She thought of Mr Webster, who wore his prisoner's suit of clothes to commemorate the anniversary of his incarceration, and it dismayed her, that Edward might not be so very different himself.

As for what would happen to her if Edward were jailed, she refused to discuss it.

'The Charterhouses, perhaps?' Edward suggested. 'Charlotte would love to have you.'

Maribel put her hands over her ears.

'You could go to my mother, I suppose.'

'That is not funny.'

'What about the Wildes? They say it is a Woman's World in Tite Street.'

It was a weak joke. The *Woman's World* was Oscar's magazine, to which he had recently been appointed editor. Maribel shook her head.

'I do not need to go anywhere,' she said firmly. 'I shall manage quite well here.'

'Alone?'

'I shan't be alone. I have Alice. Not to mention Lady Wingate and goodness knows how many other lonesome lady companions. This building is packed to the gills with widows aching to commiserate with me.'

Edward smiled. In truth, Maribel was afraid. It was not just the change in the other occupants of Cadogan Mansions, the sidelong glances and hurried ascents of the stairs. Since Bloody Sunday they had received a number of intimidating letters, several of them written anonymously, from citizens eager to inform them of the particularly low opinion in which they held Socialists in general and Mr Campbell Lowe in particular. Most came through Edward's parliamentary office but a few, including one that itemised in careful detail the series of punishments the writer considered appropriate for offences of this nature, which he deemed Treason with a capital T, were addressed directly to Cadogan Mansions. It was discomfiting to think that these people knew where she lived.

There were a great number of letters. It was no longer possible to deal at breakfast with all of the envelopes that came with the first post. Radicals of all descriptions wrote to express their support, friends their baffled affection. Witnesses offered testimony. Fellow marchers sent accounts of their own encounters with the police. Socialist groups praised Edward's actions and invited him to lecture. A letter came from his constituency, signed by hundreds of well-wishers, another from Webster requesting a thoroughgoing interview for the *Chronicle*.

'I have done a little digging, as newspapermen must,' Webster wrote. 'Though I doubt the meticulousness of many of my competitors, one must presume that they have done the same. Your father's afflictions, the family's subsequent financial difficulties, it would be hoped that these and other equally private matters might remain private. Alas, privacy is seldom the privilege of the infamous, and infamous, regrettably, is what you have become. I, however, continue as your advocate and, if I may be so bold, your friend. The cause for which you have battled so fiercely is my cause too, your fight my fight. Grant me the privilege of standing with you shoulder to shoulder. Let us share with the world the truth about you, your family, and your struggle for a better, fairer world, in your own words.'

Edward tore the letter up, incensed at least as much by Webster's synthetic bonhomie as by the expectation that he would wish to disclose private family matters to a newspaper of dubious reputation. The truth was that Webster's letter touched a nerve. So far the press had refrained from publishing Edward's history but privately there were many who had reason to recall his father's violent descent into insanity. Already several distant relatives and a number of Vivien's friends had written to Edward to rebuke him for his misguided actions, the misery he was causing his poor mother, who had surely suffered enough. Propriety prevented outright accusation but it was there all the same in the spaces between the words, the shadow of his father's madness, the taint of inheritance. Nobody doubted the publicity that Edward's trial was bound to attract. At least until that was over Edward Campbell Lowe and his reputation would be dissected and discussed, his felonies and his failings picked over until there was no meat left on them. It was not difficult to imagine careless remarks to a curious newspaperman, whispered insinuations. The years in the asylum were long past and not exactly a secret but, as Edward knew, they were shameful enough to cause damage. His reputation, after all, was hardly one of solid respectability.

She did not tell him, then, about Ida. She said nothing of her own moment of madness with Ida's husband, her ruinously ill-judged confession. How could she? He had expressly told her that there could be no more contact with her family. She had agreed. Of course she had. Both of them understood only too well the scandal that would engulf them if she were ever to be exposed. If Edward's own skeletons were regrettable, hers were nothing short of catastrophic. If the truth were to be discovered his career would be over. And not just his career. Sometimes, late at night, when she lay awake smoking and staring up into the darkness, she tortured herself with imagining Edward at the breakfast table opening the paper, the slackening in his features as he read about her baby, the baby she had never told him about, and she had to press her fingernails into her palms to stop herself from crying out.

Edith had never sent her Ida's address. Presumably she believed it was better for Ida, better for both of them. Edith had never understood anything. If Maribel only had Ida's address, she thought, she could write to her and explain. She could confess the terrible foolishness of her impulse to confide in Ida's husband, the overwhelming urge she had felt to tell him something secret so that she might somehow be closer to Ida. She could implore her to intercede with her husband, to make him see how absolutely crucial it was that he never tell another soul.

Days passed. Maribel took to chewing her nails. She smoked cigarettes as though she meant to devour them in a single inhalation, lighting one from the burning stub of another. But however many cigarettes she smoked, however much she wrote letters and busied herself in the flat, however often she told herself that there was no point in stewing on things one could not change, the worry continued to bubble up inside her until she thought she would burst from it. Once at Inverallich the vet had pressed the tip of a knife into the stomach of a colicky horse, discharging a whistle of foul-smelling gas. If she could only be sure of Ida, she thought as she bit at the tattered skin around her thumbnail, if she could know beyond doubt that neither she nor her husband had said or ever meant to say anything, that their discretion was absolutely to be depended upon, it would be like that. It would finally let out the fear.

Meanwhile she scanned the newspapers desperately, her eyes raking the print for any reference to the Member for Argyllshire. At breakfast every morning she watched Edward's slow fingers as he sorted the envelopes and she had to fight the impulse to snatch the letters from his hands. Every morning she prayed for a letter from Ida, the hope in her so sharp and vain that it blistered her stomach. But when at last Edward handed her her pile and she looked through them, the longing in her was met with a rush of guilt and apprehension at least as fierce as any hope, and the blister in her stomach burned like an ulcer.

25

CHARLOTTE'S ARM WAS MENDING well and the doctor had granted his permission for her to rise in the afternoons and receive visitors, as long as the arm in its cast was secured in a sling. Charlotte had quickly abandoned the doctor's calico in favour of brightly coloured silk scarves, which she pinned at the elbow with a brooch. The effect was rather dashing. On Monday afternoon Maribel arrived to find the arm swathed in a scarf printed with pink cabbage roses, and a pair of ladies whom she knew a little as the wives of Arthur's school chums already ensconced in Charlotte's yellow silk sofas. The conversation stopped abruptly as she was shown in. Only her unwillingness to cause embarrassment to Charlotte prevented Maribel from turning round and going home.

Half an hour of idle prattle did little to ease her mind. The ladies painstakingly steered the conversation away from the icebergs of politics and economics, but it seemed to Maribel that, for all their fixed smiles and fastidious politeness, Edward might as well have been there with them, his rear out and his trousers around his ankles. They would surely not have felt more disgusted by him, and more mortified on her behalf, if he had defecated right there and then, in front of them, on Charlotte's elegant Oriental carpet.

It was difficult to imagine a less prudent time to enquire after Ida. Maribel bit her lip, her toes clenched with impatience. The hands moved slowly around the clock and still the ladies showed no sign of going home. Someone remarked on the weather, someone else upon the prettiness of Charlotte's tea tray. The conversation faltered. Spoons clinked against saucers. Maribel set her cup down on the table.

'I don't suppose you ever heard from your Good Samaritan?' she said with studied carelessness and she gave a little shrug to underscore the casual nature of her enquiry. Charlotte did not answer immediately. She was distracted, preoccupied with the matter of more hot water for the tea. She frowned as the maid fumbled with the pot, slopping a little on the lacquered table, sighing as the flustered girl mopped ineffectually at the spill. With her good hand she absently made circles on the curve of her belly. Maribel hesitated, lighting a cigarette. The ladies wrinkled their noses.

'The Shawl Lady,' Maribel said again. 'Did she ever write?'

The tone of idle curiosity was more difficult to pull off the second time. Maribel could feel the perspiration under her arms. Charlotte frowned at her.

'I told you, didn't I? I am quite sure that I told you.'

'You didn't tell me.'

'This is the lady who came to my rescue at the Academy,' Charlotte explained to the other ladies. 'She gave me her shawl so afterwards I naturally wished to return it but, like Cinderella and the glass slipper, I had no idea who she was.'

'I hope you sent a footman to every house in the kingdom to find the girl it would fit,' Mrs Norton asked.

Charlotte laughed.

'Fortunately Maribel is of a more practical bent,' she said. 'We left my address with the Academy in case the Shawl Lady enquired. And she must have done, because she came to collect it on Monday.'

'She was here?' Maribel said.

'Well, of course. I should have invited her here earlier if I had had any notion of how to find her.'

Ida had been here. She had been in Charlotte's house. Maribel thought of her standing in the hall with its polished walnut table and its silver bowl of flowers and the thick curving banister with its coiled finial, and the thought of it changed the taste of the air. Maribel frequently visited on Mondays. If Edward had not been hurt she might have been here, might have sat on this yellow silk sofa and drunk tea with Ida out of Charlotte's forget-me-not cups.

Except that Ida had always hated tea. Their mother had insisted that she learn to endure it, had considered the drinking of tea a social skill like needlepoint and playing the piano, but Ida had emptied her cup into a pot plant when Mrs Bryant was not looking. Was it possible, Maribel thought suddenly, that Ida had chosen a Monday for her call because she had hoped to find Maribel there too? The idea was fanciful, of course, for there was no way Ida could possibly have known about Maribel's Mondays, but although she dismissed it as absurd, it left behind a residue of brightness, a faint golden gleam.

'What kind of a person was she?' Lady Brooke asked.

'A doctor's wife. Quite respectable, if a little patched and darned around the edges.'

Maribel fumbled another cigarette from the case on the table, striking a match, sucking the smoke down hard into her lungs. Like all exquisite pleasures, it was almost pain.

'Was that sensible?' Mrs Norton said. 'I mean, giving out your address like that. She could have been anyone.'

'Don't be absurd. It was the Academy, not the Clapham Omnibus.'

'They allow all sorts of people into the Academy these days.'

'On the contrary, it turned out that we were practically acquainted,' Charlotte said. 'You'll not believe this, Maribel, but it turns out that the Shawl Lady is none other than Mrs Dr Coffin!'

Maribel coughed so violently that Mrs Norton was obliged to pat her on the back.

'The unfortunately named Dr Coffin, from the Wild West, the one the boys worked themselves into fits over? The Shawl Lady is his wife. Isn't that marvellous?'

'Isn't it,' Maribel said faintly.

'She even apologised that it was her, and not her husband, who had been there to assist me. Apparently he is something of a whizz with broken bones. He once set a cowboy's leg in the arena in the middle of a show.'

'Buck Taylor!' Mrs Norton declared. 'That was the cowboy's name, don't you remember? It was all over the newspapers for days. The West London Hospital had to create a special waiting room because he received so many visitors.'

'Buck Taylor,' Lady Brooke agreed. 'Wasn't it said that if he died half the housemaids in London would die with him, of broken hearts?'

'Then thank Heavens for Dr Coffin,' Charlotte said. 'It is hard enough to find good servants as it is.'

The ladies laughed. Maribel leaned forwards towards Charlotte.

'The doctor's wife,' she said. 'Did – did she stay long?'

Charlotte shrugged. 'No more than half an hour. She seemed in rather a hurry.'

'Half an hour?' Mrs Norton said. 'To collect a shawl? That is no hurry, my dear. I should think she took one look at the house and decided to hold out for a reward.'

'I told you, she was quite respectable. We talked for a short time. I returned her shawl and, yes, gave her a small token to express my gratitude. Of course I did, she had been very kind. Then she went away.'

'I don't suppose she left you her address, did she?' Maribel said. 'It's only – well, I should like to write to her too. To thank her. I should have made a terrible mess of things without her.'

'That's nonsense and you know it.'

'All the same. You have the address?'

'Actually, no. I never thought to ask her. She has her shawl back, after all, and I already have a rather good doctor of my own.'

Mrs Norton chuckled. Maribel stared into her teacup, trying to compose herself. The raw spot in her stomach burned and she swallowed a mouthful of tea. The liquid tasted sickly, too heavily smoked, like wood ash mixed with syrup. It occurred to her that perhaps she did not much like tea herself. Most certainly she did not like tea like this, thick with boredom and self-satisfaction and a fine puckered milk-skin of disdain. Maribel did not know how Charlotte, who was clever and witty and inquisitive and the dearest person she knew, could endure it. She thought of Edward, who only the previous evening had despaired to her of progress in the House.

'Members of Parliament are no better than ladies at tea,' he had raged. 'Brought up from birth to skirt awkward issues, to leave unfortunate truths unspoken. Infinitely preferable to say nothing, to do nothing, than to display lack of breeding by embarrassing one's fellow guests.'

Edward was no lady. William Morris, safely in exile on the remote Isle of Socialism, might berate him as too well mannered by half but Edward had never flinched from saying what he believed should be said and, in doing so, he had made himself as unpopular in the House as any Irish member. Now he faced gaol, because the genteel tea-sippers of Westminster were afraid that, if they gave so much as a heel of bread to a starving man, the wretched would rise up as one and take for themselves the wealth of the capitalist classes which their labour had earned.

The conversation had drifted, the Shawl Lady forgotten. Maribel squeezed the tips of her fingers hard between her thumb and index finger, turning them yellow, and prayed for the other ladies to leave so that she might talk to Charlotte alone. Charlotte poured more tea.

'Will you be well enough to travel to Sussex for Christmas, Mrs Charterhouse?' Mrs Norton asked.

'I should go if I were three-quarters dead or answer to the children for the consequences. The Christmas rituals at Oakwood have been polished to a veritable gloss, right down to the order of the stockings on the mantel.'

'How Arthur must love it,' Lady Brooke said.

'You have never seen a man happier. This year he is scheming to dress one of the barns as the stable at Bethlehem. There have been frantic letters for weeks about gaslit stars and the practicability of securing a newborn lamb in the middle of December.'

'Do you remember the year he decorated the ponies with mistletoe and holly and had them led into the drawing room after lunch like Spanish mules, with all the presents in panniers on their backs?' Lady Brooke said, shaking her head.

Charlotte laughed. 'Neither my mother nor the carpet have ever truly recovered.'

Mrs Norton turned to Maribel.

'Will you spend Christmas in Scotland, Mrs Campbell Lowe?'

Maribel contemplated Mrs Norton and something inside her broke open.

'Not if my husband is in prison,' she said.

Mrs Norton's neck mottled red. She took a sip of tea, choking a little in her haste, and coughed, her fist pressed against her lips. On the mantel the Dresden clock chimed out the hour.

'You must have read that he has been arrested for his part in Sunday's protest?' Maribel asked in the same conversational tone. 'That he is to stand trial?'

'Well, of course there has been some – in the newspapers and suchlike – a mention or two –'

'Assault and unlawful assembly. Those are the charges, even though he was unarmed and attacked without provocation by a policeman who kicked him in the stomach and split open his head. It is most puzzling. Perhaps you can explain to me how an assembly can be deemed unlawful when the Home Secretary has no constitutional power to declare it so?'

'Maribel, dearest —'

Maribel shook her head at Charlotte.

'The *Times* has declared my husband a disgrace to the House of Commons because he upholds the legal right of ordinary men to protest, to speak and to be heard. And yet somehow they contrive to feel no shame at the disgrace that nearly half of men in this country are ineligible to vote. The disgrace that Members of Parliament continue to perform their roles unpaid and therefore the vast majority, when they trouble to attend the House at all, do so only to represent the interests of the privileged classes, that nearly one hundred men and women were taken to Hammersmith Hospital with serious injuries last Sunday because the House bestowed upon itself the power to declare a legal meeting illegal and brought in the Life Guards to drive their point home. My husband, a disgrace to the Commons? How dare they? It is the Commons that disgraces him.'

There was an uncomfortable silence. Then Lady Brooke cleared her throat, patting her chest with the tips of her fingers.

'You have heard, I suppose, that young Archie Stanhope is to marry an American girl?' she said, leaning towards Charlotte. 'Pretty as paint and, oh, the pots and pots of money.'

'Those American girls are a menace,' Mrs Norton said, rallying. 'Brandishing their dollars like farmers on market day.'

Maribel set her teacup back on the tray and stood. She was filled with a strange exhilaration.

'Charlotte dearest, it has been such fun. I do hope I shall have a great deal more time for gay little parties of this kind once my husband is safely behind bars. Until then, I am afraid it is time I went home.'

26

EDWARD WAS IN A good mood. He whistled as he dressed for dinner and, when Maribel went in to him, he took her face between his hands and kissed her full on the lips. Maribel looked at him, at the sleepy contentment that softened his mouth and glowed like sunshine in his brown eyes, and she knew where he had been. She turned away, busying herself with gathering up his socks, the shirt that he had discarded on the floor.

'Leave those,' he said. 'Alice will get them.'

'It's no trouble.'

She twisted the clothes into a ball, wanting and not wanting to catch the smell of him in that place, and dropped them on the button-backed chair. Edward leaned towards the mirror, fumbling with his tie.

'Let me do that,' she said. 'So you had a good day?'

'Not bad at all. I lunched with John Worsley which is always a pleasure. He is having a ghastly time with Webster, you know. The *Chronicle* board is positively up in arms.'

'You look distraught,' she said drily.

Edward grinned. 'Webster is not a man it's very easy to feel sorry for. I met with Hyndman this afternoon. There is to be another demonstration in the square this Sunday. It would seem that the Home Secretary has misjudged the mettle of the working man.'

Maribel thought of the press of protesters, the staves and the truncheons and the wild plunging of the police horses, and her stomach tightened.

'Oh, Edward, surely you mustn't – ?'

'The conditions of my bail forbid it. Asquith made that quite clear.'

'Thank heavens.'

'It will be different this time. No one wants more blood.'

'How can you be so sure? If Warren was prepared last time to mobilise the army –'

'We can stop Webster from pulling any more stunts for a start. Hyndman and I are to meet with him tomorrow.'

'With Mr Webster?'

'Don't look so horrified. Webster may be a publicity-infatuated blackguard but he remains one of the few supporters we have. He needs to be made to see sense, not just for our sake but for his own. The man's in very real danger of losing his position.'

Maribel stared at Edward.

'But you despise him.'

'I despise a great number of people with whom I am obliged to cooperate.'

'You are not considering his interview surely?'

Edward shrugged. 'I don't want to, God knows, but Hyndman thinks it might help. Certainly it would give us some leverage with the *Chronicle*.'

'Edward, no!'

Her voice was shrill. He turned to look at her but before he could answer there was a knock at the door.

'Yes?' Edward said impatiently.

Alice peered into the room, her face creased with perturbation. Maribel took a deep breath.

'Sir, ma'am, I'm ever so sorry to bother you but there's a – there's someone at the front door. He's asking to see you, ma'am.'

'To see me?' Maribel said, glancing at the clock. 'Are you quite sure it is not my husband he wants?'

'No, ma'am. It is definitely you. He showed me – he has one of your photographs.'

Ruined Virgins and Other Vile Abominations. Maribel had a sudden image of Victor's photographer in the red silk room, the pink tip of his tongue between his teeth, the livid scarlet of her rouged nipples. In several of the pictures he had draped the sheet over the curve of her hip so that she was covered only by her hand, her fingers tucked between her thighs. *He claims they are Art but Arthur says they are basically naked ladies.*

'A gentleman caller at this time of the evening?' Edward said. 'Bo, my dear, how many more scandals do you think we can withstand?'

Maribel tried to smile. Her hands shook and she clasped them together. This is it, she thought. This is where it begins.

'Alice, it is past six o'clock,' she said, fighting to keep her voice steady. 'Please ask whoever it is to come back another time.'

'I already tried that, ma'am. He wouldn't budge. Just pointed at himself and at the floor. It didn't seem as if he spoke English, if you know what I mean.'

Maribel stared at her.

'Are you saying the gentleman is a foreigner?'

'Yes, ma'am.'

'Well, who is he? Where is his card?'

'He didn't give one, ma'am.'

'Who pays a call and does not give a card?'

'The thing is, ma'am – he's a Red Indian.'

They made an unconventional tableau, Edward in his elegant evening suit in front of the fire, Maribel still in her walking costume, the Indian swathed in a dirty scarlet blanket. When Alice showed him in, the red man hesitated on the threshold, his head bowed, and she clicked her tongue at him as though he were a child, gesturing with a jerk of her head towards the fireplace. The Indian's eyes flickered unhappily from Alice to Maribel and back to Alice and he coughed, a deep hacking cough that rattled like a stick between his ribs. Beneath the blanket he wore a shabby tweed overcoat with a stained hem and soft moccasins that were almost worn through. The coat had lost the buttons from its fraying cuffs and the empty buttonholes fell open like little mouths. His head was bare. His black hair was unkempt, strands escaping the plaited rope that fell almost to his waist. In his hands, pressed like a shield against his stomach, he held a dog-eared piece of cardboard.

'Do you know him?' Edward asked Maribel quietly.

Maribel studied the Indian's face. He had a long nose, the end rather flattened, and heavy brows, and his brown complexion had a grey sheen like the bloom on the furniture at Inverallich where the struggle was always against the damp. There was a smear of something dark on one of his cheeks. The Indian coughed again, burying his face in his blanket. She shook her head. Her relief made her feel something like affection for him.

'I don't think so. He looks terrible. Shouldn't we give him something to eat?'

Edward nodded. 'Alice, bring some wine and biscuits, would you?'

'Edward, not wine, surely,' Maribel protested. Since the Wild West's arrival in London it had been much remarked upon in the newspapers that Indians had no biological resistance to liquor, that they knew nothing of moderation where drink was concerned and, when intoxicated, were quick to turn savage. During their time in the capital several of the Indians had been arrested by the police for drunkenness and disorderly behaviour.

'Tea,' she said to Alice. 'With sugar. Or even soup if we have some. See what you can rustle up. The poor creature looks half starved.'

Alice nodded, closing the door behind her. The Red Indian startled at the click and tugged his blanket more tightly around his shoulders. He appeared to be shivering, whether from cold or fright Maribel could not tell.

'So,' Edward said. 'How can we help you?'

He stepped forward, smiling and holding out his hand to the Indian. The Indian hesitated. Then, without speaking, he placed in Edward's outstretched hand his dog-eared piece of card, pointing to the stamped address on the back. Edward unfolded the card. Inside the cardboard frame was a photograph of three Red Indian children standing outside a wigwam. One of the children held a hoop, another a stick. The third scratched his head, an expression of bewilderment on his face. It was a charming composition.

'It is one of yours, certainly, Maribel,' Edward said, passing it to her. He smiled at the man. 'You are with the Wild West?'

'Wild West,' the red man said, nodding vigorously. In the warm room his smell had grown stronger. 'Wild West.'

'But the Wild West show packed up days ago,' Maribel said. 'Weeks, even.'

The Red Indian leaned towards her, speaking urgently in his own language, his fingers bunched together at his lips as though he would pull the words from his tongue. She gazed at him helplessly, her palms up in a gesture of incomprehension. Feverishly he gestured at the photograph and then at the window, his hands extended as though stretching for something beyond his reach, before bringing them back to his own chest, one pressed on top of the other. His mahogany brow gleamed with perspiration.

'Wild West,' he said again, coughing violently.

'I do believe the poor devil has been left behind,' Edward said.

'Left behind? Surely that could not happen?'

'Cody did not keep them prisoner. Perhaps this chap chose the wrong moment to wander off.'

Maribel glanced at the Indian. She leaned towards Edward.

'You don't think he's dangerous?' she murmured.

'Contagions, maybe. He has a filthy cough. Otherwise not in the least. Look at him. He is not here to steal our teaspoons. He wants to go home.'

Maribel extracted a cigarette from the box on the table. Edward struck a match and she leaned forward, setting the tip of the cigarette into the flame. The Indian watched longingly as the smoke coiled into the air. Glancing at Edward, Maribel offered him the box. The Indian took one, rolling it between thumb and forefinger. Edward struck another match but the Indian shook his head hurriedly and slid the cigarette into his pocket.

'You are lost?' Edward asked, enunciating his words carefully. He pointed at the Indian and then at the window. 'You wish to return to Buffalo Bill, to the Wild West?'

'Wild West,' the Indian repeated, nodding frantically.

'What is your name?'

'Yessir. Wild West.'

Edward sighed. There was a knock on the door.

'Yessir.'

Alice pushed the door open with her hip, manoeuvring a large tray upon which were set a plate of soup, some bread and a piece of cold chicken. The Indian stared at the food.

'Thank you, Alice,' Maribel said. 'He can eat next door while we discuss what to do with him.'

'Yes, ma'am.'

'And stay with him, Alice. We don't want him alarming the neighbours.'

Alice's mouth tightened. 'Very well, ma'am.'

She jerked her head at the Indian, gesturing at him to follow. The Indian glanced uncertainly at Maribel.

'Go on,' she said.

The Indian swayed a little, fixing her with his dark unfathomable eyes. Then he turned and followed Alice out of the room.

Maribel thought of the stories Mr Molloy had told her about the tests of endurance to which young Indian boys were subjected as part of their initiation into manhood. One tribe with whom he had lived for a time put dry sunflower seeds on the boys' wrists and lit them. They burned down to the skin, causing painful sores, but if the boys knocked them off or cried out, they were derided as girls. Indian boys learned early to disguise what they were thinking. It had not helped them, in the end.

'I suppose we will have to cable Cody in Birmingham,' Edward said. 'Have someone come for him.'

'But that might take days. What on earth are we to do with him till then?'

'Poor devil. I wonder where he has been until now.'

'The streets, by the smell of him.'

'God only knows what he has been through.' Edward ran a hand through his hair. 'Do you suppose a bed might be found for him upstairs?'

The top floor of Cadogan Mansions was a warren of small rooms for the servants who worked there. The allocation of accommodations was conducted according to a strict hierarchy, with the most comfortable rooms going to those employed in the largest and most expensive flats.

'For a Red Indian? The servants in this building would more likely offer lodging to a wild bear. There must be a mission that might have him, just for tonight?'

'And tomorrow?'

The words were out of her mouth before she could stop them.

'Dr Coffin,' she said.

'Who?'

The perfect simplicity of it made her giddy. 'The medical officer of the Wild West,' she said. 'He lives here in London. Near the showground, I think. We must take the Indian to Dr Coffin.'

'Bo, slow down. You know this unfortunately named gentleman?'

'I met him once at the Wild West with Major Burke. Then just last week it turned out that Charlotte's Shawl Lady, the one who was so wonderful when she broke her arm, was his wife. Charlotte didn't get an address, the woman didn't leave one, but surely it wouldn't be so very difficult to find out where he lives. I mean, you know people, don't you? People who could help.'

Edward steepled his fingers, tapping them against his lips.

'Think about it, Red,' Maribel urged. 'The Indian is clearly unwell. He needs care from someone who knows what to do.'

'It's worth a try. Webster might know something, I suppose. His newspaper was all over the Wild West. Of course I'd have to do his interview then. No unreciprocated favours with Mr Webster.'

'No!'

'Heavens, Bo, it's an interview, not an Inquisition. And Hyndman's right. A bit of judicious cooperation with the *Chronicle* might help us. We don't exactly suffer from an excess of support among the Fourth Estate. At least Webster is prepared to stick his neck out. His Defence Fund has been a godsend.'

'You aren't to talk to him, you hear me? You mustn't. The man doesn't care for you or for your party. You know it's true. He is interested only in selling newspapers. He will twist your words until he hangs you with them.'

'Isn't that a little over-dramatic? I am not a fool, Bo. Webster will not extort from me any more than I wish to give him.'

Maribel's hands were trembling again. She clasped them together as though in prayer.

'Red, I beg you. Don't do it. Please. You think if you feed this beast it will go away satisfied, but it will not. It will just get hungrier and hungrier, until it has stripped every scrap of meat from your bones.'

'Bo –' He squeezed her hands, his face creased with impatient affection. 'Can we talk about this later? We have an ill Red Indian in our flat. He needs a bed, proper medical care. I wonder if he shouldn't be in hospital.'

Maribel stared at him.

'The West London Hospital. That's where they took the cowboy when he broke his leg. Surely they will know where we can find Dr Coffin?'

'Perhaps. Someone should take responsibility for the poor devil.'

'If I write to them now, we could have a reply by morning.'

'Very well. And I shall see if I can't find somewhere for him to sleep tonight.'

For a shilling Edward acquired a bed for the Red Indian in a lodging house near Victoria Station. It should have cost tenpence but the landlady had given the Indian a disparaging once-over and told Edward it was extra for foreigners. Edward, who had tried three other such establishments already, had handed over the money without complaint.

As soon as they had gone Maribel wrote to the hospital. She sealed the letter and called for Alice to hurry, so that she might catch the evening post. It was only as Alice tugged on her gloves that she thought to write to Charlotte. She scribbled hastily as Alice eyed the clock.

'Here,' she said, handing her the second envelope. 'Hurry, won't you?'

Alice nodded and bustled out of the room. Maribel listened to the receding thump of feet on the stairs, the dull thud of the door that led out into the street. Then the room was still, silence settling on the surfaces like face powder. Slowly Maribel rose and crossed the hall to her bedroom. She ran her fingers over the heavy silk drapes that framed the bed, the fat feather counterpane. She felt curiously light-headed. For a moment she stood at the window, her forehead against the cool glass, looking down into the empty street.

In the hall the clock struck the hour. With an effort Maribel recalled herself. It was getting late and she was not yet dressed. Abandoning her walking costume on the floor, she slipped on her wrap. At her dressing table she lifted the lid of her jewellery box and took out her garnet necklace. Against her palm the stones gleamed, bright beads of blood.

She undid the clasp and ducked her head, reaching up to fasten the necklace around her neck, but the clip was fiddly and she could not keep it open long enough to catch the ring at the end of the chain. She wished Edward were there to help her. She tried again, pulling back the catch with her thumbnail, but, though she fumbled with it until her arms ached, she could not fasten it. Sighing, she let her arms fall, the necklace abandoned in her lap, and leaned forward, gazing into the mirror. Her reflection stared back, its expression as impassive as the Indian's. For a moment they considered one another. Then Maribel looked away. But even as she busied herself with the jumble of hairpins in their porcelain box, she had the strangest sense that her reflection watched her still and, worse, that it knew exactly what she was thinking.

27

AMONG THE LETTERS IN the morning post were a thin white envelope inscribed with the name of the West London Hospital and a thick cream one from Charlotte. Maribel opened the one from the hospital first. At the centre of the page, bracketed with pleasantries, was the address of Dr Coffin in London, SW. Maribel stared at it, one finger tracing the curve of the number. Ida's house. She was going to see Ida.

'See here,' she said when she could trust her voice, handing the letter to Edward across the breakfast table. 'I told you the hospital would know where to find Dr Coffin.'

Edward peered vaguely over his newspaper as she opened the letter from Charlotte.

'And Charlotte has agreed to lend me the brougham,' she announced. 'So there is no need for you to come with me.'

She was glad when Edward nodded without remark. Her plans had been careful. While it was plainly quite impossible for her to take the Indian by herself in a public cab, a private carriage was another matter. The journey might be managed in a morning, so Charlotte would not be inconvenienced if she had visiting engagements after luncheon, and, to sweeten the deal, Maribel had also suggested that she bring the Indian first to Chester Square so that those boys of hers who wished to might have their photograph taken with a real live Indian.

Regrettably he wears no warpaint, she had written, *as that seems to have been sent on to Birmingham ahead of him, but he has as ferocious a visage as any boy might wish for, not to mention hair to his waist (and a filthy head cold so you are under no circumstances to risk it yourself when you are so near your time).*

She had signed off the letter before her fingers could get the better of her, smudging the still-wet ink in her haste as the words she longed most to write danced in the air and in the spaces between her ribs. *Ida Coffin, the doctor's wife, is my sister.*

Edward rose and, bending down, kissed Maribel on the forehead.

'I have to go,' he said and, when she tipped up her chin to bid him goodbye, she saw from the abstracted expression on his face that he was already somewhere else.

'Promise me,' she said, catching his hand. 'No interview.'

Edward frowned at her.

'Bo —'

'Please. For my sake. Are things not difficult enough already?'

His frown softened.

'I'm sorry, Bo. I know this is not easy for you.'

'No interview. That's all I ask. You are a fine, good, brave man, Red. Your actions speak for you more eloquently than any newspaper article ever could.'

Edward regarded her thoughtfully. Then he kissed her again.

'Very well,' he said. 'No interview.'

For once Maribel was grateful for the dismal English climate. Had it not been for the Indian's nasty chill she was certain that Charlotte would have insisted upon accompanying them to Earls Court. As it was, it was the nursemaid who brought the boys to the mews behind Chester Square to meet them. The children wore feathered war bonnets and fringed chaps and galloped about on cloth-headed horses. The horses, affixed to broomsticks, had button eyes and ribbon bridles and luxurious manes of looped yarn. Above their heads the boys brandished wooden tomahawks. They capered and whooped about the stable yard, their feathered tails flying, their cries echoing off the cold cobbles.

When it came to the photograph the boys clambered onto the steps of the carriage, the Indian stiff as a totem between them. The boys had insisted upon him abandoning his overcoat which they considered quite unseemly for a real live Indian brave and, even from behind the camera, Maribel could see that the poor man was shivering. The horses shook their heads in their traces, their breath making clouds in the chill air. From his seat on the box John the coachman murmured at them soothingly in his soft Irish brogue. He sat with his back very straight, his dark cloak spotless, his eyes set on something very far away.

The boys raised their weapons and bared their teeth. Maribel took the photograph.

'All done, my little Sioux,' she said.

'Just one?' pouted Bertie, the eldest of the three. There was a smut on his cheek and his fair hair stuck up from his forehead in grassy tussocks.

'Just one. I must take our Indian warrior to the doctor.'

The boys leaped from the steps, pushing and jostling.

'Attack!' the littlest one whooped. 'Attack the Deadwood Stage!' and the nursemaid was obliged to bear him away before the lacquer was chipped by the assault on the imaginary pale-faces cringing inside.

The Indian travelled on the box beside John. Alone inside the carriage Maribel pressed a finger into the buttoned hollows of the leather upholstery and tried to master the butterflies in her stomach. The doctor had replied to Edward's letter. He would be there to receive them. He had said nothing of his wife, of course, but surely, Maribel thought, he would have told Ida she was coming. It was not every day that a stranger delivered a Red Indian to your door.

The traffic was atrocious. On Finborough Road the gas company were repairing the mains and the surrounding streets were crowded with conveyances impatient with the long delay. John was an able driver, skirting drays and hand barrows and traders with their donkey carts, squeezing through arches and lanes hardly wider than the carriage's wheels, but still Maribel tapped restlessly with her toes on the floor of the brougham, as though her own nervous energy might power them through the traffic more swiftly. When the carriage stopped completely for several minutes in a narrow street, she pushed down the window, unable to contain her exasperation. In the middle of the thoroughfare, and impervious to the vehicles obstructed by her trade, a white-aproned dairy maid milked her cow directly into the jugs of several waiting customers.

It was almost noon when they finally drew up in front of the doctor's house. John called out to the horses, then jumped down from the box to open the door for Maribel. As he folded down the steps she fussed with her skirts, her gloves, her cigarettes which she put first in the bag she wore around her wrist, then in her pocket, then once more in the bag. John waited as she straightened her hat and smoothed the line of her coat collar, his expression blank. His was a strikingly kindly face. The previous week two Irishmen had been arrested in Islington, accused of plotting to assassinate the Queen during her Jubilee procession. The men had been in possession of several dynamite bombs provided for them by the Americans. There were no bombs for the Red Indians, no attempts to blow up the White House, the House of Representatives in protest at the illegal seizing of land by the capitalists. It was a great deal simpler to take the natives' part when they were not your natives.

On the pavement she fiddled again with her collar, patting her hair into place beneath the brim of her hat. It was a respectable street. There was no sign of the mean, dirty-yellow terraces that huddled about the showground. The houses were good-sized, solid and white, fenced in with glossy black railings of wrought iron. The pavement was kerbed and adorned with a row of spindly fruit trees, so new that they were hardly more than sticks. Maribel thought of the devastated orchard at Inverallich and she tugged hard at the cuffs of her gloves, pulling the kid taut. Despite the season, one of the trees was flowering, its leafless branches dotted with frail white blossoms like torn scraps of paper. Maribel reached up and took one. It smelled of coal dust and of cold. She crushed it between her gloved fingers, dropping it onto the ground.

The door was answered by a small, round woman wearing a sprigged dress wrapped about with a canvas apron. There were smuts on her face and her hair was dishevelled. She stared at the Indian, her mouth open. 'Well, I'll be blowed,' she said cheerfully, shaking her head. 'You'd best come in.'

Maribel and the Indian followed the woman into a small and spartanly furnished parlour at the rear of the house. When she walked she rolled a little from side to side, as though she had rockers for feet.

'You'll have to excuse us,' she said. 'We've the sweep today and we fair don't know if we're coming or going.' She left them to wait, Maribel on an upright horsehair chaise, the Indian leaning against the window frame. He was shivering more vigorously now and several times his head jerked forward, as though he fell asleep standing up. In the cold white light of midday his pallor was ghastly.

Now that she was in Ida's house Maribel felt calm, almost happy. She looked out of the window into a small garden, its twin brick paths scattered with crumpled yellow leaves. The flower beds were winter-bare, spiked with hard-pruned rose bushes. In the centre of a rather muddy lawn a stone cherub on a plinth held up an amphora. A plane leaf adhered to its chest like a mottled shirt front. There was a wrought-iron bench, a low table. There was clematis on the wall and what looked like honeysuckle across the low branch of the old plane tree, drab and straggly in winter but pretty, she imagined, when in flower, their blooms cascading in soft veils, their sweet perfume scenting the air. It might be a pleasant place to sit when summer came.

She could hear muffled voices in the hall, the bang of the sweep's hinged brushes in the brick chimney. The Indian coughed, a low unresolved hacking. Maribel stared at her gloved hands in her lap. It did not seem so impossible, now that she was here. She would explain to Ida exactly what had happened, that confiding in her husband was the closest she could come to confiding in Ida. She would hold Ida's hand and it would be the way it had always been. If she asked Ida not to tell then she would not tell. Edith wept and confessed everything but Ida had understood the importance of secrets. She had always understood everything.

On the other side of the wall a baby began to wail. *I lost a son. He was six weeks old.* Suddenly she was not sure where she was going to start.

The door opened.

'Mrs Campbell Lowe? How good of you to come.'

She had forgotten the mellifluous voice, its actorly quality. *Then you know our grief.* There was no longer a mourning ribbon on his watch chain. She stood, held out her hand. It shook a little.

'Not at all. How do you do, Dr Coffin?'

The doctor was even slighter than she remembered him. His steel-rimmed spectacles made his eyes look larger than they were. Had he worn spectacles before? In her agitation she could not recall. The tip of his nose was pink. Around his neck he wore a stethoscope with ivory earpieces and a trumpet made from polished wood.

'Quite well, thank you,' he said. 'So this is our runaway.'

He crossed the room to the Indian, who stared at him stupidly and then closed his eyes. The doctor lifted his eyelids, one after the other. Then, taking his wrist, he set two fingers on the Indian's pulse.

'Do you know him?' Maribel asked.

'By sight, certainly. I examined them all when they first arrived in London. We could not risk contagion. This one was in good health, though I recall some inflammation from a poorly healed fracture of the right fibula.'

Gently he steered the Indian to a wooden settle. There was a similar one at Inverallich in the back hall, its chest seat stuffed with picnic blankets and broken croquet mallets. The Indian sat, his head lolling against its panelled back as the doctor took the stethoscope from around his neck, settling the earpieces in his ears. He pressed the wooden trumpet against the Indian's chest and listened. In her own throat the pulse beat like a poem, steadily, the words measuring out the silence: *Where is Ida? Where is Ida?*

The doctor lowered the stethoscope. He frowned.

'His lungs are congested and his fever is very high. Has his condition deteriorated since yesterday?'

'I'm afraid so. He coughed a great deal but he did not seem feverish. Only cold and very hungry.'

'He ate?'

'Like a starved man.'

Dr Coffin nodded gravely.

'Thank you for bringing him. Colonel Cody will be most grateful for your trouble.'

'It was nothing. I am glad that we are able to return him to where he belongs. He must have been very afraid.'

Without a fire the parlour was unpleasantly cold. She shivered, rubbing her arms briskly with her hands. The doctor cleared his throat.

'Well, I must not keep you,' he said. 'Our Indian friend has taken up a great deal too much of your time already.'

'Not at all.'

'Goodbye then, Mrs Campbell Lowe.' He held out his hand. 'And thank you.'

Maribel hesitated, a tightness in her throat. Surely he would think it rude not to offer her a cup of tea. Where was Ida? His hand was still extended. She shook it. She could not think what else to do. The doctor opened the parlour door.

'Mrs Elliott?' he called and he nodded at Maribel, standing aside so that she might pass through. Maribel did not move.

'I am rather thirsty,' she said. 'Do you think perhaps I might have a glass of water?'

'Mrs Elliott!'

'I don't wish to put anyone to any trouble. Perhaps if you could direct me to the kitchen?'

Across the corridor a door opened and the stout woman who had let her in put out her head.

'What is it now, sir?' she asked testily.

'Have Billy bring round the trap. And tell him to be quick about it. We'll need blankets too and a hot-water bottle if you can manage it. We must get our Indian to the hospital. I am sorry to be uncivil, Mrs Campbell Lowe, but if I could ask you to excuse us —'

'Why not take the brougham?'

Even as she said it she knew she should not. Charlotte had appointments and she had sworn to have the carriage back by one o'clock at the very latest, but that was before she had known how ill the Indian was. A trap would be cold and uncomfortable and might worsen his condition. Besides, Charlotte never managed to stay cross for long.

The doctor shook his head.

'You are very kind but we have imposed upon you quite enough already.'

'I insist. You will take him to the West London, I assume?'

'That's right.'

'Then that's hardly any way at all. John can take you and collect me on his way back.'

'I couldn't –'

'Please don't argue, Doctor. Think of the poor Indian.'

'Well, I suppose – if you are quite sure?'

'Perfectly.'

'Then thank you. Mrs Elliott?'

He leaned down, placing a hand on the Indian's arm. The Indian half opened his eyes. The doctor murmured something and slid his arm beneath the red man's, gently raising him to his feet. The housekeeper bustled in, a folded blanket in her arms which she handed to Maribel, so that she might take hold of the Indian's other arm. Maribel followed as they supported him through the hall to the front door. His legs moved unsteadily, as though the bones had softened.

At the door Maribel gave John his instructions.

'And the mistress?' he asked.

'Don't worry, I'll settle things with her.' Maribel turned to the doctor. 'You will let us know how he does, won't you? We should like to know.'

This time the Indian travelled inside the brougham, the doctor beside him. Mrs Elliott shook her head as the carriage rattled off down the street.

'Today of all days,' she muttered to herself as she turned back towards the house.

'Mrs Coffin,' Maribel said, hurrying after her. 'Will she be home soon, do you think?'

Mrs Elliott did not turn round.

'Friday's orphans. She'll not be back a while yet.'

'But you expect her for luncheon?' Maribel persisted. 'The carriage will be an hour or more, I imagine.'

'She didn't say nothing about no luncheon. But then we wasn't expecting visitors, not with the sweep and all. You'd best wait in the back parlour.'

'The back parlour? Don't you think – I mean, I hate to be rude but it's perishing in there.'

Mrs Elliott stared at her, dumbfounded.

'We've the sweep.'

'So you said. Do you think I might wait in the kitchen?'

The kitchen was warm, the range lit. Maribel sat in a bentwood rocking chair, a patchwork cushion at her back, as Mrs Elliott rolled out pastry and cut it into circles for jam tarts. It was plain that the housekeeper thought the arrangement most improper but Maribel did not care. She rocked backwards and forwards, backwards and forwards, until the pine dresser with its willow-patterned china swayed and her eyelids grew heavy and marmalade cats ate crumpets with honey and the door slammed and Ida took off her hat and shook out her plaits because she was still only eleven and wore a sailor suit of serge to her job at the zoo.

'Mrs Elliott? I am home.'

Maribel blinked sleepily. Ida stood in the kitchen door. She wore a plaid coat with brass buttons and the same ugly brown hat she had worn to the Academy. Her freckled face was pink from the cold. She sighed as she peeled off her gloves.

'Please tell me the sweep is almost done,' she said. 'It must be colder in the hall than in the street.'

Mrs Elliott cleared her throat, jerking her head towards Maribel.

'Hello, Ida,' Maribel said, the smile swelling in her, pulling at the corners of her heart, full to bursting with the warmth of the kitchen and the pinkness of Ida's cheeks and the sweet warm smell of jam tarts baking.

Ida gaped.

'I am so very glad to see you,' Maribel said softly.

Ida's hands twisted her gloves into a rope.

'Mrs Elliott,' she said without turning round, 'perhaps you might check on the dust sheets in the front parlour.'

'I've already done it, ma'am.'

'Then perhaps you might do it again.'

Clashing the pots in the sink Mrs Elliott glared at the clock on the mantel.

'Them jam tarts'll need taking out in a minute.'

'I'll take care of the jam tarts.'

Mrs Elliott sucked the insides of her cheeks. Then she wiped her wet hands on her apron.

'Three minutes past,' she said. 'Or they'll burn.'

Ida nodded, her neck hardly moving. There was a stiffness about her, a held-in quality, as though her back hurt. As Mrs Elliott pitched out of the room, closing the door behind her, Maribel rose to her feet.

'Ida,' she said, holding out her arms. 'Oh, Ida.'

Ida took a step backwards and her round cheeks hardened into corners. Maribel reached out and touched her arm but Ida shook her off.

'What in God's name are you doing here?'

'I brought the Red Indian. Didn't your husband tell you?'

'No.'

'I can't believe I'm here. After all this time. You look just the same.'

'What is it that you want from me?'

'To see you. To talk to you. Ever since I found out you were here, in London –'

'It's not enough for you that your husband is to go to prison? You want to drag us all down with you, is that it?'

'Ida, don't. Listen to me. Let me explain. I said something to your husband –'

'How dare you? How dare you come here? This is my house.'

'The Indian was ill. I – I thought we could talk.'

'About what, Peggy? There's nothing to say.'

332

'Ida —'

'Please go.'

'Ida!'

'How shall I explain it to my husband if you are still here when he gets back?'

'He already knows. We agreed that I should stay.'

Ida's face was white.

'What did you say to him?'

'Nothing. At least nothing about us. I thought we might tell him together. He took my carriage. I said I would wait.'

Ida put her hands over her face. She did not speak.

'I can hardly believe it,' Maribel said. 'You, married. I think perhaps I thought you would be eleven for ever.'

Ida was silent.

'I'm glad for you. He seems a good man. I should like to tell him, if he is to be trusted. He can be trusted, can he not?'

Ida gave a little cry, her hands hard against her face. When she took them away again Maribel could see the white imprints of her fingers on her forehead.

'Get out of my house,' she said and the words were hard and unexpected as a slap.

'Come on, Ida,' Maribel protested. She laughed shakily. 'Don't be like that.'

'Get out of my house. Get out and don't ever come here again.'

'Don't say that. You don't mean it. How can you mean it?'

Anger shrivelled Ida's face like salt, shrinking her eyes and pressing black lines around her mouth.

'Why did you come here, Peggy? Have you not disgraced us all enough?'

'Oh, Ida, I never meant —'

'What does it matter, what you meant? All your life, you have done exactly what you wanted to and left others to pay the price. The scandal when you left, the whispers and the nudges and the way that people looked at us in church and in the street, as though we were infectious, contemptible – but why should you trouble yourself about that? You thought us all beneath contempt yourself, you never pretended otherwise. You were the special one, the bright shining star. The rest of us were ordinary. You could not be expected to concern yourself with us.'

Maribel stared at Ida. She sounded like Edith, like Lizzie.

'Ida, it wasn't like that. I had to get out. I had to. If I had stayed –'

'They wouldn't let me go to school.'

'Oh, Ida. I didn't know.'

'Well. You never asked.'

'I tried to write. I wanted to. I thought of you all the time. It was only –'

Ida closed her eyes, shook her head. Then she reached up and unpinned her hat.

'Don't,' she said. 'I don't care about any of it. I don't care about you. I just want you to go away. To go away and never come back.'

The hat was made of felt with an upturned brim and a bitter-chocolate ribbon fastened in a rosette. Ida touched a damp fingertip to the rosette, brushing away a smut, and set the hat on the dresser. She did not look at Maribel. Instead she undid the brass buttons of her coat. The buttons were stiff and she grimaced as she forced them through the buttonholes. When the coat was undone she took it off, folding the arms inside the lining and laying it over the back of the rocking chair. Then she opened the door. She stood in the doorway, her arms crossed over her chest.

'Goodbye, Peggy.'

Maribel bowed her head.

'You are right,' she said quietly. 'I thought I was a star. Ellen Terry and Sarah Bernhardt and Lillie Langtry rolled into one. I went to the stage door of every theatre in London.

I thought if they could only see me –' She stared down at the table, at a knot in the wood like a staring eye. 'One part. One part in a year. A theatrical career of thirteen words. I sold myself to a man I did not care for because he promised to make me famous, and afterwards, when he had tired of me, I sold myself to any –'

'Stop! I don't want to hear it.'

'I had a baby. They made me give it away. I'd never told anyone until –'

'That's enough!' Ida cried, banging the flat of her hand against the pine dresser. And then again, more quietly, 'That's enough.'

Maribel swallowed and the tears fell unchecked down her cheeks.

'Ida, I am so sorry. I didn't mean – you were never like the others. You always understood. That's why I want you to know all of it. All of my mistakes. I want to show you how sorry I am for what I did, that I was wrong about so many things. I hurt you and I never wanted to. Ida, I thought I'd lost you. Now that I've found you I – don't send me away. I love you, Ida. Tell me it is not too late to set things right.'

She reached out, placing her hand over Ida's. Ida stared at it. Then very slowly she slid her hand away.

'But it is,' she said. 'It is too late.'

'Don't say that.'

Ida turned away.

'I don't want you here. Please leave now.'

'Ida.'

Ida glanced at the clock and frowned. Snatching up a dishcloth she yanked open the door of the range, releasing a rush of acrid-smelling smoke, and snatched out a tray of tarts. They were burned, blistered with black scabs, the pastry scorched to charcoal around the edges. Ida dropped the tray into the sink. It was only as she turned that Maribel realised that she was pregnant.

'I asked you to go,' Ida said. 'I won't have you here when my husband gets home.'

'But I can't go. The carriage –'

'Then take a cab. Take the Underground train. Fly for all I care. Just go.'

'Ida, please. Don't do this. I am your sister.'

Ida shook her head. She did not seem angry any more, only tired.

'Edith is my sister,' she said. 'Hester and Lizzie and Maude are my sisters. Not you. Not any more.'

'You can't choose your sisters. We agreed that, remember?'

'I didn't choose. You did.'

Maribel was silent. Ida bit her lip. Then she looked at Maribel, directly at her, for the first time.

'I am happy,' she said quietly. 'Don't take that away from me too.'

28

A T EDWARD'S TRIAL THE visitors' gallery was packed
with his supporters. There was a ripple of attention as
Maribel entered the court and, escorted by Mr Morris,
made her way to her seat. She carried herself very upright, her
chin thrust out like the prow of a ship. Charlotte had made
her promise she would wear her black walking costume, a dress
Charlotte deemed suitably penitential for the occasion, but
Edward did not like her in black. Instead she wore a dress she
had bought in Paris the previous winter and had altered to suit
the season's fashion, a striking bronze silk with a high neck and
puffed sleeves that emphasised her narrow waist and suffused her
pale skin with gold. Her dark hair was carefully dressed and
the pearls around her neck gleamed. In the dingy police court
she shone like a lamp.

Charlotte had sent her apologies. Arthur had argued that,
with her arm in plaster and the baby coming, a public gallery
was no place for her, but the truth was that he considered
Edward's conduct indefensible. So did Charlotte, come to that,
but Maribel knew that she would have come all the same if
Arthur had not forbidden it. Maribel did not blame her. She did
not want to make things worse between the two of them. Nor
did she want Charlotte there if Charlotte was not unequivocally
on Edward's side. Irrational as it was, she clung to the hope
that, if she could only crowd the courtroom with enough of
Edward's supporters, so that the very air was charged with

their faith and determination, the power of their will might just force an acquittal.

Maribel took a seat in the front row, between Mr Morris and Mrs Marx Aveling. She did not know Eleanor Marx Aveling well but she had made her acquaintance in the months since missing her lecture in Fitzroy Square and she knew what everyone knew, that she had been her father's favourite and had helped him with the translation of *Das Kapital* into English, and that she was not married to her husband, who already had a wife. They nodded at one another without smiling and Maribel noticed the bandage on Mrs Aveling's right hand, the heavy eyebrows that looked as though they had been drawn on with a burned cork. Mrs Aveling had marched with the others to Trafalgar Square. Although she had evaded arrest, she had been injured badly enough to be taken to hospital. Edward admired her. He was also of the opinion that a little of her went a very long way.

Mr Morris took a book from his pocket. His whiskers were wild and he appeared to have slept in his suit. Opening the book he slid a stiff white invitation card from inside its front cover.

'Thank you for asking me,' he said, smiling at her, and she smiled back, the queasiness in her stomach easing a little. She was glad then that she had sent them, that she had not allowed Charlotte to talk her out of it.

Mrs Campbell Lowe
At Home
Bow Street Police Court

She had sent the cards to everyone she could think of, including all the newspaper editors in London. Mrs Besant had remarked approvingly upon her drollery and several of Edward's friends from the SDF had applauded her disdain for the English legal system. Henry, Edward's brother, had hugged her and asked whether there would be dancing. As for Edward's mother, she had raised an eyebrow and asked if it had been Edward's idea. It was Maribel's impression that Vivien rather wished it had been her own.

'But, dearest, why?' Charlotte had protested. 'Aren't things difficult enough? Making light of the arrest can only provoke the party further. It might even make things come off worse for Edward.'

'I am not making light of it.'

'Then what are you doing?'

'I am trying not to be afraid.'

It was the truth. The visiting cards made her feel braver. It comforted her that she could be the kind of person who made such a gesture, who might countenance the prospect of her husband's imprisonment without fear or, more shamefully, shame. There was something else, though, something more important which she only partly understood herself. By sending out the cards, she pledged herself unequivocally to her husband and to his cause. She would not attend her husband's trial as an observer, an outsider, but as a participator. The invitation cards declared her collusion. It was as close to the dock as she could get.

The intensity of her feelings startled her. Throughout Edward's parliamentary career she had always remained peripheral, detached. It was not that she disagreed with his politics. She was as distressed as he by the plight of the poor. She was sickened by the wretchedness of the slums, the poisonous factories, the half-lives of those compelled to labour at ill-paid and back-breaking work until they dropped from hunger and fever and exhaustion. When Edward talked of a nation whose greatness was defined not by the power of its capitalists, or by the size of their fortunes, but by the education and refinement of its masses, by the universality of enjoyment and the absence of poverty, she felt a tightening in her heart, like a fist clenching. It was just that there had never been any comfort for her in politics. She had no faith in Parliament and hardly more in the impassioned crusade of the grass-roots Socialists. At those meetings she had attended it had struck her forcefully that the speakers were not the advocates of the very poor. Yes, the Socialists called for the relief of the distress of the unemployed, and vehemently, but they would have it relieved according to the gospel of Socialism or not at all. They would rather the destitute starved than filled their mouths with the bread of capitalist charity. They were floored again and again by the ignorance of the indigent masses, their inarticulacy, their lack of curiosity, their torpor, and afraid of them too, of their squalor and their territorialism and their brutishness. They talked of the plague of evil bred by poverty, the degradation of humanity, the retrograde evolution that was turning the slum-dwellers of the East End back into savages. The problem with the Socialists was not that they wanted to transfigure the structure of society. It was that they wanted to transfigure the poor.

Edward's arrest had not advanced her faith in politics. But in the desolate days after her meeting with Ida she came to understand Edward's stubborn dedication to the cause in a new light. He did not expect to win. He fought with all his strength, knowing that the most he could hope for were small triumphs, progress that at best edged two and a half paces forward for every two it took back. He fought because not to fight was impossible. Edward's Socialism was not an intellectual construct. It was as much a part of him as his lungs, his liver. He could no more stop fighting than stop his heart from beating.

She had known as soon as she left her that she would never see Ida again. At first she refused to believe it, closing her ears to the bleak voice that cried like the wind in her head, but, as the days passed, she did not have the strength to withstand it. The misery was a darkness in her that would not lift. She walked around the flat as though drugged, her feet heavy as stones. She picked things up and stared at them, startled to find them in her hands. She could not settle. She wanted to hate Ida, to rage at her for her cruelty, her savage coldness. She wanted to plead for her forgiveness, to prostrate herself at Ida's feet, to weep and weep until Ida melted in the hot flood of her tears. And yet, even in the darkness, she knew that she would do none of these things. There was no hope. She would never sit beneath the flowering honeysuckle in Ida's garden on a warm spring afternoon. She would not eat jam tarts with Ida in her cramped kitchen or hold Ida's child in her arms. Ida did not want to see her. She would not change her mind. Edith had been a weeper and Lizzie a fearful sulk, prone to hours of wounded moping, but Ida had always been as stubborn as a mule. Once she had decided to be angry there was no reasoning with her, nothing to do but to leave her because she would not budge and she could last longer than anyone.

There was no hope and yet time passed, day following night in its habitual pattern. As the trial drew closer, Maribel threw herself into the preparations. She wrote letters to Edward's supporters, checked his speeches, proofread his articles. There was solace in occupation. Slowly the darkness in Maribel began to shift, allowing pale gleams of light. It was then that she understood that nothing had changed. She loved Ida. She could not stop loving her just because Ida wanted her to. She would keep on loving Ida, however painfully, because Ida was not a tumour to be cut out. She was in Maribel's blood, in the marrow of her bones. That Ida no longer loved her back changed nothing.

'Let's go to Inverallich,' she said to Edward one evening. 'Tomorrow morning, on the first train. You can ride. We can walk. Just a few days. We wouldn't even have to tell anyone we were there.'

Edward was tired, his face pale. When she brought him a glass of whisky she stood behind his chair, rubbing his shoulders through the cloth of his evening coat. He leaned back against her, his red-gold hair bright in the firelight, and she saw, for the first time, several threads of silver at his temples.

He shook his head. 'We can't.'

Maribel did not protest. She knew it was true. There was not time. The lawyers would object. It was possible that the terms of his bail did not even permit it. All the same, she longed to go, for Edward's sake. At Inverallich Edward would be free. He would breathe in the air of the place he loved, sharp with peat and heather and the snow that gathered itself for winter in the clefts between the mountain tops, and it would settle inside him and take root and it would succour him in all the dark nights to come. Besides, when there is nothing that can be done, and the knowledge that there is nothing that can be done is too much to bear, it is always better to do something.

The proceedings were late to start. Someone in a gown made an announcement in legal language designed to obscure understanding. There was a complication but it was not clear to Maribel whether the delay was temporary or if the trial would have to be postponed. Beside her Mr Morris frowned over his poem, biting the end of his pencil. A week after Edward had been arrested, at a second demonstration at Trafalgar Square, a man had been killed, an Alfred Linnell, junior clerk to a solicitors' firm in Cheapside, and Mr Morris had promised a poem for his funeral service. Maribel peered over his shoulder. The poem was called 'A Death Song'. She could not make out all the words, his writing was cramped and very messy, but at the end of every verse, he had written the same refrain:

> *Not one, not one, nor thousands must they slay,*
> *But one and all if they would dusk the day.*

Maribel thought of Edward, his broken head and his bruised stomach and his dogged indefatigability, and she thought: Not him. You can't have him.

Around her the audience stirred restlessly on the hard benches. People coughed or rustled in bags or muttered to one another in low voices. Mrs Aveling nursed her injured wrist in her other hand, her eyes closed, her fingers idling with the edge of the bandage. A man seated behind Maribel leaned forward and patted Mr Morris on the shoulder and murmured something Maribel did not catch. Mr Morris nodded without looking up, his pencil tapping at the blue corner of his notebook.

'Linnell's name will never be forgotten,' the man sitting behind her said to his companion, and all along the bench there were murmurs of assent and approbation as though a man's name was the beating heart of him, his crowning achievement. She had finally completed a short letter of condolence to Mr Linnell's mother only to discover that he did not have one, nor any other family to speak of. His funeral would be paid for by Mrs Marx Aveling, out of funds raised to pay the fines of those arrested. It would not be a quiet send-off. The Socialists planned to march with the coffin from Soho to the burial ground in Mile End. Mrs Besant had already arranged for a banner to be sewn that could be carried at the front of the cortège: KILLED IN TRAFALGAR SQUARE. They hoped that hundreds would attend the graveside, that thousands more would line the route of the procession in support.

And yet of all the men Mr Morris had spoken to, only one could remember ever meeting Linnell; he'd said simply that Linnell had seemed to be a nice enough chap, that he'd kept himself to himself and never been in any trouble. When Maribel had remarked on how sad that was, Morris had protested that, on the contrary, it was a blessing. For once, instead of the usual roll call of felons and layabouts and troublemakers, the Socialists had an irreproachable martyr. The funeral would be a call to arms, the poem a hymn to the struggle for righteousness, an elegy for the sacrifices of the ordinary working man. Alfred Linnell, a man of no particular party, who until his death had been perfectly obscure, would stand as a symbol for those who sought to build a future founded upon equality and beauty and happiness.

Maribel hoped that he was right. More than that she hoped that there would be someone at Mr Linnell's graveside who knew what he had liked to do on a Sunday afternoon, that he had felt the cold and liked marmalade and knew how to whistle, that he had a way with dogs and had once ridden a bicycle without holding onto the handlebars.

The gallery was growing warm. At his table beside the dock a clerk shuffled papers. On the steps behind them there was the clatter of feet, the murmur of voices, as a flurry of latecomers was admitted to the visitors' gallery. Mrs Aveling glanced over her shoulder. When she frowned, her eyebrows joined together to draw a thick black line above her eyes.

'What the devil are they doing here?' she muttered. Maribel looked round. There were murmured apologies as Mr Webster and Mrs Besant made their way to two empty seats near the back of the gallery. As they sat she whispered something to him and he nodded, brushing at the lapels of his coat with his fingers. 'I suppose you saw this morning's *Chronicle*?'

'No. Why?'

'Never mind. It was all nonsense anyway. Not worth wasting your time on.'

'What was?'

Mrs Aveling shook her head. 'I shouldn't have mentioned it.'

'But you did.'

'Yes.' Mrs Aveling considered Maribel for a moment. Her dark eyes were shrewd. 'There was a piece in this morning's paper about the trial. A leader. The usual hyperaesthetic rant.'

'And?'

'It is Mr Webster's wholly unconsidered opinion that, while Mr Burns is a gold-hearted working man and martyr to the cause, your husband is nothing but a charlatanic toff with an insatiable appetite for attention. Talk about the pot calling the kettle black.'

Maribel blinked at Mrs Aveling. Then she twisted round again in her seat. Mr Webster was deep in conversation with Mrs Besant, leaning towards her so that Maribel could only see the side of his head. Mrs Besant nodded and then said something to the man on her other side. He nudged her, jerking his chin towards Maribel. Before she could turn back Mrs Besant caught her eye. She smiled, a twisted fleeting smile of something that might have been sympathy or apology. Maribel did not smile back. The thought of Webster hunched like a carrion bird behind her caused her stomach to turn over.

'As I said, it's nonsense and unimportant nonsense at that,' Mrs Aveling said. 'Sound and fury, signifying nothing. No one thinks he'll hang on much longer at the *Chronicle*. That's the real reason for the leader, of course. Webster has convinced himself that your husband is one of those conspiring with Lord Worsley to get him out.'

'What? How do you know?'

'The League keeps a careful eye on Mr Webster.'

'But that's absurd. Edward would never – and, as for John Worsley, he has gone out of his way to defend the wretched man.'

'No one is saying it's true. But Alfred Webster is a preacher's son with two years of formal schooling to his name and an ingrained mistrust of the upper classes.'

There was a commotion in the court. There seemed to be some confusion, a door at the side of the courtroom opening and shutting, whispered altercations between several men in robes. Maribel thought she caught a glimpse of Edward's face in the shadowed hallway, but she could not be sure. She leaned forward, gripping the rail. Mr Morris's book fell from his lap, the invitation card dropping from between its pages. He leaned down to retrieve them both. Maribel looked at the card and she was filled with a sudden cold terror that this was the reason for the delay, that the card was in breach of some inviolable court regulation and that the consequences for Edward would be vicious and irredeemable.

Then the judge took his place and the court was called into session. Edward and John Burns were brought to the dock and the charges read and opening statements made. No explanation was given for the delay. It was a long time before Maribel's pulse slowed and she was able to listen with some contrivance of attention to the proceedings of the court. Even then she was uneasy, troubled by the lapse in her concentration, afraid that for too many vital minutes she had failed to collect her energies on Edward's account. That was the problem with doing something. There was always the danger that it was the wrong thing to do.

29

THE TRIAL WAS BRIEF. Though acquitted of assault, both Edward and John Burns were found guilty of unlawful assembly and sentenced to twelve weeks' imprisonment at Pentonville without hard labour. As the verdict was read out Edward looked up to the visitors' gallery and, for a moment, his eyes met Maribel's. Then he was led away. Mrs Aveling laid a hand on Maribel's arm but she hardly felt it. She hardly felt anything.

'He will be out in no time,' Mr Morris said encouragingly. 'No hard labour, that's the main thing.'

Edward, who had done nothing, who had entered Trafalgar Square peaceably and unarmed, who had struck no one and had raised his arms only to shield his face from the blows of the police, was to be imprisoned. He would be confined alone in a cramped unheated cell. He would be forbidden to speak. It was unbearable to think of him shivering in the bitter chill of November nights, the damp and itch of the meagre regulation blanket, the cries and the curses and the stink of the bucket in the corner and the dirty straw on the floor. It was worse still to imagine him condemned to silence, his head bowed over his miserable work. Prisoners in Pentonville were permitted to use their voices only once a week, at chapel on Sundays, and then only the words allocated to them by the hymn book. Those spared hard labour were forced to pick oakum, pounds and pounds of it until their fingers bled. Edward's fingers had been what she had noticed about him first. She had tried not to notice their faces but hands were different. He had always had beautiful hands.

'Of course, he won't serve the full twelve weeks,' one of the men said. 'He'll get time commuted for good behaviour.'

'Good behaviour? Campbell Lowe?' another joked and several of the men laughed.

'If the Commons did not break his spirit, it will take more than Pentonville to do it,' a third man said and there were hoots of agreement and more laughter and the shuffle of boots on the wooden floor as people gathered up their coats and umbrellas and made their way out of the visitors' gallery. In the lobby they nodded at Maribel and those who knew her shook her hand, but awkwardly, without quite meeting her eye, and muttered their commiserations into their mufflers.

'Well, that's that then,' she heard one man say to his companion as he stepped into the darkening afternoon and she realised that it was, for them.

They would not abandon Edward, of course. They would write letters to the *Times* and publish articles in the *Commonweal* and speechify in Battersea and Clerkenwell, words heaping upon words, a citadel of proselytisation and poetry and propaganda in which they might shelter, leaving Edward coatless in his frozen cell.

'Go home!' the organisers of the march had said, passing the word around the disordered ranks of protesters as the cavalry pressed their horses forward and the Guards with their bayonets occupied the square, 'Go home!' but Edward had not gone home. He would not go home now. Edward, who had not turned back at the police line, who had not surrendered or slipped away but who had stood firm, knowing himself defenceless, and who had fallen, because the fight was not only on his tongue but in his blood and in his heart.

Outside the police court Maribel waited with Mrs Aveling as

Mr Morris went in search of a cab. It had grown dark and a raw breeze eddied scatters of litter and dead leaves. Around them the offices were emptying. Clerks in cheap overcoats hustled along the crowded pavements, their heads lowered. On the other side of the street Maribel saw Mr Webster walking with Mrs Besant. Beneath a street light he paused, fiddling with his gloves. Mrs Besant said something and he turned abruptly, his gaze meeting hers across the choke of traffic. Maribel thought of him smirking in the warm parlour of Green's hotel, his face fat with self-satisfaction, and she knew that she had never hated another person so entirely in all her life.

Without stopping to think she stepped off the kerb, forcing her way between the jam of carriages.

'Careful there, ma'am,' a cabman admonished. She did not hear him. The rage roared in her ears, blocking out everything but Mr Webster and his hateful milky eyes.

'Was that what you wanted?' she cried as she pushed her way towards him. She knew that she was shouting, that people were looking, but she didn't care. 'Now that they've locked him up are you satisfied?'

Mr Webster contemplated her and shook his head. It seemed to Maribel that he was trying not to smile.

'Madam,' he said, 'your husband understands the rules. He broke the law. He must take the consequences.'

'Does that include having his name blackened in the gutter press by a man who claimed to be his friend? You are a monster, Mr Webster, a shameless, cowardly, self-seeking monster. I don't know how you sleep at night.'

Mrs Besant leaned forward and took Maribel gently by the arm.

'Mrs Campbell Lowe —'

Furiously Maribel shook her off.

'This has nothing to do with you!'

Mrs Besant pressed her lips together.

'I'll be at the office first thing,' she murmured to Webster. 'Mrs Campbell Lowe, I can't tell you how sorry – if there is anything we can do to help . . .'

Maribel did not answer. Mrs Besant hesitated. Then she walked away.

'You are making the most terrible fool of yourself, you know,' Mr Webster said softly.

'Is that so? You don't think it is you that is the fool, spitting out your poisonous opinions as if they matter, as if you matter? No one cares what you think, Mr Webster. Not any more. Your career is over and you're the only person in London who doesn't know it.'

Webster's smile shrivelled. 'You venomous little bitch –'

'That's right, resort to vile insult. Isn't that how you've always done things at your dirty little rag of a newspaper? No wonder John Worsley can't wait to be rid of you. I hope he sees to it that you never write another word as long as you live.'

She wanted to spit in his loathsome face. Instead, she wheeled around before he could answer, pushing her way back into the traffic, the blood drumming in her ears. Mrs Aveling frowned at her as Maribel rejoined her on the other side of the road.

'What was that about?' she asked.

'Someone had to say something. That brute was supposed to be on Edward's side.'

'I applaud your spirit. But tread carefully. The problem with newspapermen is that they tend to have the last word.'

Maribel did not reply. Her hands were shaking and it occurred to her that she was very cold. Clumsily she fumbled for her cigarettes. 'Might I?' Mrs Aveling asked.

Placing a cigarette between her lips Mrs Aveling leaned in as Maribel struck a match, cupping her gloved hands to protect the flame. In the hiss and flare of the lucifer the tips of their cigarettes touched. They inhaled together, the flame hardening to scarlet as they drew it up the paper. When Maribel pulled away, dropping the match to the ground, a tiny scarlet curl of burning tobacco from her cigarette clung to the end of Mrs Aveling's.

'I didn't know you smoked,' Maribel said.

'Zealously.'

Mrs Aveling closed her eyes, drawing the smoke deep into her lungs. There were blue veins in her eyelids and her finger-nails were yellow. They smoked in silence, the smoke twisting and thickening about them, veiling their faces. There was no sign of Mr Morris or the cab. As she smoked, Mrs Aveling regarded Maribel from beneath the rim of her hat, a small frown notching the skin between her eyebrows.

'I liked your invitations,' she said at last.

'I'm afraid it was not much of a party.'

'I don't know. Nearly everybody came.'

'I should have chosen a more congenial venue. And served punch.'

Mrs Aveling smiled. Maribel tried to smile back but the exhaustion was too strong in her. She swayed a little, pressing the back of her hand to her brow.

'Come back with me to Sydenham,' Mrs Aveling said on impulse. 'Just for tonight. Edward and I should be very glad to have you.'

Edward and I. The ache was in the ordinariness of it. Maribel shook her head.

'You are very kind. But I want to go home.'

'All of this has been very difficult for you. Are you sure it is wise to be alone?'

'No. But I think it would be easier by myself.'

Mrs Aveling considered her for a moment, smoke issuing in a long, thin stream from between her lips. Then she leaned forward and, to Maribel's surprise, kissed her lightly on the cheek. Her lips were very dry.

'I was wrong about you. I always thought you were one of those decorative wives.'

'Decorative is not so bad.'

'All the same, I should resist the temptation to judge by appearances. It is hard enough to prove our worth to men without having to fight the same petty prejudices in our own sex. We owe it to each other to look beneath the surface. To notice the small daily struggles.'

Mrs Aveling's vehemence startled Maribel. She blinked wearily and took a long drag of her cigarette.

'It infuriates me when others think they know me because of my father,' Mrs Aveling said. 'What is it that we have to do to prove that we are more than our fathers' daughters, our husbands' wives?'

She held her hands out towards Maribel, palms upwards. It was plain she expected an answer but Maribel was too tired to think what it could be.

'Your father was a great man,' she said.

Mrs Aveling let her hands drop.

'Yes,' she said. 'He was.'

She ground the end of her cigarette out beneath her heel, and it was as though she extinguished the conversation with it. There was a silence, no longer comfortable. Whatever intimacy had existed between them was gone. Maribel took a last sharp pull on her cigarette, the tobacco so hot and harsh that it closed her throat, and let it fall.

'At last,' Mrs Aveling said, gesturing with her chin towards the kerb.

Mr Morris had finally secured a cab. He stood with the door open, waving at Maribel with his book.

'Go on,' Mrs Aveling said. 'Or you will lose it.'

Maribel hesitated. She thought of touching Mrs Aveling's arm, of kissing her on the cheek, but she could imagine doing neither. Without the cigarettes they were strangers.

352

'Goodbye, then,' she said. At the door of the hansom she turned, raising her fingers in farewell, but Mrs Aveling was already gone.

Alice served supper on a tray in the drawing room. She had drawn the curtains and banked up the fire and put a folded blanket at the end of the chesterfield and the room was warm and cheerful, but there was still a hollowness to it, a hollowness that found its echo in Maribel and held its note, as sharp and insistent as the ring of a glass. She ate a little, forcing herself to swallow, and drank a glass of wine. Then, pushing the tray to one side, she lit a cigarette. She could hear Alice moving about in the bedroom, setting out her nightclothes and pulling the curtains and turning down the bed. There was the muffled pad of feet on thick carpet.

A little later Alice knocked at the door. In one hand she held an earthenware hot-water bottle wrapped in a cloth, in the other an envelope which she set on the mahogany side table beside Maribel.

'This came for you, ma'am,' she said. She glanced at the tray and frowned. 'Is that the best you can manage?'

Maribel looked at the plate, at the congealed wax-yellow potatoes, the black-green wilt of the cabbage. The untouched lamb chop, grown cold, was iced with white fat. She nodded. Alice tucked the hot-water bottle under one arm and hefted the tray.

'There's apple charlotte if you'd like it,' she said.

Maribel shook her head. She wanted to tell Alice that she had no further need of her, that when she had finished with the bedroom and the tray and whatever else there was she could go to her room, but the effort of words was beyond her. Instead she leaned her head against the buttoned back of the chesterfield. The fire hissed and, in the corner of the room, the grandfather clock counted time, catching its breath before each tick as it always did.

How many evenings had she spent in this way, curled on the sofa in front of the fire while Alice busied herself in the narrow kitchen and Edward gave a speech or ate a dinner or did whatever it was that Members of Parliament did when they were obliged to return to the House for a late vote? Ida would be in her kitchen now or perhaps in the cold parlour, sitting on the hard settle with its lumpy horsehair cushion. As for Edward –

Her stockinged feet found the folded blanket at the end of the sofa and she reached down and pulled it over herself, and the softness of the wool and the familiarity of its smell that was cigarette smoke and laundry soap and the faint river-water scent of wind from being aired outside was a consolation more exquisite than any she could have imagined, a consolation so pure that it drew the poison of the day from her blood as a mouth draws the poison from a wasp sting, with infinite tenderness. She clasped the blanket against her cheek and, though she did not weep, her eyes spilled with tears. She grieved for Edward and for Ida and for the ordinary comforts that could no longer bring solace but were instead a betrayal, because they were hers alone.

When Alice put her head round the door the fire was almost out. Maribel sat on the floor, her elbows on her knees, staring into the embers. The air was blue with cigarette smoke.

'Is there anything else, ma'am?'

Maribel did not answer. Alice hesitated. Then she crossed the room, leaning down to touch her mistress on the shoulder. Maribel turned slowly and blinked, like a child waking from sleep. Between her fingers a cigarette smouldered, burned nearly to the stub. Alice took it from her and put it out in the overflowing ashtray on the side table.

'It's late,' she said gently, her Yorkshire vowels stretching the words like dough. 'Would it not be time you were getting to bed?'

Maribel said nothing but she allowed Alice to help her to her feet. In the bedroom the lamp was already lit. With her customary plain competence, Alice unclasped Maribel's pearl necklace, unfastened her lace collar, unbuttoned her dress. Maribel watched, expressionless, as Alice folded her chemise and rolled her stockings into neat balls. She did not move, could hardly remember how it was done. She let Alice guide her arms into her nightgown, sat where Alice set her on the stool before her dressing-table mirror, watched her reflection without curiosity as Alice loosened her hair and, dropping the pins into a saucer, brushed it out in strong smooth strokes. Maribel closed her eyes. She did not move. She sat with her hands clasped in her lap as her hair crackled and shivered, alive with its own electricity. Neither of them spoke.

Alice stopped brushing. She leaned forward to return the silver-backed brush to its place on the dressing table. Maribel caught her wrist. The fear in her was sour and urgent, like vomit.

'Not yet,' Maribel whispered.

Alice hesitated, the brush still in her hand. She looked at her mistress's reflection in the mirror. Maribel looked back at her for a moment. Then she dropped her eyes. Very gently Alice placed her free hand on Maribel's shoulder, smoothing the soft fabric of her nightgown. Her hand was warm. Then once again she began to brush. Maribel closed her eyes and all the loneliness in her rose up to meet the rhythmic pressure of the brush against her scalp.

Very softly Alice began to sing. She sang a song Maribel half remembered from her childhood, a lullaby with a simple swaying melody about a baby who would not sleep. Alice's voice was low and sweet. She sang the song through three times as she brushed and Maribel, who had fought the fetters of family so bitterly, who had battled and bitten and torn with her nails to be free of it, leaned into her warm solid body and succumbed at last to childhood. She was nearly asleep when Alice put her arms about her and half led, half lifted her to bed, drawing the counterpane up and smoothing the sheet away from her face.

'Goodnight, ma'am,' Alice whispered and she turned out the lamp.

Very quietly Maribel began to cry. Alice hesitated. Then she knelt by the side of the bed. Maribel could feel the warm heaviness of her through the bedclothes. She bowed her head, clasping her hands together so that her forehead rested on her knuckles as Alice recited the bedtime prayer familiar to all Christian children:

> *Angel of God, my guardian dear,*
> *To whom God's love commits us here;*
> *Watch over us throughout the night,*
> *Keep us safe within your sight.*

30

I N THE MORNING THE breakfast table was laid for one. Alice brought tea and a boiled egg which Maribel pushed away. Alice said nothing. She moved around the room with an expression that was neither stern nor cheerful but something uncomplicated in between. When she took away the uneaten egg she nodded and, though she said nothing, there was comfort in it.

After breakfast Maribel sent Alice out to buy the newspapers and went back to bed. When she rose again it was evening and the bed was strewn with newsprint. She did not bother to get dressed. She sat in her wrapper on the sofa, staring at the wall. Then she went back to bed. The next morning she did not get up at all. Alice brought the newspapers to her bedroom and set them in a stack by the bed. It was not until a little after two in the afternoon that Maribel called to Alice to help her dress. In the hall she bundled on her coat and hat, not troubling to check her reflection in the glass.

'You can get rid of the newspapers,' she told Alice, tugging on her gloves. 'I shall be back by six.'

The door to Lady Wingate's flat was open before she reached the bottom of the stairs. The old lady peered out, leaning heavily on a cane. She wore a dark green dress, rather worn in the skirt, and, pinned at her neck, though a little off-centre, an emerald the size of a robin's egg. Her shawl, a heavy wool patterned with orange and purple checks, appeared to be a picnic blanket.

Maribel nodded at her, pulling her fur tippet more tightly around her shoulders.

'So they put your husband in prison,' Lady Wingate said.

'Yes.'

'I told him he would get himself in trouble. A Member of Parliament breaking the law, brawling with police. It doesn't do, you know. I hope he is ashamed of himself.'

'He is in prison. Some would call that punishment enough.'

Lady Wingate tsked, shaking her head. 'Of course the scandal will do nothing for the reputation of this building.'

'Chin up,' Maribel said. 'If it is that bad they will throw us out. They might even be obliged to lower the rents.'

The old lady contemplated Maribel, her bird's face cocked on one side. Her eyebrows were pale and sparse and clumped with face powder.

'I always knew that boy was incorrigible,' she said. 'Right from the start. It's the Celt in him. Too wild by half. Handsome, though. Could whistle the birds down from the trees.'

'I shall tell him you said so.'

'They'll let you visit him, will they?'

Maribel bit her lip. 'Not now. Perhaps after Christmas.'

There was a silence.

'Well,' Maribel said. 'I should post these.'

'My father used to say that good behaviour was the last refuge of the inglorious,' Lady Wingate said. 'But then my father was a notoriously bad egg.'

She stared into space, her mouth slackening as though she had fallen asleep. Then she blinked and shook herself, like a dog emerging from a pond. The skin swung in mottled wattles from her neck, but in their creased pockets of skin, her eyes were as quick as a child's.

'My husband was an irreproachable man,' she said. 'A pillar of society. He bored me half to death.'

Her smile was gleeful. Shuffling backwards, she pulled in her head and closed the door.

'Spain?' Charlotte leaned forward, taking Maribel's hand in hers. 'Maribel, you are not thinking clearly.'

'On the contrary, I have never been clearer in my life.'

'Dearest, you are still in shock. This trial has been a terrible ordeal. You need to rest, recuperate. Perhaps if you were just to give yourself a little time –'

'I don't have time. Not if I am to do this and be back before Edward gets out.'

'But Spain? You cannot honestly mean to go to Spain alone?'

'I would not be alone. I shall take Alice with me.'

'Alice, the Yorkshire girl?' Charlotte protested. 'But what good is that? You might as well take Kitty.'

At the mention of her name Kitty looked up from the tower she was building with wooden blocks on the floor. The tower wavered and fell. Kitty wailed, banging at the rug with her fists.

'Kitty, my lamb, that is a quite awful noise,' Charlotte said, and Kitty took a deep breath and shouted louder, pressing her face into the rug. Clumsily, obstructed by her plastered arm and swollen belly, Charlotte leaned down and placed a yellow brick on top of a blue one.

'Come,' she said, picking up a red brick and holding it out to her daughter. 'How tall do you think you can make this one?'

Kitty lifted her face from the rug. Her cheeks were red.

'As tall as Papa?'

Charlotte laughed. 'Perhaps, if you are very careful. Shall I?' she asked, reaching down to put the red brick in place.

'No, me,' Kitty protested and she took the brick from her mother's hand. Her eyes narrowed with concentration, the tip of her tongue caught between her front teeth, she balanced it on the tower. The resemblance to her mother was sudden and striking.

'It's too soon,' Charlotte said abruptly. 'I shan't let you go.'

'Does that mean you won't lend me the money?'

'It means I absolutely shouldn't. You are being hasty.'

'I am being decisive.'

Charlotte looked at her friend helplessly.

'What does Edward say?'

'I have not told him yet.'

'Dearest –'

'I do not want to worry him.'

'Will it not worry him more to discover you have gone alone to Spain?'

'I won't be alone. And I shan't go without telling him, of course I shan't. I couldn't. But what else am I supposed to do? Did you see the papers this morning?'

'That will calm down now the trial's over. There's no more story to tell.'

'Are you sure about that?' Maribel said. She took a folded sheet from her pocket and handed it to Charlotte. 'This was in this morning's *Chronicle*.'

Charlotte scanned the page, the frown deepening between her eyebrows. The last paragraph she read aloud, her eyes round with disbelief.

'"The dandyish Laird of Inverallich, who divides his time between a luxurious home in Belgravia and his ancestral estate in the Scottish Highlands, was led from the dock in handcuffs. His equally flamboyant wife was in court to hear the judge pass sentence. Attired in a gold silk gown more suited to the ballroom than the courtroom, the exotic Mrs Campbell Lowe whispered with Mr William Morris throughout the proceedings. Her disregard for the proprieties of English law was further underlined by the discovery that she had, in advance of the case, sent out At Home cards, inviting her friends to attend the trial as though it were a private soirée. A senior figure in the Liberal Party told this newspaper that he considered her actions 'to be an outright mockery of the due process of the law, casting yet more disgrace over what is already a profoundly disgraceful affair'." But that's poisonous.'

'Isn't it?'

'How could they? All that spiteful innuendo – they've twisted everything. I thought the *Chronicle* was supposed to be on Edward's side.'

'So did Edward.'

'You poor darling. I'm so sorry.'

'It's my own fault. I should have listened when you told me to wear black.'

Charlotte sighed, dropping the cutting on the table. 'This isn't why you want to go away, is it? Because of this?'

Maribel shook her head firmly. The urge to confess was very strong. 'Of course not.'

'Because they'll lose interest. By tomorrow there'll be another story. There always is.'

And this time it will be mine, Maribel wanted to say. The story I've never told you, that I've never even properly told my husband. An old, old story and the end of everything.

'I don't have a choice,' she said instead. 'There isn't any more money. I have been over and over the books and every time it only comes out worse than before.'

'It's a bad time, everyone says so, but things will look up.'

'Not at Inverallich. Whatever I do we just seem to fall further behind.'

'Surely you can borrow?'

'Again? Perhaps. But for how long? It might be years before we are back to where we were before the storm.'

'But a mine in Spain? Isn't it rather a long shot?'

'Of course it's a long shot. But if we are right, and the mine exists, it would solve everything.'

'And if it does not?'

'Then I will have tried. I cannot wait here doing nothing, Charlotte. I shall go mad. And at least in Spain I shan't see the newspapers.'

The crash of bricks made her jump. Opposite her Charlotte froze, ready for the howl. Instead Kitty frowned, her hands on her hips, her neat front teeth pressing down on her lower lip.

'Dash it all to heck,' she said.

Charlotte covered her mouth with one hand, holding back her laughter. Maribel smiled. Charlotte would lend her the money, she was sure of that. Tomorrow she would book a passage to Spain. The certainty of it steadied her. It would not be easy. It was a long journey and, in winter, an uncomfortable one. Perhaps she was wrong. Perhaps the mine would not be there. Perhaps it would be exhausted, the last of the gold dug out long ago.

Or perhaps it would save them. Whatever happened it would save her. She could not stay in London, alone in the empty flat, woken at dawn with the dread of the morning newspapers. The journey would give shape to the empty days, a purpose, a goal, however far-fetched. She would forget London and perhaps, if she were lucky, Mr Webster would forget her. Charlotte was right. There was always a new story. Something else would come along and by the time she came back it would all be forgotten. By the time she came back she would have learned to be strong. Two days before the trial, walking by the river, she had hailed a passing cab. She reached the corner of Ida's street before she found the presence of mind to ask the driver to turn round. She could not stay in London.

Clearing a space among the scattered debris, Kitty began again. Charlotte smiled and leaned forward, lifting the lid of the teapot to peer inside. This afternoon her silk-scarf sling was scarlet, patterned with gorgeous paisley leaves in violet and black. The tips of her fingers protruded from its vivid carapace, pale as roots. 'Is that stewed enough for you?' she asked.

'Could you stain a floor with it? Then it's perfect.'

Charlotte poured as, at her feet, Kitty added bricks to her tower. It leaned dangerously to the left. Maribel took the proffered cup carefully, for fear of agitating the air. Charlotte watched her daughter for a moment. Then she turned back to Maribel, touching her gently on the knee.

'How are you? Truly?'

'I am all right. Truly.'

'I wish I had been there with you.'

'It wouldn't have made any difference.'

'It would to me. Oh, Maribel, don't go to Spain. Come and stay here with us for a while if you can't bear the flat. Just until things settle.'

'And Arthur?'

'Nothing would please him more.'

It was an outrageous lie and they both knew it. Maribel clasped her friend's hand in hers and raised it to her lips.

'Thank you. But I am going to Spain.'

'Dearest, I beg you, think about this sensibly. What knowledge do you have of mining? Surely it is more practical to send an agent to investigate on your behalf. Then, if the mine does miraculously exist, as soon as Edward – next year you and Edward can travel out there together.'

'And what if the agent stakes his own claim and cuts us out entirely? Charlotte, I have made up my mind. You will not talk me out of it, however hard you try.'

Charlotte shook her head. 'You know, if it is occupation you are after, I could find plenty for you here.'

'Or you could come with me.'

Her face screwed tight, Kitty reached out and placed a blue block on the top of the tower.

'Look, Mama, look!' she hissed in a stage whisper, tugging

on her mother's skirts. The tower swayed slightly but it did not fall. Charlotte smiled, putting a finger to her lips.

'Hush, my lamb. The grown-ups are talking.'

'Well?' Maribel said.

Charlotte contemplated her broken arm, her pregnant belly.

'The perfect travelling companion,' she said.

'You would be.'

Charlotte looked up, caught by the seriousness in Maribel's voice.

'There is more to this than the mine, isn't there?' she said softly.

Maribel stared into her cup of tea.

'I told you,' she said. 'I need to do something. Twelve weeks –'

'I know.'

The tower tottered. Then it fell. Kitty picked up the brick nearest to her and threw it across the room.

'Kitty!' Charlotte said sternly. 'If you cannot behave you will have to go back to the nursery.'

Her daughter glared balefully at the bricks.

'You're not playing,' she said.

'That's because I only play with good little girls.'

'No it's not. It's because you're talking. You're always talking.'

'Kitty!' Charlotte said again, making an apologetic face at Maribel. 'Mrs Campbell Lowe is our visitor. We must make her welcome.'

'It's not fair. It's my day to have you. Why does she have to come on my day?'

'I should go,' Maribel said.

'I won't hear of it,' Charlotte protested. 'Kitty, that was very rude. Apologise to Mrs Campbell Lowe immediately.'

Kitty glowered at the carpet.

'Kitty?'

'I beg your pardon.'

Kitty's face was thunderous. Maribel suppressed a smile.

'Thank you, Kitty,' she said gravely.

'Now go to the nursery and think about what you have done.'

'Mama –'

'I said now, Catherine Charterhouse!'

Kitty sucked in her cheeks. Then slowly she made her way out of the room, scuffing at the carpet with the toes of her shoes.

'And make sure to close the door properly behind you.'

The door closed, a little too loudly.

'It's my fault,' Maribel said. 'I spoiled her afternoon.'

'Kitty has to learn that she is not the only fish in the sea.'

'Still.'

'We are dining with the Woodwards tonight, for our sins,' Charlotte said. 'I suppose it is too much to hope that you are going too?'

'Much too much.'

'I wish Arthur would not insist on accepting them.'

'You should have him arrested. Then they would no longer ask you.'

'Ah.'

They were both quiet, staring into the fire.

'It's funny,' Charlotte said at last, 'I never knew anyone go to prison before Edward. And yet, with perhaps one exception, he is also the only man I have ever met who acts entirely according to his conscience.'

'You'll make other convict friends. Jane Morris says that it's only a matter of time before her husband is arrested. It seems that these demonstrations have made a dervish of him.'

'Well, there you are. Mr Morris was my one exception.'

'Jane seems to think that prison will be good for him, that he will finally have the chance to write uninterrupted, but then she has always had an uncanny ability to discover silver linings to her husband's misfortunes. She told me once it was having Mr Rossetti at Kelmscott that inspired him to his finest work.'

Charlotte smiled sadly. 'At least Edward has a wife who deserves him.'

Maribel thought of Mr Webster. 'I wish you were right,' she said.

'Don't be absurd. Look at you two, how devoted you are to one another. Perhaps it is because you don't have a swarm of children under your feet, or perhaps you Europeans are simply better at it than us English with our wretched –'

'Charlotte, dearest, what is it?'

Charlotte shook her head, fumbling a handkerchief from her sleeve.

'It's nothing. Something in my eye, that's all.'

She pressed the handkerchief hard against her eyes with the tips of her fingers. Then she blinked and took a deep breath.

'So silly,' she said. 'I can't imagine what has got into me.'

'Has something happened?'

'I'm tired. That's all.'

'Then promise me that you won't go to the Woodwards tonight, that you'll stay here and have supper in bed.'

Charlotte shook her head. 'Arthur wants us to go. Please don't worry. I shall be quite better after a little rest.'

When they bid one another goodbye Charlotte held her close for a moment, the silk sling like a wing across her back. Then she smiled and turned away.

In the square, though it was not yet four o'clock, darkness had already begun to gather behind the iron railings and there was a night chill to the air. Maribel walked slowly, her arms tucked inside her muff. It had always pained her to keep secrets from Charlotte, who loved her and whose constancy was unquestioned and unquestioning. It had never occurred to her that Charlotte might have secrets of her own.

31

CHRISTMAS HAD COME AND gone by the time their small expedition arrived in the Val de Verriz. The road, such as it was, brought them to the north end of the oxbow lake and to Ferrixao, the first of the clusters of houses that clung to its shore.

The inn was small and spartan but by then they were accustomed to discomfort. Two days later, Maribel rose before dawn and, with the men, made the uphill trek from the village. It was very cold. The laden mules plodded slowly through the damp mist, their heads down. Wizened leaves clung to their hooves. Maribel held onto the saddle and tried not to hope. Behind her the men walked in silence.

Some hours later the guide stopped to set up camp and brew tea. They were high up by now and, far below them, the pale lake steamed with mist. In the distance Maribel could just make out the roofs of the tiny houses at the southernmost end of the lake, the rough stone jetty with its fishing boats. Meiriz. The convent had been a mile from the village, hidden in a stand of trees. She squinted her eyes, gazing at a dark patch on the hill. Then, shivering, she turned back towards the fire.

She drank her tea quickly, a little distance from the men. They would complete the last two miles of the journey by foot. After half a mile, Maribel wasn't sure she could go on. The route was steep, leading up through a thick forest of chestnut trees. If there was a path Maribel could not see it. The ground was sodden and spongy with moss, sucking at her feet and leaching water into her boots. The roots of the trees snaked beneath the moss, tripping her up. She longed to stop, to smoke a cigarette, but she had left her pack at the camp and, like a fool, her cigarettes with it.

The guide skirted a thorn bush. Ahead of him the trees opened up to a flat grey sky.

'Careful,' he said, raising his hand, and as Maribel caught up with him, she stopped, her damp feet suddenly forgotten, and the breath caught in her throat.

'There it is,' he said. They stood together at the lip of the chasm as she gazed in wonder at the vast bowl dug out from the flesh of the mountain, perhaps one-third of a mile across and just as deep. It was as though the landscape had been broken open. Beyond the vertiginous drop a cliff rose like a great wave, its crest frothed with tangled undergrowth. As Maribel stared the low winter sun pierced the clouds, bleaching white stripes on the dingy sheet of the sky. In the sudden light the dark earth of the cliff glowed red, and the pebbles embedded in its surface winked and sparkled.

'A placer working, as I live and breathe!' Muñoz, the engineer, cried, the spittle spraying from his mouth, and for the first time in days Maribel did not think to flinch. 'What engineers the Romans were!'

It had been agreed that Maribel would spend a single night at the camp, before returning to the village the following day. As the guide and Muñoz looked for the easiest way down into the gorge, she stayed at the edge of the chasm, gazing into the vast red mouth of the mine. The ground was cool and muddy and she sat alone, a rug around her shoulders and another spread beneath her, tracing the faint trail of goats up the dizzying cliff, the sun-sharp patterns of quartz like constellations of stars. Later that afternoon Muñoz returned from his investigations and, spittle flying, eagerly pointed out for her the evidence of ancient endeavour, the cuttings and sluices and seams where the Romans would have had their waterways. They would have washed the hillside for gold, he said, using for the most part the same techniques employed by miners nearly two millennia later. Maribel nodded and waited for him to go away. She observed how small trees had contrived to take hold in the narrow steps and fissures of the wall, the roots gripping the red earth like fingers.

The very existence of the mine seemed to her a miracle. In London, as she had busied herself with plans and packing, she had endeavoured not to dwell on the folly of her quest. The frantic flurry of organisation brought with it a kind of euphoria. Standing in the lobby of Cadogan Mansions as Alice supervised the loading of their boxes, she had been filled with a rush of hopefulness, and when Lady Wingate emerged from her flat to complain about the racket, she had seized the old lady by the hands and kissed her firmly on the cheek. The shock on Lady Wingate's face had made her laugh out loud.

But as she and Alice made their slow way by sea to the port of Vigo and then by train into the interior of Galicia, and the discomforts of their journey eroded her spirits, her confidence had begun, little by little, to seep away. Again and again she had taken her notebook from her pocket so that she might read to herself the words she had copied from Pliny and, with every rereading, the absurdity of their enterprise had struck her more forcefully. Why, when she could have gone anywhere, had she come to this godforsaken place in the middle of winter? Surely only a lunatic would take as the foundation of his business enterprise the musings of a natur- alist penned two thousand years before and travel hundreds of miles in pursuit of what even a generous observer would have to concede was little more than a hunch. Try as she might, she could not recover the soaring sensation she had experienced at Inverallich when she had first read the descriptions of Pliny's Lusitanian gold and known, beyond all doubt, that he wrote of the Val de Verriz.

For the first time in years, she had thought of the old woman sent by Victor to take care of her during the two months she spent at the convent on the lake. With his habitual disregard for accuracy, Victor had described the old woman as a lady's maid, but though she had never before seen a lady, she was kind. She had lived in Meiriz all her life and had never travelled beyond the Val de Verriz. She told Maribel all the stories her grandmother had told to her: the girl lost in the mountains who had returned to the village as a white bird, the mule that had warned the farmers of an earthquake, the monster with the head of a dragon that lived in the black depths of the lake and who, one night, had crept onto the land and stolen a baby girl from Meiriz to be his wife. The gold mine that had caused kings to weep.

'I have come in pursuit of a fairy tale,' Maribel wrote to Edward but she tore the letter up and wrote instead of small things that she knew would amuse him, the daily successes and setbacks of the journey, descriptions of the places they passed through, droll pen-portraits of their fellow passengers. She liked to think of him reading her letters and smiling.

She missed Edward horribly. Every evening after supper, wherever they were, she wrote to him, her own spirits rising a little in her attempt to raise his. Night after night, as Alice sighed in the bed beside hers, she fell asleep thinking of him, of his body against hers, the warmth of his hands on her belly, his breath on her neck, but she did not dream of him. She dreamed of her son. In London it had been easy to pretend that she had forgotten him. There was nothing there of his, nothing to remind her of the curl of his fingers, the downy curve of his tiny skull. In London she had not felt the weight of him in her arms, or, if she had, it had been late at night, when she was alone, or at Charlotte's where, amid the clamour and jostle of the nursery, no one noticed if she was quiet, holding herself tightly until the steadiness returned.

Spain was different. In Spain the wood in the grates smelled of him. The whitewash on the walls, the iron bedsteads, the crucifixes and the portraits of the Virgin painted on ovals of tin, all of these were his. In the market squares, along the busy quays, in the alleys behind their lodgings, she heard the gull shriek of children's voices and they were all his. When the boys crowded around them at the staging inns, their dirty hands held out for coins, she could not bear the closeness of them. She had to give money to Alice to make them go away.

Had it not been for Alice she might have abandoned the endeavour altogether. Alice, whose Yorkshire temperament had in London tended to a plain kind of pragmatism, refused from the outset to take to what she balefully referred to as Foreign Parts. Her inability to make herself understood incensed her but, though Maribel attempted to teach her the rudiments of Spanish, she would not learn. She said she had no memory for nonsense. Instead she shouted in English, stubbornly determined that if she only spoke loudly enough, the Spaniards would be shamed into comprehension. Though she remained servant enough to complain only when asked, she wore the perpetual expression of a woman taken to the limits of endurance.

At first Maribel found her attitude disconcerting, even distressing. She had not expected Alice to enjoy the uncomfortable journey any more than she had expected to enjoy it herself, but she realised, long before the ship docked at Vigo, that she had expected to find solace in Alice's placid imperturbability. On Spanish soil at last and required to kill time before the train to Orense the following morning, she tried to persuade the maid to walk with her in the public garden, to climb the Monte de la Guia to the hermitage at its summit, to sample the little boat-shaped wafers known as *barquillas*, anything to pass the hours.

Alice refused all invitations. Instead she remained closeted in her room on the pretext that the luggage required her attention. At dinner she poked like a child with a stick at the food on her plate.

'What is that?' she asked Maribel, the corners of her mouth turned down.

'*Polbo à feira*. Octopus. It is a speciality of the region.'

'I can't eat that.'

'Of course you can. It's delicious.'

Alice poked again at her plate and shuddered.

'But it – it has *suckers*,' she whispered and Maribel had to bury her face in her wine glass so that the maid would not see her laughing.

The next day they travelled to Orense to meet Sr Muñoz. They left word at his hotel but he did not come. Nor did he send a message. Maribel passed the day in low spirits, the conviction that they were set on a fool's errand stronger in her with every slow hour.

'He won't show his face, most likely,' Alice said, triumphantly glum. 'Thought better of it, or got a better offer. You can't take a foreigner's word for anything.'

At supper that evening, the landlord proposed a stew of pork. Instead Maribel asked for *percebes*, the goose-necked barnacles considered a great delicacy by Galicians. Alice stared in dismay as the plate of shells was set in front of her.

'What in the name of heaven is that?'

Maribel did not answer. Instead she picked up one of the shells and extracted from it a leathery tube from which she proceeded to squeeze the flesh of the barnacle. It slithered out in a squirt of salty juices. Maribel picked up the morsel with her fingers and popped it in her mouth.

'Delicious,' she said, though the truth was that she had never understood Victor's passion for *percebes*. 'Try one.'

'I shan't.'

'Don't be such a baby.'

'I'm not hungry,' Alice said, pushing her plate away.

'Suit yourself.'

The next day there was still no sign of Sr Muñoz. Alice sucked her cheeks and said nothing. She did not need to, Maribel thought bitterly. She could not have expressed herself more eloquently if she had painted 'I told you so' across her forehead. That night Maribel ordered clams. The maid's pitiful expression when they were brought to the table was not as consoling as Maribel had hoped. While Maribel bent her head to her plate, sucking the flesh from the shells, Alice sat up very straight and ate some of the rough Galician bread. They did not speak.

'My father raised sheep,' Alice said at last. 'In the Dales.'

'Yes. I believe you told me.'

'Every spring there'd be lambs rejected by the ewes and it would be our job to feed them with a bottle. The first time my brother Davy was old enough he gave his lamb a name and petted it like a lapdog. He went soft in the head over that creature. At night he'd sneak down and let it in the kitchen so it could sleep in the warm. My sisters and me, we told him not to be foolish, that it was just a lamb like all the others, but he didn't listen. The day it was slaughtered he took out the box that had our hair ribbons in it and cut them up with a pair of scissors. Scraps of coloured silk all over the floor, there were.'

'Poor child.'

'Poor us. It wasn't our fault we was right.'

They sat for a while in silence. When Alice asked if she might be excused from the table Maribel did not object. She sat alone, doggedly eating her clams. It was not a good dish. The sauce was too salty, the onions bitter and undercooked. When she had finished the landlord brought a greasy custard tart and a tiny cup of strong black coffee. She drank a little wine. When at last she went upstairs she found to her astonishment that Alice had contrived for bathwater to be heated and a bathtub brought to their room. As Maribel soaked, she listened to Alice humming to herself as she put away her clothes.

When yet another day had passed without word from Sr Muñoz, Maribel was almost in despair. They would wait three more days, she decided. If by then he still had not come they would go home. She said nothing to Alice. They took their places at the supper table in silence. As the dish of baked chicken was placed in front of her, Alice's expression was unreadable. Her hands closed together as though she were about to pray, she looked at the plate. Then, without a word, she took up her fork and began to eat. When the plate was empty she wiped her oily lips on her napkin and remarked with a shake of her head upon the stringiness of the meat. It was the first time that day that Maribel had smiled.

By then she was certain that Sr Muñoz had no intention of coming to Orense. It was a surprise, therefore, the very next morning, to hear that he had indeed arrived in town, and even more of a surprise to discover that he positively brimmed over with enthusiasm. Sr Muñoz was not a young man by any reckoning but the notable modesty of his achievements had served only to amplify his certainty that great things lay ahead. He had a head too large for his body. His hair was astonishingly abundant and, when he spoke, his tongue fell over his mossy teeth, disbursing sprays of spittle. He had been delayed, he explained, by the process of submitting claims which must be done properly if the profits were to be fairly allocated. As he went on to outline the other preparations he had made for the journey to the Val de Verriz, it was as if not only the existence of the mine was firmly established but the capital needed for its operation were already safely in the bank. Maribel returned to her lodgings more cheerful than she had been since leaving England.

They stayed in Orense only as long as was necessary for Sr Muñoz to complete his preparations. The remainder of the journey to the Val de Verriz was completed by diligence, a rickety, creak-wheeled conveyance pulled by four ill-tempered mules whom, in the absence of a whip, the driver encouraged to greater effort by throwing handfuls of pebbles at their heads. The passengers were a motley lot, for the most part travelling salesmen or priests, which as Maribel wrote to Edward amounted to much the same thing. Crammed into the small wagon like puppies in a sack, they eyed Maribel and Alice with undisguised curiosity and made what space they could around them, as though the women's sex was something that might be caught.

The two women were obliged to press close together. Maribel grew familiar with the warmth of Alice's thigh, the dense pad of flesh that cushioned her hip, the faintly musty smell of her shawl. Sometimes when the wind came up and cut through the seams of the wagon, Alice spread the shawl so that it covered both of their laps. Sometimes, exhausted, they slept, their heads on each other's shoulders. On the last day of their journey, when they were almost at Ferrixao, the diligence hit a rock, dislodging a wheel from its axis. The passengers were hurled sideways, their limbs flailing, striking their heads against the sides of the carriage. When at last the damage was repaired and the journey resumed, Maribel reached beneath the shawl and took Alice's hand. Alice held it tightly. They travelled in this manner, hand in hand, until the diligence drew to a stop outside the inn that would be their final destination.

Maribel spent a single night with the men at their camp near the mine. Then she returned to Ferrixao. It was another dull day, the damp chill of the Galician winter undercut by a sharp breeze, but, when she reached the village, she could see Alice seated on a rough bench outside the inn. The maid rose as soon as she saw her mistress approaching, gathering her shawl about her shoulders as she hurried towards her.

'Well?' she said. She eyed the mules suspiciously, keeping a safe distance. She had refused to ride a mule herself. She said that foreign animals bit. 'Are we rich?'

Maribel laughed. The mule guide gestured at the inn and she nodded. She watched as he had the boy tether the beasts outside the inn and unload the luggage from the panniers. The innkeeper came out, yawning and rubbing his head. His hair was rumpled, the buttons of his shirt wrongly fastened so that it gaped over his paunch, revealing a strip of thickly furred belly. Beneath his stomach, like a sling, he wore a sash of black fabric, rather stained.

'I am not sure about rich,' she said. 'But we found the mine.'

'That is good news.'

'It's better than good. Muñoz was so overcome I feared he might drown in his own spittle.'

Alice made a face but, beneath the twist of her mouth, Maribel thought she was smiling.

'They think it will take perhaps a week to collect sufficient samples of the earth. Then we shall take them to the Mining College in Madrid for the assay.'

'We are stuck in this godforsaken place a week?'

Maribel rolled her eyes good-humouredly. 'We are and we may as well make the best of it. Don't tell me you would rather be digging sheep out of the snow in North Yorkshire?'

'There's nothing wrong with Yorkshire.'

'That's a matter of opinion.'

Alice curled her lip, crossing her arms over her chest. Exasperated, Maribel gestured down the hill towards the great still lake which, beneath the dull sky, gleamed pewter grey, its shores softened by thick forests of bulrushes. In several places the local fishermen had cut paths through the rushes and there, on the silent water, flat-bottomed boats idled, painted in bright colours long flaked and faded by the sun. Beyond the lake, as blurred as buildings in the London fog, rose the dark forms of the Asturian mountains.

'Look, Alice. Look properly. Can you honestly tell me it is not beautiful?'

Alice shrugged. 'Beauty is as beauty does. When I look properly do you know what I see? The food stains on the tablecloth, for one, and the fingerprints on the glasses. There's not a plate or a dish here an English dog would care to eat from. As for the fleas in the mattresses, I can see those clear as day.'

'Alice Tweddle, you are impossible!' Maribel cried. 'I am back for five minutes and already the complaining has begun. Well, I am not listening. I am in too good a humour for your ceaseless doom and gloom. Make sure my luggage is safely unloaded. I am going for a walk.'

Without waiting for Alice's reply she set off towards the lake, following the path that led away from the village and around the base of the hill. She walked briskly, not looking back. Before long Alice and the inn were out of sight but she continued to walk, enjoying the stretch in her muscles after the uncomfortable journey. Near the lake the path turned abruptly, leading down to a narrow strand of pebbled beach. Reeds grew in the quiet tea-brown water, and, along the shore, tiny waves licked at the worn grey stones. The slip and clatter of the pebbles as she walked reminded her of Inverallich and of Edward. She thought perhaps everything reminded her of Edward these days.

Gathering up her skirts she bent down, picking up and discarding stones until she found one of the right shape. She looked at it, flat and smooth on the palm of her hand. Then she closed her fingers over it, holding it in her fist like the stone of a fruit. She did not throw it. Though Edward had spent hours trying to teach her she had never mastered the skill of skimming stones. Instead she held it until it was no longer colder than her hand. As it warmed it seemed to soften. She opened her fingers. A flat grey pebble, flecked with white, an oval with one end more sharply curved than the other and a dent at the centre. Like an ear, she thought, and she set it to her own ear to listen to it. The silence in it was whole and desolate.

She threw the stone into the lake. It landed neatly, sending tiny waves shimmering through the surface of the water. She lit a cigarette. Then, with the cigarette in her mouth and her hands in her pockets, she walked slowly along the edge of the water away from the path. She was not yet ready to go back to the village. As the waves reached the beach the hem of the lake frilled.

In a few weeks Edward would be released. They would unlock the door and he would step, blinking, into the disordered bustle of a London street. At Pentonville all the prisoners were kept in solitary confinement. When they exercised with other prisoners in the high-walled yard they wore specially designed caps with flaps that covered their faces, the slits for their eyes cut only wide enough to ensure they did not fall. At Sunday chapel the pews were arranged in rows of high-walled cubicles. Such solitude could make a man mad. There were stories told of the prisoners who believed themselves to be the Devil, or God, or the Emperor Napoleon. Edward would stand outside the prison, his hand shielding his eyes as he contemplated freedom, conversation, the unfamiliar feel of his own good clothes against his skin. The light would be a shock to him. The outside of the prison, with its classical columns and porticos, was painted a startling white.

Would they have changed him, those desolate days and nights, marked off in scratched lines on the cell wall? Edward was a man of principle but he was still a man, formed of flesh and blood. The miserable regimen would starve his body and torment his mind. That was its purpose. His suffering might harden his will or it might break it but surely it could not fail to shape him. Before the trial he had said that he did not regret what he had done, had claimed that, granted the opportunity to go backwards in time, he would do it all again. The assertion had roused in her both tenderness and consternation. She thought of Mrs Besant, who, years before, had been sentenced to six months in prison for publishing a book by the American birth control campaigner, Charles Knowlton. In the event she had not served her time. The case had been overturned on appeal but the scandal had allowed her estranged husband successfully to argue that she was an unfit mother and to press for sole and permanent custody of their two children. She had never seen them again. Arthur and Mabel Besant were almost grown up now and still lived with their father. Meanwhile their mother worked tirelessly on behalf of the poor and their children, as least half of whom would never grow up at all.

Beyond the stand of bulrushes the beach curved to the left, opening up the prospect towards the south. Maribel squinted through the veil of smoke. Far out on the water men were fishing and beyond them, in the distance, a cluster of cottages huddled around a jetty on the low slopes above the shore. Some way away, where the hills folded in on themselves, among the dark bars of winter trees it was just possible to make out the line of a wall, painted white. Victor had chosen the convent for its isolation. The buildings were low, one-storey stone constructions set among groves of orange trees and enclosed on all sides by high white walls. If it had not been for the old woman Maribel would have never known the lake was there. The old woman laundered and pressed her clothes and her bedlinen, tidied and cleaned, and brought Maribel's meals from the refectory. She had a monkey's face, wrinkled as an old apple, and a mouthful of ill-assorted teeth that seemed to move in her jaw when she spoke. Maribel did not know where she slept or if she ever went home. When Maribel woke in the night, she was always there in the hard chair, her lips moving wordlessly over her teeth as she counted the beads on her rosary. In the darkness the bells had tolled softly, summoning the unseen nuns to prayer, and the newborn child beside her had stirred, crying to be fed.

She had not thought that she had come to this place because of the child. She only knew that, on the long journey, as her faith in the mine failed, the fact of the convent across the lake held her steady. Her grief was as familiar to her as the shape of her hands, the ache of it old and unfailing. The pain had not grown sharper as they neared their destination. Perhaps it could not. But it came to her more often and more unexpectedly. The arch of a bridge, the shape of a glass, the smell of food or of a log burning in a grate, such particulars could summon the pain into her throat with all the urgency of vomit. At those times she ached for Edward, the longing in her so strong that she had to bite the insides of her cheeks to master it.

It was a comfort to wake in the dark mornings in the spartan inns that marked the stages of the diligence, to jolt and shake for another day over the mud-rutted trails. To have undertaken the expedition in the warm embrace of summer, to travel through the hills bright with wild flowers, to watch the women washing their linen in the streams, the shepherds piping their sheep from the hills in the pink dusk, to lie beneath the sky on those long blue nights as the heat of the day evaporated, distilling itself into the white heat of a thousand brilliant stars – such a journey would have been unbearable. She endured the many discomforts without complaint. White she was cold and bruised with travel and the lice moved in her mattress she thought of Edward and his closeness was a consolation.

It began to rain, a light persistent drizzle. A fine muslin of cloud rucked in the curves of the hills and obscured the houses of Meiriz. She might have written to the convent from England but she had not. There would have been no purpose to it. It had been years. Even if they remembered the child, they would never tell her where he was. Besides, where was the help in knowing? Details would only whet the edges of her grief. Loss was formless but places were fixed. The precision of longitude and latitude, of distances in miles, was too absolute to be borne. To know exactly how far away he was, how close he had always been, that would be unendurable.

Still, late at night and especially after Vigo when they were on Spanish soil, when the wine was uncorked and the joints of her limbs sang with the giddy effervescence of too many cigarettes, she had allowed herself to imagine meeting him. He would be nearly twelve years old, dark and gangly, the bones sharp at the back of his neck but the curves of his face still soft with childhood. She would hold out her hands and he would set down his suitcase and step towards her cautiously, and she would take his face between her hands and kiss his cheek and he would smile and frown and rub at the place where she had kissed him with the back of his hand, and the part of her which had always been broken would not be broken any more. When she permitted herself these imaginings she squeezed her eyes tight, holding herself suspended in that moment, the swell in her chest, the diffident affection pinking his cheeks. The feeling was exhilarating, swooping upwards in her stomach like the high point on a swing. It did not matter that she did not know what came next. The trick was to think of something else before the swing began to drop.

In the rain the match took reluctantly. She hunched her shoulders, cupping her spare hand around the tip of her cigarette as she sucked in the flame. Above her, a tumble of rocks led to a narrow trail along the lip of the hill in the direction of Ferrixao. Her cigarette clamped in her mouth, her skirts bunched in her one hand, she scrambled up the rocks, her boots slipping a little on their rain-greased skin.

By the time she reached the trail the rain was falling in earnest and cloud veiled the lake. She hurried back towards the village. In a field that sloped up from the path several young boys were picking stones, gathering them in the pockets of oversized canvas aprons. They worked in silence, their hair slicked flat by the rain, their narrow bodies hunched over the weight of their cargo. Her cigarette had gone out. She stopped to relight it, watching the children as they stooped over their work. Their clothes were worn, their wooden shoes fat with mud. The rain fell harder, sticking their shirts to their backs. She could see the curves of their ribs through the wet cloth, the ridges of their spines.

The paper of the cigarette was wet too. She pulled in her cheeks, frowning with the effort of making it catch. In the field one of the boys straightened up, his fists on his hips, and stared at her. She smiled. The child called out something in Galego and the taller boy who worked beside him turned round to glance at Maribel. She thought she heard the word *cigarillo* as the taller one replied, lobbing a stone in the younger boy's direction. When the younger boy ducked the taller one laughed and returned to his work. The younger boy's jaw jutted. He glared at Maribel as though he dared her to laugh too. His hair fell over his face and in his famished old-man's face his dark eyes were huge. Then he too bent down and began once more to gather stones.

Blinking the rain out of her eyes, Maribel hurried away.

32

THE VISITORS' PARLOUR WAS a small room dominated by a polished oak table, its feet carved to resemble the clawed paws of a lion. On one whitewashed wall a large fireplace was presided over by a heavy iron chimney, an unlit fire neatly made up in the grate. The hearth was spotless. Opposite the fireplace, above a stiff row of high-backed oak chairs, a discoloured Jesus writhed on a wooden crucifix. There were no other adornments, except for plain iron sconces set at intervals into the wall, each bearing a half-burned candle, and a plum-coloured velvet curtain strung at shoulder height on the far wall. The velvet looked dusty, paler on the outward creases of the curtain where it had been bleached by the sun. It was hard to think of the room filled with sunlight. The two small windows were barred.

Maribel smoothed her skirt, shaking fragments of straw and dried mud from its hem. Then she sat down to wait on the chair nearest to the door, her hands folded in her lap. Her throat was dry. It had shaken her, how little she remembered. She had prepared herself for the avenue of trees, the wide gates, the grove of orange trees. Instead the farm cart that had brought her here had deposited her on the far side of the convent. She had entered through a side door into a high-walled passage which led directly to this room. It was like entering a prison.

She sat, her hands making patterns in her lap. It was very quiet. No one came. She longed to smoke a cigarette but she was afraid that in a convent smoking might be forbidden and she had no wish to provoke the nuns. She shifted on the chair. The wooden seat was slippery and uncomfortable. Later she stood, contemplating Jesus. His ribs protruded from beneath his yellow skin and brown blood streamed from his hands and feet and from his temples. The crown of thorns around his head was fashioned from twisted metal, the thorns sharp as razor blades. Beyond the window bells rang out. The end of sext, she thought, with a jolt of recognition. Her heart beat faster and, for something to do, she began to walk around the table, touching each of its corners with her fingertips as she passed. She thought of Edward, one bead on a string of felons, circling the prison yard. Beyond the door she heard footsteps. Suddenly she could not remember what it was she had thought to say.

There was a knock at the door.

'Yes?' she murmured and the word stuck like a wafer to the roof of her dry mouth.

A convent servant opened the door. She was slight and pale-faced, barely more than a child. She carried a tray with a carafe of water and a glass which she placed on the table. Gratefully Maribel poured herself a little water and drank. The girl did not speak. Instead, her head lowered, she scuttled across the room. Groping behind the purple curtain she pulled a cord. The curtain opened bouncily, like a puppet theatre, Maribel thought, except that behind the curtain was an iron grille, perhaps one foot and a half square, framed in curled iron brackets. The criss-crossed bars were beaten flat, leaving only small holes in the metal. At the centre of each cross was a tiny flower. The maid curtsied briefly, her eyes on the floor, and hurried from the room. The iron latch of the door clicked shut behind her.

'My apologies,' a voice said softly in Spanish from behind the grille. 'We have kept you waiting.'

Maribel hesitated. Then, her glass clasped tightly between her hands, she approached the grille.

'Prioress?'

'The Prioress cannot receive visitors without an appointment.'

'I see.'

'You may talk to me.'

The voice was husky, deep enough almost to have been a man's. A smoker's voice. There was a silence. Maribel wished she could smoke. Instead she took a sip of water. Her hand was unsteady.

'What is it that brings you here, my child?'

Maribel swallowed, placing her glass on the table. It should be easier, she thought, to talk to oneself, without the requirement to disregard the expressions on another's face, the tightening of the lips, the faint pinching of the skin between the eyebrows.

'I –'

She bit her lip sharply, moistening her lips with her tongue, but still the words did not come. On his cross Jesus twisted his head away from her, his mouth wide with anguish. Maribel put her hands over her face. The voice said nothing. After a while she opened her fingers and looked at the grille. She thought perhaps she could make out a gleam of white behind the iron lattice. Perhaps, if she placed her hand flat on the metal she would feel the warmth of the nun's breath against her palm.

'I – I cannot see you,' she said.

'But you know that I am here.'

'I think it would be easier for me if I could see you. If you were in the room.'

'That is not permitted.'

'So we must talk through the wall, is that it? Like Pyramus and Thisbe?'

The joke was a poor one, poorer still in her rusty Spanish. Her throat tightened, apprehension binding her stomach to her spine.

'Ours is a closed order. We must remain within the confines of the priory.'

'And I cannot come in?'

'Not without the express authorisation of the Bishop.'

Maribel took another sip of water. She thought of Victor, who had always claimed to know everyone who was worth knowing.

'Do not be discouraged,' the voice said gently. 'Sometimes it is easier to say things only to oneself.'

It startled Maribel, to hear her own thoughts spoken aloud. Slowly she ran her finger around the lip of her water glass. It was a heavy tumbler, unskilfully blown. Large bubbles were trapped in the thick glass like fish in ice. She set it on the table.

'My sister was here,' she said quietly. 'Eleven years ago.'

'Your sister was a novitiate?'

'She was a visitor. For three months. The Bishop must have been –' she hesitated, searching for the word in Spanish – 'accommodating.'

The voice on the other side of the grille said nothing.

'My sister did not live with the nuns. The Bishop was not so accommodating as all that. She spent her confinement in the cottage beyond the wall, the one beside the orange grove, and there she bore a child. A boy. When he was only a few weeks old they took him away. She let them take him away.'

There was a lump in her throat. She turned away from the grille, interlocking her hands and pressing the knuckles hard against her lips. Beyond the high barred window the sky was the inscrutable white of polished stone. She stared at it for a long moment until the lump was gone, her attention fixed upon the floating motes of dust as they darted and spun over the surface of her eyes. Then she cleared her throat.

'Now my sister is very ill. The doctors hold out little hope. It is a matter of months, perhaps even weeks. She has made her confession, performed her penance. She should be at peace. Instead she cries in anguish for her lost child. It was to soothe her that I promised I would come here, to see if you might have any information as to the boy's whereabouts, so that she might know him before it is too late. Of course, there is a chance that the child – that it is already too late, but, if he lives, I beg you, help me to help her. She has money. She wants to make amends. It torments her that she will die without knowing she has done what she can for him. Without his – forgiveness. She would help you, help your convent, if you were able to help her.'

The silence in the room was suffocating. Maribel did not look towards the grille. She kept her gaze fixed upon the window. When she blinked there were dark stripes in the orange of her eyelids.

'So,' the voice said at last, 'she intends to make the child a bequest?'

'Yes, of course. But this is not simply about money.'

'No. She seeks to acquaint herself with the boy.'

'It is her dying wish.'

There was another long silence. To occupy herself Maribel picked up the glass of water. She took a sip, then another. The water tasted stale.

'Your sister,' the voice said abruptly. 'She has other children?'

The glass slipped in Maribel's hand. Unsteadily she set it down.

'No,' she said.

'But she is married?'

'Yes. She is married. And very respectable.'

'And this respectable husband of hers is a good man?'

'A very good man.'

'I think perhaps the child is not her husband's son? That he knows nothing of the boy?'

Maribel hesitated a fraction too long.

'She is angry at him, perhaps? Perhaps she resents him for not giving her another child?'

'That is absurd. It has nothing whatsoever to do with him.'

'You are right. And yet it would seem that she seeks to bequeath him her torment.'

'She is dying. She wishes to atone for her sins.'

'But at what detriment to those she leaves behind? If she lights this tinderbox she will see only the pretty flames. It will be her husband who must afterwards sift through the charred remains. He and the boy.'

'There may be difficulties, of course, but they can be overcome. And does the boy not deserve to know his mother?'

'Perhaps the child already has a mother.'

Maribel faltered. She rubbed at her temples with her fingertips as though she might smooth out the disordered tangle of her thoughts.

'His real mother,' she said.

'To what end, child? So that he might experience the grief of her abandoning him a second time?'

'Death is not abandonment.'

'Do you think a child understands that?'

Angrily Maribel shook her head.

'You are twisting everything. She seeks to heal, not to hurt. The boy is her child, her flesh and blood. He is a – a part of her.'

'No. After eleven years it is his absence that is a part of her. The amputated leg continues to ache. That does not make the leg real.'

'The boy is real.'

'Yes, if he lives. But her husband, the very good man, he is real too.'

'And so is my sister. Her suffering is real.'

'I do not doubt it. It is when we suffer that it is especially hard to remember that our actions continue to have consequences. Even those we carry out to punish ourselves.'

The glare of the white sky through the barred windows hurt Maribel's eyes. She put a hand over her face.

'He is her son,' she whispered.

'She has managed to live without him for eleven years. She must know how it is done.'

'Just because one learns to endure does not mean one is obliged to do so.'

'Perhaps not. But when it is such a hard lesson, it is better to learn it only once.'

Once again the silence spread itself implacably between them. Slowly Maribel shook her head.

'"Judge not, that ye be not judged",' she said. Her heart was very heavy. 'That is what I was taught as a child. And yet you, a daughter of God, would judge my sister, of whom you know nothing.'

'I do not seek to judge her. Only to guide you, who loves her well enough to come here in her place.'

Outside birds had begun to sing, a restless flurry of peeps and whistles. Somewhere a door banged. Maribel felt exhausted, empty of words. At the base of her skull a headache began to tremble.

'Then you will not help me?' she asked at last.

'I have done what I can.'

'You have not told me where I might find the boy.'

'No. I have not done that.'

'And you will not?'

'I cannot.'

'For the love of peace –'

'It is not as you think. The cottages by the orange grove are not a part of the priory. They were once, a long time ago, but not for a century at least. For some time they were used by pilgrims on their journey to the cathedral at Santiago but that was long before my time. The pilgrims no longer come this way and the cottages are empty. They say they are falling down.'

Maribel stared at the grille.

'I don't understand.'

'Whatever arrangements were made for your sister and her child, they will have been undertaken privately. They will have had absolutely nothing to do with us.'

Maribel thought of the old woman with her monkey face and her rosary beads. She had taken the child. Maribel had hidden her face then. She had not had the courage to look. She thought of Oedipus on his mountain, of Moses lifted from his rush basket in the reeds by an Egyptian princess. She thought of the Irish babies during the Great Hunger, abandoned in the ruined fields to be pecked by crows. She thought of Victor and of all the people that he knew and the desolation spread through her like ink.

'You knew from the start that you could not help me,' she said. 'You knew you could not help me and yet on you went, on and on, preaching and sermonising and –' She broke off, her voice no longer trustworthy. Taking her cape from the chair where she had left it she put it on.

'Forgive me, child,' the voice said quietly. 'Here in the priory we speak little. It is hard to resist the lure of conversation.'

'I should like to leave now.'

'Of course. I shall call for the servant to see you out. May the Lord bless you and keep you and may He make His light to shine upon you, today and all the days of your life. And may your sister find peace. Amen.'

Maribel did not reply. From behind the lattice she could hear the scrape of a chair being pushed back. There was a rustle of skirts, the faint echo of boots on a stone floor. Then it was quiet.

Beyond the window the birds sang. Maribel wrapped her arms around the pain in her chest and wept.

33

T HE RAIN HAD STOPPED. In their attic room in the inn
at Ferrixao the pale sunlight made patterns like lace
on the single dirty pane of the window. Maribel knelt,
dragging the trunk containing her camera from its place beneath
the narrow iron bed. Inside she had wrapped the camera case
in a blanket to keep it from damage. She unfolded the blanket
and, opening the case, lifted the camera from its nest of padding.
Despite the care with which she had wrapped it, it had grown
dusty. She blew on it briskly and polished it with a clean cloth,
working the rag carefully into the hidden cavities of the lens
casing. When she peered at Alice through the viewfinder the
maid scowled, scratching ostentatiously at the red bites on her
wrists.

'Be careful,' Maribel said. 'A face like that could crack the lens
clean through.'

Alice stuck out her tongue. Then she picked up Maribel's
cape, shaking it out before holding it up for her mistress to put
on. Maribel slipped her arms through the slits. Alice assessed
her appraisingly, smoothing out the creases at the shoulders,
and fastened the clasp at the neck.

'Be careful yourself,' she said. 'You are still weak, you know.'

On the journey back from the priory a storm had blown in.
By the time the mules reached the inn at Ferrixao Maribel had
been soaked through. She had spent the following day in bed,
unable to stop shivering. Alice had stayed with her, feeding her

spoonfuls of soup and watching her while she slept. 'Nonsense,' Maribel said. 'I am quite recovered.'

'You are white as a sheet. You're to take it slow, you hear me? And no getting into trouble with Johnny Foreigner.'

'Here I believe they call him Juan Extranjero.'

'They can call him whatever they like,' Alice said briskly. 'It's not as though he's going to understand a word they say.'

The morning was still, the clouds parted to reveal strips of silvery sky. In the field above the lake the boys were once again picking stones. They worked slowly, hunched over, their hands reaching into the earth with weary regularity. Maribel watched as one boy straightened up, straining against the weight of the stones in his apron. They hung from his thin frame like a pendulous belly. 'Excuse me,' she called in Spanish.

The boy turned. He had close-set eyes and a smear of mud across his right cheek.

'Excuse me,' she said again. 'Might I speak with you?'

The boy did not answer. Slowly he emptied his bellyful of stones into a large flat basket. Then, putting his fingers in his mouth, he whistled at another boy who was working a little distance away. As the second boy looked up Maribel recognised him as the boy who had thrown the stone. He was taller than the others. She took a few tentative steps towards him. Further up the field other boys were working. Though she squinted she could not see if he was among them, the boy she had seen the last time, the boy with the huge eyes.

'I should like to photograph you,' she said, holding out the camera. 'All of you. If you will let me.'

She spoke slowly so that the boy might understand her. When he did not reply she rummaged in her satchel and pulled out a parcel, wrapped for her by the innkeeper. The paper was shiny with grease.

'Are you hungry?' she asked. 'I brought food.'

The boy eyed the parcel. Then he said something in Galego. It was not like Spanish. She did not understand him.

'Bread and sausage,' she said, holding out the parcel. 'For you. From the inn at Ferrixao.'

She pointed back towards the village. The boy hesitated. He was very thin. His Adam's apple protruded sharply from his throat, as though he had swallowed one of his stones. Behind him the other boys had stopped working. They watched him, their arms slack against their sides.

'Please,' she said. 'Take it.'

The boy chewed his lip, his eyes flickering between her face and the parcel. The greasy paper gleamed.

'Come on,' she encouraged and, taking a step towards him, she placed the package in his hands. He stared at it. She tugged at the string, unfolded the paper. When the boy saw the quantity of sausage his eyes widened and the stone in his throat moved up and down.

'It is for all of you,' Maribel said, sweeping out her arm to include the other boys. They clustered together, nudging one another, their old-men's faces pinched with suspicion and curiosity. She smiled tentatively at them, encouraging them to approach. The boy's brow furrowed. He gestured at the food, the question clear without words.

'Because I should like to photograph you,' she said, digging around once again in her satchel. 'Photograph. Like this.'

The picture she showed him was of Mr Molloy, the translator from the Wild West. He had not known she was taking it. He leaned against a five-barred gate, his hat tipped back and his thumbs hooked into the pockets of his waistcoat, his habitually sardonic expression softened into thoughtfulness. The boy stared at Mr Molloy. His dirty fingers hovered over the man's face, stiff with wonder and the desire to touch.

'The camera makes the picture,' she said, miming. 'It will make a picture of you.'

The boy's frown deepened. He gazed at the picture of Mr Molloy. Then he shook his head, muttering something in his unintelligible language. Hearing him, the boys began to turn away.

'Wait,' Maribel cried and at that moment she saw him. He stood slightly behind the others, his hands loose at his sides, and his gaze from beneath his unkempt fringe of hair was steady and unblinking. She stared back at him and her stomach turned over.

'I can pay you,' she said.

She dipped into her pocket, holding out a handful of coins. The tall boy sucked his teeth. Then he reached for them. Maribel shook her hand and closed her hand in a fist. From between her fingers she took a single coin.

'This one now,' she said. 'The rest after.'

The boy hesitated. Tearing a fragment of paper from the food parcel, Maribel wrapped the rest of the money in it. She set it on a flat stone.

'For you,' she said, pointing from the boy to the money. 'After.'

There was a pause. Then he nodded, gesturing at the boys. They murmured to one another, their flanks pressed together like cattle. The tall boy shouted something and they began slowly to inch closer. Their clogs were solid with mud.

'You can keep this,' Maribel said to the tall boy and she held out the photograph of Mr Molloy. The boy hesitated. Then, his eyes on the ground, he nodded and took it, sliding it under his canvas apron.

She photographed them separately. The poses were intimate, taken very close. The low cloud filtered the light to a soft dust that caught in the black mops of their hair and lit their dirty faces. She paid no attention to the lake, the majestic sweep of the mountains against the silvered sky. Beside the intimate topography of the boys' faces, the landscape felt flat and artificial. She did not know how much of the greed was hers and how much the camera's but with each shot she moved closer, the lens opening up like a mouth, caressing, laying claim to the smear of dirt across a cheekbone, the fleck of sleep in the corner of a dark eye, the tiny scar of a blemish in the dent of a temple. The intimacy was exquisite and yet she felt invisible, the essence of her all in the box that she held to her face, the whole world suspended in the circle of its lens.

She saved the boy with the dark eyes until last. At first he was awkward. He squinted and shifted, biting at his lips, unable to keep still. His eyes slid from side to side. He stretched his neck to look at the other boys in the field. He frowned. He opened his mouth to say something and closed it again. He twisted his fingers together, looked down at his feet. She said nothing. She waited.

The boy was weary. The day was mild, the respite from his work unexpected. Little by little the tension in his shoulders eased. His full lips parted and the little frown that notched the space between his eyebrows softened. His head lolled a little. He regarded the camera without curiosity and the steadiness of his gaze was at the same time vulnerable and veiled, childish and unimaginably ancient. He was disquietingly beautiful. His mud-caked hands, his ragged clothes, his thin hunched shoulders attested to the centuries of back-breaking labour endured by the poor peasants of this mountainous part of Spain, to hardship and hunger and the certainty of hardship and hunger to come, and yet in the artlessness of his beauty there was a nobility, a disquieting grace that made a costume of the rags and the mud.

Though she moved closer and closer, her face pressed hard against the camera, she could not reach him. He gazed through her to a place she did not know and there was no distress in his eyes nor any hopefulness either. He did not preen for her as the other boys had, tugging at their ragged clothes and trying on faces. He wore his beauty and his poverty equally, as though neither belonged to him. Like a besotted lover the camera lingered over the particulars of his face, the bent arch of an eyebrow, the crumpled whorl of an ear, the fine down along the sharp line of his jaw, everything that was not him forgotten. His eyes were almond-shaped and so dark a brown that they were almost black. They gleamed, opaque, bright with silver scraps of sky, and in their fathomless depths was nothing and all the truth in the world.

That night Maribel could not sleep. A little before dusk Sr Muñoz had returned, the panniers on the mules fat with earth from the mine, and the next day they would travel together to Madrid for the assay. It would be several days before the Mining College could assess the potential value of their endeavours in Galicia. Maribel turned over, seeking a comfortable position. The moon was full, the dirty window at the foot of the bed iced with light. She curled into the dark shadow of the eaves, straining for sleep. It did not come. She craved a cigarette.

At last, the restlessness too strong in her, she rose, slipping on her heavy wrap. In the other bed Alice slept soundly, her dark hair tumbled on the pillow and her nightgown buttoned up beneath her chin. She breathed heavily, her mouth slightly open, the shadow of a dream flickering over her face. She looked very young.

The trunk containing their clothes made for a makeshift table. Striking a match Maribel lit a cigarette and then, hurriedly, fearful of burning her fingers, the tallow lamp. The wick was reluctant and the light burned in a tight bud of flame before it caught, blooming gold against the whitewashed wall. Maribel set her writing case on the lid of the trunk and took out paper and a pen before propping the slope.

She had not written to Edward for several days and the lid to the inkwell was stiff. She smoothed the paper, drawing her cold feet up underneath her. The night air insinuated itself through the place where the window had warped in its frame. Beside her the lamp guttered a little, spitting fat. She inhaled, drawing smoke into her chest until her lungs cramped. She held the smoke inside her for as long as she was able. Then she exhaled. She dipped her pen.

My love,

It is that hour of the night when ghosts roam and the certainties of daylight grow vague as dreams. In the
village the street is empty, the houses shuttered and dark. The dogs are quiet at last, the birds not yet up. Everyone sleeps. Somewhere beyond the slumbering mountains our mine sleeps too, waiting like a princess for us to kiss her from her ancient slumber. I think perhaps I am the only person in all of Spain who does not sleep, my smoky little lamp the single gleam of gold in the black Spanish night.

But it is not quite dark. The moon is full. Do you remember how, in Mexico, the moon was yellow and so heavy and swollen it seemed barely to hang above the horizon? This moon is as small and neat as a silver shilling and so sharp it prints shadows on the bare earth. I reach out through the dusty little window and I take it in my cupped hands. For you, I whisper, and I think that perhaps, in all the years I have loved you, I have never loved you as dearly as I do tonight. Sleep safely, dearest one, and, if you should wake, do not despair but gaze out beyond the bars of your window so that you might see what I see, that all we have need of is already ours. Our mine may yet yield nothing but we shall always have the moon.

Your M

'You look happy,' Maribel remarked to Alice as they waited to board the diligence for Orense.

'Well, of course I look happy. It's over, isn't it?'

'Yes. It's over.'

It was a dank grey day and the mules at the traces of the ancient conveyance looked thinner and more dispirited than she remembered them. She glanced up at the roof of the coach where their boxes were lashed alongside the jute sacks of earth from the mine. In the doorway of the inn Sr Muñoz pumped the hand of the innkeeper and made extravagant promises to return with glad news. The driver of the diligence whistled. Sr Muñoz gave the innkeeper a final triumphant clap on the back and bounded across the muddy churn of the yard to swing himself aboard the conveyance.

As the diligence bumped along the poor road away from the village Maribel looked back towards the inn. Slowly the tumble of buildings shrank and slipped behind the curve of the hill until they were no longer visible. Maribel settled into her seat. She would never come back, she was certain of that.

They stayed in Madrid while tests were carried out on the samples Sr Muñoz had collected from the mine. Although he remained resolutely optimistic until the last handful of earth had been ground and blasted to a fine dust in the crucibles of the Mining College, Maribel allowed herself only one wild moment of hopefulness in the moment before the engineer assigned to their assay announced the results of their analysis. She knew before he spoke that the mine was infructuous. Whatever the earth had once yielded had long been exhausted. There was not one trace of gold in its ancient clay.

Sr Muñoz seemed bewildered. He shook his head angrily as though plagued by flies, unable to comprehend either the possibility of failure or the pig-headed stupidity of the scientific instruments. Maribel only shrugged. Early the next morning they made their farewells to Sr Muñoz and began the long journey back to England. 'The mine was always a million to one chance,' she said to Alice as the train jolted northwards over the ill-closed Spanish points. 'A grand and crazy dream. I don't suppose dreams are meant to come true.'

'You would tell me that now, ma'am, after all you have put me through?'

Maribel grinned. 'Were it not for the joy of tormenting you, Alice, I should have turned back at Plymouth.'

'You are a wicked woman, ma'am. Still, at least next time you drag me to abroad I shall know to bring my own sandwiches. Not to mention several pounds of proper English tea.'

'I shouldn't worry. The mine is a dud, after all. I have no plans to return.'

'Not here, perhaps. My brother Joe was like you. The itchiest two feet ever laced into a pair of boots. There'll be another somewhere soon enough, you mark my words.'

'You would do that? You would come away with me again?'

Alice rolled her eyes. 'Ma'am, what choice do I have? I saw them snails you ate straight from the shells. If I don't go with you who will stop you from losing your head and going native?'

The two women were silent, staring out of the window. It had begun to rain and streaks of water snaked in diagonal lines across the glass. Maribel lit a cigarette.

'Tell me about Joe,' she said.

'Not much to tell. The boy thought he was David bleedin' Livingstone. Never shut up about Africa and finding the Nile and whatnot. He'd not managed a month apprenticed when he ran off to join the navy, stupid bugger. Sorry. Broke our mam's heart.'

'Did he make it to Africa?'

'Never got past Portsmouth. Influenza.'

'I'm sorry.'

Alice shrugged. 'Weak chest. He'd have made a rotten explorer.'

'I suppose one must admire him for trying.'

'He was a stupid bugger. No other way of saying it.'

The whistle screamed, the brakes doing noisy battle with the tracks as the train pulled into a station. A family got into their carriage, a fluster of boxes and bags and children chattering like starlings in rapid Spanish. They spread a picnic, offering food to Maribel and Alice, who declined politely. Maribel took out her book but the words swam before her eyes. Her thoughts were all of Joe Tweddle with his weak chest, who strove for Africa and died without ever getting his feet wet.

34

EDWARD AND JOHN BURNS were released from Pentonville Prison at seven o'clock on a dark Saturday morning in February, less than a fortnight after Maribel returned from Spain. The two men had served ten of the twelve weeks of their sentences, having earned remission for good behaviour. Though the early hour had been chosen deliberately by the authorities to ensure the prisoners' quiet release, an enthusiastic crowd awaited them outside the gates of the prison. As they stepped out into the street they were greeted with a barrage of noisy cheers. Several men in heavy boots threw their hats into the air and others thrust food into the freed men's hands, hunks of bread and slices of pie which the two men bit into ravenously before adjourning to breakfast in the coffee shop on the other side of Caledonian Road.

While they were still eating Maribel arrived in a hansom, stepping down amid a flurry of applause from the knot of supporters still gathered on the pavement outside. She had risen early, anxious to be punctual, but somehow, with one thing and another, she found herself delayed, and by the time she was ready to leave the flat, the cab driver had been waiting for the best part of an hour. She had spent the journey huddled in the seat, fighting impatience at his cautious progress and the strong urge to return to Cadogan Mansions. Her grey silk dress was too obviously good, her hat too fashionable. She wished now that she had worn her brown walking suit after all.

She paid the cabman and turned to go in. Edward was sitting with John Burns at a table in the steamed-up window, the words 'MURPHY'S COFFEE HOUSE' in time-worn gold lettering in an arch above his head. The sight of him in his familiar long black overcoat at the crude wooden table, his red-gold head bent over a plate of bacon and eggs, caused her to catch her breath. It was only then that she understood how afraid she had been that he was gone from her for ever. Inside Edward kissed her and she pretended not to cry. He was thin and very pale, dark smears of exhaustion beneath his eyes. He smelled different. There were crescents of dirt under his fingernails. She shook John Burns's hand and toasted their health in tea so strong it left a stain on the inside of the cup. Mr Hyndman of the SDF arrived with two other men whom Maribel did not recognise. They were both young, one barely more than a boy. The proprietor brought more chairs and a basket of fresh rolls. When it was time to leave he refused to allow Maribel to pay the bill.

Outside, a handful of men still loitered on the pavement. Two or three pushed forward as they emerged from the coffee shop, shouting questions.

'Don't stop,' Hyndman murmured to Edward. 'They're none of them on our side.'

'Are there any left that are?'

Hyndman grimaced, steering him round the corner to where a hansom was waiting.

'Courtesy of Mrs Aveling,' he said.

Mr Burns looked at Edward.

'That's it, then,' he said with a crooked smile.

Edward took Burns's hand. His lips were pressed very tightly together.

'*Adios, amigo.*'

'Till next time.'

'I suppose so.'

They looked at each other, their hands still clasped. Then Burns turned away, the two young men following close behind him. Edward watched him go as Mr Hyndman helped Maribel into the cab. Then slowly he turned and climbed in beside her.

On the pavement Hyndman raised his hand in a salute. The cabman touched his whip to the horse's neck and with a jingle of harness the cab jolted forward. Edward flinched. Gently Maribel stretched over and placed her gloved hand on his. He pressed it, sliding his fingers between hers. They did not speak. The brim of Maribel's hat was broad and low, its edge nudging Edward's shoulder. He shifted away from her a little to avoid crushing it. Impatiently she pulled the hat off, dropping it at her feet. He looked down at her and very faintly he smiled. Tucking her other hand into the crook of his arm she pulled him close, setting her head on his shoulder. The prison smell of him mixed with the worn leather of the hansom seat, the wool of his coat. He rested his cheek on the top of her head. His breath was slow and very careful.

The cab rattled south along Baker Street, the panorama of brightly coloured shops and restaurants unspooling before them like a bolt of cloth, but she closed her eyes, the world contained in the warmth of his lean thigh against hers, the lurching slant of his shoulder, the weight of his head. The pressure of his fingers between hers stretched the tendons, pulling the skin tight around her knuckles. When she squeezed his hand he set his other one on top of hers, clasping it tightly, so that she felt the throb of the pulse in her fingers, the steady thump of her heart.

The adjustment to ordinary life was not as easy for Edward as either of them had hoped. The injuries to his skull caused crippling headaches, while the blows to the stomach had resulted in internal inflammation that refused to heal. The pain kept him from sleeping.

Several times Maribel rose in the night to find him sitting alone and in darkness in the drawing room at Cadogan Mansions, staring out over the empty street. He said it was the silence that woke him, that in prison the nights had echoed with the tramping of men up and down their cells, the mysterious code of rappings by which prisoners communicated with one another repeating themselves in patterns over and over again until one's skull sang with it. He talked of the twisting and turning of those interminable nights, the frequent rising from his narrow bench, the restless pacing, the ritual touching of the few articles in the cell, always in the same order, the counting to one thousand, to one hundred thousand, the weariness of lying down only to rise again moments later and begin all over again. In the darkness he had reflected on every base thing he had ever done. He had shouted and wept and cursed like a drab and beaten the walls with his fists until they ached, until at last he fell into a thin uneasy doze that seemed to last only a minute or two before he was roused again by the sounding of the morning bell. He had marked the passing of the nights on the wall by his bench with a bent pin he had found hidden in his salt box. It helped him, he said, to think of the man who had left it. It was the closest he could get to a conversation.

On those nights Maribel did not try to persuade him back to bed. She brought a blanket to put around his shoulders and sat with him, her legs tucked up beneath her, as he yielded to the spate of words dammed up for ten solitary weeks. In the light of the street lamp his hair was bronze, his face a sulphurous yellow. The winter dawns were late and it was still night when they returned to bed. In the darkness they made love quietly, tenderly, their cheeks pressed together as though they were dancing.

As soon as he was able Edward began to work. The day after his release several boxes were delivered to Cadogan Mansions from the offices of the Socialist League, filled to the brim with files. Maribel urged him to take time to recuperate but he told her that he had wasted enough time already. It was plain that he was not well. Several times she came into the drawing room to find him asleep in his armchair, his glasses crooked on his face, the floor around his feet littered with dropped newspaper clippings and sheaves of memoranda.

He had been free six days when he returned to Parliament to attend a disorderly debate on public meetings. Despite his imprisonment he had retained his seat in the House but, from the moment of his arrival, it was plain that he had categorically forfeited the support of his fellow Members, his own party among them. In the Palace of Westminster it was universally agreed that Edward Campbell Lowe was, as the *Times* had opined, a disgrace to the House. His actions were condemned as braggadocio, the intolerable posturings of a rabble-rouser and political sensationalist. Even those who had supported him in the past had to concede that he had shown himself to be, without question, an enemy of law and order. Such a man, it was agreed, had no part to play in the democratic constitution of their great Empire.

The Liberals were not foolish enough to vilify one of their own in public but when a Conservative backbencher accused the Member for Argyllshire of being nothing short of a revolutionary, there were murmurs of assent on both sides of the House. Edward stood, begging the Speaker's indulgence. In an impassioned speech he declared that if to be a revolutionary was to wish to improve the wretched condition of the poor, to seek a fair wage for fair hours, to demand on their behalf a properly democratic manner of government, to fight for the payment of Members of Parliament and to resist with every fibre of his being the illegal suppression of free speech, then, yes, he was indeed a revolutionary.

The speech, though eloquent, found little favour with the floor. Edward sat down to booing on both sides of the House.

Later, on his way out of the Chamber, he found himself walking beside the Prime Minister.

'Well, well, Mr Lowe,' Lord Salisbury said mordantly. 'And where exactly do you intend to erect your guillotine?'

Edward raised an eyebrow. 'In Trafalgar Square, of course,' he replied.

Salisbury's mouth moved in its thicket of whiskers but he said nothing. The next day the *Herald* carried a caricature of Edward in his prison uniform floating back towards Pentonville Prison in a balloon filled with his own hot air. When he next encountered Salisbury in the House his greeting was answered with a brief and chilly nod. It was clear that the Prime Minister considered it unseemly for the shamed to make jokes, even at their own expense.

'I have a new title,' Edward remarked drily the next day as he leafed through the newspapers. '"Disgraced". "The disgraced Mr Campbell Lowe" and here "the Disgraced Member for Argyllshire". That one sounds like the title of a *Punch* cartoon.'

'Don't speak too soon.'

'Hang on a moment. In the *Chronicle*, our friend Mr Webster has ploughed his own furrow and gone for "dilettante". Well, that's good. Whatever one's views of the man one must admire his refusal to swim with the current. Oh no, I'm wrong. Here is "disgraced", two lines down.'

Maribel shook her head.

'I can't believe Lord Worsley allows him to hang on. If I had known that brute would still be editor when you got out I would never have given him such a piece of my mind.'

Unable to contain herself she had confessed her outburst to Edward soon after he got out of prison. To her surprise Edward had been sanguine. It turned out that Mrs Aveling had written to him at Pentonville, expressing both support for his endeavours and admiration for his wife's candour and her dauntless spirit. It was plain, she had remarked, that the two of them were perfectly matched.

Edward smiled. 'That, my dearest Bo, is utter rot.'

'I'm still sorry. He might have deserved it but you don't. Things are already difficult enough without me making them worse.'

Edward took her hand and pressed it to his lips. 'Well, don't be. Mr Alfred Webster is an abomination and it was about time someone told him so. I just wish I'd been there to hear you do it. Mrs Aveling tells me that the fearless crusader for justice quaked in his boots like a schoolboy.'

Maribel smiled reluctantly. Though she could scarcely allow herself to believe it, it seemed that perhaps there was, after all, nothing to fear. Once the spiteful coverage of the trial had abated, there had been no further mention of Edward in the *Chronicle* until his release, which was reported in a short paragraph at the bottom of page 5.

'It's a shame, of course,' Edward mused. 'Webster may be a double-dealing bastard, but, despite everything, he is a Socialist. Those leaders of his attacked me not because of my principles but because he doubted my seriousness. He is the only newspaperman in London who has ever wanted me to be more myself.'

Edward was called to a meeting with the most senior members of the Liberal Party. While the whip was not formally withdrawn it was made perfectly plain to Edward that the party considered him a liability and that he could no longer count on their support. It was suggested that, if he were to decide to stand at the next election, he would be obliged to do so as an independent candidate.

Edward was not surprised. He no longer considered himself a Liberal either, or even a Radical. Though he scrupulously fulfilled his parliamentary duties he avoided Westminster. He spent most of his time in his constituency. A miner and secretary of the recently established Ayrshire Miners Union, a man by the name of Keir Hardie with whom Edward had become acquainted from his work with the Scottish Land Restoration League, had tried and failed to gain Liberal support for his candidacy in a by-election for the nearby constituency of Mid Lanarkshire. The experience had convinced him and many of his fellow miners of the need for an independent party representing the interests of labour and he had written to Edward to solicit his support. Convinced now that the Liberals neither could nor would do anything to relieve the misery of the working classes, Edward offered it eagerly. The prospect of a Labour Party filled him with new hope. Though both the Socialist League and the SDF promised to boycott the event, he agreed to chair a founding conference in Glasgow in May.

Unwilling to be left alone again in London, Maribel travelled with him. At Inverallich she attended increasingly fractious meetings with the estate's financial advisers. When the accountants were gone, she pored over the books, trying to see what might be done to improve their parlous situation. She drew the line at the endless round of wearisome political rallies but she acquired a typewriter and taught herself to use it, so that, afterwards, she might transcribe Edward's illegible scribbles into serviceable minutes.

She typed up the accounts of the overcrowded villages of Motherwell and Coatbridge where the roar of the furnaces and the steam hammers never ceased, so that the ground trembled beneath one's feet and, at night, the sky above the town burned scarlet. She noted the tight rows of thrown-up houses, where the miners' families lived ten to a room and tuberculosis was rife, the unflagged dirt floors, the open sewers, the filthy skin of black dust that overlay everything. She hesitated as she made out a note in the margin that Edward had underlined and marked with an asterisk: '*Everyone either very young or very old, for age follows so hard on youth in Coatbridge.*'

The next time he went to the mining villages she went too. She took her camera, a bag filled with food and candles and matches, and, reluctantly, a young man in heavy boots whom Edward insisted accompany her as guide and guardian. She made the boy wait at a safe distance while she held up the camera for the thin, bow-legged children, so that they might look through the viewfinder and see how the plates slid into the holder. As she stood over them she could see the lice crawling in their hair.

She photographed them as she had photographed the boys in the field at Ferrixao, very close. She did not flinch from the stink of unwashed bodies, the scabs on their cheeks and fore-heads, the crusted snot around their noses. She did not bring handkerchiefs or Bibles. She did not try to comb their hair. They stared into her lens and she met their gaze, steadily and without judgement. When she was finished she had the young man distribute the food and the candles and a handful of pennies from a purse she had given him to keep safe.

Back in London she waited in the darkroom as their faces gathered shape, their eyes darkening and deepening. It was not true what they said, that the wretchedness of poverty extin-guished the human spirit. In time, perhaps, it would but for now, though the children's faces were all pinched, depleted by the deficit of light and nourishment, there was no uniformity of character or expression. Beneath the weariness there was the wariness and insolence that one might have expected from street urchins, there was sullenness and slit-eyed calculation, but there was hope too and humour and eagerness for praise. A boy with sores about his mouth laughed unguardedly, his eyes pressed into half-moons by the wideness of his smile, while a girl with thick brows and hair in strings about her face thrust up her chin in swaggering defiance, her shoulders up and her jaw set like a prize fighter. One of her teeth was broken. Only the tilt of her eyes betrayed her youth and the uncertainty of her challenge.

Maribel bent over the baths of chemicals, the taste of the fumes sharp in her mouth, and with her tongs carefully lifted out a print of a pale-haired child. The child had a high brow and wide-set eyes and might have been beautiful had it not been for the cleft palate that split her upper lip to the nose, peeling it away from her gums. The fleshy nakedness of her exposed mouth was shocking, almost obscene. Propped on the sill of the blacked-out window the boy from Ferrixao watched her work. She set the print to dry, standing back to consider it.

'Any good?' she asked him.

The beauty of him still caused her heart to turn over. Frowning, she turned back to study the girl. Two days previously she had received a letter from Constance Wilde in which she wrote of an acquaintance of hers who owned a gallery in Duke Street. It seemed that the gentleman, who had recently inherited the business from his late father, wished to mount an exhibition of photographs and had asked Constance if she knew any photographers whose work might be suitable.

I recall from our last conversation that you have certain misgivings about this latest project but, should you be interested in showing it, I should be delighted to effect an introduction. Mr More is remarkably open to new ideas and when I mentioned your portraits he showed himself so eager I feared he might snap my arm off at the elbow.

Maribel stared at the girl. As yet she had not written a reply. She shook her head at the boy, wiping her hands on her stained apron.

'I need a cigarette.'

Taking cigarettes and matches from her satchel she pushed

open the door. The tall windows of the corridor were lemony with spring sunlight and she squinted, her eyes unaccustomed to the brightness. On the wall opposite, the ranks of sailor-suited moppets pouted winsomely at her, ribbons and ringlets arranged in charming cascades.

Despite her avowals to Mr Pidgeon she had not found another darkroom. She had made some half-hearted investigations but darkrooms for hire were uncommon creatures in Chelsea, still less on such reasonable terms as those extended to her in Turks Row, and the prospect of struggling to a studio in the likes of Ealing or Hackney had not filled her with enthusiasm. Then Edward's trial had begun and she had not thought of photography.

When she returned from Spain, her impatience to develop the images from Ferrixao had overcome what remained of her indignation. She had returned to Turks Row with a determined nonchalance, resolved to deflect any enquiries from Mr Pidgeon with breezy evasion. She need not have worried. For several weeks she had seen only the boy Thomas. When at last she had encountered the photographer it had been on the pavement outside the studios. He had not seemed surprised to see her. He had only raised his hat and muttered something lugubrious about the unseasonal lateness of the daffodils.

There was no sound from the studio today. She leaned against the wall, striking a match, drawing the flame through the cigarette and right into the ache at the centre of her chest. Recently the urge for a cigarette had begun to wake her in the night and it was not until she had smoked two and some-times three in quick succession that she was able to get back to sleep.

She ground her finished cigarette out beneath her heel and returned to the darkroom. The image of the girl with the cleft lip was almost dry. She considered it, her eyes straining to adjust to the night-time gloom, her hand held up to obscure the child's deformity. She was unsure why the image affected her, whether it touched something deep in her or only titillated her with the shock of disgust, like a freak at a fair. Carefully, holding it by its edges, she nudged open the door so that she might see it in the light. In the doorway of his studio Mr Pidgeon stood with his hands upon his hips, his glasses set low on his nose.

'Ah, Mrs Campbell Lowe. Good afternoon.'

'Good afternoon,' she replied in a tone intended to be both polite and discouraging. She tilted the image towards the window, studying it in the primrose light. Above the mutilated mouth the child's pale eyes and paler complexion shone with hidden light. With her thin eyebrows and a long delicate nose she had the look of a Lippi madonna. Maribel felt a flicker of hopefulness.

'Sun's out at last,' Mr Pidgeon said. 'Perhaps we shall have something of a spring after all.'

'Perhaps.'

'I thought I should – the thing is, I have received a letter from Mr Webster. He wishes to take the studio for a few days next month. I have written down the dates.' He took a folded piece of paper from his pocket and held it out to her. 'You may wish to – that is, if you thought that it might make for awkwardness . . .'

Maribel took the piece of paper. 'Thank you.'

Mr Pidgeon nodded.

'That one of yours?' he asked, gesturing at the photograph.

'Yes.'

'It is an impertinence, I know, in the light of past circumstances, but – might I see?'

'No. No, I don't think so.'

Mr Pidgeon was silent. Then he cleared his throat.

'If that's all, Mr Pidgeon?' she said, pushing open the door to the darkroom.

'Good day, madam,' the old photographer said sadly as the door closed heavily behind her.

*

By the time Maribel finally left the darkroom the faint warmth of the spring sunshine had given way to a clammy dusk. She peered out of the window and was startled to see that the street below was thick with fog. In the milky blur the gaslight pulsed like an anemone. She could hear the warning shouts of an unseen coachman, the clatter and jingle of the carriage. A passer-by in a dark overcoat loomed into brief solidity and was gone. Somewhere, its bells muffled and thin, a church clock chimed the hour.

She hastened along the corridor, not troubling to switch on the light, and pushed the key to the darkroom back through the slot in Mr Pidgeon's door. A narrow ribbon of light caught on the hem of her skirt, illuminating the scuffed toes of her old boots. She had turned away when a fit of coughing seized her. She tried to swallow it but it was too strong for her. Though she hurried to the steps the door opened.

'Goodnight, Mr Pidgeon,' she croaked, the cough still lodged in her chest.

'Mrs Campbell Lowe? I did not know you were still here.'

'I cannot stop, I'm afraid. I am horribly late.'

'Before you go, I wonder if I might beg your tolerance in a small matter?'

Maribel hesitated, one hand on the iron balustrade. 'If this is about my account –'

'Your account? No indeed. I have something I should like to give you.'

'To give me? Mr Pidgeon, I hardly think –'

'Please. I did you a considerable wrong. Permit me to make amends.'

'I do not –'

'Please. It will only take a moment.'

She sighed. Then slowly she turned back towards the studio.

The room was very bare, the usual family scene dismantled. The rocking horse had been pushed back against the wall, a crumpled dust sheet obscuring all but its rump. The doll's house was nowhere to be seen.

'I don't suppose you would care for a little refreshment?' Mr Pidgeon asked.

He opened a cupboard to reveal, between stacks of battered buff files, a decanter of sherry and several glasses. When Maribel shook her head he poured himself a glass and, taking a small sip, led Maribel to a screen behind which were several powerful lights, set about with white reflectors. He switched one on. On the wall were hung several large exposures of what appeared to be family portraits. He gestured at her to come closer. She looked without curiosity, then looked again.

The portraits were indeed of a family group, father, mother and son, and, though perhaps a little blurrier than some of their counterparts, differed little in composition from the many thousands of such portraits taken in studios across England. The father, stern-faced and heavily bewhiskered, stood stiffly to one side of his seated wife, stout as the Queen in diamonds and black silk. At their feet the child, dressed in a sailor suit, sat cross-legged, his hair brushed neatly across his brow and his hands in his lap. It would have aroused in Maribel not the faintest curiosity had it not been that all three family members, father, mother and son, were quite plainly Mr Pidgeon's assistant, Thomas.

Mr Pidgeon watched her, sipping at his sherry. Then, putting down his glass, he took one of the images from the wall and handed it to her.

'For you,' he said. 'With my compliments.'

Maribel blinked. Technically the picture was quite remarkable. It was also very funny.

'I don't understand.'

'A triple exposure, madam. Each image taken separately on the same plate. To create a convincing ensemble requires care and accuracy but curiously little skill.'

'It is extraordinary.'

Mr Pidgeon shook his head. 'It is a trick,' he said.

'Well, yes, but all the same –'

'Anyway, it is yours. And now you must go. I do not wish to detain you further.'

'Was it a commission?'

'No. It –' Mr Pidgeon hesitated. 'Some months ago, you told me that spirit photographs were hoaxes, tricks played upon the credulous. Perhaps you remember.'

'I remember.'

'I am a Christian, Mrs Campbell Lowe. I take solace from the knowledge that those who depart this world do not leave us but only pass into the next room, where, when the time comes, we shall be reconciled. I, like many others, have long harboured hopes that science would help us to gain a better understanding of God's mysteries, so that we might see Him through a glass less darkly. Like them I have deplored the pseudo-scientific cynicism of the so-called psychical researchers who make it their business to discredit those miracles made possible by such technological advances. I cannot help thinking that if such people had been around when the Lord was creating the world, He would have abandoned His efforts in disgust.'

Mr Pidgeon paused, his fist against his chest, and cleared his throat. His tone, when he resumed speaking, was soft.

'In the past few months, however, I have come to see that the quest for evidence, for proof, though doubtless well intentioned, is – misplaced. The Lord does not ask us to comprehend His mysteries, far less to prove them. He asks us to have faith, *the substance of things hoped for, the evidence of things not seen.* The opposite of proof. It is through our faith, not photographs, that we find truth and, through truth, comfort. The faith that requires proof is no faith at all.'

'And this?' she said, gesturing at the photograph.

'It is difficult for some to accept that, on occasion, the camera does indeed lie. I wished to make it easier.'

'I see.'

'Besides, it was rather diverting.'

Maribel smiled. Mr Pidgeon twitched his mouth and looked away.

'It is difficult sometimes to know what is truth and what is only beauty,' she said after a while. 'Or the lack of it.'

'I'm afraid I don't quite follow.'

Maribel blinked. 'Hold this.'

Handing the photograph back to him, she tugged at the buckles of the satchel on her shoulder and slid out a thin cardboard portfolio. Quickly, before she could change her mind, she spread its contents across the table.

'Yours?' he asked.

She nodded, standing to one side so that he might examine them more closely, her arms folded defensively over her chest. Already she regretted the foolish spontaneity of her decision. It hardly mattered what he thought, of course, the opinion of a jobbing portraitist was not worth a jot, a fraction of a jot, but all the same she watched him, scouring his face for any trace of a reaction. Eventually he straightened up.

'Well?' she demanded, despite herself.

'Where did you take these?'

'Mostly in Coatbridge. Some in Motherwell. In Scotland.'

He nodded thoughtfully. 'They are unusual. Raw. Very – candid.'

'But are they any good?'

'Some are. Some are very good. This one in particular.'

He reached over the girl with the cleft palate and picked up an image of a tow-headed boy who peeked up at the camera from beneath a rickety table. Maribel frowned at the picture. It was not one of her favourites. The dreaminess on the child's face gave him a fey look, while the playful pose struck her as uncomfortably sentimental.

'You think so?' she said doubtfully.

'The way the light falls, the lift of his knee here, the hands around the tin cup, it contrives to be charming, despite everything.'

'I never meant it to be charming.'

Mr Pidgeon smiled as though she had said something witty and put his finger to his lips.

'I shan't tell if you don't.'

Maribel shook her head. 'You don't understand. These are the children we have destroyed. The great capitalist's bastard sons. That tin cup? Gin. The boy was drunk. Ten years old and unable to stand up straight. He said his father gave it to him, that it was the only pleasure he had in life. That there wasn't anything in the world could ever make him give it up.'

'So the camera lies,' Mr Pidgeon said with a shrug. 'It doesn't matter. The boy himself, drunk or sober, is quite immaterial. What matters is the image, the moment you have created, the boy you have made. This boy belongs to all of us. We are each free to tell his story in whatever way we choose.'

35

FREDERICK MORE'S GALLERY WAS a small shop tucked beneath the overhang of a crooked Tudor-beamed residence in Duke Street. Under his father's management it had specialised in oils of the eighteenth century and, even blank-walled, the low-ceilinged rooms were stuffy and old-fashioned. It did not surprise Maribel that the son wished to wield a new broom. What puzzled her more was why he wished to champion the most controversial of the modern arts when it was plain that he had not the least artistic impulse in him. His questions to her were all about Edward and in particular whether it was true that the Queen had referred to him as 'that insufferable Anarchist'. As for the photographs, he gave them only a cursory glance before inviting her to participate in an exhibition scheduled to begin in less than two weeks. It came as little surprise, then, to discover that the exhibition had been set up as a favour to Walter Edridge, a doctor and aspirant photographer of landscapes whose wife was a cousin by marriage of More's, and who had made vague undertakings of investment in the gallery if the show was a success.

So small an exhibition would likely have passed quite unnoticed had it not been for a letter to the *Times* from a group of painters, objecting in the strongest terms to the effrontery of those who presumed to claim photography as Art. It was not Art, the painters stormed, to *'set down facts as they exist. There is in Photography no skill of hand or eye, no trace of the artist's imposition of self upon his subject, that draws upon the highest flights and darkest reaches of the soul. Photography is no more Art than the making of a garment in a factory is Art, which creates a product through the mundane manipulation of a machine.'* They declared it a betrayal of London's artistic traditions that an eminent gallery like the More dared to present the empty images of the camera as a creditable pretender to paint and charcoal. Mr More's late father, they insinuated, would be turning in his grave.

This letter inspired several others, three-quarters of them purple with violent agreement, and, though it was not long before the editor tired of their tub-thumping, the exhibition of photographs at the More Gallery received a good deal of publicity. Frederick More might have lacked his father's aesthetic sensibilities but he had a nose for business. He hastily arranged a late opening for the gallery on the first night of the exhibition and invited not only the contributing photographers but all the gentlemen of his acquaintance to stop by for a glass of Moselle cup on their way to their clubs.

Maribel, who had begged Henry and Charlotte to attend so that she might not have to stand alone in a deserted room, was astonished to find the gallery crowded with people. Near the door a huddle of newspapermen crowded around Mr Edridge, who opined on the importance in photography of noble and dignified subjects, such as mountains and cathedrals. He had introduced himself to Maribel that afternoon as the pictures were being hung and had been unable to conceal his surprise that her work had been included. She had been unable to discern whether he considered it shocking or only rather infra dig.

Henry pushed through the throng towards her, a glass of cup in each hand. He was dressed formally, in white tie and tails. Onyx studs gleamed in his starched shirt front.

'You look as though you could do with one of these,' he said. 'Or perhaps both.'

Maribel laughed and took one of the glasses gratefully.

'Is Teddy here?' he asked.

She shook her head. 'He's on his way back from the Black Country. He had to speak at a meeting of chain-makers.'

'But he is coming?'

'Oh yes. He cabled last night. He plans to come straight from the station.'

She touched her hand to her pocket, feeling the corners of the folded paper there. That afternoon Edward had sent a second telegram, directly to the gallery. She had opened it reluctantly, certain that he had been detained. It read only *THINKING OF YOU SHALL BRING MOON.*

'Which ones are yours?' Henry asked, looking around him.

She gestured towards the back wall. He craned his neck, raising himself on tiptoes.

'I can see only hats. Shall we?'

'In a minute,' she said, sipping her drink. 'There's no hope of lifting a glass in that crush.'

'Have you sold many?'

'I shouldn't think so. From what I gather, this lot have come to sneer, not buy.'

'What nonsense. Once they see your work they won't be able to help themselves.'

Maribel smiled and shook her head. 'Thank you for coming,' she said.

'I wouldn't have missed it. Although I can't stay, I'm afraid. I have promised faithfully that tonight I won't be late.'

'It must be something special if you are prepared to make a promise like that.'

'Buffalo Bill is back in town and Berkeley Levett has been prevailed upon to host a farewell dinner. It would appear that the Prince of Wales wants one last chance to win back some of the family inheritance before the old cowboy hightails it home to the prairie.'

'The Wild West is finally going home?'

'Not home exactly. They have a summer season booked in New York City.'

'No peace for the wicked, then.'

'No, but then Cody is very serious about his wickedness.'

Maribel smiled. Henry leaned closer, lowering his voice.

'He has asked me to keep an eye out for his Miss Clemmons while he is gone. It would seem that he is not entirely convinced of her affections.'

'He is hardly entitled to them, given that he already has a wife.'

'If he finances her new show, as she is pressing him to do, he will be entitled to them several times over. That creature is perfectly shameless. I know quite well she has had other gentleman friends while Cody's been out of town. Trouble is, one can't quite bear to tell him. He's as smitten as a schoolboy.'

Maribel's glass was empty. Henry took it from her, setting it with his on the ledge of a nearby window.

'Sharpen your elbows,' he said. 'We are going in.'

It was nearly eight o'clock when the crowd began to thin. Maribel looked about her, searching those faces who remained. Near the door the Wildes conversed with the Mansfields, Oscar paying not the least attention to Constance's repeated blandishments that they should leave, and Jane Morris smiled at a gentleman that Maribel did not know.

At the back of the gallery a handful of people still examined her photographs. She scanned them quickly, looking for Charlotte. The Ferrixao boy returned her gaze impassively. Until today she had not been sure whether it was right to include him in the exhibition. The picture was the best she had ever taken but, as she had watched the photographs being hung, she could not evade the feeling that she had betrayed him, that, to serve her own vanity and commercial advantage, she had offered up to public scrutiny something precious and profoundly private.

On the other side of the gallery, beside a huge print of Whitby Abbey, Edward leaned back a little from Mr Edridge, who, in full flood, swept his arms about him in great arcs. Edward looked tired, travel-worn. There was no sign of Charlotte.

'I shall be there unless I am actually in labour,' she had promised, patting her huge belly. Perhaps the baby was indeed on its way. It was due any day. Perhaps at this very moment Charlotte clamped the hand of the nurse, her back arched and her screams pressed into the pillow so that she might not frighten the little ones upstairs. It was too silly to worry about her, of course, who had more children than the old woman in the shoe. Knowing Charlotte she would be telling the doctor his business and dictating the next day's menus as she laboured. All the same Maribel was distracted, her smile uncertain as she shook Mr More's hand and congratulated him upon the attendance.

'Madam, it is not my work they have come to see,' More said, raising her fingers to his lips. 'Thank you for entrusting my modest gallery with your immodest talent. May we enjoy a long and profitable partnership.'

His expansive manner hung loosely on him, a borrowed suit several sizes too large. Over the toothy clutter of his smile he scanned the room, his eyes pale and narrow.

'Ah,' he purred, his outstretched arm nudging Maribel to one side. 'Mr Webster, what a pleasure. You are acquainted, perhaps, with Mrs Campbell Lowe?'

Maribel's heart shrivelled.

'Mr Webster,' she said curtly.

'Madam.'

His eyes held hers, cold and opaque. Like a dead fish, she thought. The idea that she had ever thought him charming sent a chill down her spine.

'So,' Mr More said, rubbing his hands, 'have you seen anything you like?'

Webster did not take his eyes from Maribel.

'Not yet,' he said.

'Then I must insist on showing you Mrs Campbell Lowe's work. She has real talent. It won't be long before she is at least as well known for her photographs as for her husband.'

'What a distressing thought.'

Mr More smiled nervously.

'You must let me introduce you to Mr Edridge,' he suggested. 'His views would interest your readers, I think.'

'No, thank you. That chap there, in the brown coat, he's one of mine. Talk to him if it's publicity you're after.'

'Publicity? Heavens, are all newspapermen such cynics?'

It was intended as a joke but Webster did not smile. Maribel felt a lick of fear at the base of her throat.

'Well, gentlemen, if you will excuse me –'

Webster stepped a little closer, blocking her path.

'It astounds me, you know,' he said, his tone almost conversational, 'the insatiable hunger you people have for notoriety.'

Maribel swallowed. Beside her Mr More rolled his eyes. This was a conversation he enjoyed.

'I am surprised at you,' she said, struggling for civility. 'I had thought as a photographer yourself you might be less old-fashioned.'

'A photographer?' More said eagerly. 'How marvellous. What are your subjects?'

Maribel had made sure to stay away from Turks Row on the days that Mr Pidgeon had rented the studio to Webster. When at last she returned she had found some thirty portraits of Webster drying on the rack. The photographs differed little in pose or composition. In all of them he looked directly at the camera, dressed in a white collar and a heavy jerkin. In the crook of one arm, he held a wooden staff. Though Webster had not gone so far as to shave his whiskers there was no avoiding the allusion to the famous Walker portrait: God's Englishman, Oliver Cromwell.

'Mr Webster is his own favourite study,' she said. 'Isn't that right, Mr Webster?'

'I don't suppose you have thought of exhibiting your work but if you were ever looking for a gallery I would consider it a privilege, a man of your reputation . . .' More tailed off as Webster turned his fishy gaze to glare at him, holding up one palm in mock surrender. 'Now is not the right time, I see. But if you change your mind –' Extracting a card from his pocket he pressed it into Webster's hand. Webster dropped it.

'Go away,' Webster said.

More laughed nervously.

'Well, you know where to find me,' he muttered, backing away. Webster watched him go. Then he turned back to Maribel. His fish eyes gleamed with disgust.

'So you would be a famous artist?' He spat out the word as though it were poisoned. 'The hubris is breathtaking.'

'Why did you come here, Mr Webster? Was it simply for the pleasure of insulting me?'

'You would think, with all you have to hide, that you would have the sense to keep a lower profile. But you people are all the same, aren't you? You think, because you are born with silver spoons clutched in your aristocratic little mouths, that the world will continue to fawn all over you the way it always has, that it will worship you like gods, however low you stoop.'

'I should like you to leave now.'

'Should you? And if I don't?'

'Then I shall scream. And Edward will have you thrown out.'

'Ah, he will enjoy that, won't he? The champion of the working man with his great Scottish estates. The Socialist campaigner whose finest act has been to conspire with his degenerate, adulterous, inbred upper-class friends to discredit me, the only Socialist newspaper editor in London.'

'Don't you think you might stand a better chance of keeping your position if you displayed the slightest trace of honour or integrity?'

'You dare to talk to me of honour? You people disgust me. For centuries you have hidden behind your titles, dispensing justice and making the laws for the ordinary people to obey, dismissing the virtues of decency and modesty and Godliness as nothing but useful curbs on the excesses of the poor working man, gags along with his pipe and his Bible and his slack-jawed forelock-tugging that will keep him quiet while you lie and cheat and squander the spoils of his miserable labour on abominations that would sicken the Devil himself. Well, let me tell you something. The world is changing. Once perhaps the gentlemen of the press were your lapdogs and your lackeys. Well, no longer. Don't think you can rely upon me to keep your shameful secrets. Your powerful friends can threaten me all they like. I shall not be silenced. The Lord cares nothing for wealth or rank. He cares for Truth and I, madam, am His humble servant, however foul His task.'

His face was so close that she could smell the stale coffee on his breath. She gazed at the sheen of sweat on his flushed cheeks, the spittle caught in white beads at the corners of his mouth, and she thought that she might faint. She put a hand out behind her, feeling the cool steadiness of the wall.

'I know about you Campbell Lowes,' he hissed. 'I know about all of you.'

'Mr Webster.'

Dizzily Maribel looked up. Edward stood beside Webster, a frown creasing his brow. Webster did not reply. Setting his jaw he pushed past Edward and was gone.

'What on earth was all that about?' Edward asked. Maribel shook her head. It felt unsteady on her neck.

'I – I am not sure.'

'I suppose it's too much to hope that he bought something?'

Maribel shook her head. 'I don't think there is any chance of that.'

The last guests were dispersing. Across the emptying room, Mr More bid a group of gentlemen goodnight.

'You've got a bloody nerve, old boy,' she heard one declare jovially as he put on his hat. 'It's the Emperor's new clothes with knobs on.'

Maribel's legs trembled and suddenly she felt close to tears. She took Edward's arm.

'Let's go,' she said.

'Are you sure you've had enough of the limelight?'

'Quite sure.'

'Then let me get the toast of London her coat.'

Edward took her to dinner at the Savoy Grill. She would rather have gone home but he would not hear of it. As soon as they were seated he ordered champagne. Maribel drank several glasses too quickly and smoked several cigarettes, trying to dull the trembling that persisted in her arms and legs, to blot out the image of Webster's fish eyes, the hatred in his twisted mouth. She had thought he had forgotten her. She had been a fool. He had not forgotten. All this time he had been hoarding their secrets like a miser, groping with his filthy hands in the darkest, most private recesses of their lives. He hated them, there was no doubting it now. He hated them and he meant to have revenge.

The waiter refilled her glass, emptying the bottle. Edward nodded at him to bring another and raised his glass. Forcing herself to smile she raised hers too and touched it to his.

'To a triumphant exhibition,' he said. 'May there be many more.'

'I'll drink to that.'

She set the glass to her lips, wrinkling her nose against the fizz of the bubbles. Her head felt fizzy too and the sick feeling in her stomach had been superseded with a kind of dull pitch, like the rocking of a boat. Tipping up the glass she emptied it in a single swallow.

'Steady on, there,' Edward said gently.

Maribel set down her glass. He reached out a hand, placing it over hers. She looked at his dear face and the tears prickled in her eyes. She blinked them away. She would tell him, she knew she would have to tell him, but she would not tell him here. Not tonight. Tonight he smiled at her across the snowy tablecloth and the light of the candles caught in the honeyed gleam of the champagne and set points of light dancing in his eyes and it was possible to imagine that life could always be like this, a perfect symphony of white and gold.

'I am very proud of you, you know,' he said.

A waiter brought Dover sole on a broad platter. They watched as he deftly peeled the fish's spine away from the delicate flesh.

'I wonder how many you sold.'

'None?'

'That's hardly likely. The place was positively heaving.'

'I don't think they were there to buy. One gentleman I spoke to asked me very politely how I dared to peddle the principles of Socialism when they would destroy the very fabric of the Empire. He seemed to think my work some kind of political propaganda.'

'Dear God.'

'It made me think the pictures must be clumsier than I had imagined.'

'Nonsense. The clumsiness is all with him. Those dyed-in-the-wool Tories only ever consider the appearance of a man. They never look at his face, let alone into his soul. You do.'

She had not expected his praise to move her so. She sipped at her champagne, swallowing the lump that rose in her throat. Edward took another mouthful of fish.

'That boy,' he asked. 'The one with the eyes. Who is he?'

Maribel shrugged. 'I don't know. Just a boy. One of the stone-pickers at Ferrixao.'

'I think of all of your photographs it is the most arresting.'

'Do you?'

'I was struck by him all over again tonight, the astonishing candour of his expression, as though he is giving himself to the camera, to you, without reservation. He meets one's gaze and one cannot bear to look away. It is as though there is a connection, a bond that has been created between him and oneself. To break it seems – this will sound overblown, I know, but I mean it truly – it feels like a kind of sacrilege.'

Something tightened in Maribel's chest. She reached out and took his hand in hers.

'Thank you.'

Edward raised her hand to his lips and kissed it. Then he set it down and took another mouthful of sole.

'Eat,' he urged. 'The fish is delicious.'

Obediently Maribel stubbed out her cigarette and picked up her fork. Edward chewed thoughtfully, leaning back to allow the sommelier to top up their glasses.

'I found myself wondering what it was that you said to the boy that made him trust you so.'

'Nothing at all. That is just how he was.'

'It was really that simple?'

'I think – I think that we understood one another. I saw something in him – something that I recognised. Does that sound overblown too?'

'No. Not overblown at all.'

Maribel smiled. I loved him, she wanted to say, but she did not. Instead she raised her glass to Edward.

'To understanding,' she said, and when his glass touched hers the note was high and pure as ice.

36

'SHE IS PERFECTLY SWEET,' Maribel said, peering at the scrunch-faced bundle in Charlotte's arms. Tufts of black hair stuck up from beneath the knitted bonnet; around her nose and wisps of eyebrow the skin was red and scaly. As Maribel watched she yawned, squeezing her eyes tight, and settled back to sleep. Her mouth was round and puckered as a kiss. Maribel patted her awkwardly, feeling the warmth of her, the tiny completeness. When she took her hand away it was as though she left something of herself behind.

Shaking the smuts from her skirts she settled herself awkwardly on the side of the bed. She wished now that she had gone home to change. The heavy dun wool of her walking costume, the stout solidity of her shoes, did not belong here among the silk and the lace and spotless white linen. They sullied the wholesome cleanliness of the air, dragging in on soles and hems not only the grime of the city but its crudity. The previous afternoon, in this very costume, she had tried to photograph a girl in Green Park. The girl had worn a scarlet dress trimmed with black lace and a purple shawl and on her head a battered bonnet of green velvet. Though it was hardly five o'clock in the afternoon, she called out to the men who passed by, a hard little laugh in her voice and her pert chest pushed out, her hands tugging suggestively at her skirts. Beneath the slackened criss-cross of her lacings, her belly was round with child.

When Maribel had asked if she might take her picture, the girl's sharp face had shrivelled. Her skin was greasy and pimpled, her eyes hard as chips of glass. There was a sore at the corner of her mouth. When she spat on the ground the smell of drink on her was very strong.

'Cost yer sixpence,' she had said, 'or a shillin' for Cock Lane,' and she cackled and hitched up her skirts so high that Maribel caught a glimpse of felted hair, dark against pale thighs. The girl's jeers had echoed in her ears as she hurried away.

'How are you feeling?' Maribel asked Charlotte. She was glad to see that her friend seemed comfortable and that she had a little colour in her cheeks. Arthur had declared the birth an easy one but a husband's view of such matters was seldom reliable.

'Never better. I can't tell you what heaven it is not to be pregnant.'

Maribel raised an eyebrow. 'I shall be sure to remind you of that in six months,' she said and Charlotte laughed and gazed down at the baby in her arms, her laughter softening into a smile of such fierce and private tenderness that it pierced Maribel's heart. 'An ounce of mother is worth a pound of priest,' Maribel murmured.

'Who said that?'

'It's an old Spanish proverb.'

'Or so your mother told you.'

Maribel smiled.

'Helena Mary Gwendolen Charterhouse,' Charlotte murmured, tracing the curve of the infant's cheek with the back of her finger. 'Such a big name for a little girl.'

'The older ones must be thrilled to have a new sister.'

'Not a bit. As Kitty asked me, what good is a baby who can't play? This one will be nothing but a nuisance until she is old enough to eat pretend cake and withstand the medical attentions of Doctor Ursie, or Nursula as the children have taken to calling her.'

Maribel laughed. 'She still harbours ambitions to be the next Elizabeth Garrett Anderson?'

'I hope that Dr Anderson's interest in medical matters extends beyond a passion for bandaging. Ursie should have been born in ancient Egypt. Mummification would be her idea of perfect heaven.'

The baby began to whimper. Charlotte crooned at her, rocking her in her arms, but the infant did not quiet. A nurse, all starched skirts and self-importance, bustled into the room.

'It's time for Baby's bottle, madam. May I?'

When Charlotte hesitated, the nurse bent down and scooped the child from her arms.

'Come now, missy,' she chided as she whisked the infant from the room. 'You will give poor Mother a headache with that infernal racket.'

Charlotte watched them go.

'Don't look so pitiful,' Maribel said. 'You'll be pregnant again before you know it.'

Charlotte mock-pouted, swiping at her friend with the back of her hand.

'There are rules about teasing a woman who is still in childbed, you know.'

'I didn't. How soon can you get up?'

Charlotte laughed and rang for tea. Without the child in her arms, the soft vagueness that had enveloped her seemed to recede a little. Maribel lit a cigarette, holding the smoke in her lungs, savouring the shiver of it in her chest, in the backs of her knees.

'Ah,' she said, tipping back her head and exhaling. 'That's better.'

Charlotte waved impatiently at the plume of smoke.

'Just don't let Arthur catch you,' she said. 'Now tell me about the opening. I can't tell you how maddening it was to miss your moment of triumph. I want to know everything.'

'There's not much to tell. There were a good deal of people there, lured in by moral outrage and Moselle cup. Most of them duly hated it. Some bought, though not as many or for as much as the oleaginous Mr More would have liked. You weren't there because you were having a baby which I consider a tolerably good excuse. That's it really.'

'If you imagine you can get away with that, young lady, you have another think coming.'

Maribel smiled. Since the exhibition's opening, the gallery had continued to attract a steady trickle of visitors. It had even secured a short review in the *Illustrated London News*, three lines of teeth-sucking ambivalence in which none of the photographers had been mentioned by name, thereby exceeding by some margin Maribel's modest expectations. Though Edridge's monumental subjects had proved more popular with the public than her portraits, she had to her surprise sold six pictures, including the boy from Ferrixao. Even after the gallery had taken its commission the proceeds would cover a substantial share of her bills in Paris when she travelled there for fittings in May.

Two days after the opening she had written to Ida. It was a short letter, little more than an expression of her continued affection and the address of the gallery in Duke Street. For a moment she had allowed herself to imagine Ida's face as she gazed at the boy from Ferrixao, the visible emotion in her expression. Then she had sealed the envelope and put it in the cigar box in the cupboard.

'I can't wait to be well enough to go,' Charlotte said. 'You know that Bertie has asked if he can come with me? He is beside himself to know a bona fide artist.'

'Hardly.'

'He made me promise to ask you if you would sign that photograph you took of them with the Indian. He is convinced that it will be worth a fortune one day.'

Charlotte rummaged among the books and magazines piled on the table beside her and pulled out the photograph. The Indian, shabby and pouch-eyed, hunched like a refugee as the boys grimaced at the camera, teeth bared, their tomahawks held high above their heads. The littlest one had moved as the shutter opened. His right arm drew a smoky trail through the air.

It seemed like a lifetime ago. Maribel thought of the Indian slumped in the wooden settle in Ida's bare parlour, of Dr Coffin's strangely beautiful stethoscope with its walnut trumpet and Ida's ugly brown hat. Briskly she stubbed out her cigarette and took the pen Charlotte offered.

'Sadly, for Bertie, it is a pretty rotten picture,' she said. Turning over the photograph she scrawled an affectionate message to the boy on the back. Charlotte read the message and smiled. Then she looked again at the photograph.

'What horrors,' she said tenderly.

'Tell Bertie I shall take a proper portrait of him next time.'

'Do tell me that means ghosts,' Charlotte teased. 'I was horribly disappointed there weren't any in this one. I had rather got the impression that they were your thing.'

Maribel shook her head, reaching again for her cigarettes. 'No ghosts,' she said, a little too firmly, and under her skirts she crossed her fingers, just in case.

On Eaton Terrace the cherry trees were in blossom, clouds of pink and white that stirred in the breeze, exhaling their faint scent. Maribel walked home slowly, enjoying the warmth of the spring sunshine on her back. It was a beautiful day. The elegant stucco houses gleamed white against the blue sky, their glossy black doors and railings as slick as oil. An open victoria spun past, drawn by a pair of grey horses, a man and a child laughing in the back. The child's coat was yellow and the crimson ribbons on her hat streamed out behind her like the tails of a kite.

At Bourne Street, reluctant to return to the flat, she turned instead towards Sloane Square, intending to stroll a little in the direction of the park. It was too fine a day for sitting at a writing desk and much too fine for the darkroom. Instead she paused at the corner of the square where a flower seller in a patched shawl and battered straw hat had set up her stall. The trestle, a plank of wood balanced on decrepit tea chests, was crowded with baskets of pansies and violets and crocuses and gold-centred polyanthus, the colours as bright as a child's painting. In a chipped white mug a mass of anemones turned up their scarlet faces to the sky.

Maribel bought wallflowers and, on impulse, a bunch of the anemones and waited as the flower seller wrapped them in paper. On the other side of the square a building was being erected and hod carriers hefted loads of bricks from a heavy dray, dark maps of sweat on the backs of their shirts. The wallflowers were heady with scent but they would not last long without water. Maribel turned for home. At the corner of the square a news-paper seller cried his wares to passers-by.

'*Chronicle*! Buy your *City Chronicle*!'

It was like a sickness, the way her heart lurched whenever she saw a copy of Webster's newspaper. She could not forget Edward's expression when she had finally summoned the courage to tell him of Webster's tirade on the night of her exhibition. He had composed himself quickly, had told her not to worry, that there was no reason to suspect that Webster knew any more than what was already widely known, that his father had owed a great deal of money and gone mad.

'As fathers do,' he had joked, but his smile came too late quite to conceal the bleak shadow that passed over his face, the presen-timent of defeat that pressed his lips together and carved a small brief dent in the space between his eyebrows. In that look she had seen the momentousness of the scandal to come which would destroy not only his reputation for truthfulness, which was the only reputation he cared for, but whatever small concessions he had still hoped to wrestle from the future for those wretched men and women who had never stood a chance.

'What if it's more than that?' she had asked him and he had shrugged.

'You mean you? But how could he possibly know? How would he have found out?'

Maribel had thought of Mr Webster's private collection of artistic portraits. She thought of Edith and Ida, and of Sir Douglas Maddox's accidental remark about a cousin in Yorkshire. She thought about the times she had scorned Webster when she might have pacified him and flattered his vanity, and of Mrs Aveling's remark outside the courtroom that newspapermen always got the last word. She thought with a shudder of the heat that had flushed her skin when they first met. Of all her mistakes that was the one of which she was most ashamed.

'I'm sorry,' she had whispered. 'It's my fault. I provoked him.'

'You think I did not? But it makes no difference. We would have provoked him just by being us.'

After that Edward had refused to discuss it again. One evening, plagued with apprehension, she had alluded to the matter obliquely as they returned from dinner. Edward's response had been angry and unequivocal.

'That's enough, Bo, do you hear me? What possible purpose does it serve to torment yourself with the imaginary ways in which Mr Webster and his ilk might one day make us suffer? Whatever he knows, whatever he decides to print, we shall survive it. Until then you are not to waste a single minute thinking about him, do you understand?'

Maribel had nodded. She had not mentioned it again, though she found herself thinking about it often. She thought about it as she opened the door of the rosewood cabinet and saw the cigar box pushed to the back of the high shelf, and on the evening, some four weeks after his release from prison, when Edward came home late, his eyes bright, his mouth soft and satiated, and she knew immediately where he had been. It pressed itself into the gaps in conversations, the stillness between breaths. In the dark wakeful hours of the night, her ragtag thoughts thrummed to the low drone of foreboding.

The newspaper stand was on her corner. As she hurried by a thickset tradesman in a tweed coat and ginger whiskers pushed past her, a coin between his fingers. The newspaper seller flipped the paper into a neat roll and presented it with a bow.

'*Chronicle*, ma'am?' he asked, peeling another paper from the pile. She shook her head but all the same glanced at the headline. Directly beneath the newspaper's masthead, in heavy capitals, were the words 'FITZROVIA BROTHEL OUTRAGE' and under that, in smaller letters, 'CRIMINAL PEERS IN PARLIAMENTARY COVER-UP'.

She closed her eyes. The smell of the wallflowers filled her nostrils, sickeningly sweet. She stood frozen and adrift in the middle of the street, jostled on both sides by passers-by, as the image in her head formed and sharpened like a print developing in its bath of chemicals: Edward, his hat pulled over his eyes, standing too close to a glossy black front door, his finger pressed to a bright brass bell.

Someone pushed past her, knocking the flowers from her arms. She opened her eyes, staring at the scatter of blooms strewn at her feet.

'Can I help you, ma'am?'

She shook her head dumbly. There was still a chance it was not Edward. The headline had said CRIMINAL PEERS, after all, and Edward was not a peer. Even as she thought it she knew she was clutching at straws. The penny newspapers claimed anyone with the merest whiff of a title a peer. But criminal? Brothels might be scandalous, especially when their clients were respectable married men, but they were not illegal. Even Webster with his Congregationalist puritanism could not make them so. All he had managed with his Sink of Iniquity scandal was to raise the legal age of consent. Unless the girls were under sixteen –

Maribel's stomach turned over. Could it be that so respectable a place as Edward's had employed underaged girls? That there were girls there held against their will? In the months after the *Chronicle*'s revelations and the subsequent amendments to the Criminal Act the newspapers had brimmed with the trials of men accused of criminal offences against minors. The guilty had been sentenced to imprisonment, years and years of imprisonment. What if the establishment in Whitfield Street had indeed broken the law? Would Edward be held accountable? Would he even have known? He was not the kind of man to take an interest in young girls. Their callowness, their inexperience, would bore him. He had always preferred sophistication to artlessness, worldliness to naivety. At parties he sought the company of his friends' witty wives, not their wide-eyed daughters.

Yet when he had come to the Calle de León she had been just seventeen years old. She pressed her fingertips to her eyes, fighting the sudden rush of tears.

A woman in a patched dress thrust her flowers at her, clumsily wrapped in their paper. The blooms were crushed and dusty.

'There you are, ma'am,' she said, patting Maribel on the arm. Her accent was Irish. 'Will you be wanting to sit down?'

Maribel shook her head. Taking a penny from her purse she jabbed it at the newspaper seller. She pushed the paper he gave her deep into the velvet bag she carried over her shoulder, and hurried away. The Irish woman called angrily after her, cursing her for her close-fistedness, but Maribel did not turn round.

The lobby of Cadogan Mansions was dark after the brightness

of the afternoon. She stumbled across the chequered floor, one hand clenched around the mouth of her bag. She could no longer pretend composure, even to herself. Webster was a newspaperman and the most dangerous kind of moral despot. Moreover, he believed himself wronged. If Edward, knowingly or otherwise, had frequented a brothel that employed underaged girls Webster would show no mercy. It would matter not a jot to him that, following so hard on the heels of his imprisonment, Edward would have no armoury with which to withstand a scandal of this kind. It would not matter that the cause for which they had fought so zealously together might be damaged by the loss of one of its staunchest advocates, that a good man might spend the last years of his life in prison. For Edward was good. He was brave and kind and fierce and funny and vain and wholehearted, his sharp intelligence countered by an intuitive tenderness, his dry wit by a gentleness of temperament, his exhibitionism by a passionate determination to extract from life every drop of joy. He had never affected to be perfect. He was as tolerant of others' shortcomings as he was scrupulous about his own. The only fault he could not forgive was cruelty.

None of that would mean a thing to Webster. Again and again Webster had demonstrated that he had neither patience nor compassion for the ordinary failings of honourable men. Edward would be dragged through the dirt, set in the stocks for spite-soaked pinch-faced hypocrites to humiliate and torment. Moral outrage was an ouroboros, an insatiable monster that gorged on its own flesh. Its appetite would not be easily sated. How soon, then, before the stories started about her? She had not been careful and Webster was thorough. How soon before he found Ida and Edith too? Perhaps he already had. What then would stop him and his kind from working backwards to Madrid, to Victor, to the photographs taken in the scarlet studio with the blacked-out windows? They would not see what Maribel had seen, that Edward was too fine a man to condemn her for her mistakes. They would be intoxicated by their own clamour of condemnation: liar, charlatan, harbourer of harlots. And what of the child, of whom Edward knew nothing? They would smash their lives as carelessly as eggs.

Lady Wingate's door swung open and the old lady peered out through the crack, her tortoise eyes blinking in the gloom. Maribel's heart sank.

'Ah. It's you.' Lady Wingate frowned and opened her door a little wider. She wore a lace cap and, around her shoulders, a moth-eaten fur stole. 'I thought it was. You clatter through here like a freshly shod pony on those heels of yours. What is wrong with you? You look as if you've seen a ghost.'

'Not at all.'

'Well, you are fearfully pale. It is hardly surprising. To judge from the manner in which you slam and stamp your way up and down those stairs you are always in the most tearing hurry. Look at you now. Positively itching to be off. Anyone would think you wished to avoid me.'

Trapped, Maribel paused on the bottom stair, one hand on the banister, the other clutching her bag against her hip. Lady Wingate eyed her beadily.

'I've just been looking at the newspaper,' she said. 'I wonder, is there any limit to your appetite for notoriety? Your wretched husband is only just out of jail.'

All the stuffing went out of Maribel then. She sagged, gripping the banister to keep herself from falling.

'I – I don't think I –'

'I suppose you thought it was your turn. That's the way with you New Women, isn't it? Anything they can do you can do better.' She shook her head, pulling her stole about her shoulders. 'These photographs of yours, the ones that have caused all the to-do. Should I be going to see them?'

'The photographs?'

'Yes, dear. The photographs. They sound rather striking, I

must say. Though I confess to having some sympathy with your critics. It is rather outlandish to claim photography as Art when the camera does all the work for you.'

Maribel swallowed. 'A good camera is a great help,' she said faintly.

'I imagine it is like working with a lathe or some such. Not Art exactly but craftsmanship of a sort.' The old woman considered Maribel, her head on one side. 'You are fortunate. When one has much to endure, work can be a great comfort.'

'I'm sure.'

Lady Wingate frowned. Then she waved a dismissive hand at Maribel.

'Well, don't let me keep you. Rush, rush, rush to whatever it is you rush to. New Women, pish. The whole lot of you will be dead of nervous exhaustion before you are forty.'

Inside the flat, Maribel leaned against the front door and tore the newspaper from the bag, her eyes scouring the page. A case of such loathsome indecency, such hideous evil, that the *Chronicle* could not remain silent. A scandal that threatened to engulf many peers, among them the son of a duke and a well-known baronet. The monstrous threats of those who feared exposure, the shameful cowardice of the police. The determination of one newspaper, led by its courageous editor, to take a stand against depravity and the grotesque abuse of power. The triumph of Truth and of Justice.

Three paragraphs of sanctimonious self-justification and then, at last, the crime itself, the very ink trembling with righteous disgust. Behind the darkened windows of a den of infamy in Bolsover Street, the *Chronicle* hissed, in the incense-choked air of secret chambers, ignoble peers of the realm had slaked their vile appetites, committing acts of unspeakable indecency with young boys.

The paper crumpled in Maribel's hands, drifting to the floor as she let herself slide down the door to bury her face in her knees. It was not him. Whoever it was, it was not him. Not yet, not this time. She did not know how long she sat there among the folds of her skirts, inhaling their comforting darkness. She only knew that she would do anything to protect him, that there was no one in the world, no one at all, whom she loved as she loved Edward Campbell Lowe.

37

MARIBEL HEARD EDWARD'S KEY in the lock as she sat before her dressing-table mirror, watching Alice's fingers twist and smooth as they made the final careful adjustments to her hair. She let out a breath and, beneath the whalebone embrace of her corset, her chest eased a little. Even by Edward's standards he was very late.

'Here he comes now,' Alice said, standing back to consider her handiwork. 'I told you there were nothing to worry about.'

When Maribel smiled the sheen of gloss on her lips caught the light.

'If only it were that simple.'

It was several days since the *Chronicle* had made its explosive allegations and London was convulsed with rumour. A month or so earlier, two boys from the Central Telegraph Office had been tried for gross indecency, found guilty and sentenced to some months in prison. The whole affair might have passed unnoticed had both the lightness of their sentences and the eminence of their counsel not aroused the suspicion of a reporter on the *Chronicle*, who had, with Webster's support, made his own enquiries. The police had been unhelpful. The brothel in question had closed down. Its proprietor had fled abroad. Though the boys had named names during their trial, their accusations were unsubstantiated and could not be made public. No arrests had been made. The *Chronicle* hinted at a government cover-up and then, as the scandal swelled, at pressure brought to bear by the authorities to gag the newspaper's investigations. So far the *Chronicle* had refrained from specific accusations but it promised that names would be forthcoming. In the meantime its leading articles raged daily against the 'perversions of a depraved aristocracy'.

The depraved aristocracy had its own theories about the identities of the guilty men. It was said that the two boys had been defended in court by a lawyer in the employ of the Earl of Somerset, equerry to the Prince of Wales, who, when the *Chronicle* story broke, was discovered to have fled to Hanover on unspecified royal business. Henry FitzRoy, the Earl of Euston, was another name whispered at society parties. Though no one knew for certain where FitzRoy was, it was rumoured that he had sailed for Peru. Most scandalous of all, and sotto voce, were the murmurings about Prince Albert Victor, son of the Prince of Wales.

Among England's most eminent families there were shudders at the unmentionable practices of the offenders, and outrage at the reckless indiscretion of the *Chronicle*. Dowagers fanned themselves busily, as though troubled by a foul smell, and declared Webster the worst kind of parasite. His refusal to be silenced was pronounced proof of his detestable lack of breeding, his newspaper disdained as a filthy rag. 'The scuttlebutt of the slums,' one of Vivien Campbell Lowe's grander friends had called it. Despite her repugnance, the old lady's knowledge of its revelations had been thoroughly encyclopaedic.

Maribel heard the hall cupboard open and close, the soft hush of Edward's shoes on the carpet. In the mirror the door handle turned.

'Goodness, what kept you?' she said gently. 'You will have to hurry if you wish to bathe. We are expected at the Howards' by eight.'

Edward's face was ashen. He sank down onto the bed, one

hand at his brow. Maribel gazed at him, the old terrors rising up in her like ghosts.

'What is it? Edward, dearest, whatever is the matter?'

Edward shook his head mutely. Alice hesitated, catching Maribel's eye in the mirror. Maribel nodded. She waited until the door had closed behind the maid, then rose from her stool to kneel before him, taking his hands in hers.

'Tell me,' she said.

He looked up at her. For an awful moment she feared that he might weep.

'It's Henry,' he said.

'Oh God, Edward. What is it? What has happened to him?'

Edward shook his head. 'He – he says Webster has his name. That they mean to publish.'

Maribel stared at Edward.

'Henry?' she said dumbly and the shock was like a fist around her lungs. Impeccable Henry, with his easy charm and beautifully cut suits, involved in something so sordid, so squalid? It was impossible. And yet she knew that it was not. Henry was not like Oscar. He did not wear his hair long. He did not dress in fur and velvet and soft collars, a silk handkerchief cascading artfully from his pocket. He did not rhapsodise with voluptuous languor about Endymion as Oscar did when extolling the shame-less Robert, or tell pretty actresses that, had they been boys, they would have ruined his life.

Henry was not showy nor was he in the least effeminate, and yet there was something in him that was not like other men. In the years that Maribel had known him he had pressed his lips to her upturned palms, had set his head on her shoulder, had smoothed her hair from her brow with the tenderness of a lover, and not once had she felt the discomfiting awkward-ness of unwanted attention. He had never once looked at her, as many men looked at her, so that she had to lower her eyes. It was not only that he was Edward's brother. There was a

444

fire in the blood of other men, even quite old men, a heat that scorched her cheeks if she came too close, as though it sought to raise an equal heat in her. That fire did not burn in Henry. Once, years ago, when she and Edward had not been married long, she had asked Henry why it was that he had not yet found a wife.

'It is not so bad as they say, you know,' she had teased him. 'With the right person.'

'Ah,' he had said. 'Therein lies the difficulty.'

'Your circle is too narrow and much too stuffy. You should come to our kind of parties. Beneath that elegant exterior you are a bohemian at heart, I know it.'

He had only smiled and shaken his head.

'Darling girl, but I like my circle. You forget that I am both narrow and stuffy myself. Besides, my mother attends your kind of parties.'

They had laughed then, Maribel a little guiltily. She had not pressed him again. Discreet, amusing and ever the perfect gentleman, Henry was much in demand. He was always escorting somebody somewhere.

'I am not the marrying kind,' he had said to her and she had assumed that he relished the liberties of bachelorhood. It occurred to her now that perhaps he had been horribly lonely. It was unbearable to think of gentle, urbane Henry ruthlessly exposed, the veil of his discretion torn away and the white light of publicity turned onto every recess of his secret life. All the same, it made her shudder. The thought of Henry touching those crude coarse boys with their gapped teeth and their greasy caps and their cunning weasel grins, of wanting to touch them, to press himself against them – it was not just that it was illegal, it was abhorrent.

Edward sighed. Extracting his hands from hers he pressed his fingertips to his forehead, massaging his frown. Silently she stood and, taking two cigarettes from the box on her dressing table, she lit them and passed one to Edward. He took it and inhaled, the red tip devouring the paper.

'What will he do?' she asked.

Edward shook his head. When he spoke the smoke came out of his mouth in ragged snatches.

'He travels to Paris tomorrow. The police have dragged their feet but, if Webster names names, there will be pressure for arrests. At least in France he is safe.'

'If? Then there is still a chance that he might not?'

'There is always a chance. The government is leaning heavily on him and I know that Euston has threatened to sue for libel if he publishes. Together that may be enough to scare Webster off.'

'Do you really think so?'

'No. No, I don't.'

'Oh, Edward.'

Edward said nothing but took another long pull on his cigarette.

'Did – did you know?' Maribel asked very quietly.

'I don't know. I suppose, sort of, I suspected that he might – I mean, at school – but one was expected to outgrow it, it was not something I – I did not think about it. I certainly never thought he'd be damned fool enough to get himself caught.'

'That's hardly his fault.'

'Of course it's his bloody fault. Ferreting around filthy back-streets with money-grubbing little rent boys. It was madness, utter bloody madness.'

Angrily Edward leaped up, crushing out his cigarette in the overflowing saucer on the dressing table. He stood for a moment, his back stiff, staring down at the tangle of hairpins in their porcelain dish, the clutter of powder puffs and matchboxes and silver-backed hairbrushes, all dully reflected in the table's glass surface. He picked up a tortoiseshell comb, running his thumb along the blade of the teeth, and set it down again. When he turned round a crease pulled his eyebrows together and his eyes were desolate.

'He'll get two years,' he said. 'With hard labour. He will never survive it.'

They were the last to arrive at the Howards' and the first to leave. Back at the flat Edward came with her to her room. She held him tightly as he pressed himself against her, his eyes closed and his face stricken with concentration. Afterwards he slept. Maribel did not. The hum of her thoughts and the ache in her lungs roused her frequently from her thin doze. In the morning the saucer by the window brimmed with butts.

She rose at the usual time and dressed in the shabby costume she wore for the darkroom. It would distract her to work. She was dizzy with sleeplessness, her thoughts swirling in her head like a snow-globe. She rubbed her eyes, staring at her pale reflection in the mirror as she put up her hair. Her reflection stared uncertainly back. Where would it stop? she thought, and then she sighed and shook her head, because there was no purpose in thinking that way. When she crossed the room the carpeted floor seemed to tilt like a ship beneath her feet.

At breakfast Edward spoke little. He stared unseeingly at the folded newspaper, the bridge of his nose pinched between his finger and thumb, blinking as though he had trouble with his eyes, and let his tea grow cold. When Alice brought the letters he reached out to take the pile but his hand hesitated halfway, suspended in the air. Edward regarded it in bewilderment, then brought it back to his plate. His long fingers crumbled the crust of a slice of unbuttered toast. His distraction made Maribel afraid.

'Will you go into the House today?' she asked him.

He shrugged. 'I might as well. I shall be no less useful there today than I ever have been.'

The wretched attempt at a joke twisted her heart. She leaned across the table, placing her hand on his. He did not look up but his fingers opened, allowing hers to fit between them. Fragments of toast lay scattered about his plate.

'We must not despair,' she said. 'Not yet. There is still a chance that Webster will not publish.'

'Perhaps I should go and see him. Perhaps, if I talked to him –'

'Surely that would only make matters worse?'

'I have to do something.' He looked up at Maribel. 'When my father went into the asylum I swore to Mother that I would take care of them both. What a magnificent job I have made of it. Inverallich hanging by a thread and Henry –'

'You have been a fine brother. A fine son. Henry too.'

'What about Mother? On top of everything . . . It is not only the scandal, Bo. If this gets out, if they press charges – Henry may never be able to come back.'

'Exile is better than prison,' she said.

Edward stared at their hands, her fingers between his. Then, gently he extricated his hand. He shook his head.

'Exile is a prison too.'

38

AFTER BREAKFAST THEY BOTH went to work. At Turks Row Maribel had a sudden dread of encountering Mr Webster on the stairs but she saw no one. The corridor outside Mr Pidgeon's studio was deserted. She knocked softly. A moment later Thomas answered the door and handed her the key.

Maribel hesitated, fiddling with the ribbon. 'Mr Webster,' she said. 'I wondered – you do not expect him today, do you?'

Thomas shook his head. 'No, ma'am. He came the day before yesterday. No customers today.'

'That's not like Mr Pidgeon.'

'Mr Pidgeon's not here, ma'am. He's got family business. Won't be back till tomorrow.'

Maribel nodded. 'Well, don't let me keep you. I shall drop the key back when I am done.'

She stood in the corridor for a moment, smoking a cigarette. Then she unlocked the darkroom and went in. She had spent the previous day photographing the fishmongers at Billingsgate and she took the plates from her satchel and set them on the developing table. Yesterday, returning from the market in the Underground train, her hair ripe with the smell of fish, she had imagined developing the prints with excitement. It felt like a lifetime ago. She tried not to think at all as she set out the chemical baths and took down the bottles of solution. Mixing them together she slid her first plate out of its cover and slipped it into the bath of developer.

Anxiety made her clumsy. The solution splashed onto her wrist, burning her skin. Cursing, she spat on the burn, fumbling on the shelf nearest the door for a rag to wrap it with. As she tied it she noticed a thick brown folder tied with ribbon, WEBSTER printed in Mr Pidgeon's neat capitals on the front. Before she knew what she was doing Maribel took it down and opened it. There, in print after print, was Webster, standing in his white collar and his jerkin with his legs astride and his milky eyes fixed upon the camera. There was a horrible satisfaction in looking at him, like a tongue probing a sore tooth. The photographs were almost all identical, differing only in the angle of Webster's head, the set of his mouth, the position of his left hand. Turning them quickly one could almost see him move.

It was only when she closed the folder that she thought of it. The idea was absurd, impossible, but, as she took up her tongs, watching her photograph begin to form beneath the stippled surface of the chemicals, it too began to take shape.

On the shelf to the right of the table there were, as usual, several stacks of covered plates awaiting development. Each stack was wrapped in brown paper and marked with the name of the customer. Standing on a chair she struck a match so that she might see them more clearly. The light snagged on the labels, BAXTER, HOLLAND, MAXWELL. She pushed them to one side impatiently. And then, as the flame burned almost to her fingers, a pile of perhaps twenty plates marked WEBSTER.

Maribel dropped the match. Very carefully she took the Webster plates and set them on the workbench. When she had rearranged the stacks so that the gap was not noticeable she clambered down and stood, one hand on the package, feeling the shape of them beneath her hand. Then, pulling out the cloth-lined box at her feet, she secreted the unexposed prints inside.

When she knocked at the door of the studio again Thomas looked surprised.

'Is anything the matter, ma'am?' he asked.

'Not exactly. I wondered if I might ask you something.'

Thomas frowned, biting his lip. 'Me, ma'am? I don't know –'

'How long have you been Mr Pidgeon's apprentice, Thomas?'

'It'll be three years this June, ma'am.'

'By now you must know almost as much as your master.'

'I don't know about that.'

'The thing is, I need some help.'

'It'd be better if you talked with Mr Pidgeon, ma'am. He'll be back tomorrow.'

'I'm rather afraid it can't wait till tomorrow. Might I come in?'

Thomas hesitated. Then, reluctantly, he opened the door. Along the back wall of the studio hung the long curtain that had provided the backdrop to Webster's photographs. In front of it stood the rocking horse and a small upright chair.

'Is this how Mr Webster photographed himself last time?' she asked. 'Astride a white steed?'

Thomas grinned awkwardly and did not answer.

'I saw his photographs in the darkroom,' she said casually. 'So many prints all the same.' She took up a position in front of the curtain, her shoulders thrown back and her hands upon her waist. 'One would have thought he would have tired of the same pose.'

Thomas ducked his head. 'Camera was set up for it. On a clock. Had to use a mark to hold the focus.'

Maribel looked at the floor. 'I think I see it. Just here?'

'A little to the left, maybe. It was a matter of the light.'

'A clock. How fascinating. But I am wasting your time. I did not come here to gossip.' She set down her portfolio and untied the ribbons. 'I came to talk about this.'

When he saw Mr Pidgeon's family portrait Thomas grinned.

'Fine, ain't it?' he said.

'It's extraordinary,' Maribel said. 'I wondered, do you think you might be able to tell me a little about it? I would pay you for your time, of course.'

Tentative at first, in the warmth of Maribel's interest Thomas opened like a flower. His knowledge was extensive, his eyes and curiosity sharp, and he grew animated, gesticulating with his hands as he talked of exposure times and emulsions and gelatin bloom. Maribel scribbled notes, possessed in turn by agitation at the multiplicity of difficulties that Thomas described and by a determination so feverish she could hardly keep up with her own hand. The difficulties would have to take care of themselves. When at last she bid goodbye to Thomas she returned the portfolio to the darkroom and locked the door. Slipping the key into her pocket she descended once again to the street.

Alice looked up, surprised, from her housework as Maribel hurried into the flat.

'Is everything all right, ma'am?'

Maribel did not answer. In the bedroom she rummaged together powder puff, hairbrush, pins, a jewelled comb, a pair of paste earrings, a pinkish salve she sometimes wore on her lips, bundling them all into her satchel. She glanced around the room, then on impulse stuffed her silk wrap in on top. She buckled the bursting satchel and snatched up her camera.

'I shall not be back for lunch,' she called out to Alice as she let the door slam behind her. Less than twenty minutes later a hansom deposited her at the entrance to Green Park. It was before midday and, though the nocturnal haunts of the park would not awake for many hours, near to the place where she had tried to photograph the girl in the scarlet dress she found an old woman slumped on a bench, a bottle ill-concealed beneath her shawl and a basket of grimy artificial flowers tucked under one arm.

At first the old woman was unwilling to answer Maribel's enquiries, but once she realised that Maribel was not from the Refuge and was prepared to enrich her by sixpence, she proved perfectly obliging and directed her to a low type of inn in an alley off Bury Street. The door stood propped open, and from inside came the sour smell of spilled beer. Maribel lit a cigarette, drawing the courage of it deep into her lungs. In the window of the house next door a green blind had been pulled down. In faded black letters it read 'LODGINGS FOR SINGLE MEN 6d'.

The girl in the scarlet dress was both less intoxicated and less forthcoming than she had been on the occasion of their previous meeting. She gave her name as Betsey, though the slight squint of her eyes as she said it suggested that it was not a name she was accustomed to. She leaned against the jamb of the inn door, smoking one of Maribel's cigarettes, and the swell of her pregnant belly lifted her grimy skirt almost to her ankles, displaying a battered pair of men's boots. Her pinched face was opaque as she listened to the proposal that Maribel put to her, her eyes narrowed against the smoke, her sharp little jaw moving in rhythmic circles like a cow's. It was only when Maribel mentioned a hansom to Turks Row that she screwed up her face, pinching out the smoked cigarette between two dirty fingers and throwing it like a dart into the gutter.

"Ow gulpy d'you fink I am? I knows a forriner when I 'ears one. 'Ow's I to know you ain't abductin' me?'

'For pity's sake, do I look like a criminal?'

The girl shrugged. Maribel glanced down at her old work dress. It was very shabby.

'We'll take the omnibus,' she said desperately. 'I can hardly kidnap you on the omnibus.'

The girl said nothing but sucked on her teeth, her hands pressed against the curve of her back as though it hurt her. She was very near her time.

'I'll only need two hours, three at the most,' Maribel said. 'You'll be back by nightfall.'

'Why me? What's so special 'bout me?'

'It was your idea in the first place.'

The girl scowled suspiciously. 'What you talkin' 'bout?'

'In the park, don't you remember? You made me an offer.'

'What offer?'

'Cock Lane for a shilling.'

39

MARIBEL WAS OBLIGED TO offer a good deal more than a shilling, and half the money upfront, before the girl was finally persuaded to return with her to Turks Row. As the omnibus neared Sloane Square Maribel lifted the shawl from around her shoulders and arranged it over her bonnet like a hood, obscuring her face. The girl eyed her suspiciously but said nothing. On Sloane Avenue Maribel slipped her arm through the girl's, clamping her to her side, and hustled her to the narrow entrance to the studio.

Thomas answered her knock almost immediately.

'The darkroom key,' he said anxiously. 'Please tell me you have it?'

'Silly me,' Maribel said, fishing in her pocket. 'I must have taken it by mistake. Let me fetch some plates. Then you can have it back. Go on, don't be shy.'

She pushed the girl ahead of her into the studio. Thomas said nothing but a notch appeared between his eyebrows.

'Thomas, this is – Violet. Violet has kindly consented to pose for me this afternoon so perhaps you might set up the lights for me while I get her ready?'

It took longer than Maribel expected to dress Betsey's hair. It was matted and oily and the girl yelped furiously several times as Maribel yanked at the knots. Once it was combed out, however, it proved to be rather fine, a dark lustrous chestnut with a slight wave. The girl pouted admiringly at herself in the mirror as

Maribel set about dressing it. She tried to remember how Alice did it, the roll of hair at the nape of the neck that gave the arrangement volume, the way she licked her finger and wrapped the hair around it to hold a curl. The effect needed to be elegant, any wantonness in it no more than the shiver of an almost-dimple, a glance held a second too long. Titian or Giorgione, never Francisco de Goya. Several times, as the hair slipped, escaping the pins, she wondered if perhaps she was mad, if the whole idea was preposterous. It would never work. But still she kept twisting and rolling and pinning. It was too late to stop now. Besides, it was always better to do something.

The final result, while hardly up to Alice's standards, was not unsatisfactory.

'Come and stand over here, Violet,' she said and Betsey rose clumsily, her swollen belly making her awkward. Since arriving at the studio the girl had been very quiet, the rolling boil of pugnacity reduced to a simmering wariness. Now she stood before the long pale curtain like a defendant in the dock, the belligerence of her expression not quite concealing her apprehension. On the swell of her stomach her hands clenched in fists.

'See this mark? I want you here, just six inches or so to the left. A little more towards that wall, that's right. And try to relax. Let your shoulders drop. Imagine you have only just been woken, that you are still half asleep.'

She tilted Betsey's head, adjusting her curls with one finger so that a ringlet brushed against her cheek. The hair would do. The difficulty was Betsey's face. It was too bony to be pretty, the nose too narrow, the jaw too sharp. Her lips were thin, her mouth hardly more than a slit. There was none of the childlike softness of seduction about Betsey. Hers was a face for haggling and for disappointment.

Maribel thought of the photographer in the crimson studio, the appraising way he had studied her with his head on one side.

'Turn away,' she said. 'Look back over your shoulder.'

Betsey scowled, jutted her chin. Maribel bit her lip. She thought of Victor's hand on her shoulder, the scorched caramel burn of the brandy on her tongue.

'Thomas,' she said, 'we need flowers. Might you be an angel and run out for them?'

'There's no need for that, ma'am. We have several silk —'

'Fresh,' Maribel interrupted smoothly. 'Perhaps it is the scent but they quite change the mood of a composition.' She extracted a crown from her purse and handed it to Thomas. 'White roses. And freesias. They must be white.'

'It is a bit early in the year for roses, ma'am.'

'Thomas, please. Roses and freesias. I don't care if you have to go to Timbuktu and back for them.'

Thomas opened his mouth to say something. Then, closing it, he nodded.

As soon as the door closed behind him she bolted it from the inside. Then she went to the cupboard behind the door and opened it.

'Do you want a drink?' she said. 'There's sherry.'

When Betsey took the glass she cocked her little finger and downed the contents in a single gulp. Then she made a face.

'It ain't gin,' she said but she closed her eyes a little, savouring the warmth of the alcohol as it spread through her chest. Taking her silk wrap from her satchel Maribel handed it to Betsey.

'Go and put this on,' she said.

Betsey eyed her consideringly, then reached out and touched the robe, gauging the stuff between finger and thumb. The girl's hands were grimy, her fingernails torn, and Maribel had to resist the urge to snatch the wrap away. She had bought it in Paris the previous season for a price she had done her best to forget. The heavy silk gleamed, its opalescent folds as unctuous as cream.

'I'm goin' to want it,' Betsey said. 'You know, after.'

'Don't be absurd.'

Betsey shrugged.

'Then I'll just be gettin' off,' she said and she reached up, fumbling at the pins in her hair.

'You can't do that!' Maribel cried. 'We agreed your price.'

'Price just changed. Take it or leave it.'

The two women stared at each other. Maribel was the first to look away. They did not have much time.

'Very well. You can have the stinking wrap. But that had better be the end of it, do you hear me, or you won't get another farthing.'

The threat sounded hollow, even to her own ears, but Betsey nodded to herself, a satisfied smirk on her thin lips. She scooped the silk wrap into her arms.

"Ow about another?' she said, jerking her head at the sherry decanter.

'Later,' Maribel said. She gestured towards the screen in the far corner of the studio. 'You can change behind there.'

Betsey let her smirk spread across her face. Then, yanking at the lacing on her dress, she tugged it from her shoulders and let it fall. Maribel caught a glimpse of heavy blue-veined breasts, pale brown nipples, the marbled sheen of her drum-tight belly. She flushed and looked away. Betsey reached out and, gripping Maribel's wrist, twisted her hand around to press her breast. With a strangled cry Maribel snatched her hand away.

'Come on,' Betsey said. 'It's what you want, ain't it? Why else you send the boy away?'

Her tone was two parts wheedling, one part menace. Stepping out of the mess of her skirts she came round to stand in front of Maribel, one hip thrust sideways. A dark line ran like a shaft of an arrow over the stretch of her swollen belly to the pelted point between her thighs.

'What I want is for you to stand over there,' Maribel said tightly. 'Exactly where I showed you.'

Betsey cupped her breasts in her raw hands, pressing them upwards. 'Flesh and blood's better than dirty pictures,' she said.

Maribel shook her head. 'Not this time. Now get over there. We haven't much time.'

It was peculiar how quickly the girl's nakedness became ordinary. Turning Betsey's back to the camera Maribel arranged the robe so that it draped from the crook of her elbows, the neckline falling to reveal the base of her spine and, below that, the cleft of her buttocks. She brought Betsey's face around, tucking her chin behind her shoulder, so that she looked out from under her eyelashes. The sherry had blurred her gaze a little. Her jaw was loose, her arms slack by her sides. Maribel took her hands and folded them together in front of her. Then she bent and moved her right foot out a little so that, beyond the ivory folds of silk, it was just possible to see the crest of her pregnant belly.

'Look towards the screen,' Maribel said. 'Imagine that the man you desire most in the world is standing in front of you, right there where the mark is on the floor. But you cannot touch him. And he cannot touch you. You have to make love to him with your eyes.'

So many years and yet the photographer's words came as readily to her lips as the Lord's Prayer. Betsey sniggered.

'What ballsack of a john pays for eyes?' she said.

Maribel picked up the decanter and refilled Betsey's glass. Then she poured a large one for herself.

'To dirty pictures,' she said, raising her glass. Swallowing a large gulp she reached for her camera and slid the first plate carefully inside. There was no way of knowing whether the drape of the curtain was right, or the tilt of the light, no way of knowing with any accuracy how it would come out. There was no way of knowing if it would work at all.

'You desire him,' she said. 'With all your body and soul you desire him. No man has ever made you feel as you feel now, liquid with the longing to touch him, to feel the kiss of his hands on your naked skin. The desire in you is so strong it burns in you like a fire. Every nerve in your body prickles with the nearness of him. You can feel the warmth of his breath on your skin. The blood in your veins is electric with it.'

All the time she was taking photographs she continued to talk in this way. At first Betsey laughed, muttering sneeringly under her breath, but as Maribel's low voice curled around the studio like cigarette smoke, relentless and hypnotic, Betsey's sneer softened. The alcohol and the warmth of the lights and the music of Maribel's voice eased the clench between her shoulder blades and tempered the sharp corners of her face. Maribel went on talking. She talked as she bent to the camera, as she opened the shutter, as she adjusted Betsey's hair or her robe or her stance. She talked as she changed the plates. When Betsey began to tire she gave her a third glass of sherry and took another for herself and all the time she kept talking, talking, as though to stop would be to give up hope.

By the time she heard Thomas's footfalls on the stone steps she had taken eleven plates. It would have to do. She glanced towards the door, checking the bolt, and thrust the remainder of the unused plates in her satchel.

'Quickly,' she hissed at Betsey. 'Get dressed.'

Betsey gawped at her, glassy-eyed.

'Hurry,' Maribel said and she pulled the wrap from her shoulders, shoving her towards the dress that lay where Betsey had dropped it on the floor. Thomas's key scraped in the lock. Bundling the wrap into a knot, Maribel shoved it into her satchel and fastened the straps.

"Ey, that's mine!' Betsey protested.

'Later,' Maribel said, gathering up the decanter and glasses and putting them back into the cupboard. 'Not here. Now get dressed.'

The door rattled but did not open. There was a silence. Then Thomas started banging.

'Ma'am? Are you in there?'

'Come in, Thomas,' she said, yanking the scarlet dress up around Betsey's shoulders. 'Now do yourself up, for God's sake.'

'I think the door is bolted,' Thomas said.

'Oh, I am sorry. Give me a moment to finish this last shot and I'll let you in.'

She grabbed Betsey's greasy shawl, and threw it at her along with her battered green bonnet. She pushed her towards the chair by the screen.

'Sit there,' she muttered. 'Put your head in your hands.'

Then, picking up her camera, she went to the door and drew the bolt. Thomas held out a bunch of tired-looking roses. Maribel took them. They smelled of coal dust and dirty water. She smiled and handed them back to Thomas.

'Thank you,' she said, 'but I fear our model is taken ill. I am going to have to accompany her home. Keep these, why don't you? For your trouble.' She picked up her satchel. 'Come on now, Violet. Steady as you go. I shall keep the darkroom key, Thomas, if I may. There is still a little work I have to do.'

40

I T REQUIRED CONSIDERABLE INSISTENCE on her part before Maribel was admitted to the office of Mr Webster. Although it was a little after six in the evening and the street outside was crowded with weary-faced people making for home, the newspaper office was as busy as an anthill. As a clerk conducted her along a dingy passage, a man pushed past her, his shirt-sleeves rolled up to his elbows, a large sheet of cardboard held like a shield over his chest. His untied shoelaces darted behind his boots as though trying to catch him up. She glimpsed a large room like a schoolroom, crowded with desks half partitioned by low carrels and stacks of papers, before the clerk showed her into a shabby office. The room was small and very spartan in its design. A desk with a green-shaded brass lamp took up almost all the available space. The floor was uncarpeted, the walls mostly obscured behind rows of shelves laden with books and ledgers and piles and piles of paper tied with black ribbon. The chair behind the desk was upholstered in worn leather.

Maribel sat down on a scuffed upright chair. She held her portfolio tightly on her lap. The clerk shut the door. From somewhere upstairs she could hear the asthmatic wheeze of machinery. Restlessly she looked about her. The window gave out onto no more than a narrow well, its brick walls streaked with damp. Behind the desk hung a number of framed letters and photographs. She hesitated, then rose to take a closer look.

The letters were mostly several years old, their ink faded, and while two or three were extravagantly complimentary, heaping praise upon Mr Webster for his moral courage, the same number again were vituperative in their condemnation of his exposures. The photographs all had Webster in them. There was one of him with General Charles 'Chinese' Gordon, another with Buffalo Bill, a third, rather blurred, with Mr Gladstone. On the desk, in a gilt frame, there was a studio portrait of Webster dressed in prison uniform, the arrows on the jacket like the prints of inky-footed birds. A narrow slot cut into the mount contained a typewritten quotation: *'This is our comfort, God is in Heaven, and He doth what pleaseth Him; His and only His counsel shall stand, whatsoever the designs of men and the fury of the people be.'*

She was obliged to wait more than thirty minutes before Mr Webster finally came to the office. He brought with him like a gust of warm air the noise and hubbub of the newspaper, which filled the room as he stood on the threshold, issuing instructions to a man with a hasty pencil and a frown between his eyebrows. When Maribel half rose from her chair he raised a hand in a gesture which was at least as much command as apology. The young man with the pencil scribbled, then set the pencil behind his ear. Webster nodded. Then, turning to Maribel, he fixed her with his milky eyes.

'Mrs Campbell Lowe,' he said. 'To what do I owe the pleasure?'

The sarcasm in his voice was unmistakable. Maribel smiled coldly.

'No doubt I have come at a bad time,' she said. 'I should have made an appointment, except that this really can't wait.'

Webster crossed his arms. 'If you have something to say, say it. I am in a hurry.'

'Very well.'

Leaning down Maribel took up her portfolio and loosened the ribbons. Her heart thumped in her chest but her hands were steady. Carefully she drew out a print and laid it on the table.

'I have come about this,' she said.

Webster frowned and took a step towards the desk. Maribel watched his face, impatience giving way to puzzlement and then to a furious disbelief as he snatched up the print.

'What the Devil –'

'I thought you should like to see it,' she said evenly.

Webster wheeled round. He brandished the photograph, his mouth working, then cast it from him as though it were poisoned. It made a low swoop before landing beneath Maribel's upright chair. She bent down and picked it up.

'It is rather good of the girl, I think,' she said. 'Less flattering of you, perhaps, but then your resemblance to Oliver Cromwell was never particularly marked.'

Breathing heavily, Webster snatched the picture from her hand. He smelled strongly of carbolic soap and stale breath. His milky eyes bulged like marbles.

'What kind of filthy trickery is this?'

'Trickery?'

'This – this obscenity, what in the name of the Devil is it?'

'It is you, Mr Webster. You and a naked woman, but not, I think, your wife?'

For a moment Maribel thought that Mr Webster might strike her.

'If you touch me I shall scream,' she said, in the same conversational tone. 'I can't imagine you would want me to scream.'

Webster looked at her, his face contorted.

'This is a libel. The man in that – you know as well as I that it is not me.'

'Oh, but it is, Mr Webster.' She proffered the photograph to him. 'Take a closer look. The costume is foolish, of course, but see how you look directly at the camera. There can be no mistaking you.'

Webster took the photograph from her. He stared at it, his jaw working. Then, very slowly, he tore it in two and dropped the pieces on to the floor. Maribel said nothing. Sliding her hand into her portfolio, she drew out another identical print.

'That's better,' she said. 'I should tell you that I have made a number of copies. I took the precaution of sealing them in envelopes addressed to several prominent gentlemen of my husband's acquaintance who I think might take an interest in such a photograph. My maid has instructions to post them if I am not home by eight.' She glanced at her watch. 'Goodness, that does not leave us much time, does it?'

Webster's neck was scarlet. Slowly, a muscle jumping in his cheek, he tore the two pieces of print into tiny scraps.

'No one will believe you,' he hissed. 'The picture is a fake and you know it.'

'A fake, is it?' Maribel studied the print in her hands, her head on one side. 'And yet it looks so real.'

'Of course it's a damned fake. What sort of madness is this? I have never seen that – that harlot before in my life.'

'Come now, Mr Webster, be reasonable. You are a married man, I understand that. The last thing you want is a scandal. You say you do not know this woman but, you see, I find that rather hard to believe. I happen to have this rather damning photograph.' She rose from her chair and walked to the door of his office, her hand on the porcelain handle. 'Perhaps we should consult your underlings. See what they think of the evidence.'

'Evidence? That? It is nothing but a concoction of lies! I tell you, I have never seen that woman before.'

'So you say. And yet here you are and here she is and from her condition one would have to assume that you are – to put it delicately – rather more than passing acquaintances.'

He lunged at her, his hands splayed, his arms jerking like a puppet's, but Maribel was too quick for him. Turning the handle of the door she threw it open. The dammed-up clamour of the newspaper office cascaded over them. At a desk beyond the door, an island in a sea of hurrying people, a clerk looked up from his papers. Maribel nodded at him. In the pool of light from his brass lamp his hands were yellow as wax. Then she closed the door. Webster twisted away, slamming his fist against the wall. The framed letters shook.

'I would be grateful, Mr Webster, if you could conduct yourself with a little more propriety,' she said. 'Now perhaps we can get down to business. I am here to make a deal.'

'I don't make deals with the Devil.'

'Oh, I think you will in this case. You really don't have a choice, do you?'

Webster was silent.

'Very good. So here are my terms. Insofar as you must report the Bolsover Street case at all, you will publish in your newspaper only the names of the gentlemen cited by the defendants in court. If any other names are mentioned, any at all, I shall make certain that this photograph is as widely distributed as I can manage, and I should warn you, my husband and I know a great number of people. Of course, it goes without saying that any further invasion into our privacy, or that of our family, would ensure a similar result.'

Webster spat in disgust, swiping at the print in her hands.

'You think that this – this trumpery will prevent me from doing my duty? The scientists that examined Hudson's work – I am certain they could prove in a minute that this was a double exposure or some other manner of cheat.'

'From a print? I hardly think so. To prove such a thing would require examination of the camera used to take the photograph, the camera slide, the plate from which the prints were made, the bath in which it was developed. Do you have access to all of those things, Mr Webster?'

'There are such things as subpoenas, you know. I could make you turn them over.'

'That is to assume I have them. Of course you could inform

the police, prosecute me in the law courts, but do you really think that would help? Once the story became a matter of public record there would be no containing the scandal.'

There was a film of sweat on Mr Webster's brow. When he drew his handkerchief from his pocket his hands shook.

'This is perfectly absurd,' he hissed. 'You cannot blackmail me. People know my reputation. I am an honourable, respected man, a good Christian and a faithful husband and father. There is not a soul alive who will believe this filth to be genuine.'

'I suppose you could take that risk, though it would seem hazardous to me, for a man acknowledged by so many of the gentlemen of his acquaintance to be infatuated with sex.'

'I – how dare you?'

Maribel shrugged. 'You are quite right. It is ill-mannered of me to repeat the private opinions of others, however widely held. I apologise. Let me ask you this instead. Do you remember a Mrs Burwood, Mr Webster?'

'Is there no end to the baseless accusations that you mean to level at me, Mrs Campbell Lowe?'

'Mrs Burwood is not one of your mistresses. Or, at least, not to my knowledge. No, Mrs Burwood was the widow you swindled when you published Mr Hudson's photograph of her without her permission. The spirit photograph, surely you remember?'

'There was no swindle, damn it, and I fail to see –'

'Mrs Burwood, like so many other bereaved and grieving widows before her, believed that her husband appeared in her portrait because she wanted to believe. The desire to believe is very powerful, Mr Webster, especially when the proof appears to be incontrovertible. There are many people out there who believe that the camera is incapable of untruth. There are a great deal more who, thanks to years of sensational revelations in the *City Chronicle*, take considerable satisfaction in the exposure of a hypocrite. These people are your pupils, Mr Webster.

It was you who cultivated in them the taste for blood, the voracious appetite for scandal and righteous disgust, the disregard for the niceties of privacy and the benefit of the doubt. You taught them well. Why would they not devour you too?'

Webster regarded her with a hatred so pure the air seemed to shrink away from it. His slit of a mouth pressed in on itself and, at his sides, his hands were clenched into fists.

'Do we have a deal, Mr Webster?'

Slowly, as though his limbs were too heavy for his body, Webster sank into his chair. He regarded the piles of paper on his desk, then, with a great sweep of his arm, sent them flying into the air. Books and bundles of documents crashed to the floor. An ink bottle smashed, spattering the wall with black. As several loose sheets drifted quietly to the floor a black puddle spread across the worn wooden boards.

'You shall go to Hell,' he hissed. 'You and your lying, cheating, fornicating husband.'

'Perhaps. It is a chance we are willing to take.'

Webster looked up, fixing her with his milky eyes.

'How does it feel to have a sodomite for a brother-in-law?'

Maribel lifted her skirts and stepped carefully over the puddle of spilled ink. For a moment she studied the photograph in her hands. Then she turned it round and placed it on the desk in front of Webster.

'I haven't the first idea,' she said. 'And I have no intention of finding out.'

41

I T WAS NEARLY THE end of summer. They stood together on the pebbled beach, her arm through his, watching the evening sun as it melted over the mountains. It was very still. Beyond the mirrored sweep of the loch the rocky slopes were hazed with purple. Inverallich was to be sold. The orchards that Maribel had planted had at last begun to flourish but the yields were no match for the mortgages. There was nothing else to be done. Already the smaller rooms of the house were packed up. There were pale squares on the walls where the pictures had hung, and the rugs lay in long rolls against the skirtings. The corridors were crowded with wooden tea chests packed with books and lamps wrapped in newspaper. The pianoforte had been sold. Its castored feet had left tiny dents in the wooden floor of the library.

By the end of the month they too would be gone. The buyer was a Mr Farquhar, Conservative Member for Richmond in Yorkshire, who had amassed a fortune in the construction of railways and canals. In the weeks before the sale he had brought an architect to inspect the property. They had talked of extending the stables, of redesigning the western facade of the house to include a clock tower. Plans had been drawn up for a folly on the island, a rotunda in the classical style. The gnarled old trees would have to be cut down.

They had achieved a good price, given the economic climate. The sale would allow them to pay off all of Edward's father's debts and leave them enough to live very comfortably. They would rent a smaller house in the constituency for as long as Edward continued to serve in Parliament. There would be an election before long and he did not mean to stand, even as an independent. The Liberal Party had finally withdrawn the whip when he, along with Keir Hardie, had attended the inaugural conference of the Socialist International in Paris as representatives of the newly minted Scottish Labour Party. Afterwards, in the midst of an angry debate in the House of Commons over the striking dockers, Edward had been challenged to declare whether he preached 'pure unmitigated Socialism'.

'Undoubtedly,' he had replied cheerfully.

Maribel had had Alice make a cake, on top of which she had inscribed the word UNDOUBTEDLY in bright pink icing.

Edward bent, selecting a flat stone. He weighed it in his hand and then, with a flick of the wrist, sent it skimming across the surface of the loch. Maribel watched as it flew, leaving a feathered trail of arrows behind it.

'It surprises me,' she said. 'How much I shall miss it.'

Edward smiled and chose another stone. 'You will miss complaining about it.'

'That too.'

'You can spend your summers in Spain and Italy just as the doctor has always said you should. It will do wonders for your health.'

'I know. But it's strange. Somehow this place – it has worked its way into my bones.'

'Like rheumatism?'

Maribel laughed as he kneaded her hand, pretending to palpate the knuckles. She caught his fingers in hers and kissed them. They were as familiar against her lips as her own breath.

'It is beautiful here.'

'Yes. It is beautiful.'

They stood together, arm in arm, watching the last honeyed

slither of the sun behind the mountains. The horizon was smeared with gold. Above them the first stars were out and the pale wisp of the new moon was a smudge of chalk dust on the darkening sky.

When it was almost dark they turned and made their way back up the path towards the house. Cora had lit the lamps in the drawing room and the light spilled out through the French windows onto the terrace. Maribel held Edward's arm tightly, dizzy with *saudade*. After Edward had signed the sale papers he had gone out for a walk alone. She had watched from an upstairs window as he stood among the mossy headstones in the family graveyard, the rain dripping from the gutter of his hat.

In the drawing room there was a tray with cake and tea in a silver pot.

'Tea?' Maribel offered. 'Or something stronger?'

'Tea is fine.'

Maribel poured the tea. She handed him the cup, touching his wrist lightly with her other hand.

'You do not have to be brave, you know. Not with me.'

Edward sipped his tea. Then, reaching for Maribel's cigarette case, he snapped it open, set a cigarette between his lips.

'The solicitors claim the contracts are watertight,' he said, striking a match. 'The tenants and feuars are protected as well as we can manage it.'

'And you?'

He shrugged, exhaling a plume of smoke.

'I have money in the bank for the first time in my adult life. I have a cigarette and a cup of tea and a beautiful wife and no meetings until Monday. If I'm lucky that selfsame wife may even offer me a slice of cake. What more could I ask?'

'It is your childhood home, Red. Of course it is awful.'

'It is not awful. It is – a relief. The tenants concern me, it's true, but I shall do what I can for them in Westminster and here with Hardie. As for the house, it had become a millstone around our necks. It will be a good deal easier to be a Socialist without it.'

'You are very philosophical.'

'There is no purpose in fighting what must be.'

'This from the man who did battle in Trafalgar Square?'

'That's quite different and you know it. Come here. Let me tell you something.'

Throwing the stub of his cigarette into the fireplace Edward put down his cup of tea and set his arm around Maribel's shoulders. She tucked herself against his chest, pulling her stockinged feet up underneath her.

'An Indian from Buffalo went fishing on the Niagara River. As he waited for the fish to come his birch canoe caught in the current and began to drift towards the falls. At first he paddled desperately, frantic to escape the pull of the water, but, though he paddled like a madman, the waters continued to bear him forward. So he stopped. He dropped his paddle and lit his pipe and leaned back to smoke it. The tourists watched him through their opera glasses. It was said that as he approached the falls it was impossible to tell what was spray and what pipe smoke.'

'Is that really true?'

'Cody said so.'

'I admire the Indian's style. But it is not yours. You never give up.'

'Nor did the Indian. That's the point. He knew better than to waste what time he had left on a fight he could not win. He accepted what had been and what had to come next and he took his pleasures where he was able. I mean to do the same.'

'But this place is your *querencia*. This is where you belong.'

'No,' Edward said and he held her tightly against him, his lips soft against her brow. 'This is where I belong.'

*

Edward's mother had not come to Inverallich that summer. She told Edward that she was not as strong as he was, that she would not be able to bear it. Edward, who had not wept for himself, wept a little for Vivien. He blamed himself. Maribel, who had never much liked her mother-in-law, hated her for that.

They took Alice with them to help with the packing. Maribel, deprived of models, took a great many photographs of her. The Scottish air brought roses to her cheeks and a kind of soft homesickness to her expression. Some of the photographs were very good. In the evenings, when Edward was out with Hardie or at rallies, the two women ate together. Cora made it clear that she considered it quite irregular but Maribel did not give a fig for Cora's opinion. Already on notice, she could hardly threaten to leave. Sometimes, after dinner, Maribel brought the atlas from the library and showed Alice the places where she meant to take her next photographs. Andalusia. Tangier. Marrakesh. She told Alice of the dark faces and vivid skies of the paintings of Delacroix, the Berbers in their white robes who seemed to have stepped straight from the agora of ancient Greece, and though Alice rolled her eyes, she followed the blue shapes of the coastlines with her fingers and tasted the unfamiliar names on the tip of her tongue. Alice would go too. There was no question about that.

Towards the end of August Henry came to stay. He was his usual charming and urbane self, if a little thinner, and still a reliably sharp-witted source of gossip. The only subject they did not discuss was Bolsover Street, though the scandal remained a topic of speculation among the upper echelons of London society: not only had Somerset's solicitor been convicted of obstruction of justice for assisting his client to flee abroad and sentenced to six weeks in prison, the rumours concerning the Prince of Wales's eldest son, Prince Albert Victor, had continued to burgeon and the royal family had seen fit to dispatch him on a lengthy tour of India while they set about securing him a suitable wife. Oscar's letters brimmed with sly supposition – he declared the Prince's notorious narcissism 'more Aphrodite than Ares' – but Henry said nothing at all. When he spoke of the Prince of Wales it was only to remark upon his enthusiastic support for the return to Europe of Buffalo Bill's Wild West, which was to undertake a second tour the following year.

'Cody intends to spend the first half of the year in Paris,' Henry said as they walked around the garden. 'There is to be an exhibition to celebrate one hundred years since the French Revolution. Let us hope the Prince can keep his head.'

The rhododendron were in flower, their colossal blooms a blaze of crimson and white amid the dark foliage. Planted by Edward's grandfather they had flourished in the poor soil, massing like an invading army around the lawn and down the drive. Maribel and Henry paused by the sundial to admire them. Within the circle of numbers on the lead face of the sundial a stooped Father Time held aloft his scythe, and beneath him the words NAE MAN CAN TETHER TIME OR TIDE. Maribel supposed the quotation was from Burns, with whom the Scotch were unaccountably enamoured. The lead was dull and spattered with bird droppings, and lichen grew in its grooved lip. She picked at it with her thumbnail, listening to the quarrelsome cawing of the rooks in the trees behind the house.

'Will the show come back to London?' she asked.

'Naturally. There is the small matter of Miss Clemmons, after all.'

'Of course. I had forgotten her.'

'If only Cody had.' He smiled, shaking his head. 'I am sure that, if you wished to, we could arrange for you to photograph the Indians again. They are rather up your street, are they not? Those extraordinary faces.'

Maribel shook her head. 'Thank you, but I don't think so. I am finished with myth-making.'

'Myth-making? His new company of Indians are Standing Bull's men. Real-life prisoners of war.'

'Perhaps in America. Here they are just actors, aren't they? Players in a flagrantly fictionalised version of their lives.'

'Aren't we all?'

They were silent for a moment. Maribel pressed the palms of her hands against the rough stone plinth of the sundial. Perhaps, she thought, he did mean to confide in her. Then he laughed and declared himself wearied half to death of fresh air and suggested they go back inside and play cards. She took his arm gladly and squeezed it, giddy with relief. There was, after all, nothing to talk about. Everything was as it had always been. When the scandal he dreaded had failed to materialise Henry had returned from Paris, a little greyer about the temples perhaps but otherwise unaltered. The excursion to France, he told those who enquired, had been pleasant but fruitless; the horses he had gone to look at for the Prince of Wales, though much praised, had proved in the event to be unsatisfactory. It was tiresome but there it was. French bloodstock dealers were, after all, French.

When the *Chronicle* ran an article in which the newspaper named both Somerset and Henry FitzRoy as clients of the infamous brothel, FitzRoy had immediately filed a case against Webster for libel. It seemed likely that he would win and that Webster might, once again, be sentenced to serve time in prison. Though he used his editorial platform to protest vociferously against the indefensible muzzling of the press by the Establishment, Webster had made no further allegations. Meanwhile his legal predicament had served as something of a warning to the proprietors of rival newspapers. The reputation of Henry Campbell Lowe, it seemed, was safe.

In the darkroom at Turks Row Maribel had dropped the

entire pile of plates onto the floor. The smash made a very satisfactory noise. Then she went to the studio to apologise to Mr Pidgeon. She hung her head as she told him that she had knocked them from the shelf as she hunted for another bottle of pyrogallic acid. When she begged his pardon the tears came easily. Plainly discomfited by so abject a display of contrition, Mr Pidgeon lent her his handkerchief and, assuring her that accidents happened, urged her to go home. Thomas would sweep up the mess. When she had recovered herself she went into the darkroom to collect her things. Thomas was kneeling on the floor, sweeping glass into a dustpan. He had looked up at her then, watching as she put on her gloves and settled the strap of her satchel across her shoulder. The intensity of his expression had made her uneasy. It had also made her want to photograph him.

In the cigar box at Cadogan Mansions, interleaved with sheets of tissue paper and hidden beneath the piles of old letters, was a sealed envelope containing the photographs of Mr Webster and his unnamed consort. For surety, Maribel had put several additional copies in a second envelope. When she deposited the envelope with the bank manager she told him it was her will.

She had brought the cigar box with her to Inverallich.

'Will you not miss this place just a little?' Maribel asked Henry when they were settled with tea in the drawing room.

'Here? I shouldn't think so for a moment.'

'It is funny. Edward feels so strong an attachment to the place, to the weight of family history here. You don't feel that too?'

'Naturally, which is precisely why I shall be delighted to see the back of it.'

'You didn't hope to be buried here?'

'And throw in my lot with the wretched bones of my fore-fathers? No thank you.'

'I suppose the tragedy of your own father −'

476

'The tragedy of my father was that he was a drunk and a bully and would doubtless have continued so had the fits not incapacitated him so thoroughly. He beat us both often, for the pleasure of it, I suppose, though he always insisted it was for our own good. The lunatic asylum was the best thing that ever happened to us.'

Maribel stared at him. Insofar as she had thought of Edward's father at all she had always imagined him to be a fine man afflicted by a terrible malady. She did not know why, quite, except that he had two fine sons.

'So you see, I have never much liked this house,' Henry said evenly. Clearing the teapot and plate of biscuits from the tray he set it between them on the sofa. 'London is where I belong, if I belong anywhere. And, talking of London, I want to hear all about this new exhibition of yours. Come on, it's your deal.'

Maribel blinked. Then, picking up the cards, she shuffled the deck.

'There isn't much to tell,' she said. 'It is an even smaller gallery than More's and consequently even less likely to sell anything.'

'But they want to show your work.'

'So they say.'

'Well, then. You are an artist now, whether you like it or not.'

Maribel grinned. 'Oh, I like it,' she said. 'I like it very much.'

Setting the remaining cards down in a pile between them, she turned the top one over. Henry picked up his hand, smoothing the cards into a fan.

'Now down to business,' he said. 'Seven of clubs, me to start.'

After Henry had gone it was just the two of them. Edward was busy with constituency work, Maribel with the packing up of the house. While some of the contents were to be sold most of

477

the furniture and the better paintings were to be shipped to London where, with the money from the sale, they would finally be able to take a house. Edward was enthusiastic about the idea, Maribel less so. She had grown fond of the flat at Cadogan Mansions and of the looseness of life there, the absence of a kitchen and proper servants, the impossibility of entertaining. In a house she would be obliged to manage staff, at the very least a cook and a housemaid, and to assume a great number of tedious domestic responsibilities. Besides, there was Alice, who was not a housemaid or a lady's maid or a cook but something of all three and, in some ways, not quite a servant at all. It was not easy to see how Alice would fit into such a household.

They did not talk of the future in those dying weeks of summer. It seemed too close, somehow, and the past already too far away. As the rooms emptied a silence settled on the house, the sweet sadness of *saudade*. Every familiar place, every ordinary occupation, bore the weight of the last time.

On their last Sunday at Inverallich Edward saddled Pampa and rode out into the hills.

'Come with me,' he said, but she only smiled and kissed him and told him to be home before dark.

'You don't want me. Not today. I would only slow you down.'

'I don't mind slow.'

'You are a terrible liar, Red, and you know it. Go on. Go and say goodbye. Say it for us both.'

'What will you do?'

'I shall pack.'

'But you've been packing for weeks. Surely there is nothing left to do?'

'Almost nothing.'

When he was gone she went upstairs. From the large window on the landing she could see the rooks circling above the trees at the back of the house. The previous afternoon Alice had gone out to the back to say goodbye to them. It was an old tradition in Yorkshire, she said, to tell the rooks of a death or departure, otherwise they would fall into a melancholy and forget to come home.

'I imagine Mr Farquhar would be grateful if they did,' Maribel had said. 'Those birds are a menace.'

'That's as maybe but it's very unlucky to lose them. The house they leave will never prosper.'

It was on the tip of Maribel's tongue to retort that, if the rooks had brought prosperity, they would not be leaving in the first place, but the seriousness on Alice's face had stopped her. Later she had paused on the landing and seen Alice standing beneath the trees, her head tipped back, and, though she could not hear what she was saying, Maribel was startled by the commotion as the birds rose up, filling the sky with a great clamour of wings and cawing. Alice had watched them without expression, her arms crossed over her chest. Then she had wiped her hands on her apron and returned to the house. It was nearly dark when Maribel saw the birds coming back to their nests. They settled quietly, without their habitual hullabaloo, folding themselves up like umbrellas beneath the canopy of the trees. It seemed that they had decided to stay.

In her bedroom Maribel opened the largest of the trunks and, from beneath a pile of blankets, carefully took out the cigar box. The satchel she used for her photography was hung by its strap from a chair. She unbuckled it and slipped the box inside.

At the door of the kitchen she paused. Cora was bent over the range. In the pantry Alice was wrapping the last of the plates in newspaper.

'I'm going for a walk,' Maribel said, taking the iron key of the boathouse from its hook. 'I shan't be long.'

She went first to the old stables and then across the lawn towards the loch. The boathouse had a dilapidated air. The paint had peeled from its plank walls and the roof was spongy with moss. The rusted lock was stiff. The doors had not been opened for a long time.

Inside it smelled of peat and mildew. A narrow wooden dock ran the length of the boathouse like a shelf above the shallow water and, on it, near the back, the little rowing boat had been propped on struts to prevent it from rotting. Maribel ran her hand over its belly, feeling the rough skin of the flaking varnish. Despite the chill in the air the wood felt warm. At the bow the carefully painted black letters had faded. She traced them with a finger. *Robinson Crusoe.*

She smiled, lifting the oars down from their nails on the wall, taking the rowlocks from their wooden box and slipping them into the iron sockets. She had always thought it was the rigorous discipline of boarding school that had made both Edward and Henry so unnaturally orderly. The boat was an awkward shape but it was not heavy and she slid the struts out from beneath it without difficulty, stowing the oars in the bow and dispatching the boat into the water with a quiet splash.

It was a more difficult matter to climb into it. Without someone to steady it the boat rocked dangerously as she stepped down and she almost lost her footing, grabbing wildly at the dock to keep herself from falling and striking her elbow painfully on an iron ring. Cautiously she sat, tucking her skirts between her knees, and, using her hands to push off, she edged the boat out of the boathouse and into the loch.

A breeze had got up. The sky was low, the loch pocked with little brown waves. The boat pitched as she leaned forward for the oars and slid them into the rowlocks. They too were rough from ill use, the grain of the wood splintery against her palms. Pushing at the mud of the loch with one oar she turned the boat round clumsily. Then, lifting both oars from the water, she leaned forward as Edward had taught her and began to row.

The strap of the satchel cut across her shoulder and beneath her arm as very slowly the boat began to move. She had forgotten how heavy the oars were and how uncooperative. As she splashed her way into open water the wind buffeted the little craft, whipping her hair from its pins. Already water had begun to collect in the bottom of the boat, darkening the hem of her dress. She lifted her feet, pressing them into the walls of the boat, and leaned forward to pull again on the disobliging oars. She could see Cora, bending to pick something in the herb garden. She looked very small.

By the time the bow of the boat scraped the pebbly strand of the island Maribel's back ached and the palms of her hands were raw. She clambered out of the boat, careless of the water that sucked at her boots, and dragged it up the shore. The wind was even stronger here, a horizontal breeze that cut through her cape. Clutching her satchel, she scrambled up the narrow beach towards the trees.

She chose a place on the far side of the island, out of sight of the house. It was a bleak spot, wind-flattened, the grass wiry and reluctant. The ground was very rocky. It was not easy to dig. The garden shovel she had brought was short-handled and lacked leverage. She had to slip her fingers under the bigger stones to loosen them, prising them out like teeth. Further down, the roots of the stunted trees twisted like thick cables, and rocks the size of flagstones made pavements in the ruins of the earth.

It was in attempting to raise one of these rocks that she broke the handle from the shovel. She dug into the earth with her hands, levering the rock up until she was able to push it clear. Beneath the rock the earth was crumbly and flecked with pebbles. When the hole was deep enough she unbuckled her satchel and took out the cigar box. The wind caught in the string, making its ends flap. She smoothed them down, holding the box tightly in her lap. Then she leaned forward and placed it in the trough she had made. She looked at the box for a long time. Taking a handful of the crumbly earth, she threw it onto the lid.

'Goodbye,' she said or perhaps she did not, because the wind whipped the words from her mouth and sent them spinning across the brown waters of the loch.

The sky beyond the mountains was a bruised purple and over the water it had begun very lightly to rain. The drops pitted the surface of the loch and the tongues of the waves were tipped with white. Rocking back onto her heels she picked up the broken blade of the shovel and covered the cigar box with earth. Then clumsily she hefted the flat rock back over the place where it had been, replacing the dug-up clods of turf and smaller stones until the rock was quite covered. By her feet a small white feather was caught in a twist of flowerless heather. She reached out, taking it in her hand. The feather's shaft was fine as a fish bone, its down tremblingly soft. Carefully she planted it in the turned earth.

At the trees she paused and looked back. Over the hills the rain had begun to fall in earnest. Clouds shrouded the slopes and turned the loch to lead. Against the dark soil the feather was very white. It shivered, its head bowed against the rising breeze. Then, abruptly, caught by a sudden gust of wind, it danced across the earth and was gone.

Author's Note

THE LONDON OF the 1880s has long fascinated me, mostly because it defies many of our assumptions about it. In the fifth decade of Queen Victoria's reign, London was the largest and richest city in the world, and the centre of an empire that encompassed one quarter of the globe. And yet it was riven by political, economic and social upheaval. The contrasts have interesting parallels with our own times. Like 2012, 1887 was a Jubilee year, marked by lavish celebrations. Like 2012, it was a time of deep recession and rising unemployment. There were strikes, demonstrations, violent riots in which shops were smashed and looted. There were even temporary camps as the homeless sought refuge in Trafalgar Square.

For the ordinary working man in 1887, without the safety net of the welfare state, the suffering was very great. The prolonged slump of 1884–7 was one of the worst of the century and the gulf between rich and poor had never been wider. In cities thousands lost their jobs. Those that were fortunate enough to keep them saw their wages slashed. The situation in rural areas was dire. Britain's determined refusal to impose tariffs on imported grain had resulted in a collapse in prices. By 1885, the British were importing an astonishing 65% of their wheat and the sum of land under wheat cultivation had shrunk by a million acres. As agricultural prices collapsed, men flocked to London in search of work that did not exist, swelling the ranks of the urban unemployed.

The grim conditions forced political change. In Parliament the radical wing of the Liberal Party pushed for social and economic reform, while at grass-roots level the Socialist ideas of Marx had begun to reach an influential audience. The first Socialist political party, the Social Democratic Federation, was established in 1881. A second, the Socialist League, a breakaway from the SDF, followed in 1885. Though both parties were tiny, their militancy alarmed the authorities. In 1885 and 1886 both parties were forbidden by the London Metropolitan Police from holding public meetings. The Socialists refused to heed the ban and their meetings were often forcibly broken up, which attracted a good deal of public attention. In 1886, with unemployment at unprecedented levels, the SDF hijacked a demonstration against free trade in Trafalgar Square; hoisting a red flag, one of their leaders, John Burns, urged the crowd to revolution. When the police attempted to move them on a riot ensued. The rioters attacked carriages in Hyde Park, smashed windows and plundered shops. The police, caught unawares, instructed shopkeepers to put up their shutters. For several days, before order was restored, it seemed that the mob had gained the upper hand.

The Socialists were not the only political group fomenting disorder in London in this period. During the 1880s, the question of Irish Home Rule dominated domestic politics and, from 1880, Irish terrorism returned to London with new boldness. The Fenians, the fraternity dedicated to the establishment of an independent Irish republic, took their name from the *Fianna*, bands of ferocious warriors in Gaelic Ireland who lived apart from society and who might be called upon in times of war. For decades they had considered terror their most powerful political weapon. The Fenian dynamite campaign saw attacks on such London landmarks as the Tower of London, Westminster Hall, Mansion House and the House of Commons. In 1883, on the Metropolitan

Railway near Paddington station, a bomb was dropped from a moving train, injuring seventy-two passengers.

Unrest in the capital reached its fever pitch in 1887, the year that marked Queen Victoria's Golden Jubilee. The celebrations were a riot of pageantry; immense crowds of Londoners turning out to cheer their monarch and her glittering procession. Several weeks later two Irish-Americans were arrested, complete with dynamite, in Islington, accused of plotting to assassinate the Queen as she made her way to the Jubilee service at Westminster Abbey. In nearby Trafalgar Square hundreds of London's poorest families bedded down around the fountains, which offered water to drink and the chance for a free wash. Though the police were instructed to move them on, their numbers continued to rise. The poverty shocked some of London's more compassionate citizens, who arranged for 'bread vans' to tour the square, handing out food. The local police superintendent disapproved of such largesse, claiming that it only made the problem worse. He described the no-good idlers whom he believed descended on the square in search of a free meal derogatively as 'loafers'.

By October the mood was sour. Under mounting pressure to deal with a situation described by the newspapers as a disgrace, the police grew more aggressive in their attempts to clear the square. There were skirmishes and arrests. On 8 November, Henry Matthews, the Home Secretary, banned all meetings in Trafalgar Square. The effect on the Socialists was electric. Long riven by factional disagreement, they found themselves at last united in common cause: the right to freedom of speech and to peaceful protest.

On 13 November, in what came to be known as Bloody Sunday, smarting from their failures of the previous February, marchers converged on Trafalgar Square in outright defiance of the ban. This time the police left nothing to chance. The marchers were ambushed before they could reach the square. There was fighting in Shaftesbury Avenue, Parliament Street and the Strand. Three thousand police officers were supported by two squadrons of cavalry from the Life Guards, while, in front of the National Gallery, a company of Grenadier Guards occupied the square itself and fixed bayonets. Mercifully they proved unnecessary. The police prevailed without difficulty against the unarmed protestors. Two hundred marchers were injured in the fracas, many seriously. Two died.

Though a second demonstration was organised for the following Sunday, the heat had gone out of the protests. Skirmishes continued till December but the efforts were fractured and disorganised. As Socialist activism directed its attentions increasingly towards the industrial struggles of the New Unionism, Bloody Sunday was to prove the high-water mark of what some Socialists had hoped would be the unstoppable tide of popular revolution.

In stark contrast to the poor camped in Trafalgar Square, 1887 saw a very different kind of encampment establish itself in the western end of the capital. In April a company of over two hundred men, women and children pitched their tents at Earls Court. Numbered among them were one hundred cowboys and ninety-seven Indians, including the Sioux chief Red Shirt, as well as 180 horses, eighteen buffalo, ten elk, two deer and five wild steers. On 9 May Buffalo Bill's Wild West opened its doors to the public. An adjunct to the American Exhibition, a trade fair for the promotion of American-manufactured products, the show re-enacted the key events of America's pioneer history and boasted magnificent and elaborate scenery. Seventeen thousand railway-carriage-loads of rock and earth were used to simulate the Rockies and planted with mature trees brought from the Midlands.

Buffalo Bill's Wild West was a sensation, rapidly eclipsing the American Exhibition next door. It was not only the ambitiousness of the show that ensured its success. The show's promoter, Major John Burke, was perhaps the world's first PR supremo. Long before the show had even left New York harbour he was in London, buttering up the editors of the capital's thirty-two newspapers and feeding them with tasty daily bulletins about the show and its exotic cast. Everything from the Indians' fear of the sea (they believed that once they lost sight of land they would surely die) to the age of the youngest cowboy (Master Bennie Irving, aged five) was faithfully reported in the press. By the time the steamer disgorged the company in Gravesend on 13 April there was not a person in London who did not know that Buffalo Bill Cody was coming to town.

Cody was adamant that the Wild West was an unvarnished picture of life on the American frontier but the show allowed itself some liberties. It was Cody who invented the war whoop we now associate with Indian braves, for he wanted their dramatic entrance into the arena to be as frightening as possible. Cody's obsession with war bonnets also meant that the Indians in the Wild West were much more gloriously feathered than they could ever have afforded to be, even in pre-Custer times. Nor did he have any scruples about exploiting the alarming appearance of his Indians to promote the show. Dressed in war bonnets and with terrifyingly painted faces, his band of Indians was conducted around the sights of London as a walking advertisement.

The Wild West made celebrities of many of its stars, including the cowboy Buck Taylor and the diminutive sharp-shooter Annie Oakley. Oakley was married, and her husband accompanied her to England, but Burke ensured that this was kept a secret. She attracted many admirers and several proposals of marriage. Cody himself was the toast of London, invited to innumerable high-society events and made an honorary member of several distinguished London clubs, including the Reform Club. The Lord Mayor even honoured him with a lunch at Mansion House.

Cody too was married, although there was little evidence of it in his behaviour. In London he embarked upon a passionate affair with a young actress, Katherine Clemmons, which he made no effort to disguise, often taking her to dinner at the Savoy after the show.

The success of the American Exhibition in general, and of Buffalo Bill's Wild West in particular, marked a fundamental shift in the relationship between Britain and America, sowing the seeds for a friendship that would shape the global politics of the twentieth century. Two and a half million people paid to see the Wild West during its six-month London run and, thanks to the efforts of Major Burke, scarcely a day went by when the newspapers did not carry a story about Buffalo Bill or his entourage. A good number were even true. Many were also exaggerated or knowingly set up for the purpose of charming the press. Though it is a beguiling story, I have my doubts as to whether one of Cody's Indians really referred to the telegraph that connected the two coasts of the United States as the 'singing wires'. Even Cody's title of Colonel was not quite what it seemed – it was not a mark of military rank but rather an honorary title bestowed upon him by the Governor of Nebraska.

Many of the Indians in Buffalo Bill's show were prisoners of war, sold in bond to Cody by the US government. Such an idea sits uncomfortably with modern-day sensibilities. However it is plain that Cody treated his Indians a great deal better than they were treated in the government reservations, where promises were routinely broken and food was deplorably scarce. Furthermore, the Wild West highlighted the plight of the displaced Indians, ensuring that the question of their future was taken up by, and debated in, the English press.

It was through his furious letters to the *Daily Graphic* on the plight of the Indians that I first encountered Robert Bontine

Cunninghame Graham. Each letter was a small masterpiece, bristling with anger and fierce irony. His Socialist leanings were immediately apparent – in one letter, written after the murder of Sioux chief Sitting Bull, he compared the plight of the Indians to the fate of the miserably paid tailors in the East End and declared furiously that 'the mere accident of a little colouring matter in skin does not alter right or wrong and that the land was theirs, no matter to what uses they put it, centuries before the first white man sneaked timidly across the Atlantic'.

It transpired that Robert Cunninghame Graham was a Scottish aristocrat, whose ancestors had long been radicals. One of his great-grandfathers had had his portrait painted with one hand pointing to a bust of Charles James Fox, a prominent eighteenth-century radical renowned for his impassioned campaigns against slavery and for parliamentary reform, and the other to the Bill of Rights. His maternal grandfather, meanwhile, was famous for having given away a valuable Allan Ramsay portrait of the Marquess of Bute because he could not stand to have a picture of a Tory grandee in the house. Cunninghame Graham's maternal grandmother was Spanish and at her urging he travelled extensively in his youth, mostly in South America, working as a gaucho on the plains of Argentina. He attempted to establish several businesses in South America, including a ranch and a maté plantation, but he had little aptitude for business and none of his enterprises proved successful.

Instead he returned to London, where the poverty and deprivation shocked him profoundly. Determined to push for reform he stood for Parliament as a Radical-Liberal. Once in the House he was a tireless campaigner, pushing hard for Irish Home Rule, land reform in Scotland, graduated income tax and a higher rate of tax on unearned income. He condemned Scotland's hereditary chiefs and landowners, despite being one himself, claiming that 'the unfortunate people starve, and the Tory government, to their cry for a meal, answers with bullets'.

Cunninghame Graham attracted a good deal of attention, not all of it favourable. While William Morris praised the 'brilliancy' of his maiden speech to the Commons, plenty more dismissed him as a dilettante and poseur. *Vanity Fair* described his appearance as 'something between Grosvenor Gallery aesthete and waiter in a Swiss cafe', mockingly claiming him 'a person of "cultchaw"'. He favoured an exotic style of dress, sporting jaunty bandannas and broad-brimmed hats, and, at Ascot, wore a gaucho knife under his dress suit. He was impetuous and chafed against the mechanisms of parliamentary procedure. In September 1887 an outburst against a series of Lords' amendments to the Coal Mines Regulation Bill, in which he protested against the unelected nature of the Upper House, earned him a brief suspension from the Commons. Two months later, in November, he was arrested and imprisoned for his role in the Bloody Sunday riots. Bitterly disillusioned, Cunninghame Graham did not stand for re-election in 1892. Instead he joined with Keir Hardie to found the Scottish Labour Party which fielded five candidates of its own, none of them successfully. The SLP, which merged with other groups in 1893 to become the Independent Labour Party, was the foundation stone of the modern-day Labour Party.

It will be perfectly clear by now that the character of Edward Campbell Lowe is modelled, politically at least, very closely on the real-life Robert Cunninghame Graham. This decision was deliberate – I wanted the politics that form the backdrop to the novel to be absolutely historically accurate. *Beautiful Lies*, however, is not at heart the story of Edward Campbell Lowe or, by association, of Robert Cunninghame Graham. The novel belongs to Maribel, and it was when I happened upon an article in a little-known literary journal that I knew I had my story.

The article that led me to Maribel was written by Jad Adams and called 'Gabriela Cunninghame Graham: Deception and Achievement in the 1890s'. It opened with a story that featured heavily in all the books and biographies of Robert Cunninghame Graham. In 1878, at the London registry office on the Strand, he had married a Chilean woman ten years his junior. His wife, Gabriela, was the daughter of a French landowner, Don Francisco José de la Balmondière, and a Spanish mother. Both had been killed in an accident when Gabriela was twelve years old. Gabriela had then been sent to Paris where an aunt enrolled her in a convent school. The Cunninghame Grahams liked to relate how they had met by chance on the Champs-Elysées, when Gabriela was startled and almost knocked off her feet by Robert's wayward horse. It was, as Robert's friend, A. F. Tschiffely, cooed in his biography of 1937, 'a case of love at first sight'.

The story was very romantic. It was also, as Adams's article revealed, a complete fiction, albeit one that had been successfully maintained long after its protagonists were dead and buried. Gabriela Cunninghame Graham died of dysentery in 1906, her husband thirty years later in 1936. It was not until 1985 that a previously undiscovered cache of family letters revealed the truth: Gabriela was not Chilean at all, nor was she called Gabriela. Her name was Carrie Horsfall and she had been born in 1860 in Masham, North Yorkshire. Her father was a surgeon. Carrie was his second daughter, and the second of thirteen children. In 1875, aged fifteen, she had run away from home and headed to London, determined to fulfil her dreams of becoming an actress. As for what had happened between then and her reappearance in 1878 as Robert's wife, Adams could only speculate.

Immediately I was smitten. I tried to find out more about Gabriela but it seemed that, beyond what had been included in the article, there was little more to discover. The fleeting references in her husband's biographies were unrevealing. I tracked down a handful of her published articles and poems. I also found a brief entry in *Study in Yellow*, a history of the influential literary journal *The Yellow Book*, that as well as recounting (again) the story of their romantic Parisian encounter, claimed that, during Robert's trial for illegal assembly after the Bloody Sunday riots, Gabriela had issued 'At Home' cards to all their friends, giving their address as Bow Street Police Court. Everything else that seemed to be known about her was contained in Adams's short article. Gabriela Cunninghame Graham was beautiful and charming (W. B. Yeats apparently referred to her as the 'bright little American'), smoked prodigiously, and had a weakness for Parisian dressmakers. She was also enamoured of mysticism and the esoteric, and wrote a biography of Santa Teresa of Avila, published in 1894.

Only her mysticism prevented me from loving Gabriela Cunninghame Graham unreservedly. I could not help finding it peculiar, even improbable, that a woman who had once summoned the courage to run away from home to go on the stage would in later life succumb to what I considered to be mumbo-jumbo. I was certain from the outset that 'my' Gabriela was a sceptic, a woman with no time for visions and emanations and materialisations from beyond the grave. Almost immediately Maribel began to take shape in my mind.

The irony of imagining the life of a woman who imagined it for herself is not lost on me but *Beautiful Lies*, though based in truth, is fundamentally a work of fiction. Unhooking myself from the real Gabriela allowed my imagination to take flight.

There is no evidence that there was ever, during Gabriela's life, a serious risk of her secret being discovered, but I could not help thinking how differently her story would have ended if there had been. The 1880s witnessed the emergence of a brand-new kind of journalism, one that laid the foundations for our modern tabloid press and that would, by the end of the decade, bring down Charles Parnell, the widely revered founder and leader of the Irish Parliamentary Party who, before scandal destroyed his career, had looked set to lead his country towards Home Rule (and from there perhaps, as some historians have argued, to all-Irish independence).

The pioneer of this New Journalism was the editor of the *Pall Mall Gazette*, William Thomas Stead. Stead, who took up his editorship in 1883, was the first newspaper editor who fully understood that the great power of the press lay in its role as a conduit between an eagerly opinionated public and a political class eager to appropriate popular issues for political gain. (He was also the first editor to introduce to English newspapers the American convention of the interview.) The son of a Congregationalist minister, Stead was a chapel-going Nonconformist and though he had little education and was described by George Bernard Shaw as 'stupendously ignorant', had a thunderous sense of right and wrong. Stead's father had considered the theatre to be the Devil's Chapel, and novels the Devil's Bible. Under Stead's leadership the *Pall Mall Gazette* soon provided a lurid alternative to both, whipping itself into sensationalist frenzies under the auspices of moral outrage and setting the tone for tabloid newspapers ever after. Stead's most infamous stunt, *The Maiden Tribute of Modern Babylon*, exposed the seamy underbelly of London's sex trade and forced Parliament to raise the age of consent for girls from thirteen to sixteen. It also resulted in Stead, who had purchased a girl of twelve for £5 in order to show how easily it might be done, serving four months in prison for trafficking in child bondage.

Stead was also largely responsible for the downfall in sexual scandals not only of Charles Parnell but of Sir Charles Dilke, another Liberal politician. Both were supposedly on 'his side', but Stead showed no qualms about their destruction; his Puritan moral code allowed for no shades of grey. Later he worked to bring down the homosexual dramatist (and friend of Gabriela Cunninghame Grahame) Oscar Wilde. It was not a climate in which one was safe harbouring secrets. In his article Adams quotes a letter written by one of Carrie's sisters after her death which underlined the fear of her family that the truth about Gabriela would be revealed. 'I shall watch the papers,' she wrote in 1906, 'for I am certain in spite of all the story will come out . . . what I want to find out is what name he registered her death in − if other than Papa and Mama's he can be charged with perjury.' The scandal that would have resulted from such a discovery would not only have destroyed Robert's political career, it would have meant social disgrace, not only for Gabriela and Robert but for both of their families. At a time when respectability was critical to a family's social, financial and professional standing, such a loss of reputation might well have proved disastrous.

In my novel Maribel is not a writer, or not with any success. She is a photographer. Photography drew me in part because of its metaphorical significance, its ability to create illusions that seem real, and partly because the rapid development of photographic technology in the 1880s propelled the camera to the forefront of contemporary culture. While artists argued heatedly about whether photography could be considered a legitimate artistic form, the majority of Victorians regarded the camera as a scientific instrument, incapable of dissembling. As the pace of scientific discovery accelerated, psychology was also advancing with rapid strides, and hypnotic experiments were revealing previously unimagined complexities in human consciousness. There was, among many, a growing fascination with the occult. Spiritualist mediums promised communication with the spirits of the dead. Though some were sceptical, many took comfort from the idea that, in an increasingly secular world, it might be possible to prove the existence of God. In 1882 a group of scientifically-minded scholars, clergymen and public figures, among them a professor of physics from the Royal College of Science in Dublin, established the Society for Psychical Research, its stated objective to conduct organised scholarly research into human experiences that challenged conventional scientific models. One of their earliest experiments concerned the use of photographic images to capture the spirits of the dead, thereby proving beyond doubt the existence of the life everlasting.

It was some time before the Society abandoned its attempts and accepted the impossibility of proof. One might argue that it hardly mattered. Cynics and atheists dismissed the pictures as frauds; the faithful had no need of evidence. Perhaps our own stories are the same. During the writing of this novel I have come to question the nature of true stories, of history, of memory. Perhaps, like Maribel, we are all the composites of our own fantasies. Perhaps, in the end, it matters less what is true, but what we are determined to believe.

Acknowledgements

I OWE A HUGE debt to all the writers and scholars whose knowledge and wisdom have provided the foundations for this novel. I cannot possibly hope to do justice to them all here but I must extend special thanks to A. N. Wilson for his brilliant history, *The Victorians*, which is as entertaining as it is erudite. Jerry White's *London in the Nineteenth Century* proved another indispensable resource, while contemporary memoirs and biographies provided wonderful first-person witness accounts of events in the book, among them *London Letters and Some Others* by George W. Smalley and *RDB's Diary 1887–1914* by R. D. Blumenfeld, both memoirs of American journalists in London, and *Reminiscences and Reflexions of a Mid to Late Victorian* by the British Socialist philosopher Ernest Belfort Bax. *Annie Besant, An Autobiography* was also a source of fascinating contemporary detail.

A range of more specialised histories provided me with an understanding of the particular world occupied by Edward and Maribel Campbell Lowe. I was ably served by a number of political histories, notably *Socialists, Liberals and Labour* by Paul Thompson, *Labour and Socialism: A History of the British Labour Movement, 1867–1974* by James Hinton, and the riveting *The World That Never Was* by Alex Butterworth. Two books in particular provided unparalleled access to the world of Victorian newspapers: Alan J. Lee's *The Origins of the Popular Press in England 1855–1914* and Lucy Brown's *Victorian News and Newspapers*. The website attackingthedevil.co.uk also proved a treasure trove of original contemporary sources pertaining to W. T. Stead and to the emergence of the New Journalism in the 1880s. The murky history of spirit photography was elucidated by two particularly helpful studies, *100 Years of Spirit Photography* by Tom Patterson and *Photographing the Invisible* by James Coates.

For information about Buffalo Bill and the London tour of his Wild West show I relied heavily on Alan Gallop's terrific *Buffalo Bill's British Wild West* with its wealth of contemporary photographs and press cuttings, and on *'Your Fathers, The Ghosts': Buffalo Bill's Wild West in Scotland* by Tom F. Cunningham. More general context was provided by such histories as Don Russell's *The Lives and Legends of Buffalo Bill*, and Sarah Blackstone's excellent *Buckskins, Bullets and Business: A History of Buffalo Bill's Wild West*. *Black Elk Speaks*, as told through John G. Neihardt by Black Elk, offered a privileged glimpse into the Indian perspective on the period by one of the medicine men of the Oglala Sioux who travelled to England with Colonel Cody in 1887.

It was thanks to *Hostiles? The Lakota Ghost Dance and Buffalo Bill's Wild West* by Sam Maddra that I gained my first introduction to Robert Cunninghame Graham. His impassioned letters, written about the plight of the Indians to the *Daily Graphic*, led me to a number of books about the Scottish Socialist MP, most usefully *Don Roberto* by A. F. Tschiffley and *Cunninghame Graham; a critical biography* by Cedric Watts and Laurence Davies. Most importantly they steered me to the article that would prove to be the inspiration for this novel, Jad Adams's 'Gabriela Cunninghame Graham: Deception and Achievement in the 1890s', published in 2007 in the journal *English Literature in Transition, 1880–1920*. I would like to extend my thanks to him, and to all the other historians upon whom I have depended so heavily during the writing of this novel.